S0-AQE-491

TRIPPIN' OVER LOVE

BOOK YOUR PLACE ON OUR WEBSITE AND MAKE THE ARABESQUE ROMANCE CONNECTION!

We've created a customized website just for our very special Arabesque readers, where you can get the inside scoop on everything that's going on with Arabesque romance novels.

When you come online, you'll have the exciting opportunity to:

- View covers of upcoming books

- Learn about our future publishing schedule (listed by publication month and author)

- Find out when your favorite authors will be visiting a city near you

- Search for and order backlist books

- Check out author bios and background information

- Send e-mail to your favorite authors

- Join us in weekly chats with authors, readers and other guests

- Get writing guidelines

- AND MUCH MORE!

Visit our website at
http://www.arabesquebooks.com

TRIPPIN' OVER LOVE

Kori Nicole Brown
LaTwaan Green
LaShell Shawnte Stratton

sepia

BOOKS

BET Publications, LLC
www.bet.com

SEPIA BOOKS are published by

BET Publications, LLC
c/o BET BOOKS
One BET Plaza
1900 W Place NE
Washington, DC 20018-1211

Copyright © 2003 by BET Publications
"The Art of Selfishness" Copyright © 2003 by Kori Nicole Brown
"A Matter of Trust" Copyright © 2003 by LaTwaan Green
"A Fateful Possibility" Copyright © 2003 by LaShell Shawnte Stratton

All rights reserved. No part of this book may be reproduced, stored in a retrieval system, or transmitted in any form or by any means without the prior written consent of the Publisher.

If you purchased this book without a cover, you should be aware that this book is stolen property. It was reported as "unsold and destroyed" to the Publisher and neither the Author nor the Publisher has received any payment for this "stripped book."

All Kensington Titles, Imprints, and Distributed Lines are available at special quantity discounts for bulk purchases for sales promotions, premiums, fund-raising, and educational or institutional use. Special book excerpts or customized printings can also be created to fit specific needs. For details, write or phone the office of the Kensington special sales manager: Kensington Publishing Corp., 850 Third Avenue, New York, NY 10022, attn: Special Sales Department, Phone: 1-800-221-2647.

BET Books is a trademark of Black Entertainment Television, Inc. SEPIA and the SEPIA logo are trademarks of BET Books and the BET BOOKS logo is a registered trademark.

First Printing: August 2003
10 9 8 7 6 5 4 3 2 1

Printed in the United States of America

Contents

A MATTER OF TRUST

LaTwaan Green

My love and my thanks to my mother, Susan, and my Aunt Shirley for being my biggest supporters. To my children, Bryan and Jasmine, for inspiring me to go after my dreams.

Oscar Green 1930–2002: You may be gone but you will never be forgotten. RIP, daddy.

Love,
Your Baby Girl

One

Alexis typed the final sentence of her article before she hit the print button. She glanced over at her desk at the porcelain Winnie the Pooh pendulum clock her boss had given her for her birthday. She sighed with relief to discover it was only four o'clock. She still had plenty of time to get ready for the cruise tonight.

As she waited for the printer to stop she glanced around the tiny office that belonged to *Black Ink* magazine. With the exception of a few diehards like her, the office was empty. Brown leather chairs rested behind cherry-wood desks. Phones remained silent beside black computer screens as their owners prepared for New Year's Eve parties being held that night. She was used to the office being filled with people laughing and talking as they went about their daily duties.

She felt the familiar tremor of excitement travel down her spine. Even after three years of working here, there were times when she found it hard to believe it was real. Her dreams of becoming a journalist had finally come true. She was a member of one of the most exclusive magazines in the country.

Alexis knew she wanted to be a journalist at the tender age of six when her mother took her to the newsroom of the

New York Times where she was working. She'd watched in amazement as people bustled back and forth carrying articles to their editors while others clicked away at their typewriters. Even then she felt the excitement in the air of people who truly enjoyed the work they did. She knew her mother would have been proud she'd followed in her footsteps.

As the last page of her article printed she pulled it off the printer and hit the button to shut her computer down. She pulled her purse from the desk drawer and slid the strap over her shoulder. She turned her monitor off as she stood up and headed for Sonya Davenport's office.

Sonya was the senior editor. Every article printed in *Black Ink* magazine had to have her final stamp of approval. Even though she sometimes sent an article back five times before she approved it for publication, everyone who worked there respected her judgment. Her attention to detail and her expectation of excellence were what made the magazine successful.

When Alexis reached her office it was empty. She stepped inside and placed her article in the in-box on the file cabinet. She headed for the door. If she hurried she could still beat some of the downtown Orlando rush-hour traffic. As she stepped outside the door, Sonya approached her.

"Alexis. I'm glad I caught you before you left."

"I was just on my way out the door," she replied with a smile. "I put the Peter Sheldon article in your box."

"How did the interview go?"

"Wonderful. Peter is an amazing man. He's funny, intelligent, and down-to-earth. After I put him at ease he really opened up to me. I think you'll be pleased with my article."

"I can't wait to read it." There was a moment of silence between them as Alexis watched her.

Her boss was attractive with her dark brown hair, pecan-tan skin, and hazel-brown eyes. She was only five feet two inches tall, but the rod of steel that braced her backbone made her seem much taller. She was dressed in one of her customary two-piece pantsuits with her hair pulled back into a French twist. She wore no jewelry other than the wedding band on her left hand.

Alexis shifted her gaze to her watch. "I have to get going."

"Big plans tonight?"

"Kavon and I are going down to Cape Canaveral to sail on his father's yacht."

"That sounds like fun."

"I think it will be."

"I'm having a party at my house tonight and I'd like for you and Kavon to stop by for a few minutes. There are a few people from the publishing industry coming that I'd like for you to meet."

"Thank you for the invitation. I'd love to stop by."

"I know you have to get going, but would you mind stepping into my office for a moment?"

"Of course not," she replied as she followed her into her office. Sonya went around her desk and sat down as Alexis took the empty chair in front of her.

"Have you had an opportunity to look over the article idea I gave you?"

She'd done more than look it over. She'd fallen in love with it. It was in connection with the series of articles she'd already done on the record industry. This time the article would be a more in-depth look at the contracts signed by recording artists that made their executive producers rich but barely paid themselves enough to cover the extravagant expenses the record companies insisted they pay out of their money.

She'd looked it over several times in the past few days, and each time she'd grown more attached to it. She knew it was an excellent follow-up to her last article. That only made it more difficult for her to refuse to do the story.

"I read over it several times."

"What did you think?"

"The story will bring a lot of attention to the way record companies handle their artists."

"Why do I sense there's a but coming?"

Alexis lowered her gaze to the floor. "The articles I've written in the past have stepped on a lot of toes in the record industry, Kavon's father, Karl Anderson, included. Things have been strained between us since he received too much unfavorable media attention stemming from my last article."

Sonya leaned back in her chair. "You're having reservations because of your relationship with Kavon?"

"Yes."

"I will understand if you refuse to do the article, but the only reason I asked you to handle this is that I feel this is a story that needs to be told. I was surprised when I found out you were dating Karl Anderson's son, because of your honesty in your articles. Being able to write about the music industry while dating the son of a record producer tells me that you are capable of being unbiased about subjects that are close to you. You even mentioned Karl in your story. That took a lot of guts."

"I put him in the article because he is as guilty as everyone else. The entertainment industry takes advantage of artists every day who have no idea they're being ripped off. I had to do the right thing."

"I know you've caught a lot of heat from people about the stories you've written for *Black Ink,* but any story that exposes the truth about any industry, whether it be music or underwater basket-weaving, faces public scrutiny. I think you did an excellent job, which is why I want you to do this story."

Alexis hesitated. She was itching to do the article but she knew she was digging her own grave. She wanted Karl's approval because of her relationship with Kavon, but there was no guarantee that he would ever forgive her for what he considered betrayal. She knew his production company, Rain Records, would have to be mentioned. It was only a question of whether she was willing to take the risk. She knew she could tell Sonya no and she would accept her answer without any further discussion, but she didn't want to. She was going to do the right thing.

"I'll do it."

Sonya smiled. "Thank you, Alexis. I know you'll do an excellent job."

"Thank you." She stood up and adjusted her purse strap. "I have to go get ready for my cruise."

"I'll see you later."

"Count on it," she replied as she headed out the door.

In the parking garage she clicked the button on her key chain to unlock the door of her candy-apple-red BMW convertible. She climbed inside, started the car, and flipped on the radio. She set the dial to 89.9 FM, allowing smooth jazz to fill the car as she put on her sunglasses. She let the top down before she pulled from the parking space and headed for the exit.

Darryl Alexander pulled his gold convertible Mercedes into the parking lot of Robin's and cut the engine. He surveyed the cars and frowned as he spotted his brother's shiny black Acura gleaming under the late afternoon sun. He shook his head as he got out of the car and headed for the back of the restaurant.

The white brick building was a far cry from the ramshackle structure they'd inherited from their Uncle Oscar four years ago. Darryl had taken one look at it and told his brother to bulldoze it, but Malcolm vowed to make it into something spectacular and he'd made good on that vow. He'd transformed the one-story dungeon into a two-story palace fit for a king.

Robin's, named after their mother, was much more than a restaurant. It was a place where people came to relax and chill after a long day in the office. When the doors opened at five o'clock, people piled in to get a good seat in front of the stage where his brother hired local jazz bands to strut their stuff. Every once in a while he changed up and hired local comedians to put on a comedy show. People from as far as Daytona and St. Petersburg drove in to enjoy the festive atmosphere.

Darryl picked up the pace as he reached the back entrance of the restaurant. He opened the back door and stepped inside. The mouthwatering aroma of spaghetti sauce greeted him. His stomach growled as he headed down the narrow corridor to the main area of the kitchen.

People were everywhere preparing meals and shouting orders. As he watched them in action they reminded him of a synchronized swimming team. Everyone seemed to move in one fluid motion as they stirred pots and poured food into glass dishes. Copper pots gleamed from overhead racks as the staff pulled them down to prepare their dishes. His stomach grumbled again as he spotted Luther, Malcolm's catering manager, issuing orders.

"Hey, Luther, where's your boss?" he questioned as he approached him.

"Finishing up a cheesecake over there." He pointed to the right.

"Thanks." Darryl headed past the boiling pots of fettuccini to the section of the restaurant where Malcolm had placed center islands. He found him standing at an island chopping pecans. A chef's hat sat askew on his head, a white apron covered his black shirt and tan pants.

"How did I guess I would find you here in the kitchen slaving away?" Darryl questioned as he strolled over to him.

Malcolm paused briefly to glance at his brother before he continued chopping pecans. "Why are you all up in my business?"

"I can't believe you're asking me that question. It's New Year's Eve and you're stuck here in the kitchen. Hello? Someone has to save you from yourself."

"Save me from myself? That's an interesting concept."

"Depends on how you look at it." He leaned against the island. "Don't try to change the subject. Answer my question."

"What question?"

"Why are you here when you should be at home getting ready to go out and get your groove on?"

"I'm catering a party tonight."

"What do you mean you're catering a party tonight?" Malcolm picked up a handful of pecans and sprinkled them over the white-chocolate-covered strawberries he'd placed on a cheesecake. "You heard me the first time." He glanced up at the clock on the wall. "I'm due to arrive there in less than four hours, so if you didn't come to help, stop pestering me."

"I wouldn't be caught dead doing manual labor on New Year's Eve."

"Or any other day of the year," Malcolm muttered under his breath.

"I heard that."

"I don't care if you did."

"Why are you being a stick-in-the-mud?"

"Why are you harassing me? New Year's Eve is just another day."

Darryl held up his hands. "You're the only person I know who feels that way, Malcolm. Tonight is the ultimate party night, and my brother is working because he has no life."

"Correction. The reason I'm working tonight *is* that I have a life."

"No, you don't. Working eighty hours a week can't be exhilarating."

Malcolm placed a silver lid over the cake before he removed his apron and tossed it on the hook beside the island. He shot an annoyed glance at his brother before he turned and headed for his office.

Darryl followed him. "I'm trying to add some excitement to your life, and this is the thanks I get?"

"Is there a reason you're harassing me today?"

"I'm only here because you're here. I swear you spend more time at this restaurant than you do at home. That's not normal for someone our age."

"Running a restaurant takes a lot of time and energy." He walked into his office and sat down in his black leather chair. "I've been here since noon preparing for this party."

"I thought your purpose for hiring Luther was for him to run the catering side of the restaurant."

"If Cecile Anderson hadn't called me to oversee this party personally I could have been more than happy to let Luther handle it."

"Mom's college roommate, powerhouse stockbroker Cecile Anderson?" Darryl questioned with raised eyebrows.

"Do you know any other Cecile?"

"No." He flopped down in the chair opposite Malcolm. "For a man who has no desire for a social life you certainly believe in living dangerously."

"Care to explain that remark?"

"You have been officially nominated as the flavor of the month."

Malcolm groaned. "Who nominated me?"

"I have no idea but I'm not surprised."

"Why not?"

"You've been a divorced bachelor for almost four years now. Those sisters will eat you alive." He smirked. "Who would have thought the daughters of record executives, doctors, lawyers, and stockbrokers would be so money hungry?"

"Having money doesn't make them any different from anyone else. Those women are looking for a man who can provide the lifestyle their fathers do, and I'm not trying to hear that. I don't plan to change my bachelor status any time soon. I was hoping my name would never make their list."

"A good-looking brother with his own restaurant and a six-figure income is a magnet. You couldn't run forever."

Malcolm narrowed his eyes suspiciously. "How do you know all of this?"

"Courtney told me."

Courtney. The mere mention of her name caused him to wince. Smart, beautiful, and a successful model, she'd been after him since he signed his name on the dotted line of his divorce papers. Like the women that were attending Cecile's party, she wanted a successful husband. A man who would take care of her whenever her career reached the finish line.

"I should have known."

Darryl noticed his pensive gaze and shook his head. "I don't understand you, Malcolm. I'd be flattered to have Courtney falling at my feet."

It was Malcolm's turn to shake his head. No matter how many times he tried to explain it to him, Darryl never understood. "Why don't you go after her?"

"I have, but for some reason she prefers the boring twin."

He laughed. "So this is about the fact that she rejected you?"

"Rejection has nothing to do with this, dear brother. Don't try to flip the script. This conversation is about you and your lack of social life."

"Call it whatever you want, but I happen to enjoy my life just the way it is, and I don't intend to change my lifestyle any time soon."

"You hate change. You have a hundred and fifty employees to help you run this restaurant and your catering business, but will you delegate some of your responsibility to any of them? No. You prefer to work like a dog so you can avoid what's really bothering you."

"Can I help it that I'm a hands-on owner? Cooking helps alleviate my stress."

"How can a man with no life have stress?" Darryl questioned with a smirk. "Why can't you admit the only reason you throw yourself into this restaurant is that Leslie left you?"

The vein in Malcolm's forehead flexed at the mention of his ex-wife's name. "I know where you're going with this, so you can stop right there. I'm tired of hearing the how-much-I-need-a-woman-in-my-life speech. Been there, done that, and won't be attempting it again any time in the near future."

"Is that why you haven't dated the same woman more than three times in the past three and a half years? It's time for you to let go of the past and start moving on with the future. Wherever Leslie is, she isn't living like a nun."

"I for one couldn't care less what my-ex-wife is doing. She left me, remember? Right after our dear Uncle Oscar kicked the bucket, leaving us his fortune. Imagine how betrayed I felt when I discovered she only married me for what she could get out of me."

"That and the fact that she left you for another man."

Malcolm exhaled sharply as he clenched his fists. "This discussion is over."

"All I'm trying to say is to stop letting her run your life. She made her decision when she left you. Let go of your anger and hostility and move on with your life."

"My issues aren't with other women, Darryl. My issues lie with trust. That's a different subject. It seems like every woman I've met the past few years has seen dollar signs attached to my name. I refuse to be used for financial gain. Uncle Oscar thought he was doing us a favor when he willed us his money, but it was more of a curse than anything else. Sometimes I find myself wishing he'd had a wife or children to leave it to so he could have spared me this grief. All I want is a real woman who is willing to love me for who I am and not for what I can do for her. I want an independent woman. Is that too much to ask for?"

Darryl shook his head as he put his feet on Malcolm's desk. "You know how many brothers I hear say that, Malcolm? Hundreds. They all claim they want an independent woman until they actually meet one and then they can't handle it. They become intimidated and move on because she has a mind of her own and doesn't need him to take care of her. Face it, Malcolm, deep down inside, all men want a woman who needs them in some way. If they appear not to need us we don't waste our time."

"That may hold true for some men, but believe me, I've dated enough gold diggers to figure out what I don't want in a woman."

"I'm just trying to look out for you. Don't bite my head off."

Malcolm's eyes narrowed. "Why is my personal life suddenly so interesting?"

"I'm heading to a slamming party and I wanted you to come along."

He shook his head as he laughed. "Liar. You were trying to set me up with someone again, weren't you?"

"Make a resolution this year to stop being so suspicious of me. I only came by because I didn't want you to bring in the new year alone. Is that so bad? I know how rough it can be when you don't have someone special to spend the holidays with."

Malcolm smiled at the sincerity in his brother's voice. How could he stay mad at him? "How are Mom and Dad?" he questioned in a desperate attempt to change the subject.

"They were fine when I visited them a couple of weeks ago, although Mom did relay a message that she wants you to visit them more often. She said once every two years is not enough. She wanted me to convince you to come to Battle Creek in the next month or so."

"You're not getting me to go to Michigan this time of year. The snow up there is probably three feet deep. Besides, the farther away they are, the more I don't have to hear about my bachelor status."

"Just do us all a favor and find a woman."

"Trust me, when I find a woman I like, you'll be the last to know."

Darryl grinned. "I'll know."

"I doubt that."

"You can't keep secrets from me, Malcolm. It's the telepathic twin thing." He stood up. "I'm just happy you'll be around a ton of single women tonight. Perhaps you'll meet the next Mrs. Alexander."

"I don't think so. I'm never getting married again."

"Famous last words."

"Trust me, I have the evidence to back mine up."

Darryl threw his hands up in the air. "I guess I have to face the fact that you're a grown man perfectly capable of making your own decisions."

Malcolm laughed as he stood up and backed away from him. "I hope I'm not standing anywhere near you when that lightning bolt strikes. It's going to ricochet."

"So I'm lying. You should be used to it by now."

"One of these days you'll learn not to dip into grown people's business."

"I doubt that very seriously," Darryl replied with a laugh as they headed out the door.

Two

Alexis placed the final hairpin in her hair as she set her brush down on the vanity. She stood up to inspect her reflection in the mirror. She admired the way her red silk evening gown hugged her curves deliciously to reveal a body that was firm and void of excess flesh.

She glanced up at the clock on the wall as she headed for her closet. She didn't have much time before Kavon arrived. She shivered with anticipation as she pulled a black shawl with a butterfly design made of diamonds from the closet door. She draped it over her arm as the doorbell rang. She grabbed her inhaler as she turned off the light and headed down the stairs.

She pulled her black purse from the hook at the foot of the stairs and slipped her inhaler inside as she headed for the front door. She slid the latch back and opened the door to find Kavon standing there with a single red rose in his hand. A huge smile spread over her face as she admired the man in her life.

With his pecan-brown skin, wavy black hair, and muscular body he was enough to make her weak in the knees. He was dressed in a black tuxedo with a crisp white shirt and a black cummerbund. He reminded her a lot of Morris Chestnut.

"Hi, sweetheart," he said as he kissed her gently on the cheek so he wouldn't smear her lipstick. "You look beautiful."

The smile on her face grew brighter. "Thank you."

"This is for you." He held the rose out for her to take it. She pressed it to her nose to inhale the fragrant scent as he held his arm out. "Ready?"

"Always," she said as she linked her arm through his.

He led the way down the walkway to the shiny black limousine waiting in her driveway. The chauffeur opened the door, allowing them to slide inside before he closed it behind them. Alexis settled back in her seat as they pulled out of her driveway and into the street.

"I love that dress on you," Kavon murmured as he nuzzled her neck. "If we weren't headed out tonight I would have shown you just how much I appreciated it."

"Stop being bad," she said with a giggle as she gently pushed him away. "If you're not careful, my dress will be wrinkled before we get where we're going."

"Believe me, that will be the least of your worries," he said as the driver approached the main highway. Alexis chewed on her bottom lip. It was now or never to tell him about Sonya's house.

"Kavon, I have a stop to make."

"What kind of stop?"

"Sonya asked me to stop by her house."

"Why?"

"There were a few people that she wanted me to meet and she asked if we could stop by for a few minutes. I already told her I would."

"You should have asked me first, Alexis. You knew we already had plans."

"I told her about our plans, but she assured me it would only take a few minutes of our time." She touched his face. "My career is very important to me."

"And I'm not?" he questioned with a touch of impatience. "We have an hour drive ahead of us and you commit us to a party? You should have told her you couldn't make it."

"I could have but I didn't." Her voice was soft. "We'll still have plenty of time to get to the yacht before it sets sail. Karl would never leave you behind."

"I know he won't leave us, but that isn't the point," he replied through clenched teeth. "We made plans to attend this cruise with my parents months ago."

"Don't you mean you obligated me to attend this cruise with your parents?" she questioned with a hint of anger in her voice. "I could have gone to Sonya's and had a wonderful time without you. It's not like I mix well with your family and friends anyway."

"Whose fault is that, Alexis? You've written articles on all of my father's business associates. Did you honestly think they wouldn't take offense to the stories you publish?"

"I reported the truth, Kavon. If they have such a hard time accepting that, then that's their problem. I can't change the facts."

"Then stop blaming me for the way they treat you. I've tried to come to your defense more than once, but it may take a while for them to warm up to you again since they don't know when something they say will show up in *Black Ink*."

"I've never taken anything I learned on my personal time and used it in my articles," she said defensively. "Only the cold, hard facts that can be proven." She touched his arm. "Are you going to tell the driver about the change in plans?"

"Fine." He picked up the phone. She listened intently as he relayed Sonya's address before he hung up. "Happy?"

"Yes."

"At least one of us is," he mumbled under his breath.

"What is your problem tonight?"

"I'm fine, Alexis. I'm just fine."

"Don't lie to me, Kavon. I know something is wrong between us. For the past few months you've picked fights over the smallest things and you've broken several dates without any explanation. What am I supposed to think? That everything is peaches and cream between us? I would have to be a fool not to see what's going on."

Kavon shot her a nervous glance. "I'm sorry, sweetheart.

I had no idea you felt that way." He touched her face. "I've been under so much stress lately from work that I haven't been paying you as much attention as I normally do. Now that I know how you feel, I'll do better."

Her eyes narrowed. "Would the sudden increase in stress have anything to do with Sydney?"

He rolled his eyes as the chauffeur pulled up to Sonya's house. "How many times have we been over this, Alexis? Sydney has nothing to do with this. You're trying to make a mountain out of a molehill."

"Am I? Things have changed between us and I know she has something to do with this. Why else would she show up at your door at two in the morning wearing nothing but a trench coat and a smile?"

"You're grasping at straws and you know it," he shot back. "I had no idea she was going to pull a stunt like that. Who knew she had a crush on me?"

"You can play innocent all you want, but hear this and hear it well. I won't stand for being mistreated."

The chauffeur opened her door as Kavon touched her arm. "Make this short and sweet, Alexis. We don't have all night. The yacht sails in less than two hours."

"You've made your point," she said as she stepped out of the car, leaving him behind. She was halfway to Sonya's front door by the time he caught up with her.

"Alexis?"

"Yes?"

"Let's kiss and make up. I don't want you to be mad at me for the rest of the night." He took her hand and kissed it. She found herself smiling despite her anger as he reached over and pulled her into his arms.

He was the only man she'd ever dated that had that effect on her. She could never stay mad at him for more than a couple of minutes. Despite their rocky relationship she loved him with all her heart. They'd been together five years and she loved every minute she'd spent with him.

"Come on, princess," he said as he led the way up the walkway to the front door. He hit the doorbell. Sonya opened the door almost instantly.

"Alexis, Kavon. I'm glad you could make it." She hugged Alexis briefly. "I know you don't have much time, so come on, let me introduce you to a couple of people." She took her by the arm and led her away from Kavon.

The next thirty minutes flew by in a blur as Sonya introduced her to several big-name people in the publishing industry. They were people who would be vital to her career if and when she ever decided to branch out into other fields. By the time she'd finally caught up with Kavon, he had a frown on his face a mile long.

"I thought you said this would only take a minute."

"Sonya got a little carried away."

"Carried away?" he questioned in anger. "I warned you about this before we stopped."

"I'm ready to go now," she replied softly, unwilling to let him ruffle her feathers. "I met quite a few people who can help me with my career in the future."

"I'm happy for you," he mumbled as he took her arm and led her to the front door and out to the limousine.

The drive to Cape Canaveral was spent in silence. The tension in the air was so thick she could almost cut it with a knife. They were five miles from their destination when Kavon glanced down at his watch and sighed impatiently.

"Now we're late."

She looked down at her watch. "We're only five minutes late."

"If we hadn't stopped we would have been there by now."

"I told you why I had to stop, Kavon."

"I just hope my father doesn't get impatient and leave us behind."

"You don't have to worry about that. Karl would never leave his precious son behind," she muttered under her breath.

"Do I detect an attitude from you?"

"Would that be enough to get your attention?"

"What is that supposed to mean?"

"Sonya is the only friend I've managed to make since I moved to Orlando, because every time I turn around you've obligated me to attend something with your family and friends. Then you have the audacity to get an attitude because I want to do something else for a change? I didn't move here for you to take over my life."

"I'm only trying to steer you in the right direction, Alexis. I want you to fit into every aspect of my life."

"By trying to turn me into someone I'm not?" she questioned as the limousine pulled up to the marina.

"We can argue about this for the rest of the night, but I don't want to bring in the new year fighting. I want to be able to get through tonight without turning it into World War Three."

"Fine with me." She stepped outside into the warm night air with Kavon right behind her. He linked his arm through hers as he led her down the wooden dock to his father's yacht.

The *Cecile* was a one-hundred-and-fifty-foot blue and white yacht with three levels. It had been decorated in honor of New Year's Eve with streamers and banners. She saw balloons attached to the upper deck and smiled. Kavon held her hand tighter as they descended the metal stairs leading up to the lower deck.

Once aboard he led her up the stairs to the upper deck where the party was being held. As they passed through the cabin door he led her down the narrow corridor to the ballroom. Once inside he paused, allowing Alexis an opportunity to look over everything.

Cecile had outdone herself with the decoration. She had opted for the customary New Year's Eve decorations of hats, noisemakers, confetti, and an array of balloons to be released at midnight. The thing that made everything so unusual was that she had made everything from the napkins to the balloons in the shape of hearts. There was a huge buffet table, in the shape of a snake, with everything imaginable on it to the left side of the ballroom. The front had been cleared for dancing. There were tables and chairs scattered throughout the room.

Everywhere she turned, couples were eating, drinking, and laughing. Others were dancing to the music from the snazzy jazz band Cecile had selected. Alexis's smile disappeared as Karl spotted them and approached.

"I'm glad you finally made it, Kavon," he said with a bright smile. "I was beginning to wonder if you were going to cancel on us."

"Alexis and I had a stop to make."

Karl's face tightened as he turned his gaze to Alexis. "Good evening, Alexis." All the warmth in his voice had disappeared.

"Hello, Karl," she replied softly.

He smiled tightly and turned back to Kavon. "Everyone has been asking for you, Kavon."

"Have they?" he questioned with a grin. "I guess I'll just have to make my presence here known. Alexis, are you going to be okay on your own for a little bit?"

"Yes," she said with a smile as she spotted his mother across the room. "I'll go over to talk to Cecile."

"I'll see you in a little bit." He started off behind his father as she headed for his mother.

Cecile Anderson reminded Alexis a lot of Sonya. She was five feet three with honey-colored skin, dark brown hair, and chocolate-brown eyes. She was dressed in a royal-blue silk dress with pearls adorning the top. Her dress combined with the jewels weaved through her hair made her look like a tiny queen as she sipped her champagne.

"Cecile," Alexis said with a bright smile.

"Alexis," she said as she turned to face her. "I'm so glad you could make it."

"I'm glad someone is," she said with a weary smile.

"Don't pay them any attention. So you stepped on a few toes, it happens in the business world all the time." She smiled. "Personally I admire your spirit. You remind me of myself when I was your age."

"I'm glad you approve."

"You haven't said anything I don't wholeheartedly agree with. The way executive producers treat the people who work for them is a shame. I'm just glad you had the courage to speak up for what was right." She smiled. "If more people did that, this world would be a better place."

Alexis couldn't resist her smile. Knowing Cecile appreciated her work was uplifting for her. "I'm sorry we're late. I had to stop off to my boss's house for a few minutes. She wanted me to meet a few people that could be vital to my career as I move forward."

"It's always good to make contacts. In my business it can make or break you."

"At least people think your career is worthwhile. They view me as a viper."

"Making judgments on what will sell and what won't isn't that hard, Alexis. Being able to write is a gift not many people possess. You're doing the right thing by sharing it with the world."

Her smile brightened. Cecile always knew the right thing to say. Her smile slipped when she noticed Karl heading in their direction. She had hoped he would have found it in his heart to forgive her for the articles she'd written, but so far there didn't seem to be any indication that he had. His greeting was as cold as ever.

"Cecile, I need to borrow you for a moment."

"Please excuse me, Alexis," she said apologetically. "I'll be right back."

"Go ahead," she said softly as Karl led her away. As she gazed around the room she caught glimpses of the other women present whispering and laughing as they looked in her direction. She knew they were talking about her articles. They were the only thing they seemed to associate her with now. It was hard for her to remember that at one time they actually seemed to like her. With a sigh and a heavy heart she turned to stare out at the moonlit water.

Malcolm's gaze traveled over the groups of men and women laughing and talking. It amazed him that no matter how many of these parties he attended they were all the same. The men stood in one corner comparing stories while they checked out the single women, wondering if they had a chance to score on the side, while the women tore one another apart in between gossiping about who was sleeping with whom.

As he looked up he caught sight of several women lurking nearby. Darryl's words echoed in his head. He'd made a huge mistake coming here tonight. From the moment the women walking in the door spotted him behind the buffet table they began stalking him like lionesses ready to move in for the kill. He nearly groaned out loud when he spied Courtney heading in his direction. He'd hoped she wouldn't be here tonight.

"Have you been avoiding me, Malcolm?" she questioned as she stood in front of him.

Malcolm arched his eyebrows. "What would make you think that?"

"I've left you several messages and you haven't returned any of my calls."

"If you left them for me at home I'm not surprised you didn't get a call back. I'm very rarely there."

"This is the first time I've seen you in months." She allowed her eyes to roam over his body. "Did Darryl tell you I bumped into him the other day?"

"No."

"Well, when I asked him about you he said I shouldn't feel slighted, because he barely sees you himself. He told me you bury yourself in your work so much you barely come up for air." Courtney held out her goblet for a refill.

"He told the truth." Malcolm poured champagne into her crystal goblet.

"How can twin brothers be so different?" She licked her lips. "You and Darryl are like night and day."

"So I've been told." He let his gaze wash over her.

With her cocoa-brown skin and almond-shaped dark brown eyes set in a heart-shaped face, he couldn't deny that she was beautiful. Tonight she was dressed in a dove-white beaded gown that hugged every curve, complemented by high-heeled diamond sandals that made her as tall as he was. He remembered his conversation with his brother. There was no denying that she was attractive, but he was willing to bet his attraction to her had more to do with the fact that she'd rejected him.

It was easy to see why Darryl was so hung up on her. He

personally believed the only reason his brother wanted her so much was that she'd rejected him.

"You really should get out more, Malcolm. You spend too much time alone."

"Managing a restaurant is time-consuming, Courtney."

"All you need is the right woman in your life and you'd make time to do other things. All work and no play makes for a very unhappy man."

He sighed inwardly. Everyone had an opinion on what they thought was best for him. Didn't they think he was entitled to run his own life? He knew better than any of them what he wanted. Why couldn't people understand that he was happy with the way his life was going? He had a very successful restaurant and he enjoyed his work. Wasn't that enough?

"Would you like to try some of my white-chocolate strawberry cheesecake? It's one of my specialties," Malcolm said in a desperate attempt to change the subject.

"No cake will touch these lips tonight." Courtney laughed as she licked her lips. "Although I might be inclined to let you sample them later if you're willing."

Well, so much for subtle hints. Whatever happened to women who waited for a man to come on to them? Were there no women left who played hard to get? He knew if he asked any one of these women out, they would jump in a heartbeat because of who he was. Knowing that only depressed him further. Who needed that kind of pressure in their life?

He shook his head as the longest pair of legs he'd ever seen on a woman caught his eye. Mesmerized, he let his gaze continue up to the red silk dress she was wearing. She was slender with wide hips and an impossibly tiny waist. He let his gaze travel farther until it landed on her face. He nearly gasped out loud as he took in the silky black hair pulled up into a loose up-do, butter-pecan-brown skin, and oval eyes. He felt as if he'd been struck by lightning as he stood there staring at her.

She was standing off from the crowd staring out at the

water. He'd been so wrapped up in making sure everything was kosher he hadn't even noticed when she walked in. He was so caught up in watching her he'd completely forgotten about Courtney until he heard her sigh with impatience.

"Malcolm? Did you hear me?"

He blinked rapidly as he tore his gaze away from the mystery woman and turned back to Courtney. "I apologize. I was trying to keep an eye on the floor."

She smiled at his explanation. "I command you to stop being so wrapped up in your work. I think you're long overdue for some rest and relaxation, and I have just the thing."

He raised his eyebrows. "Oh?"

"My mother is throwing my father a fiftieth-birthday party on the nineteenth and I was wondering if you would like to be my escort."

"I'd love to but unfortunately my schedule is booked solid for the next two months. I'm sorry."

Her smile slipped. "The only way I'll ever get you out of that restaurant is to call you to cater a party for me. That way you can't refuse."

He completely tuned Courtney out as she droned on about the party she wanted to give. His attention was firmly locked on the young woman standing by herself. He knew he was wrong for staring at her but he couldn't help himself. His gaze was drawn to her like a magnet. He wanted to know who she was, but how could he introduce himself without making his intentions known?

He smiled when he realized she didn't have a drink in her hand. His heart skipped a beat as he came up with a way to meet her without being obvious. Without giving himself a chance to second-guess, he reached over and picked up a drink tray.

Courtney frowned slightly as she placed her right hand on her hip. "You haven't paid attention to a word I've said. I may as well be talking to myself."

"I'm working, Courtney. Cecile is paying me to do a job." He lifted the tray above his right shoulder. "I need to circulate another drink tray before the natives start getting restless."

"Go ahead."

He sighed in relief as she turned and stalked away without another word. He turned to Luther. "Luther, watch things here for a few minutes while I circulate another drink tray."

Luther nodded in response as Malcolm headed around the front of the table.

He felt butterflies take flight in his stomach as he left the buffet table. His reaction shocked him. He'd always been confident when approaching women before. What was so special about this one that she made him feel like an inexperienced schoolboy?

He circulated the room several times, allowing people to take drinks as he passed by. He'd passed her five times already, but she was so preoccupied with her thoughts she never even looked up. He realized he would have to take matters into his own hands or he could never accomplish his mission.

"Champagne?" Malcolm questioned as he placed the tray in front of her.

She jumped slightly before her caramel-brown eyes met his. She smiled. "No, thank you. I'm trying to change my bad habits for the new year."

"Is that one of your New Year's resolutions?"

"No."

"At a time when people are making resolutions for the coming year?"

"How many people really keep their resolutions?"

Malcolm frowned as he pretended to rack his brain. "I can't think of one person."

"See my point? I prefer to think of this as a lifestyle change that happened to occur around the new year."

"Are you enjoying the party so far?"

"You've been to one, you've been to them all," she said with a smirk. "Believe me, they don't change much from year to year."

"Why do you come?" he questioned in amusement.

"To be honest with you, I really didn't want to be here tonight, but since my boyfriend insisted, here I am." Her eyes narrowed as she turned them away from him. He wished he knew the source of the sadness he saw in her eyes.

"You mean you don't enjoy the company of this crowd?" he questioned with mock surprise in his voice. "Don't let them hear you say it too loudly or they'll throw you overboard."

She heard the sarcasm in his voice and grinned. "At least I wouldn't have far to swim, since we're still in the harbor. I might even be able to make my best friend's New Year's Eve party."

"You really don't want to be here, do you?"

"No, I don't," she said softly. "Unlike a lot of these women I have a fulfilling career outside of looking for a husband to take care of me."

He arched his eyebrows. "What do you do?"

"I'm a journalist for *Black Ink* magazine."

He whistled. "You must be very good."

"I'd like to think so," she replied as her eyes locked with his. "I get to cover a wide range of subjects, and the pay is good. Besides, I truly enjoy the work I do."

"Enjoying your job is always a good thing," he said as he shifted the tray to the other hand. Out of the corner of his eye he saw Courtney shooting daggers at him with her eyes as she talked with her friends, but he didn't care. He was enjoying this conversation.

"I see gauntlets are being thrown," she commented as she threw a glance in Courtney's direction.

"You noticed?" he questioned with a laugh.

"Not very much escapes me," she replied as she turned back to him. "I've noticed her hounding you."

"You noticed me?" Malcolm's voice was filled with surprise.

"I've been to enough of these parties to notice a new face when I see one."

"You don't mix well with this crowd, do you?"

"No. The women seemed to be threatened by me, which is why I'm always standing over here alone in the corner while they tear me apart with their snide remarks."

"And that doesn't bother you?"

She shrugged. "Why should it? They don't even know

anything about me other than whatever their small minds tell them."

"Well, you're not alone anymore," he said as he took a glass of ginger ale from his tray and placed it in her hand. "You are allowed to drink sodas, aren't you?"

"What if I told you I didn't drink sodas?"

"Then I would have to walk over and get you an iced tea."

"Long Island or regular?" she questioned with a grin.

"Whichever one you desire, Miss Lady."

"Miss Lady, huh?" she questioned in amusement. "You're extremely polite to be a waiter."

He knew he should have corrected her and let her know that he wasn't just a waiter, but he decided against it. For once he was relieved he wore the same outfit as the rest of his staff. He was enjoying his conversation with her and he didn't want to ruin it by telling her too much too soon. It was refreshing to talk to someone who had no clue who he was but was still interested in talking to him. That let him know her interest in him was sincere.

"Part of my job description entails getting along well with other people. If I didn't put the customer first I wouldn't have a job."

"Do you enjoy what you do?"

"You mean being a waiter?"

"Yes."

"I love my job. I get to interact with a lot of different people on a daily basis. My brother is always teasing me about my work, but that's because he doesn't understand my passion for it. I genuinely enjoy what I do." Malcolm broke off with a shrug.

"People never truly understand passion," she said softly as their eyes locked.

Malcolm was lost in the milky depths of her eyes as he stood staring into them. She was different from every other woman he'd ever met. He'd learned a lot about her character in a few short sentences and it left him hungry for more. He was dying to know what she was thinking as her eyes searched his face, but they revealed nothing.

"I'm sorry I had to leave," Cecile apologized, interrupting their private moment. "I don't know what my husband would do without me."

"Don't be sorry for leaving me alone," Alexis replied with a smile. "I was just enjoying a delightful conversation with . . ." Her voice trailed off as she turned to face him.

"Malcolm."

"Pleased to meet you, Malcolm, I'm Alexis," she said as she extended a perfectly manicured hand.

"The pleasure was all mine, Alexis." Her named rolled from his tongue as if he'd been saying it his entire life.

"Malcolm has been keeping me company."

"Thank you, Malcolm," Cecile said with a warm smile.

"I'd better get back to my post before the others start to look ugly at me."

Alexis laughed. "I'm sure your boss won't object too badly if you're out here keeping the guests happy."

Cecile's brows knitted together in surprise. "Didn't Malcolm tell you that—"

"He is very pleased to be your *waiter* tonight," he interrupted. The last thing he needed was for her to blow his cover. "I really must return to the buffet table. Thank you for allowing me to take up some of your time, Alexis." He saw Cecile raise her eyebrows curiously as he turned to walk away, but she didn't say another word as he turned around and headed for the buffet.

The moment he was behind the buffet he felt his heartbeat return to normal. His attraction to her left him puzzled and unbalanced. He'd gone over to her hoping it would help cure his curiosity; instead it only helped to strengthen it. He wanted to know more about her.

"Luther, if you'd like to take a break, this would be a good time to do it," Malcolm said as he placed the nearly empty tray down. "Things are only going to pick up later on."

"Thanks," Luther said as he shot Malcolm a questioning gaze. "Are you okay, Malcolm?"

"I'm better than I've been in years," he said with a broad smile. He took one last look at Alexis before he began filling empty champagne glasses.

Three

Alexis watched Kavon as he laughed and talked with his friends. He'd been blatantly ignoring her for the past two hours, and she was furious with him. As much as she loved talking to Cecile, she didn't come to this party to talk to her. The only reason she came was to spend time with him so that they could get their relationship back on track. This was the first time he'd ever distanced himself from her, and his actions only caused her to worry even more about their relationship.

Her gaze settled on Karl as he sipped his champagne. Her mood instantly darkened. She had hoped time would be enough to resolve the hostility he felt over her articles, but she was wrong. His reaction to her earlier tonight proved that the grudge he held for her was as strong as ever.

He'd warned her he would find a way to break her and Kavon up if she printed her article. Not one to let threats bother her, she'd gone ahead with it. Now that the dust had settled, he was acting on his promise and she was powerless to stop him. She wanted to tell Kavon what was going on, but he would never take her word over his father's. She would have to come up with a plan of her own if she was going to save their relationship.

Without her being aware of it, her gaze turned from Karl to Malcolm. All of the single women in the room seemed to be gravitating toward the buffet table tonight. She'd been to enough of these parties to know food wasn't that interesting to them. No. Their sudden interest in the buffet table had to do with a certain handsome waiter behind the serving spoons.

Malcolm. She watched as he laughed and talked with an elderly gentleman as he spooned soup into his bowl. His baby-smooth milk-chocolate skin combined with flawless features, a low Caesar cut, and a muscular build were a feast for her eyes. She'd tried hard to keep her gaze from traveling in his direction, but she couldn't prevent it. She'd always had a weakness for tall, well-built men. The fact that he was handsome was an added bonus.

She hated to admit that she was curious about him, but she couldn't lie to herself. Talking to him earlier was just enough to pique her curiosity. She was interested in learning more about him. For once in her life she wished she were bold like some of the other women present. She would have the courage to walk over to him and strike up a conversation without any regard to Kavon standing in the corner acting as if he didn't know her.

As if he sensed her gaze, Malcolm looked up and caught her eye. Instead of looking away, she met his gaze head-on. The combination of mystery and humor in the depths of his smoky eyes intrigued her. She couldn't break his gaze. He smiled at her, revealing deep dimples in his cheeks. She imagined what it would feel like to rub her hand against his baby-smooth skin.

She blinked rapidly as her face flushed bright red. She smiled softly as she turned back to Cecile. It was the only way to get her thoughts back on track. She shouldn't fantasize about a man she didn't even know.

"Alexis, are you okay?" Cecile queried softly.

"I'm fine, why do you ask?"

Cecile's eyes narrowed as she studied her face. "Your face is flushed."

How could she admit it was flushed because she was having sinful thoughts about Malcolm? "It's a little warm in here."

"I agree but there's a little more than that going on. You can't fool an old bird like me." Her eyes flickered in the direction of her son. "Is it Kavon?"

"Partially."

"The two of you having problems again?"

"Yes. I seem to be invisible to him tonight."

"I just hope Kavon wakes up and realizes what he has before it's too late," Cecile muttered under her breath.

There was a hidden message there that Alexis couldn't decipher. Was Cecile trying to tell her something inadvertently? It was the first time she'd ever heard her say something about Kavon that wasn't in his defense.

"Stop staring at me like I sprouted horns. I love Kavon dearly, but he has a lot to learn about life." Cecile glanced down at her watch. "We should have left two hours ago. At this rate we'll be bringing in New Year's Eve still docked in the harbor. And all because my husband is waiting for a last-minute guest . . ." Her voice trailed off abruptly as her eyes narrowed into angry slits.

"Is something wrong?" Alexis was puzzled by the sudden change in Cecile's demeanor.

"I'll be right back." Cecile didn't wait for a reply as she headed in the direction of the ballroom door.

Alexis, afraid her gaze would return to Malcolm, turned to watch the moon shining over the water. She took a sip of her soda and enjoyed the view until a familiar velvety laugh forced her to turn around. She wished the floor would open and swallow her the moment her eyes landed on Sydney Bradshaw, the woman she was sure was responsible for the tension in her relationship.

Barely five feet tall, with chocolate-brown curls, a peach-oval face, and dark brown almond-shaped eyes, everything about Sydney appeared regal and expensive. She was dressed in an emerald-green dress with black heels. She wore a matching bracelet and necklace set designed like snakes with diamonds representing the scales and emeralds for the eyes.

"Sydney." Karl's voice boomed as he held out his arms. "I'm so glad you could make it." Sydney laughed again as she fell into his embrace.

Alexis tore her eyes away from Sydney and Karl to stare at Kavon. It was a useless gesture. Kavon's gaze was firmly locked on Sydney as she laughed and talked with his father. Alexis's temper simmered just below boiling as she walked over to where Kavon was standing.

"Now I know why you haven't paid me any attention this evening."

"I had a lot of catching up to do tonight, Alexis." Kavon's eyes remained firmly locked on Sydney.

"I'm sure you did. You couldn't wait for Sydney to arrive."

"Stop being ridiculous," Kavon admonished her as Sydney broke away from Karl, her eyes searching the room. The moment her eyes found him, a huge smile spread across her face. Alexis felt his body tense as Sydney approached them.

"Hello, Kavon," Sydney said with a bright smile. "How are you?"

"Wonderful," he said as he returned her smile. "I thought you were going to Paris with your parents."

"I was on the plane when your father called me up and insisted I be here tonight. Who was I to say no to such a passionate plea?" She touched his arm. "Now that I'm here I'm glad I changed my mind."

Alexis's eyes moved back and forth between Kavon and Sydney as they gazed into one another's eyes as if they were the only two people in the room. The knot that had settled in her stomach earlier reappeared with full force as she realized what was going on. How could she ignore the truth any longer when it was blatantly staring her in the face?

Her anger reached the boiling point when she became aware of the other women in the room laughing and grinning with one another as they looked in her direction waiting to see how she would react. A wave of nausea washed over her as she realized everyone else in the room was aware of Kavon's involvement with Sydney. She didn't have to hear their catty remarks to know what was being said. Kavon had given them what they'd wanted from her since she became a social outcast: her head on a platter.

She stared at Kavon without really seeing him. His betrayal cut her to the quick. In her eyes he'd subjected her to the ultimate humiliation. Something she would never be able to forgive him for. She cleared her throat softly. Kavon jumped slightly as he turned to face her. She saw a flicker of emotion she didn't recognize in his eyes as she extended her hand to Sydney.

"Hello, Sydney. How are you?"

The warm look in Sydney's eyes turned icy as they roamed over Alexis as if she were an animal that needed inspection. Her smile disappeared as her lips flattened into a furious line. Alexis knew she was remembering their argument of a few weeks ago when she had showed up at Kavon's apartment in the middle of the night. For a moment she thought Sydney was going to say something to her when she turned back to Kavon and placed her hand on his arm.

"I have yet to see the rest of the yacht. Care to give me a personal tour?"

"If Alexis has no objection." He looked Alexis in the eye for the first time since Sydney had walked in the door.

"Why would I mind? Just continue to do what you've been doing all night. Pretend I'm not even here." Without another word she turned and headed for the door. As if he called her name out loud, she glanced over to see Malcolm staring at her with a mixture of anger and sympathy on his face. His face was the last one she saw as she headed out the door.

Kavon pulled Sydney into his arms the moment they were alone. "I couldn't wait to get you alone. I've been thinking about you all day."

"Oh, really?" She stepped away from him. "Then why was Alexis's face the first one I saw as I walked across the room?"

His eyes skipped away guiltily. "Can we not discuss this now?"

"Why not, Kavon? I was tempted to lay everything out on the table when I saw her standing there clinging to your side like a little puppy."

"Why didn't you?"

"I'm not into scenes." She folded her arms. "We agreed two months ago you were going to tell her the truth. Why are you dragging your feet on this?"

"I was trying to come up with a way to tell her the truth without hurting her too badly. She's really been there for me the past two years."

"And your point would be what? You and I have been seeing each other for six months. Obviously you didn't care about her as much as you thought, or you never would have gotten involved with me. I'm sure by now she's figured out there's something wrong with your relationship anyway. Tell her the truth."

"Don't do this, Sydney."

"Do what? Force you to stand up and be a man about this? I'm tired of sneaking around like I'm dating a married man. You're not married to her, Kavon. How hard can it be?"

"It's not that simple."

"You better make it that simple. If it's over and I'm the one you want to be with, tell her that. If I were in her position I would want to know. I'm not going to let you have your cake and eat it too. Make your choice." She smiled softly as she traced her fingers lightly over his chest. "I'm sure Daddy won't be pleased if you upset me."

Karl wouldn't be happy with him either. For nearly two years his father had been trying to form an alliance with Sydney's father, Daniel Bradshaw. Daniel owned one of the biggest recording companies in the country. He would make a powerful ally for his father's company if he sealed the deal with Sydney.

"You're serious about this, aren't you?"

"I'm as serious as a heart attack, Kavon. I refuse to share you a moment longer. Do whatever you have to do to make this right, or I walk away without a second glance."

"Sydney . . ."

She held up her hand. "Nothing you can say or do will

change my mind on this. Make your choice and live with it, although I will warn you in advance. When the new year comes in, you'll either be kissing me or it's sayonara for you." Without another word she turned and walked out the door.

Alexis folded her arms under her chest as she stood on the lower deck staring out at the moonlit water as they headed out to the Atlantic Ocean. The weather was unusually warm even by Florida's standards, but she was grateful. At least she wouldn't have to suffer alone in the cold.

Her heart ached with every beat. How could Kavon do something like this to her? She'd left New York to move to Orlando because of him. She'd given up her old life to give him what she thought he needed, and this was his repayment? How could she forget the past three years and start over when her life had revolved around him for so long? She'd lost the man she loved to someone else. It didn't seem fair that he would be able to walk away from this unscathed and she would be left to pick up the pieces of her life.

She remembered the day they had met in the New York Public Library as if it were yesterday. She was working in the library as a part of a work-study program when he'd approached her about finding a book for his English class. She'd helped him find the book he needed, and after a lengthy discussion she'd agreed to tutor him. He never would have obtained his MBA if it weren't for her. Now that he no longer had a use for her, he was pushing her to the side.

A lone tear slid down her cheek. She brushed it away quickly. No matter what happened, she would never let him see her cry. She would never give him the satisfaction of knowing just how much he'd hurt her.

She heard a door close behind her, but she didn't bother to turn around. Even after she heard the footsteps approaching she remained locked in place. It was only when she heard the footsteps stop a few feet away that she whirled around to confront the intruder.

"I thought you might like some champagne," Kavon said as he held out a glass.

"Is that your way of easing your conscience after placing my head on the guillotine?"

"For what it's worth, I didn't plan this."

"Is that supposed to make me feel better?"

Kavon dropped his head beneath her penetrating gaze. "This wasn't the way I planned for you to find out."

"Find out what, Kavon? That you've been seeing her behind my back?"

He looked up as he held out the glass again. "It's your favorite."

"I don't want it, you keep it."

He set the glass down on a patio table. "Suit yourself."

"Did you really think a glass of champagne was going to ease your conscience?"

"My conscience doesn't have anything to do with this."

"I forgot, you first have to have one for it to bother you."

"We can fight about this all night but it won't change anything, Alexis. Things haven't been right between us this past year. You had to know it was leading up to this."

"Our relationship started going downhill when your father hired Sydney."

"I never meant for this thing with Sydney to take off the way it did. Our relationship started off as strictly business. The more we worked together, the more I found myself becoming attracted to her."

"Is that supposed to make me feel better? That it just happened? That's an excuse I would expect from a teenager, Kavon. Although this does help explain all of the broken dates, the fights and petty arguments. I finally know where you were all the nights you claimed to be working late."

"I was working late."

"On what?"

"Touché."

"Why embarrass me like this? I deserved to know the truth before tonight, Kavon. You didn't have to bring me here in front of all your friends and family to flaunt your new girlfriend in my face."

"I had no idea my father invited her tonight. If I had known, I would have skipped the party this year."

"And leave me in the dark for how much longer?"

"Until I figured out the best way to break the news to you."

She shook her head. "What you were going to tell me? How about the truth, Kavon? What did you think I would do? Get down on my hands and knees and beg you to stay? Trust me, I have more dignity than that."

"In a way, I'm glad my father took things out of my hands. If not, I would still be living a lie." He paused as he dropped his head. "This gives me a chance to clear the air between us, Alexis. To tell you that I love Sydney and she's the one I want to be with."

Alexis felt her heart shatter into a million pieces the moment the words left his mouth. How dare he say this to her after all the time she'd invested in their relationship? She'd helped him pass his classes in his senior year of college. Now that he'd made it, so to speak, he was leaving her for someone who'd probably never done anything for him except sleep with him.

She felt a mixture of fury and hatred well up inside her as she stared at him. "Am I supposed to just drop off the face of the planet because you think you're in love with Sydney? I moved away from everyone and everything I loved to be with you, and all you can say to me is, so sad, too bad, I fell in love with someone else? How dare you!"

"I wanted to tell you before now, but I kept putting it off because I didn't want to hurt you. I regret that things happened the way they have, but it's given me the opportunity to be honest about the woman I love. I still love you but I'm not in love with you." Alexis turned away from him as he continued. "Are you going to be okay?" he said.

"Okay? Would you be okay if the roles were reversed?"

"No," he replied softly. "Do you need anything before I head inside?"

"I don't need anything from you."

"I want us to remain friends."

She spun around to stare at him. "Friends? How can you

even fix your mouth to ask me that after tonight? Why would I want to have anything else to do with you?"

"Alexis . . ." he began as he took a step in her direction. She held up her hand. "Don't come anywhere near me."

"Are you sure you don't need anything?"

"There is one thing you can do for me." She saw the puzzled look on his face.

"What?"

"Tell Karl congratulations."

"Excuse me?"

"Relay the message. He'll know what I'm talking about." She turned away from him then.

"Alexis—"

"Go back to Sydney," she said as she blinked away her tears. Without another word, Kavon turned and walked away, leaving her alone.

Four

Malcolm stood behind the buffet table catching bits and pieces of gossip as they came his way. He'd learned a lot in the past hour. The vultures couldn't wait to start talking about Alexis and the articles she'd written about the entertainment industry. From what he gleaned from their conversations, she'd caused a lot of controversy with her no-holds-barred journalism. They hated her because she had the guts to risk her neck for what she believed.

When she told him she was a journalist for *Black Ink,* he never made the connection. He'd read several of her articles, so he understood why the people at this party were up in arms. She'd made a lot of valid points and she didn't hide the truth. His respect for her had grown by leaps and bounds now that he'd met the woman behind the words.

Alexis. His heart skipped a beat just thinking about her. Their conversation echoed in his head. He'd only talked to her a few minutes, but it left him wanting more. His eyes narrowed as he watched Kavon and Sydney laughing and talking with several other people. He'd known Kavon since they were children. Even then he'd never liked his attitude.

As much as he wanted to go over and slap the taste off Kavon's prep-school mouth, he restrained himself. He couldn't lose his head and make a bad situation worse by allowing personal issues to take over.

He poured champagne into empty glasses as his gaze searched the room for Alexis. He was hoping she would have returned by now, but who could blame her if she never did? Why would she want to watch Kavon in the arms of another woman?

His stomach tightened with anger. Alexis was probably somewhere crying her eyes out over a man who clearly didn't deserve her tears. He removed his jacket. He was going to take matters into his own hands.

"Luther, watch things here for me." He didn't wait for a reply, so he didn't see the surprised look on Luther's face as he turned and headed for the door.

Outside, he searched the entire middle and lower decks before he finally found Alexis lying on a lounge chair with her legs tucked neatly under her. She wasn't crying as he'd expected. Her eyes were closed as the breeze blew over her. She reminded him of a life-sized doll with her delicate features.

As if she sensed him standing there she opened her eyes and peered up at him. He saw the pained look there. It caused a bolt of fury to shoot through him. Why did the good people always end up with the no-good ones?

"I agree completely," she whispered with a soft smile. It was then that he realized he'd spoken his thoughts out loud.

"I shouldn't have voiced my opinion."

"Even if I agree?"

"It wasn't my place."

"Don't worry about it."

"Want to talk about it?"

She shook her head. "Not really."

"Want me to just hold you?" he dared to ask.

"Yes," she said softly as he extended his hand. Without the slightest trace of hesitation, she placed her hand in his, allowing him to help her to her feet. The moment she was standing, he pulled her into his embrace.

"Malcolm, maybe this isn't such a good idea."

He tightened his embrace. "When you break down, it will be better if someone is holding you. It helps anchor you."

She looked up at him. "You seem to know a lot about this."

"I've had my heart broken a time or two."

"I refuse to cry over Kavon."

His breath caught in his throat as he caught a whiff of her perfumed hair. The scent was intoxicating. His body hardened. It was a reaction that completely took him by surprise. It had been so long since a woman had affected him this way, he was at a loss. He knew he should have let her go and walked away with his mind intact, but his urge to protect her was so strong his heart refused to listen. He forced his thoughts to remain neutral as he steeled his body against her.

"You'll feel better. Trust me."

Alexis lifted her head and smiled warily. "If I had a dime for every time I've heard those words I would be filthy rich."

"Are you sure you don't want to talk about it?"

"I don't think the details of my heartbreak and humiliation would interest you very much, although I do thank you for caring enough to ask." She dropped her head. "Just hold me."

As he tightened his arms around her, the dam of tears she'd been holding back emerged. He remained silent as the tears slid down her face and uncontrollable sobs racked her body. Nothing would make her feel better except time. His anger for Kavon deepened every time a sob caused her body to tremble. Her tears soaked his shirt, but still he held her. She needed him to hold her up and he was willing to be there for her.

He looked up when he heard footsteps approaching. Cecile froze in place as her eyes locked with his. He saw the sympathy there for what her son had done. She had opened her mouth to say something when he shook his head. This wasn't the time. Having her there would only make things worse. As if Cecile understood, she nodded before she turned and walked away.

Alexis cried until she had no tears left to cry before she finally met his eyes again. Her makeup was streaked across her face, and her eyes were still moist, but to him she was the most beautiful woman in the world. "Why me?"

"Bad things happen to the best of us."

"How could he throw me to the side like this?" she whispered almost to herself.

"Kavon is a fool." He gently brushed the remaining tears from her cheeks.

"You think so?" Her voice was filled with uncertainty.

"He doesn't realize a precious jewel when he sees one." Their lips were so close they were nearly touching.

He wanted to kiss her even though he knew he shouldn't. It would only complicate things. He was trying to come up with a way to break the awkward silence between them when her lips touched his.

All of his resolve went out the window as the pressure of her lips against his enveloped him. She moaned as her lips parted slightly, allowing him further access. Before he could stop himself his tongue slid into her mouth. Her arms wrapped around his neck as their tongues began an intricate dance.

The scent of her perfume filled his every breath. Her breasts were crushed against his chest. Unable to help himself he ran his fingers through her hair, pulling away carelessly the hairpins holding it in place. Her hair fell to her shoulders in a cloud of silk. The more he tasted her, the more he wanted her. Passion held his body rigid as if he'd been struck by lightning.

His feelings of euphoria were quickly replaced by the reality of the situation. It was all he could do not to tear himself away from her when he realized what he was doing. He had to handle this delicately. If he didn't he would cause more harm than was already done. He'd come out here to comfort her, not to seduce her. He was filled with shame at his weakness.

He summoned every ounce of willpower he possessed to remove his mouth from hers. She whimpered slightly and attempted to pull him back into her embrace, but he stepped just beyond her reach.

"I can't do this, Alexis. It won't get us anywhere."

Alexis's eyes, which only moments before had been filled with passion, turned icy. Her face flushed red with embarrassment before she turned her back to him. "You must think I'm the biggest tramp alive."

"No, I don't," he replied honestly. "I think you've been through a lot tonight and you're looking for an outlet. This may seem right now, but you'll only regret this later. You can't erase Kavon this way."

"I don't give a damn about Kavon," she hissed. "He's in there with Sydney enjoying his New Year's Eve. I'm the one struck here against my will."

He didn't have to see her face to know her tears had returned. The bitterness in her voice pierced his heart. He took a step in her direction. "Alexis?"

"Please go, Malcolm. You've done enough." Her fingers gripped the metal railing.

"Alexis—"

"Please just go and leave me alone. I've made a big enough fool of myself for one night." Her voice was choked.

His heart felt heavy. Instead of helping her through her pain, he'd succeeded in making a bad situation worse. He wanted to reach out to her but he wasn't sure how to do that now. In a matter of seconds she'd placed a wall around herself he had no idea how to get around.

For a moment he stood there watching her as her hair blew in the breeze. His need to protect her was so strong it shocked him. Never in his life had he felt the need to watch over a woman and keep her safe. His emotions were foreign to him and he couldn't understand why he felt the way he felt, but he knew he couldn't discount his feelings or pretend they didn't exist.

"I can't leave it like this between us, Alexis."

"Of course you can. Do what most men do and walk away."

"I'm not like most men, damn it," he replied in frustration. "I can't pretend this didn't happen."

"Of course you can," she said as she turned tortured eyes to him. "It's what men do best."

"All men are not alike, Alexis."

She held up her hand to silence him. "Just leave, Malcolm. I need to be alone for a while."

He wanted to argue with her, but he realized that would only make everything worse. He decided he would grant her wish for now, but he wasn't going to give up on her that easily just because she asked him to.

"I'll leave you alone for now, but I won't just disappear, Alexis. This isn't over."

She didn't reply as she turned away from him as if she hadn't heard him. His heart was heavy and his mind was full as he took one last glance at her before he headed inside.

more objections, Miss Lady," he said as he removed his keys from his pocket and unlocked the door of the Acura she'd been leaning against.

"This is your car?" She couldn't hide the note of surprise in her voice.

He lifted his eyebrows. "Yes. Is there a problem?"

"I'm just a little surprised."

"Because I'm a waiter?" Malcolm questioned with amusement.

"That wasn't what I meant."

"I wouldn't take offense if you did." He laughed. "In addition to genuinely enjoying my job, the pay is good."

Alexis didn't reply as she slid inside the car. The leather was buttery smooth against her skin as she settled back into the passenger seat. The interior of the car was a deep cream color and smelled of citrus. Malcolm closed the door behind her and headed for the driver's side. He climbed in and started the ignition.

"Where to, my lady?" he questioned in a fake English accent, causing Alexis to laugh.

"Are you always this comical?"

"Of course," he said as he put the car in drive. "I get to drive beautiful women home all the time."

"Flattery will get you nowhere, mister."

"Are you sure about that?" There was a hint of mischief in his voice.

"Yes," she replied as he reached the front entrance.

"Where to?"

"Lake Sheen Reserve."

"Isn't that in Orlando?"

She didn't miss the note of surprise in his voice. "Yes. Is something wrong?" The moment the words left her mouth they both burst out laughing.

"Those words seem to be floating around a lot tonight."

Alexis felt her mood lighten despite the disastrous night. A few hours ago she couldn't wait to get home. Now that she was enjoying Malcolm's company, she found herself wanting to spend more time with him. By the way he'd come to her aid when she needed someone and their intimate kiss, she felt as if he were an old friend instead of the stranger he was. She felt comfortable and at ease with him.

As she glanced over at him she wondered if she would be interested in him if the circumstances were different. Just being with him tonight, she sensed he was caring, sensitive, and immensely passionate. Those were admirable qualities in any man. She wanted to know more about the complex man beside her, but she refused to ask him the questions she wanted answers to, for fear of opening a door that would be hard to slam shut. Just the thought of Malcolm holding her in his arms caused her heart to flutter with excitement.

Surprised by her thoughts, she turned to stare out the window. How was it possible that she'd just broken up with Kavon a few hours ago and already her mind was filled with thoughts of another man? A man she knew virtually nothing about.

Malcolm reached over and flipped on the radio. The majority of the ride they spent in silence as the songs from the past filled the car. They were only a few blocks away from her gated community before he finally spoke again.

"You're awfully quiet."

"I was just thinking about tonight."

"I know this is one New Year's Eve I'll never forget."

"I can agree with you on that," she replied softly as he pulled up to the gate of her small community. "I can't believe we're already here."

"All of the stimulating conversation helped," he joked as she reached in her purse and produced the gate key.

As he slid the pass into the slot, Alexis realized her time with him was just about over. She sighed softly when she realized this would probably be the last time she saw him. She couldn't figure out if she was relieved or disappointed. Tomorrow she would begin picking up the pieces of her life to start from scratch. Having Malcolm there would be a distraction she didn't need. As the gate slid open she tried to ignore the small part of her heart that wanted him to stick around.

Malcolm pulled into the driveway of Alexis's home and cut the ignition as he looked at the house that loomed before him. It was a two-story beige Spanish-style home with arched doorways, several balconies, and a red-tiled roof. The grass had been recently trimmed as well as the shrubs that grew around the downstairs windows. Two metal candle lanterns and soft patio lights decorated the walkway that led up to the front door. There was a heavy wooden door with stained glass in the middle adding a touch of elegance to the front of the house. He could see several lights on inside, giving the house a warm, cozy look.

It was time for him to let her go, but he found he didn't want to. Their kiss earlier had left him wanting more of her, but he knew that was impossible. Even if he was considering the possibility of trying to pursue a relationship with her, which he still wasn't sure he was, he doubted she'd even be open to the idea. She'd just come out of a long-term relationship with a man who dumped her for someone else. It would take time for her to heal.

For a moment they sat there in silence. It was after five o'clock in the morning. She probably couldn't wait to crawl into bed and shut out the rest of the world, but he found himself wanting to spend more time with her.

"Have you ever thought about planting rosebushes near your front door?" The moment the words left his mouth he wanted to kick himself for asking such a stupid question.

"I considered it a year after I moved here, but I didn't have the space they require."

"How long have you been here?"

"Going on three years." She pulled her house keys from her purse.

"Hold on." He got out of the car and went around to her door. He opened it and held out his hand. She placed her hand in his, causing a tremor of heat to surge through his bloodstream.

"A true gentleman."

"My mother spent enough time beating it into my head."

"Would you like to come in for a few minutes?"

"Sure." His voice was calm but his heart was racing out of control. He wanted to be with her right now more than anything else in the world.

He couldn't resist a smile as she led the way up the walkway. She opened the door, allowing him to walk inside ahead of her as she closed and locked the door. As he walked inside he checked out the interior. The walls were painted in vivid tones of yellow, terra-cotta, and blue. Instead of looking tacky, it fit in with the decor of her home.

The den to his right was painted in a beautiful terra-cotta. He could see an overstuffed sofa, love seat, and chair set in a soft beige color. There were several bone-white shelves and cabinets built into the walls. He saw several black art pieces and woven Indian blankets adorning the walls. Above the white mantel there was a huge painting of a black leopard, highlighted by several hidden lights, which took up most of the wall.

Everything was cozy and comfortable and he immediately felt at home. He had no idea what he'd been expecting her home to look like, but it certainly wasn't this.

Alexis looked up at him shyly. "I decorated it myself."

"You did a wonderful job."

"I love vibrant colors. It makes a home look lived in."

"It certainly does," he said as he stepped inside the den.

"Would you like something to drink?"

"Sure."

"Tea okay?"

"Yes."

She smiled. "Make yourself at home."

His eyes roamed around the room at the art she'd selected. His gaze landed on several silver picture frames lining the mantel. Curiosity got the better of him as he headed for the fireplace. They were several pictures of Alexis during her childhood. Even as a child she was beautiful. The picture that held his interest was the one of an ebony-skinned woman and Alexis. The women had her arm wrapped possessively around her shoulders. The strong resemblance between them led him to believe the woman was her mother.

Embarrassed by his nosiness, he began checking out the

rest of the room. The house was immaculate. The only thing that seemed to be out of place was a ball of fur in a wicker basket in the corner of the room. With a frown on his face he went over to it. He was about to reach down and touch it when the fur moved and stretched, producing two tiny black eyes.

"A Pomeranian," he said as the dog gazed up at him and gave a halfhearted yelp before it turned over and resumed its position.

"I see you've met Frisky."

He raised his eyebrows. "Frisky?"

"Believe it or not, she used to be a long time ago." She laughed. "She's nearly fifteen years old, so I guess she figures she's entitled to some rest and relaxation. All she does now is sleep."

"An ankle biter," he joked as he took the mug from her outstretched hand.

"She gave that up a long time ago." She rubbed Frisky with her foot. "She belonged to my mother."

"I checked out your pictures on the mantel. I hope you don't mind."

"I put them there for people to see." She headed over to the sofa. He followed her and sat down on the love seat.

"Is the woman on the picture with you your mother?"

Her smile was sad. "Yes. It was the last picture we took before she died five years ago."

"I'm sorry." He wished he could bite his tongue off for asking.

"Don't be."

"Do you have any other family?"

"No. My mother's parents died long before I was born and I never knew anything about my father or his family, because he disappeared right after my mother got pregnant. When she died, I became an orphan."

"Have you ever thought about trying to find your father?"

"There's no point. Sometimes you're better off not knowing." She turned to him. "What about you? Do you have a big family?"

He wanted to kick himself. Why had he brought up the

subject of family? "I have a small family. My parents are still alive. I have a sister, Brandy, who is expecting a baby in a few weeks, and a twin brother, Darryl, who drives me up the wall."

"A twin?"

Malcolm smiled as he thought about his brother. "Yes. We have a lot of ways alike, but sometimes we're so different I swear aliens have abducted him and replaced him with a clone programmed to make me miserable. Despite our differences we get along great."

"Did you grow up here?" Alexis questioned as she sipped her tea.

"Yes." He sipped his drink. He was greeted by a slightly sweet, tart flavor. "I haven't had green tea in a long time."

Alexis smiled as she tucked her legs beneath her. "My mother used to fix me a cup of tea before she put me to bed. I can't go to sleep without it now."

"Some habits are hard to break."

She hesitated for a fraction of a second. "Thank you for bringing me home, Malcolm. I'm glad you talked me into it."

He smiled. "My mother would be proud all of her lessons finally paid off."

"Oh?"

"My mother has beat into my head I should always be kind and help damsels in distress."

"Am I a damsel?" she questioned with amusement.

"As close as I'll ever come."

"You make me laugh. Something I haven't done in a long time."

"Is that a good thing?"

"A very good thing." She paused. "I want to thank you for everything you've done tonight, Malcolm. I don't think I would have made it without you."

The look of tenderness in her eyes was nearly his undoing. He wanted to go over and crush her in his arms and kiss her until the sun came up. She'd touched something in him tonight he thought had died a long time ago. Emotions he wasn't aware he was capable of feeling again. What shocked him the most was that after so many years of being emotionally bankrupt where women were concerned, his attraction to her didn't frighten him.

"I'd better be going," he said, breaking the awkward silence between them.

She glanced down at her watch. "I didn't even realize it was nearly six in the morning."

"See what good conversation will do for you?" he teased as he pulled his keys from his pocket and stood up. Alexis stood and stretched her arms wide before she followed him to the front door.

"Thanks again for everything, Malcolm."

His name sounded like music coming from her lips. "You're welcome, Alexis." He pulled her into his arms.

He knew he should have stopped at that, but he couldn't help himself. His desire for her overruled the sensible side of his brain as his lips tenderly touched hers. She didn't resist as he slipped his tongue into her mouth. As he stood there exploring her mouth, they were the only two people in the world. The feel of her tongue against his caused his blood to boil. He felt a throbbing ache in his groin. He didn't know what was happening to him, but he knew he didn't ever want it to stop.

Alexis pulled away from him all too soon. As her eyes locked with his, he wondered why she was different. He felt the carefully constructed walls he'd built years ago crumbling down around him. Why out of all the women in the world did he have to fall for this one? He was the last thing she needed in her life right now.

"Good night, Alexis," he whispered softly as he brushed away a stray hair from her forehead before he stepped outside the door.

"Good night, Malcolm," she replied softly as she closed the door behind him.

Six

"What is wrong with you this morning?" Darryl questioned as he slam-dunked the basketball into the basket. "Brandy would give me a better run for my money and she's eight months pregnant."

Malcolm smiled at the mention of Brandy's name. "How is she?"

"It's a shame you have to ask me how your own sister is doing." Darryl shook his head as he bounced the basketball with his right hand. "She's as big as a house right about now."

"How much longer does she have to go?"

"According to her doctor, another three weeks."

"I'll have to go see her sometime this week."

"Please do." Darryl twirled the ball around on his finger. "Ready to lose?"

"Nah." Malcolm wiped the sweat from his brow and headed for the bench. He didn't know why he was trying to fool himself. He was on the court but his heart wasn't in it. His mind was on Alexis and the heat he felt when he held her in his arms.

For three years he'd been able to keep at a comfortable distance all of the women who passed through his life. He was always able to find some flaw with them to keep him from getting too close. That prevented him from having his heart broken. In one night Alexis had changed all of that.

The feel of her mouth, so warm, moist, and giving, was burned forever in his memory. He wanted to hold her in his arms again and soothe all of her pain and misery. For the first time since his ex-wife left him he felt a tremor in his heart.

"Earth to Malcolm. What's up with you this morning?" Darryl questioned as he sat down on the bench next to his brother. "You've been acting strange all morning."

"I'm just tired." Malcolm took a swig from his thermos. "Last night wore me out."

"I know you didn't go there. If you were out like me getting your groove on, I would accept that excuse in a heartbeat. Since you were stuck playing waiter you need to come up with one better than that. Something else is bothering you."

"I have no idea what you're talking about." Malcolm averted his gaze from his brother. "Perhaps I'm upset because I can't be a party animal like you."

Darryl grinned. "Don't try to flatter me to get me off your case. By the way, how was the party? I'm surprised to see you in one piece this morning."

Malcolm wiped his forehead. "Those women nearly tore me apart last night. Every time I turned around, Courtney was in my face."

"I don't see what the problem is. You have a supermodel practically throwing her body at your feet and you're turning her down? Opportunities like that only come once in a lifetime."

"After last night I don't think she'll speak to me again." His voice drifted off as he thought about Alexis and how different she was from Courtney. She was just as beautiful, but it was her quiet confidence and independence that drew him to her. He admired the passion he saw in her eyes when she talked about her work. He understood the way she felt all too well.

"Who is she?" Darryl slapped Malcolm on the leg with a wet towel.

"Who is who?"

"The woman who has you grinning like the Cheshire Cat."

"I wasn't aware I was grinning."

"Who is she?"

Malcolm groaned. Darryl wouldn't leave him alone until he gave him some information. "Her name is Alexis."

"Beautiful name. Now what about the women behind the name? I want to hear all of the details."

"If you're looking for details you won't get many, because there really isn't anything to tell. I met her at Cecile's party last night. That's basically it."

"I thought you weren't looking for another debutante looking for a six-figure husband."

"She's not like that."

"How do you know that after only one night?"

"I never told her who I was and she's still interested."

"Come again."

"She assumed I was a waiter and I played along with it. She has no idea who I am."

"Get real, Malcolm. Every woman in a fifty-mile radius knows who you are."

"Not Alexis. She moved here less than three years ago from New York, and from what I gather she hasn't gotten out much."

"So you're going to play it low-key with this one?" There was genuine surprise in Darryl's voice.

"Why is that so surprising? I'm not one who flaunts what I have anyway."

"That's not your style. You're usually Mr. Honesty, Malcolm. Don't you think not telling her who you are is dishonest?"

Malcolm shook his head. "For the first time I have a chance to get to know a woman without my background and family standing in the way. I think this is going to work. I get to be a normal person for a change."

Darryl narrowed his eyes as he shook his head. "I should have known a woman had something to do with screwing up your game this morning. There is no way I could beat you like I did today otherwise."

"I told you, I'm tired."

"We'll drop it for now but I'm not letting you off the hook that easily. You owe me a real game." He picked up his gym bag.

"Where are you heading off to?"

"I have a date."

"Anyone I know?"

"No." Darryl said as he averted his gaze. "Just someone I bumped into today."

Malcolm laughed as they approached their cars. "Whatever you say, Darryl." Unlike Darryl he never pried into his brother's private life. And today he was anxious to be rid of him so he could call Alexis and ask her out.

"I'll catch you later," Darryl said as he hurried over to his Mercedes convertible and hopped inside.

Malcolm grinned as his brother drove off. If the situation were reversed, Darryl would still be asking questions. He opened his car door and slid inside. He had flipped open his cell phone to call Alexis when he realized he'd never gotten her number. Dismay settled over him. How was he going to call and ask her out if he didn't have her number?

As he sat there pondering the answer to his question, Cecile's name popped into his head. He could call her and ask her for Alexis's number. He was about to dial Cecile's number when he realized he needed to come up with an excuse for wanting Alexis's number. Frustration set in as he racked his brain. Tired of trying to come up with an excuse, he just decided he'd ask for the number and go with the flow. He flipped his phone open and dialed. Cecile picked up on the second ring.

"Hello?"

"Hi, Cecile, this is Malcolm." He rolled his window down. "How are you this fine day?"

She laughed. "Tired. I'm not as young as I used to be."

"I know the feeling."

"I want to thank you again, Malcolm. Everything turned out beautifully last night. You can look for me to call you whenever I have catering needs in the future."

"I'm glad you approved of my selections." He tapped his fingers on the steering wheel.

"Now that we've gotten the formalities out of the way, to what do I owe the pleasure of this phone call?"

"What makes you think I didn't call you to talk about last night?"

"I already cut your check."

Malcolm laughed. It was now or never. "I was wondering if you had Alexis's telephone number."

Cecile hesitated for a fraction of a second. "How is she?"

"She was pretty torn up last night."

"Kavon was wrong for the way he treated her. Alexis has really been there for him the past two years. He never would have made it out of grad school if it hadn't been for her." She sighed. "If I'd known what was going on, I would have canceled the party."

"Don't beat yourself up, Cecile. I got the impression Alexis already knew there was something going on. What happened wasn't your fault."

"Then why do I feel so damn guilty?"

"You really like her?"

"You're too kind." Cecile laughed lightly. "You have a pen handy?"

Malcolm pulled one from the armrest. "Go ahead."

Cecile gave him the number. "I wanted to call her this morning but I knew she was probably worn out from last night."

"You should call her. I have a feeling it would mean a lot to her."

"You think so?"

"Yes, I do."

"I'll call her later on this evening." He heard the smile in her voice. "Thank you for the pep talk, Malcolm."

"Any time, Cecile."

"I'll speak with you later, Malcolm. Good-bye."

"Good-bye, Cecile." He disconnected and stared down at the piece of paper with Alexis's number on it. He couldn't prevent the huge grin that spread across his face as he flipped open his phone again and dialed her number.

*　　*　　*

The sound of Frisky's barking aroused Alexis from a deep sleep. With a moan she ran her fingers through her hair as she sat up. She gently rubbed her sleep-heavy eyes as she peered over at the clock. Shock spread through her when she realized it was nearly six-thirty. She'd slept the entire day. As she glanced down at her wrinkled dress, memories of the night before flashed through her mind.

She rubbed her eyes once again as she peered down at the tiny dog sitting expectantly next to her bed. With a laugh she reached down and rubbed Frisky's head. Food was the only thing strong enough to rouse Frisky from her resting place.

"You must be starving." She stood up and headed for the kitchen. She opened a can of dog food and dumped it into Frisky's bowl before she headed back to her bedroom. She went into the bathroom and without glancing in the mirror turned on the faucet and poured half a bottle of vanilla-scented bubble bath into the flowing water. She peeled off her gown and stepped into the thick fluffy bubbles. She flipped on the spa jets and rested her head against the back of the tub.

As the jets massaged her tired muscles she let her thoughts drift to Kavon. It was hard for her to believe he'd done her the way he did. Had anyone told her he would throw her to the side like this, she would have told them they were lying. She had given him far too much credit for caring about her feelings than he deserved.

She felt a slight cramp tighten her stomach. Her period was just about due, wasn't it? She frowned as she realized it was a few days late. Her heart nearly stopped as a lump formed in her throat. Her period was never late. It came like clockwork every month on the same day.

She tried to swallow the lump in her throat as she considered the possibility that she might be pregnant. That was the last thing she needed right now in light of everything that was going on. Surely fate wouldn't be that cruel to her, or would it? She bit down on her lip. She would have to make a doctor's appointment as soon as possible to make sure she wasn't pregnant.

The sound of the telephone ringing interrupted her

thoughts. She sighed as she stood up and wrapped a towel around her as she headed for her bedroom. She picked up the cordless phone and hit the talk button.

"Hello?"

"What happened to you last night?" Kavon demanded.

Anger rose in her throat like bile. "I left so you and Sydney could enjoy the rest of your morning."

"Why bring her into this, Alexis?"

"Why? You were the one who put her there, Kavon. Don't turn this around."

"I didn't call to fight with you, Alexis. I only wanted to make sure you were all right. You disappeared as soon as we docked."

"I guess you expected me to hang around so I could revel in your happiness. Did you want me to ride home with you too?"

"You could have taken the limo home, Alexis. I would have made other arrangements. I came out to find you gone and had no clue where you were. Just because we aren't together anymore doesn't mean I don't still care about you. I know you probably hate me right now and I don't blame you for that, but I needed to know you were okay. I still love you."

Alexis didn't even reply as she hit the disconnect button. She threw the phone down on the bed. Despite her anger her heart ached as Kavon's voice echoed in her head. She would have to call the phone company tomorrow and have her number changed. It was strange thinking of him as the enemy, but that's exactly what he was to her. She reached over to flip the ringer off when the phone rang again.

"What do you want?" she demanded as she answered the phone.

"Alexis?"

Her heart skipped a beat when she recognized his voice. Her first thought was, how had he gotten her number? She hadn't given it to him, or had she? There were a lot of things about last night she didn't remember or chose to forget for one reason or the other.

"Malcolm?"

His voice was sensuous and deep as laughter erupted. "I'm flattered you recognize my voice."

A smile crept across her face. "How could I forget it?" Memories of his smiling face filled her mind, pushing every other thought away.

"You seem a little angry."

"I apologize for answering the phone the way I did, but I've had some annoying phone calls today."

"Just remind me never to get on your bad side."

"Sure."

Malcolm hesitated a fraction of a second. "I was calling to find out if you wanted to catch a movie with me tonight."

"A movie?" Alexis repeated.

"Yes."

"What did you have in mind?"

"I was thinking about the Ritz Theater down by the boardwalk. They run old movies that television doesn't do justice to."

It was her turn to hesitate. Her skin grew warm as she thought about the way his lips had felt against hers. She wasn't sure what would happen if she was with him again. As if he sensed her doubts, he quickly continued.

"I know you just broke up with Kavon, but I like you, Alexis. I would love the opportunity to get to know you better if only you'll give me the chance. Agree to go out with me tonight and if at the end of the night you decide you don't want to see me again I'll leave you alone. Deal?"

How could she refuse such a passionate plea? "I'd love to, Malcolm."

"I'll pick you up at eight."

"I'll see you then. Good-bye," she said as she hung up the telephone.

She quickly finished her bath and searched through her closet for something to wear. She could barely contain her excitement as she went through her blouses and pants. She couldn't remember the last time she'd been out on an actual date.

She changed her outfit three times before she finally set-

tled on black jeans, a white ruffled blouse, and black thick-
heeled sandals. She pulled her hair back into a ponytail and
put on lipstick. She misted her body with perfume and stood
back to admire her reflection for a moment before she
headed for the living room.

She was pacing back and forth in front of the fireplace
when the sound of the doorbell startled her. She glanced
down at her watch as she headed for the front door. After
making sure it was Malcolm, she threw the door open. He
was dressed in a black muscle shirt and a pair of blue jeans.
He looked even better now than he had the night before in
his uniform. He held a large basket with flowers overflowing
from it in his hand.

"Hi," she said softly as she stepped aside to let him enter.

"Hi." He stepped inside the foyer. "These are for you."

"They're beautiful." She took the basket from him.

"I didn't know what you liked, so I asked the florist to
give me one of everything."

"Thank you, I love it." She buried her nose in a white rose
before she set the basket down on the small table next to the
door.

"Are you ready?"

"Yes," she said as she picked up her purse and followed
him out the door.

Malcolm took Alexis's hand in his as they strolled from
the movie theater. The moon was shining brightly, illuminat-
ing the streets with an almost eerie glow. Other than a few
more couples leaving the theater, the streets were empty. A
smile spread across his face as he thought about the wonderful evening he was sharing with Alexis.

It was the first time in forever that he'd actually enjoyed a
date. Unlike his other dates who expected fancy dinners and
Broadway plays, she was content to have pizza and catch a
movie. He felt relaxed and at ease, and for once Robin's was
the furthest thing from his mind.

"What are you thinking about?" Alexis questioned as she

looked up at him. Despite her being nearly six feet tall, he still towered over her.

"What makes you think I'm thinking about anything?"

"You have a goofy grin on your face."

"For your information, I was thinking about the movie and about you."

Her face flushed red as she turned away. "What about me?"

"I was thinking about how much I really hate to see this night end. I'm enjoying every moment I spend with you."

"Then don't let it end. Let's go for a walk on the boardwalk," Alexis suggested as they approached the car.

Malcolm smiled. "That sounds like a wonderful idea." He led her past the car and down the street to the boardwalk. After buying an ice cream cone from a vendor closing up for the night, they began a long leisurely stroll.

There was a comfortable silence between them. He didn't feel pressured to keep a conversation going. Just being in her presence was enough for him. He knew he would have to tread the waters carefully. Alexis was someone who could seriously endanger his bachelor status.

She paused as they reached the stairs leading down to the beach. She leaned against the railing and closed her eyes as the wind whipped strands of her hair across her face. Malcolm smiled. She looked so content and peaceful.

"A penny for your thoughts," he whispered. A smile spread across her face as she opened her eyes.

"I was thinking about how much I love the beach," she replied softly. "I grew up in New York where there weren't any beaches, but every summer my mother would rent a house in South Carolina for a weekend even though she couldn't afford it. We would swim and lie out in the sun like we didn't have a care in the world. Those are some of my most precious memories of her."

"You loved your mother, didn't you?"

She nodded. "Very much. It was hard for me when she died. The only reason I got through it was because of my best friend, Tiffany. She forced me to get up and keep living.

She forced me to realize there was nothing I could do for my mother."

"It's hard to lose someone you love."

"You're telling me."

His heart lurched in his chest at the sadness he heard in her voice. He wanted to banish away those feelings and replace them with feelings of love and happiness. He quickly changed the subject. "You're a long away from home if you grew up in New York."

"To be honest with you I only moved here because Kavon wanted me to. He approached me at one of the lowest points of my life and I fell head over heels in love with him." She blinked rapidly. "I guess the love was kind of one-sided."

"Kavon didn't realize what he had."

"As I think about it now I realize that he only tried to tear me down because he realized I would eventually leave him behind. He was all about himself. He never really cared about what I wanted. Whenever we went somewhere, no matter where we went he was always the one who chose. I wasn't an equal partner in our relationship. He used me as his trophy girl."

"He didn't give you enough credit, Alexis. I think you're a wonderful young woman with a bright future ahead of her."

"I'm glad you think so," she said shyly. "What about you? You know all about my sordid affair with Kavon. Why aren't you taken?"

Malcolm took a deep breath as he turned to stare at the waves. "I married my high school sweetheart the day after graduation, much to my parents' horror. They wanted me to go to college and get a formal education, but I wouldn't listen to them. I thought I had everything I needed to make it. Leslie and I were happy for a time, but my work schedule got in her way. She wanted to party her life away, and eventually she left me for someone else. I poured everything into that relationship only to come out empty-handed." He turned to her. "I understand where you are right now. I've been there and done that."

"Casualties of war," she replied softly as she touched his arm.

"We just fell in love with the wrong people."

"How did you find the courage to go on after your relationship ended?"

"I threw myself into my work even harder. In the meantime my parents, my brother, Darryl, my sister, Brandy, and every one of their friends tried to fix things by attempting to set me up with different women. I can't tell you what a disaster that was. Every time I went to someone's house I knew there would be some unattached female waiting. I finally had enough and told everyone to mind their own business. So far it's worked for nearly four years."

Alexis laughed. "Was it really that bad?"

Malcolm cracked a grin. "Worse."

"Oh."

He slid his arm around her waist. "This is the first time in two years that I've actually enjoyed a date."

"Really?" Her surprise was evident in her voice.

"Yes. I've shied away from women because I was afraid of being hurt again."

He could see the curiosity in her eye as she looked up at him. "Why did you ask me out, Malcolm?"

"You were down-to-earth," he replied honestly. "You don't know how many women out there would turn their nose up at a man in my position."

"There's always room for improvement, Malcolm. You could always go back to school."

"I know . . ." He let his voice trail off. He wanted to tell her everything but he sensed it was still too soon. She was starting to open up to him. If he told her the truth about his background and his family, she would put her guard up and he'd never get anywhere. He felt a twinge of guilt in the back of his mind for what he was doing, but as he stared at her beautiful face he realized this was for the best. He would tell her everything when he was sure it wouldn't matter to her anymore.

His thoughts shocked him as he realized he wanted her

around. This wasn't going to be a onetime thing if he had anything to do with it. He couldn't explain it but he knew deep in his heart Alexis was going to become a permanent person in his life.

"Ready to head home?" he questioned as he gently touched her face. She nodded as he took her hand and led her back down the boardwalk.

The radio was kicking out all the old jams he'd grown up listening to as he drove back to her house. Several times he and Alexis sang along with the songs as they tried to remember the artists who sang them. In no time at all he pulled up to Alexis's and cut the ignition.

His heart sank when he realized they were at the end of the evening. He felt a lump settle in his throat as he remembered what he'd said to her earlier. No matter what he told her he had no intention of never seeing her again. He was going to do whatever was in his power to convince her she needed him in her life.

"I'm glad I let you talk me into going out tonight, Alexis. I really had fun."

Alexis laughed. "Isn't that supposed to be my line?"

He laughed. "Equal opportunity is the name of the game." He got out and headed around to open her car door. He reached for her hand and helped her to her feet before he closed the door behind her. He didn't release her hand as he slowly walked her to the front door.

"It's beautiful out tonight," she said as she looked up at the star-studded sky.

"It fails in comparison to you." He touched her face. "I really want to see you again, Alexis."

Her eyes widened in surprise as she looked up at him. "Why?"

"Do I really need a reason other than I want to get to know you better?" He pulled her into his arms.

"I don't think that's a good idea, Malcolm."

He lifted her chin with his index finger so that he was staring into her eyes. "Why not?"

"I don't want to get involved with someone again this soon after Kavon."

"We can go as slow as you want to go, Alexis. I won't rush you into anything. I know you just broke up with someone you loved, and I respect that. I won't rush you into anything."

Alexis exhaled deeply. "Malcolm, I just don't want to—"

He placed his finger up to her lips to silence her. "What happened in the past has nothing to do with here and now. I want you to be a part of my life and I feel it's only fair to warn you that I always get what I want, Alexis. Always." His voice conveyed his determination.

"Malcolm, you don't understand that I'm—"

"A beautiful, desirable woman that I want to get to know better," he interrupted as his eyes locked with hers. "Please give me a chance to make you happy."

Alexis stared up at him as if she couldn't believe what he was saying to her. He saw the mixture of pain and sadness surface in her eyes. They were emotions he wanted to banish from her life forever if only she'd give him the chance. No one, least of all her, deserved to go through life miserable.

"Alexis?" She remained silent. He was about to get down on his hands and knees when she finally nodded in consent. Warmth and tenderness spread through him as he pulled her into his arms. "You'll never be sorry."

A soft smile touched the corners of her mouth. "I know."

"Thank you for giving me a chance." He gently pressed his lips against hers.

"You're welcome," she whispered softly. "Good night, Malcolm."

"Good night, Alexis." He watched her as she walked inside and closed the door behind her.

Seven

Alexis held a blue chemise top up to her chest as she peered in the mirror. She was trying to decide what would look best with her black jeans, but everything she held up looked the same. Sonya, lying across her bed leafing through a romance novel, finally sighed in frustration.

"Why don't you go with the red top and call it a day, Alexis?" she offered as she threw the red blouse at her. "I'm tired of watching you go through tops."

"I just want everything to be just right, Sonya. I really like Malcolm."

"So I noticed." She sat up. "You never went through twenty outfits for Kavon."

"Only because Kavon told me what to wear before we went out." She picked up the red chemise and held it up. "Do you really think this blouse is the best?"

"Yes, I do. You're being paranoid for no reason."

"I have a lot to be paranoid about," Alexis replied before she could stop herself.

"What's going on that you haven't told me about?"

She sighed. She wanted to keep it to herself until she knew for certain whether or not she was pregnant, but she couldn't hold on to it any longer. "I think I may be pregnant," she mumbled.

"From Kavon?"

"No, the man on the moon."

"Why do you think you're pregnant?"

"Besides the fact that my period is missing in action, I've been tired lately and my appetite has increased a little."

"That sounds like the symptoms of early pregnancy." Sonya frowned. "How long have you been having these symptoms?"

"Since New Year's Day."

"That was almost three months ago, Alexis. You need to make an appointment with the doctor as soon as possible."

"I knew I needed to make an appointment months ago, but I kept putting it off because I'm afraid to know the truth."

"The truth will be a lot easier to swallow once you know for certain what the outcome is."

"What if I'm pregnant, Sonya?" she questioned as she sat down on the bed.

"I trust you to make the right decision whatever that may be." She pulled her into her embrace. "Guard your heart in case you are pregnant and Malcolm doesn't want the responsibility."

Alexis sighed deeply as she looked up at her best friend. "I'm praying for a false alarm."

"Sometimes prayers do come true." Sonya held her out at arm's length. "Whatever happens, I'll be here for you."

"I know you will, I know you will."

Malcolm took Alexis's hand as they left the parking lot. It was a beautiful day for the Jazz Festival. The weather was warm and there wasn't a cloud in the sky. As far as the eye could see, people were stretched out on blankets as they enjoyed the music and food. Alexis eyed the picnic basket on his arm and felt her stomach rumble with anticipation of whatever he'd packed.

"There's a picnic table over there," Malcolm said as he pointed in the direction of a huge oak tree.

"Where?" Alexis questioned as she placed her hand up to shield her eyes from the sun.

"Malcolm, how are you?" an elderly gentleman questioned as he and a woman approached them.

"I'm fine, Sam. How are you, Monica?" Malcolm replied with a smile as he shook the man's hand.

"We're doing fine."

"Sam, Monica, I'd like for you to meet Alexis."

"Hello, Alexis," Sam said with a bright smile.

"Pleased to meet you," Monica said as she took her hand in hers.

"The pleasure is mine," she said politely as she noticed a family of four claimed the table Malcolm had spied moments before.

"Sam is one of my father's oldest friends." He turned back to Sam. "I had no idea you were in town."

As she stood back and watched him in action she began to wonder about him. It wasn't the first time she found herself wondering about the man she'd spent the past three months with. Being with him had allowed her to see a side of him she never guessed existed. In a matter of minutes the man with whom she'd spent countless hours frolicking through the park and eating hot dogs on the beach had disappeared. In his place was a polished, classy guy no one would ever believe was only a waiter in a restaurant.

She shrugged off her thoughts as she focused on the music vibrating in the background. The funky, sexy beats combined with the mellow March weather were an irresistible combination. The spring concert was in full effect. Everywhere she looked she saw couples moving and grooving to the beat of the music. She wanted to dance but Malcolm wanted to wait until after lunch.

She turned her attention back to Malcolm and the man he was talking with. "How are your parents, Malcolm?" Sam questioned.

"They're doing wonderfully."

"I talked with your father before we left. This is the only time of the year we get an opportunity to travel south."

"I would imagine traveling can be quite hard for a doctor."

"It is but I still make the time to do the important things in life." He patted his wife's arm affectionately as he turned to Alexis. "I'm glad you were able to get Malcolm out of that restaurant for a day. He works much too hard to be so young."

"Stop bothering Malcolm, Sam," Monica chided as she punched him lightly on the arm.

"Working eighty hours a week is not healthy for someone so young. I know there is such a thing as loving your work, but that is ridiculous."

"Well, Sam, Monica, as much as I've enjoyed this conversation, I'm sure Alexis is probably starving by now," he said quickly. "We've been trying to find a spot in the shade."

"Try that way." Sam pointed to his right. "If you don't mind sitting on the grass, we just passed a nice shaded area under a tree."

"Thanks."

"No problem."

Malcolm led Alexis in the direction Sam pointed out. "I apologize, sweetheart. I didn't realize I would run into so many people I knew."

"Can you blame anyone for coming out and enjoying the music in this weather?"

"I think Gerald Levert being here today had a lot to do with it." He spread a blue-and-white-checkered blanket down beneath the tree and set the picnic basket down.

"He's not until later this evening."

"Tell that to all the women out here." He plopped down and patted the seat beside him.

"Ha, ha." She sat down. "How do you know so many people?"

"A lot of these people frequent the restaurant."

"You're going to have to take me to . . ." Her voice trailed off. She was almost embarrassed to admit she didn't know where he worked. She tried to remember if he'd given her that information or not before she finally broke down. "Where do you work, Malcolm?"

He placed a finger to her lips. "You heard Sam. I work too much. Today I'm not thinking about work, because I'm too busy thinking about you. Let's enjoy this delicious food before we shake our bodies to the music."

"What's in the basket?" she questioned as she placed her hand on her growling stomach.

"Ham and cheese sandwiches complete with lettuce, tomatoes, onions, and mayonnaise, homemade potato salad, shrimp salad, raspberry bottled water, and fresh strawberries for dessert."

"Sounds delicious." She licked her lips.

"Don't do that too many more times," Malcolm whispered. "It gives me ideas."

"Maybe that was the intention." She picked up her sandwich and took a small bite.

He groaned. "Are you trying to drive me crazy?"

Alexis smiled. The sexual attraction between them was so thick you could cut it with a knife. Other than a few kisses here and there and a few snuggles, they hadn't gone any further. She wasn't sure she was ready to take their relationship to the next level, and Malcolm respected her wishes. Sometimes it was hard for her to be so close to him and keep her resolve. Malcolm was the sexiest man she'd ever known.

She glanced over at him several times as they ate lunch. She tried to ignore her feelings of guilt for not telling him the truth about the possible baby. She knew she would have to tell him soon. She'd attempted to tell him in the past two months, but every time she got the nerve to tell him, something always spoiled the moment.

She placed a spoonful of potato salad in her mouth. She was starting to get paranoid about every little change in her body. Lately she'd been so fatigued it was hard to keep her eyes open. She'd gained a few extra pounds the past few months that she couldn't seem to shake. It wasn't anything unusual, but when you added the disappearance of her period it had her nerves on edge.

"Still have room for dessert?" Malcolm questioned as he produced a huge strawberry covered in whipped cream.

Alexis moaned slightly as she leaned back on her arms.

"I'm going to weigh five hundred pounds if you have anything to do with it."

He placed a strawberry up to her lips. "We're going to work this off when we shake our bodies to the music. Besides, strawberries are full of nutrients and they're sweet like you. How can you go wrong?"

She opened her mouth, allowing him to place the strawberry on her tongue. She closed her eyes as she savored the taste. He was right. The strawberries tasted like sugar even without the sweetness of the whipped cream.

"They are delicious."

He raised his eyebrows. "You doubted my word?"

"Never." She stretched out on the blanket and closed her eyes. "I wish I could stay out here forever."

"Don't you think you would have to come in when it got cold?" Malcolm teased as he traced a finger down her leg.

"You know what I meant."

"I can only go by what you say." Malcolm stood up. "Stay here. I'll be right back."

Alexis cracked open one eye. "Where are you going?"

"Trust me." His smile was devious as he disappeared into the crowd. The cool breeze combined with the mellow music was soothing to her as she began to hum along.

"Alexis?"

For a moment she thought she was dreaming when she opened her eyes to find Kavon kneeling beside her with a smile on his face. It was the first time she'd seen him since New Year's, and she was at a loss for words as she stared up at him.

"Aren't you going to say something?" he prompted.

"Kavon," she mumbled as she found her voice.

"How are you, Alexis?"

She ignored his question. "What are you doing here?"

"I'm enjoying the concert like everyone else."

"You who always said these concerts were for people who couldn't afford Broadway plays?"

Kavon laughed. "So I changed my mind? Sue me. I'm starting to discover a lot of new things about myself lately."

"Forgive me if I don't shed a tear."

His eyes wandered over her. "You look fabulous."

"Did you expect me to look like a ragamuffin because you weren't around?"

"Never. Ever since I met you, you've always carried yourself like a queen." He reached out and brushed a strand of hair away from her face.

She jerked away from him as if his touched burned her. "What do you want?"

"May I join you?"

"You have got to be kidding."

"No. I'm not."

"Why aren't you sitting with Sydney? You know, the woman you love so much?"

"Sydney doesn't care much for concerts."

"La-di-da for her."

"Why are you being so bitter, Alexis? This isn't like you."

"Did you expect me to break out the champagne, Kavon?" she questioned as she cut her eyes up at him.

"For your information, Sydney and I broke up."

"Two tears in a bucket."

"Aren't you curious about why we broke up?"

"No."

"I broke up with Sydney because she wasn't you. At the time I thought she was the woman I wanted, but I never realized I was making a huge mistake until the damage was already done."

"Tell it to someone who cares, Kavon. I don't."

Kavon touched her arm. "You're the only woman I've ever loved."

"Love?" She laughed. "You wouldn't know love if it reached out and slapped you in the face."

"I know I messed everything up, but I want to make it up to you, Alexis."

"There is nothing you can say or do that will make everything all right. I'll never forgive you for what you've done to me."

"You and I belong together, Alexis. We've always been able to work through our problems before. This shouldn't be any different."

Alexis glared at him as she stood up. "I won't dignify that with a response. This conversation is over."

"What's wrong, Alexis?" Malcolm questioned as, having just returned, he slipped a protective arm around her waist.

"What's going on here?" Kavon demanded as he turned his gaze to Malcolm.

"Why are you harassing Alexis?"

"You're here together?"

"Yes."

Kavon turned to Alexis. "You've already started dating again?"

"Did you expect me to wait around for you?"

"I expected a lot more loyalty from you than this."

"You have a lot of nerve talking to me about loyalty. At least I had the decency to wait until we broke up."

Kavon's jaw tightened. "I'd prefer we talk about this in private."

"I prefer we not talk about this at all. I don't owe you any explanations, Kavon."

He narrowed his eyes as he peered at Malcolm. "You couldn't wait to step in and play hero, could you, Malcolm?"

"Why blame me for your mistakes? You created this situation, Kavon. Live with it."

"Why should I live with it? It's never too late to win back the woman you love." He slapped his hand against his forehead. "My bad, you wouldn't know that, because Leslie wouldn't have anything else to do with you after she told you it was over."

Malcolm's jaw tightened. "You of all people should never mention her name, Kavon."

"Why not, Malcolm? Don't want Alexis to know what a failure you were at your last relationship? What is this, revenge against me or is it competition?"

Alexis looked back and forth from Kavon to Malcolm as if she didn't know either one of them. She'd learned a lot in those few sentences and she didn't want to know any more. She was caught in the middle of something she had nothing to do with it and it angered her. They were using her as a pawn. She didn't say a word as she turned around and quickly walked away.

The air was stifling as she walked through the crowd. She had no idea where she was going, but she knew she had to get away from them. She should have known her relationship with Malcolm was too good to be true. Now she would be alone all over again, but at least this time she hadn't gotten too involved. She was nearing the vendors when Malcolm finally caught up with her.

"Alexis, would you wait a minute?" He took her by the arm.

"Leave me alone, Malcolm," she mumbled as she tried to jerk her arm away from him.

"Why are you mad at me? What did I do?"

"You and Kavon are fighting over something that has nothing to do with me, Malcolm." She searched his face with her eyes. "Is he the man your ex-wife left you for?"

Malcolm averted his gaze. "Yes."

"Why did you keep that away from me, Malcolm? Why didn't you tell me you knew Kavon before New Year's Eve?"

He took a deep breath. "I didn't feel it was important, because that had no bearing on my relationship with you. Kavon and I both grew up here and our paths have crossed more than a few times. What happened between Leslie, Kavon, and me happened a long time ago and it has nothing at all to do with you."

"How do I know that? How do I know you aren't just using me to get back at him for what he did to you?"

"Do you really think that?"

She dropped her head. "I don't know what to believe anymore."

"I would never use you or any other woman to get back at Kavon. You have to know how much you mean to me, Alexis. I care about you."

"Then why hide the truth?"

"I didn't hide the truth." His voice was filled with frustration. "I didn't bring Kavon up because I knew how hurt you were because of the way he treated you. What happened between him and me has no bearing on my relationship with you."

She seemed to digest his explanation for a moment before she jerked her arm away. "Leave me alone, Malcolm."

She was filled with even more doubt than before. It hurt her that Malcolm hadn't told her something she considered very important. Kavon, the man she'd spent the past two years with, was responsible for the breakup of his marriage. Was he only using her as a means of revenge against Kavon? She was so confused by the thoughts swirling around in her head she could barely think straight.

She was nearing the parking lot when she felt her lungs tighten in her chest. She stopped as she reached out to steady herself using a picnic table. She tried to calm down and take a deep breath, but to no avail. Her lungs burned from their effort to breathe. It was only then that she realized in her haste to escape she'd left her purse with her emergency inhaler behind.

"Miss? Are you okay?" a young man sitting at the picnic table questioned as he stood up. She tried to tell him what was wrong, but the words wouldn't form. She pointed to her throat and gasped. Her lungs were filled with liquid fire.

"Help!" the man shouted. "I need some help over here! She can't breathe."

She could feel the light shrinking around her as Malcolm reached her side. She looked up at him, helpless, as she felt her knees going weak. The last thing she was conscious of was the fear in Malcolm's eyes as she slumped over in his arms.

Eight

Malcolm glanced up at the clock on the ugly yellow wall in the hospital waiting room. He'd been there nearly an hour, and not one person had updated him on Alexis's condition. He placed his fingers on his temples. A major migraine was starting in the back of his head, but he refused to let the pain get the better of him. Alexis needed him.

He couldn't put into words the fear he had felt when she went limp in his arms. He stood there holding her as the people around him shouted for her. His voice was paralyzed as he held her. Luckily the paramedics on duty for the concert weren't that far away. It had taken them less than a minute to reach them, but to him it felt like an eternity.

The paramedics sprang into action immediately. As they examined her they spouted a ton of medical jargon into their walkie-talkies. Malcolm was a novice but he was able to deduct she'd suffered an asthma attack and it was pretty serious.

He sighed deeply as the past few weeks played through his mind. Robin's was all but forgotten as he took strolls along the beach, went to movies, ate ice cream on the boardwalk, and ran around barefoot in the park. For the first time in his life he was like everyone else and he'd never been happier. Alexis had given his life new meaning.

Alexis. Guilt for keeping her in the dark about his identity gnawed at him. He should have come clean and told her everything when she discovered he and Kavon knew each other, but he couldn't bring himself to do it. If she found out he'd been lying to her about being a waiter along with the Kavon thing . . . He shuddered as he thought about the possible repercussions. It was something he didn't want to think about. He had to wait until she let him in.

He knew she'd been keeping him at a distance, and he respected that in the beginning. Now as time was moving on he wanted to get closer to her. He wanted to be an important part of her life, and he couldn't do that if she constantly kept her guard up. The more he tried to get her to drop her guard, the more she resisted.

How ironic that after all this time of keeping people away from him, someone was flipping the script. Someone he cared very much about. If only he knew how to get past the walls she'd built. He was still working on it but he knew he had to find a way, because she was in his heart now and he refused to let her go without a hell of a fight.

Shock spread through him as he realized just how much he cared for her. The hours and days spent with her had only strengthened the emotions he'd experienced the night they met. He wasn't sure if it was love but it was definitely the beginning of something wonderful.

He looked up when he heard footsteps approaching the door. He hoped it was someone coming to update him on Alexis. Instead of a doctor he came face-to-face with Kavon. His jaw tightened and his fists clenched as he stood up.

"What in the hell are you doing here?" he demanded.

"I wanted to know how Alexis was doing."

"Like you really give a damn."

"For your information, I love Alexis. She and I were together five years." Kavon eyed him warily. "You can't just erase our history because it isn't convenient for you."

"Convenient?" His laugh was sarcastic. "This coming

from a man who threw those years away for another woman. You have a lot of nerve even showing your face here."

"I don't have to explain anything to you." Kavon waved his hand as if to dismiss him. "You are of no consequence to me."

"I should be." He took a step in Kavon's direction. "You had your chance with Alexis and you blew it."

"Judging from her reaction earlier, she had no idea we knew one another." He narrowed his eyes. "How much have you told her about yourself, Malcolm? Did you tell her the real reason Leslie left you for me?"

Malcolm took another step in his direction. "You have a lot of nerve talking to me about Leslie. You destroyed my relationship with my wife."

"I merely gave her what she wanted, Malcolm. Everyone knew you weren't man enough for her. She left you because you were married to that damn restaurant. Do you really think this time it will be different? A couple of months with Alexis won't change who you are. In a few months you'll return to Robin's, and Alexis will be back at square one."

"You don't know anything about me, Kavon. You live in a dreamworld if you think I'd listen to anything you had to say. Forcing my wife to lie on the stand that I abused her wasn't enough? Do you have some vendetta with everyone around you that discovers happiness?"

Kavon smiled. "Happiness has nothing to do with this. This is about rivalry. You're just upset because you've never been able to beat me at anything. I've always won and I always will."

"You really think this is a competition?" Malcolm's voice was filled with disbelief. "Alexis is not a toy you put up on a shelf when you get tired of it and pick it up when you decide you want to play with it again. She is a human being with feelings, but I guess you wouldn't know anything about that because you're incapable of having feelings."

"You're wasting your time, Malcolm. All I have to do is whisper a few sweet nothings to Alexis and she'll fall right back in my arms. I have her wrapped around my little finger.

It's always been that way and now won't be any different."
Kavon smiled smugly. "I've always had a way with the
women in your life. Leslie all but begged me to take her out
of her misery."

"You son of a—" Malcolm began as he lunged at Kavon.

"Mr. Alexander?" a male voice from the doorway called,
causing Malcolm to freeze in place.

"Yes?" he replied, his eyes never leaving Kavon. "How is
Alexis?" He finally forced his gaze to the doctor as he approached him.

"She's fine. Her asthma attack didn't cause her any real
harm. I'm going to prescribe some medication for her, but
you need to make sure she follows up with her regular doctor. Asthma can be very tricky sometimes."

"I will."

"As long as she takes her medication you don't have anything to worry about."

"When can I see her?"

"They're moving her to another room. Just to be on the
safe side I want to keep her here overnight to monitor her
condition. As soon as she's settled in her room I'll send a
nurse out to get you."

"Thank you, Doctor." Malcolm shook his hand. He felt a
sigh of relief overcome him when he realized that she was
going to be okay. He said a silent prayer of thanks.

"I'm glad she's okay," Kavon said softly as he sat down
on the sofa.

"Why should you care?"

"I don't recall asking for your input."

"Whether you did or not, I offered it to you."

"Say whatever you want, Malcolm. The cards are in my
favor. Alexis has been with me for the past five years, not
you."

"And you think she'll just let you walk right back into her
life after what you did to her on New Year's Eve?"

"She'll take me back in a heartbeat." His voice was filled
with confidence.

"In your dreams."

"Why am I even talking to you?" Kavon questioned as he eyed him warily. "You of all people would never understand my relationship with Alexis."

Malcolm went over to him and grabbed him by the collar. "I don't have to understand it to know that if you don't stay away from her, I'll make you sorry you were ever born. Her asthma attack was your fault, Kavon. Yours. She doesn't need you in her life. She has me and I'm not going anywhere. If you know what's best for you, you'll go and stay gone, because if I lie down and dream you are anywhere near her I'll be on you like white on rice. Understand?"

"You think threatening me is going to work?"

"I'm not threatening you, Kavon. I'm making you a promise."

"Mr. Alexander?" a female voice from the doorway called. He looked up to see a nurse standing there.

"Yes?" he questioned without turning Kavon loose.

"The doctor says you can see Ms. Williams now."

"Thank you." He pulled Kavon's shirt tighter. "When you walk away, let it be the last time either one of us sees your sorry face. If you don't I promise I will make your life a living hell."

"You can threaten me all you want but you can't keep me away from her."

"You've been warned." Malcolm released him as he walked away. He would deal with Kavon in his own time. Now was the time to see Alexis and get some answers.

Kavon's face was a mixture of jealousy and fury as he watched the nurse lead Malcolm down the hall to the woman he loved. The woman he hadn't realized just how much he loved until he nearly lost her.

He knew about the severity of her asthma. On several occasions she'd experienced the attacks but never anything as severe as the one he'd witnessed today. When he saw her go limp in Malcolm's arms his heart nearly leaped from his chest. He couldn't lose her that way. Fate wouldn't be that cruel to him.

The relief he felt now was overwhelming. He'd made a big mistake when he walked away from his relationship with her, but it wasn't too late. Those words weren't in his vocabulary. He clenched his fists as he stared at the doorway of the waiting room. "You may have won the battle, Malcolm, but I will win the war." He smiled softly as he headed for the door.

Alexis exhaled deeply as she leaned back against the pillows on her bed. She was a little groggy from the medication, but otherwise she felt fine. She breathed a sigh of relief that her attack wasn't more serious. She knew she shouldn't have allowed Kavon to get her so upset, but she couldn't help it. Knowing that he and Malcolm had been playing her for a fool caused her blood to boil.

She sighed deeply as she closed her eyes. She wasn't pregnant. That fear had been laid to rest when the doctor examined her. She'd questioned him about her symptoms, but he'd informed her that she was suffering from stress, not pregnancy. She felt her heart leap in her chest to think that it was all just a false alarm. She was free to go on with her life without any ties to Kavon.

She opened her eyes and nearly jumped out of her skin when she came face-to-face with Malcolm. She'd been so wrapped up in her thoughts she hadn't heard him come in the door.

"What are you doing here?" she questioned as she turned away from him.

"I came to see how you were doing."

"Why? Have you suddenly developed a conscience?"

"That's not fair, Alexis. You know I care about you."

"Do I?"

"You should. My being here for you should speak for itself, Alexis. Believe me, if I was trying to get revenge against Kavon, I wouldn't be using you to do it." He lifted her chin so that she was facing him. "Give me more credit than that."

"I'm so confused about everything, Malcolm. My entire life has been tossed upside down and I have no idea how to fix it."

"Let me help you." He caressed her face. "Let me be here for you."

"Every time I turn around you're sneaking up on me. How do you do it?" she questioned in a teasing voice.

"I do my best to keep you on your toes." He touched her face. "Don't think I'm letting you off the hook that easily. Why do you keep pushing me away, Alexis?"

She swallowed hard as two tears slid down her face. It was the moment of truth. It was time to tell him about her worst fears, but the words wouldn't come. She'd buried her emotions for so long it was hard to let go and tell him what was deep in her heart. He placed his finger under her chin and turned her head back toward him.

"I want the truth, Alexis. I want to know why you're keeping a part of yourself away from me."

"I was afraid," she whispered softly.

"Afraid of what?"

"Every time I love someone or something it leaves me, Malcolm. I loved my mother and she left me. I loved Kavon and he left me for someone else. I figured if I kept my distance from you, whenever the time came for you to move on it would be easier on me. It was the only way for me to avoid being hurt again."

"Look at me," Malcolm demanded as he turned her chin around. "I'll never intentionally hurt you, Alexis. You've become very important to me. Nothing you could say or do would make me leave you. I'm not Kavon. I'm here for the long haul and I'm not going anywhere. All you have to do is call me and I'll come running."

"I can't help it, Malcolm. My whole life has been one disappointment after the other."

"You never have to worry about disappointment or heartbreak again. I'm here to protect you now."

Alexis felt a tear slid down her cheek. "Imagine how shocked I was when I found you knew Kavon. That was enough to throw anyone for a loop."

"Don't worry about him. Kavon will leave you alone or he'll have to answer to me."

Alexis looked up at him as she cracked a smile. "Did you threaten him, Malcolm?"

"Yes." He pushed a strand of hair from her forehead. "I

told him if he even breathed the same air as you I would beat him to a pulp."

"You actually said that to him?"

"Yes. I meant every word of it." He bent over and kissed her. "I can't believe I've been so blind I couldn't see what was right in front of me. Will you forgive me for being so blind and stupid?"

"You have nothing to apologize for. If anyone should be asking for forgiveness, it should be me."

Malcolm placed his finger up to her lips. "Let's forgive each other and get this thing on the right track." He smiled.

Alexis smiled softly. "Thank you for being here for me, Malcolm."

"You're welcome." He kissed her tenderly on the lips. "Now, for the record, what is your favorite ice cream?"

Nine

The doorbell rang relentlessly. Alexis cracked open one eye as she peered at the clock. It was only seven in the morning. Who in the world would be ringing her doorbell at this time of day? She knew it couldn't be Malcolm. They hadn't crawled back from playing miniature golf until almost two o'clock this morning.

As she thought about Malcolm a soft smile covered her face. He was treating her like a queen. She'd never felt so cherished and loved her entire life. For the past few weeks they'd done everything from playing pool and miniature golf to catching movies and rollerblading at the roller rink. Every time she looked around he was popping up for no reason. He sent her flowers at the office that made her the envy of all the women who worked with her. For the first time in her life she was thankful for the flexibility her job granted her.

She buried her head under her pillow. The pillow was thick enough to drown out the sound of the doorbell and allowed her to fall back to sleep. She dreamed she was in Malcolm's arms. He was holding her and kissing her. She felt his fingers brushing against her cheek. She moaned as she turned over. It was then that she realized she wasn't alone. She screamed as her eyes snapped open and she bolted from the bed.

"It's only me." Kavon held up his hands.

"What are you doing here?" she demanded as she inched away from him.

He didn't answer her as his gaze traveled over her body. She suddenly felt naked in the nightgown she was wearing. She quickly pulled the sheet from the bed and wrapped it around her.

"I rang the doorbell but you didn't answer. I was worried about you, so I let myself in to make sure you were okay."

"How did you get in here?"

"My key."

Why hadn't she remembered she'd given him a key right after she moved in? He hadn't used it once to her knowledge and she'd soon forgotten about it. As she stood there staring at him she nearly freaked out. All this time he had a key to her home. The one place she'd always been sure she was safe.

"Give me a good reason why I shouldn't call the police, Kavon."

"I just wanted to check up on you."

"A phone call would have sufficed."

"You changed your number."

"Exactly."

He shook his head as a smile spread across his face. "I left myself open for that one."

"I'm still waiting for an answer, Kavon." She eyed the telephone.

"Don't go ballistic. I only want to talk to you."

"Everything that needs to be said between us has already been said."

"No, it hasn't, Alexis. I know that you may not believe this but I want another chance to be in your life. I know I hurt you New Year's Eve and I apologize for that, but I love you, Alexis, and I want to make this right. The past few weeks have been hell for me. I can't eat, I can't sleep, and I've been screwing up at work."

"Screwing up how?"

"I've been late to several vital meetings. I've messed up a couple of important business deals. My father is angry with me. Rain Records has been suffering because of my stupidity." He looked up at her with tortured eyes. "My entire life has been tossed upside down since you and I split."

Alexis stared at him in disbelief. After the careless way he'd thrown her aside he wanted her forgiveness. "You don't care anything about my feelings, Kavon. The only reason you're saying this to me at all is that you found out I was dating Malcolm."

"I tried to get you back before I found out about Malcolm, Alexis."

"Ask me if I care," she snapped. "I'm very happy and I'm not going to let you ruin it."

"You're actually happy with him?"

"I'm very happy."

"How much do you really know about Malcolm, Alexis?" he questioned as he stood up.

"What I do and don't know is none of your business."

"I think it is my business. You're allowing yourself to be caught up in a fantasy world, Alexis. He's feeding you lines and you're falling for them because you very vulnerable right now. I don't want to see you get hurt."

"See me get hurt?" she questioned sarcastically. "Isn't it a little late for that?"

"I can't help how I feel, Alexis," Kavon said with a smirk. "Malcolm is using you to get back at me."

She shook her head. "Malcolm would never do that."

"Did he tell you that?" Kavon questioned with a smug smile. "You actually believed what he told you? After he didn't tell you he knew me? He and I have been competing against one another since we were four years old. He'd been looking for a way to get back at me since his ex-wife left him for me. He blames me because Leslie wanted me, and now he's trying to even the score."

"Say whatever you want, Kavon. Malcolm has been here for me in ways you never were."

"Really?" He shook his head. "What has he told you about his background? Did he tell you about the real reason his ex-wife left him? Did he tell you about the restaurant he loves so much?"

Alexis stared at him as if he were an alien from another planet. "Get out, Kavon." She pointed to the door.

"I will when I'm done here." He reached down on the floor and picked up a gift bag. He tossed it on the bed. "I didn't want it to come down to this, but you've given me no other choice. Everything you ever wanted to know about Malcolm is in there, Alexis. Don't be a fool and get sucked into a world of lies. He's leading you on."

"At least he's man enough to stand up for me, Kavon. That's more than I can say for you."

He frowned. "What is that supposed to mean?"

"You've never stood up for anything in your life. Your father leads you by the hand like a puppet. He's the reason we aren't together anymore. He finally made good on his promise."

"What promise?" he questioned in confusion. "What in the world are you blabbing about?"

"Your father told me if I printed another article he would break us up, and I didn't listen. He succeeded in what he set out to do. All he has to do is say jump and you say, how high? Maybe one day you'll grow up and stop being manipulated by him."

"My father had nothing to do with this, Alexis."

"Oh, yes, he did. He had a lot to do with it. He'd better get ready because there is another article coming out in a few months that I'm sure he'll love just as much as the others I've written."

Kavon's face went blank. "You're writing another article?"

"Yes, I am. It should hit the newsstands in the next couple of months."

His mouth opened and closed but no words came out. He stared at her in disbelief. "I can't believe you're being this vindictive. You're just writing this article to get back at me, aren't you?"

"I accepted this article before you broke up with me, Kavon. You're not going to make me feel guilty about it."

"Just like all the other articles you've written since we've been together." He shook his head. "I can't believe you're doing this."

"Believe it. I'm not going to relax my principles because it doesn't suit you."

He looked as if he was going to say something but changed his mind as he pointed to the gift bag on the bed. "There is everything you ever wanted to know about your precious Malcolm. I assure you, there is a lot you don't know about him."

Alexis stared at the bag as if it were a snake. "You've said what you wanted to say; now get out before I call the police, Kavon."

"Alexis—"

She reached over and picked up the phone. "Get out."

"This is not over, Alexis." He took one final look at her before he walked out the bedroom door.

Ten

The gift bag lay on its side on the seat next to Alexis as she sat there staring at Robin's. She didn't even know why she'd brought it with her. All she had to do was close her eyes to see its contents in living color. The lies, the deceit, all of the cards were on the table now and she couldn't ignore them.

A chill washed over her despite the warm spring weather. Her heart ached and tears stung her eyes as she faced the proof of his betrayal. For all of his talk about honesty and truth he'd been lying to her from the very beginning.

Why had he done this to her? she asked herself for the hundredth time. Why had he deceived her this way? The more she questioned his actions, the angrier she became at herself. She had no one to blame for this but herself. She'd jumped from one relationship to another without pausing to put things into perspective. She was too busy enjoying herself to realize she was being pulled into an illusion.

Their relationship had seemed so perfect because she wanted it to be perfect. For once in her life she wanted something to work out in her favor, so she ignored the fact that Malcolm always carefully diverted the conversation whenever she asked about his job or his friends. She ignored the fact that she'd never been to his house or that despite them talking about everything under the sun she'd never been to his apartment. She'd been so desperate for happiness she'd stuck her head in the sand to avoid seeing the light.

She picked up the gift bag and got out of the car. She knew the restaurant wasn't open yet, but she knew he was there, because she'd seen his car when she pulled up. She headed for the back entrance and tried to knob. The door opened effortlessly. She walked down the long corridor to the main area of the kitchen. It loomed before her empty and sterile in the early morning air. She stood there for a moment allowing her eyes to adjust to the dim lighting before she weaved her way through the islands and stove until she came to a corridor she assumed led to Malcolm's office.

Her heart sank further when she saw the golden plaque beside the door with his name on it. Even with all of the evidence in front of her, there was a piece of her that still wanted this to be a big mistake. She sighed deeply. She had to do what she had to do.

She placed her hand on the knob and opened the door. Malcolm was sitting behind a large mahogany desk with his feet propped up. His mouth dropped open in shock and his feet fell to the floor as she walked through the door of his office.

For a moment they stood in a face-off. Neither one was sure what the other was thinking. Malcolm's expression gradually turned from shock to relief.

"Alexis, what are you doing here?"

"I could ask you the same question but I already know the answer, so I won't go there."

His gaze widened as he turned away from her to face the chair in front of his desk. "Darryl, would you excuse us?"

Her eyes widened as a mirror image of Malcolm stood up. Her eyes traveled up and down his muscular frame. They were identical in every way. Darryl met her gaze and returned it with one of his own. She saw the curiosity in his expression as he stared at her.

"Darryl." Malcolm's voice was sharp. "I need to be alone with Alexis."

Darryl frowned slightly as he cut his eyes at his brother.

"Call me later." He picked up his jacket from the back of the chair and shot another curious glance at Alexis before he headed out the door, closing it behind him.

Malcolm remained silent for a moment before he spoke. "How did you find out?"

"Kavon." She tossed the gift bag on his desk. "He couldn't wait to rub this in my face."

The nerve over his left eye twitched as he studied the contents of the bag. "Kavon went too far this time."

"Why, because he told me the truth?"

"He wouldn't know the truth if it reached up and slapped him." He crushed the bag with his hands.

"I guess this restaurant is a lie too?"

"No." He stuffed his hands in his pockets. "Robin's is very real."

"How long were you planning to keep me in the dark? Were you going to keep lying to me until you decided to move on?"

"I had no intention of ever leaving you, Alexis. I wanted to tell you the truth, but I couldn't figure out how to break it to you without hurting you."

She laughed bitterly. "You know, that's exactly what Kavon said to me on New Year's Eve."

"I'm not Kavon, Alexis. I didn't tell you about my background because I wasn't sure you could handle it. I've been agonizing over it for months."

"You lied to me, Malcolm. That's the one thing I can't tolerate."

"I never lied to you, Alexis. I merely omitted a few details about my background. Things that shouldn't matter one way or the other."

"You think that justified you lying to me?"

"I never lied to you." His voice was filled with frustration.

"Omitting details is the same as lying." She stared at him. "I guess I should believe you now because you've been so honest with me until now, haven't you? You've listened to me pour out my heart about everything and you never said a word to me about any of this." She waved her hands around. "I trusted you and you betrayed that trust."

"You don't understand the entire situation, Alexis."

"I understand enough." She paused as she exhaled deeply. "I'm through being lied to. Good-bye, Malcolm." She was almost at the door when Malcolm pulled her into his arms. "Let me go."

"Not until you listen to me," he whispered against her ear. "I'm not letting you walk out that door without hearing me out."

"There is nothing you can say to me that will change my mind," she said stubbornly as he guided her over to the chair.

"You are going to give me a chance to explain myself, Alexis. You already made up your mind before you walked in the door. I deserve the right to explain myself without interruptions."

Alexis glanced down at her watch. "You have five minutes."

"When you and I met I didn't tell you who I was, because I knew my background would get in the way. I never intended for this to drag out as long as it has. I only wanted a chance to get to know you without the complications my life would bring. I wanted to be able to walk on the beach and stroll through the park and lead a normal life for once. You were the most amazing woman I'd ever met in my life and I didn't want anything to ruin that."

"Then why didn't you tell me later on?"

He dropped his head. "You've been keeping me at a distance, Alexis. I was afraid that if I told you the truth you would walk out of my life, and I couldn't let that happen. I didn't want my money to destroy the one relationship I truly cared about. I knew that no matter what, I couldn't lose you." He looked up at her. "If I'd given you my background in the beginning, would you have gone out with me?"

She averted her gaze. "Probably not."

"All of my life I wanted to find someone who cared about me, Malcolm, not Malcolm the restaurant owner. I thought I found that woman in my ex-wife, but I didn't. There have been several women since then, but they always saw dollar signs. I knew you were different, from the moment we met. You thought I was a lowly waiter and you were still interested in me. I knew I'd found the woman I'd searched my whole life for. At first not telling you who I was enabled me to get to know you, but as time went on I became afraid I would lose you if I told you everything. Especially after the day of the concert."

"You're saying all of this is my fault?" Alexis questioned in disbelief.

"No. It's my fault for not being honest with you."

She remained silent for a moment before she spoke. "I understand why you didn't tell me, but I can't forgive you for lying to me, Malcolm. I can't have a relationship with someone I don't trust."

He swallowed hard. "What are you saying?"

"That when I walk out that door it's for the last time. No matter how much I care for you, I have to walk away now before I get hurt."

Malcolm took her hand. "Don't do this, Alexis. I had my reasons for doing this."

"Reasons?" she questioned bitterly. "There is never a good reason for lying to the person you claim to care about." She pulled away from him as she stood up.

He pulled her into his arms and kissed her passionately. At first she tried to push him away, but his will was stronger than hers. When he finally released her she felt light-headed and weak.

"I love you, Alexis."

Her eyes widened as she stared up at him. "What did you say?"

"I've loved you from the moment I laid eyes on you, Alexis. I tried to lie to myself that I didn't love you, but I can't deny it any longer. I love you and I'll go crazy without you in my life. What I did I did for you, for us."

"Oh, Malcolm," she said as her eyes filled with tears. "I love you too," she said as he reached out and pulled her into his arms. Together they fell back on his desk. He held on to her as if his life depended on it as he rained kisses on her face.

"I love you so much," he said as he gently pushed her hair from her face. "I never thought I could feel this way about another woman, but you showed me that I could. You gave me hope, Alexis."

"Did I?"

"Yes," he whispered softly. "All you have to do is open up your heart to me and I'll make you happy, Alexis. Please open up your heart." She held on to him as he nuzzled his face in her hair. "Let your guard down, Alexis. Let me in."

"It's hard, Malcolm. All of the things that have happened to me—"

"Are in the past. Give me a chance to make you happy."

"You already have." She smiled. "I'm so glad we've finally found each other."

"I never intended to hurt you, Alexis. You have to believe that."

"I know that now," she said with a smile. "When I walked in here tonight I had every intention of walking out the door and never seeing you again. I realize now I've always known there was more to you than met the eye. I sensed you were different from the other men I've dealt with in the past."

"Does this mean you forgive me for not being completely honest?" Malcolm questioned as he traced a finger down her face.

"Yes," she replied softly.

"Thank you," he said as he kissed her lips gently.

"Now of course you know you're going to do all of the cooking from now on," she said with a laugh.

"It will be my pleasure," he said as he kissed her again.

Eleven

Kavon paced back and forth across his office. There were several accounts on his desk that needed his attention, but for once he didn't care. The only thing he could think about was New Year's Eve and the way he'd treated Alexis.

It had been nearly two months since he'd seen her, and his heart was aching. He knew she was nearing her due date for her article and there wasn't anything he could say to stop her from printing it. She would go ahead with it the same she had with all the others.

He dropped his head as he came to grips with the error of his ways. He wanted to blame everything that had happened on Malcolm, but deep in his heart he knew he had no one to blame for this but himself. He'd destroyed the one relationship that meant the world to him. He would give everything he had to have her back in his life. The sound of someone knocking on his door interrupted his thoughts.

"Why did you turn the Joe Montgomery account over to Simon?" Karl demanded. "What in the hell were you thinking?"

"I did what was in my authority to do. If he can't handle the account he shouldn't be working here," Kavon snapped as he sat down in his chair.

"What is your problem this morning?" Karl questioned as he sat down in the chair facing his son.

"Alexis is my problem."

Karl frowned. "I thought you were finally over her, Kavon."

"I will never be over her, Dad."

"What about Sydney, son?"

"I don't want Sydney, Dad."

"Why not? Her father is a powerful ally to make in the record industry. An alliance between the two of you would seal the deal, especially when you take over Rain Records."

"What if I don't want to take over the company?"

"When the time comes you will," Karl countered confidently. "Now I want to know what's wrong with you. It's not like you to turn an account over to someone else."

"Do you really care?"

"Everything in your life matters to me."

"I found out Alexis is writing another article about the recording industry."

Karl's eyes widened as he stared at his son. "Tell me I didn't just hear what I thought I heard."

"You heard me the first time, Dad. Alexis is writing another big article. It will surpass her last one."

"Why in the hell would she do that?"

Kavon raised his eyebrows. "What does she really have to lose? She's already a social outcast amongst all of our friends, no thanks to you."

"She started this, not me. Don't try to turn this around on me."

"You helped put her on the list, Dad. I can't believe I was so blind I couldn't see what was right in front of my face."

"Which is?"

"You broke us up as revenge for the article she printed about Rain Records, didn't you?"

"I did no such thing." Karl's voice was filled with outrage. "I had nothing to do with you breaking up with Alexis."

"Yes, you did. You planted the seed and it took root. All of your talk about getting together with Sydney was just a petty stab of revenge at Alexis." He shook his head. "I can't believe I hurt her over this."

"How long have you known about this article?"

"A few months," he admitted honestly.

"A few months?" he questioned incredulously. "And you've just decided to tell me about it?"

"I needed time to figure out what could be done about it, if anything. Alexis can be extremely stubborn when it comes to her writing."

"If you got back together with her, would she still write the article?"

"I have no idea." He shook his head slowly. "I don't think she will ever take me back after what I did to her."

"Nonsense. Alexis is no fool." He leaned back in his chair.

"What are you saying, Dad?"

"Just leave everything to me, son. I'll handle Alexis."

Kavon heard the superior note in his father's voice as he swung around to meet his gaze. "What do you have up your sleeve?"

"Nothing for you to worry about, son. I want you to concentrate on your work. I have a few deals on my desk that I'd like to pass your way, but I can't do that if you're not focused."

"I'll try to get back into the grind of things." He sighed. "I know I've been messing up lately."

"You haven't done anything that can't be fixed, son. I'll make sure you get your focus back."

Kavon's smile was tired. "Are you sure?"

"Have I ever been wrong before?"

"No."

"Then trust me on this." He stood up. "I'll think of something to do about the Alexis situation. I'll give you my plans by the end of the week. I'll see you at dinner tonight."

"Sure," Kavon muttered angrily as his father left the room. He realized for the first time that his father ruled every aspect of his life and there wasn't a damn thing he could do about it.

Twelve

Alexis arranged the basket of fresh roses on her mantel and stood back to admire them. Ever since she and Malcolm had started dating he'd sent her a dozen fresh roses every day. Her home smelled and looked like a flower shop. She smiled. It was one of the things she loved about him.

She glanced down at her watch. He was due any minute now. They were going to take a ride down to Daytona with Sonya and her husband, Matthew, to shop at the flea market and hang out at the beach for the day. She felt a tremor of excitement race down her spine as she thought about the fun they would have.

When the doorbell rang a few minutes later she headed for the door and opened it without thinking about what she was doing. She was surprised to see Karl standing on her doorstep. He'd never visited her in the three years she'd lived there.

"Karl, what are you doing here?" she questioned wearily. Whatever his reasons for being there, she didn't trust them.

"May I come in?" As if he sensed her hesitation, he continued. "This will only take a minute of your time."

"Please make it quick. I was on my way out," she said as she opened the door wider, allowing him to step inside the foyer.

She motioned for him to go into the living room before she followed him inside. He sat down on the sofa as he glanced around.

"Would you like something to drink?" she questioned out of politeness more than anything else.

"No, thank you. I won't be here long." He cleared his throat. "I know things have been strained between us the past few months, but I came here hoping we could put our differences aside and come to an understanding."

Alexis's eyes narrowed suspiciously. "I'm not sure I understand your request."

"My son hasn't been the same since he broke up with you. He won't eat, he won't sleep, and he's screwed up several important deals. For the first time in my son's life he's been late for everything, and that's unlike him. I have to do something to rectify the situation." His eyes met hers. "I was hoping you would go back to him. Give him a sense of purpose again. Help my son get his life back on track."

Alexis laughed as she shook her head. "You can help him get on track by butting out of his life for a change. Kavon is a big boy capable of taking care of himself if given the chance. As far as your proposal is concerned, my answer is no. I refuse to be a part of any manipulating schemes."

His eyes widened in disbelief. "You're refusing to help me with this?"

"I can't go back to Kavon after the way he treated me. I would be a fool to consider it."

Karl laughed as he shook his head. "You're doing exactly what I always figured you would do. I warned Kavon that the day he needed you most you would turn your back on him."

"I'm turning my back on him?" she questioned in disbelief. "After he humiliated me in front of everyone you have the nerve to talk to me about not being there for him? Wasn't he supposed to be here for me when he placed my head on the chopping block New Year's Eve? When you invited my replacement so he could flaunt it in my face? Am I supposed to ignore that out of the kindness of my heart?"

"I knew you were lying to him about caring about him.

This proves it. How can you fall out of love with someone in a couple of months?"

"I haven't fallen out of love with your son. I love him and I always will, but we can never have what we had in the past. I've grown a lot in the past few months. I can't go back to being a trophy on his arm."

Karl stared at her as if she'd grown another head. "I suppose you're still going to write your article on my production company?"

Her eyes locked with his. "I should have known that's what you were coming here about." She shook her head. "For your information, my article is already printed and should hit the newsstands in the next couple of days. And it's not completely about your production company, it's about production companies in general, although Rain Records is mentioned."

He stood up. "If you go ahead with this story you'll be sorry, Alexis. I promised you that the last time but you didn't listen. I made your relationship with Kavon disappear. Don't think I won't hesitate to make your life a living hell. I have friends in high places. I will make sure your name is mud in this town before this is over with."

"Do you really think threatening me will accomplish anything? You tried that the last time and it didn't get you anywhere then. What makes you think things have changed?"

"For someone who claims she grew up so much, you have no concept of what it's like in the real world. I have enough money to make your life miserable." He smiled. "Don't think I won't hesitate to make it happen."

"Say whatever you want, I'm printing my article."

"You will be sorry."

"You may leave now." She headed for the front door and opened it.

He strolled toward her with a tight smile. "Remember what I told you, Alexis. If you print this article it will be your last."

"You can't intimidate me into doing what you want me to do."

"Why not?" he questioned with a smirk. "It's the American way."

"Alexis?" Malcolm's smooth voice queried as she turned to face him. She'd been so busy showing Karl the door she hadn't noticed Malcolm and Sonya come up the walkway.

"Malcolm." Her voice was soft as he wrapped his arms possessively around her shoulders.

"Karl."

"Malcolm," Karl replied flatly.

"Karl was just leaving us."

"Remember what I said, Alexis." He brushed past Sonya as he headed down the walkway.

"I'm glad that's over," Alexis said as she closed the door behind him.

"What was that all about?" Malcolm questioned as they headed for the living room.

"Karl came here to threaten me about printing my article."

"What did he say?"

Alexis nearly smiled when she saw his jaw clenched with anger. "Don't worry about it. I'm not about to let him intimidate me."

"What did he say, Alexis?" Sonya queried softly as she sat down on the sofa.

"He came here under the pretense of asking me to take Kavon back. When I refused he threatened to make my life miserable."

"Is there anything Karl can do?" Malcolm's voice was filled with concern.

Sonya spoke up. "No. Karl can't do anything, because we've taken all the necessary precautions. There isn't anything in her article that can't be backed up with cold hard facts." She turned to Alexis. "We can stop the article from hitting the newsstands if you want. It's not too late, you know."

"I refuse to let Karl intimidate me. He has to pay for some of the dirt he's done. This is the only way that will happen."

"I admire your courage," Malcolm said as he pulled her into his arms. "Not many people have the guts to stand up for what they believe."

"I can't back down on this, Malcolm." He kissed her lightly on the lips. "I just hope you'll still be around when my article hits the wire. Believe me, this won't be pretty."

"Don't worry about me, sweetheart. I'm here for the long haul."

Sonya rolled her eyes as they kissed again. "Can we pleased get started? I don't want my husband to melt before we get where we're going."

"With all due respect, Miss Lady, he'll be in good company."

"Flattery will get you nowhere, mister," Alexis said with a smile.

"We'll see about that," he replied as he ushered them out the door.

Thirteen

Alexis paced back and forth across her living room. The magazine article hit the newsstands that morning and she was waiting for the aftermath. She knew it was only a matter of time before the phone started ringing off the hook. She glanced up at the clock. It was a little after nine o'clock. Malcolm said he would be over first thing in the morning, but so far he hadn't appeared. She was wondering what was keeping him when the phone rang. She swallowed as she reached over and picked it up.

"Hello?"

"Your article is the talk of the town, Alexis." Sonya's excited voice came over the line. "Everyone is talking about your honesty and your insight. We have sold a record number of magazines and it's only nine o'clock. I can't believe it."

"I'm glad," she replied with a smile. "I was a little nervous about how people would react."

"You have no reason to be, Alexis. You did an excellent job on this. As soon as you get into the office tomorrow we'll have to talk about a raise in salary. You deserve it."

"Thank you, Sonya," she said as the doorbell rang. "I'd better go, Malcolm's at the door."

"He's probably coming to congratulate you on your success."

"I certainly hope so. I'll talk to you later, Sonya."

"Bye, Alexis."

She felt giddy as she headed for the front door. She checked the peephole and swallowed hard when she saw Kavon on the other side. She flung the door open in anger.

"What in the hell were you thinking, Alexis?" he questioned as he held up the magazine. He brushed past her and stepped inside.

"I wrote an honest story about the way record companies cheat the people who work for them."

"You mentioned my father's production company several times, Alexis. My father is about to have a coronary. Ever since we opened this morning, our phones have been ringing off the hook. I can't believe you would do something like this to me."

"You?" she questioned in anger. "Why do you always think that everything has to be about you? This article had nothing to do with you, despite what you think. Sonya approached me with the story idea and I accepted. I wrote my story and I won't apologize for the way it came out."

"I don't know how my father's company will survive this."

"That's a personal problem. Karl should think about that when he's cheating people out of their money. He's sailing in yachts and sailboats. He has homes in three states. The people who work for him have peanuts compared to him. I don't apologize for doing what's right."

"You heard the lady," Malcolm's voice interrupted as he walked in the room. He looked wonderful in a lime-green muscle shirt and a pair of black jeans. She felt her mouth water as she watched his muscles ripple beneath the shirt.

Kavon looked back and forth from Alexis to Malcolm with a stupid expression on his face. Malcolm walked over to her and put his arm around her waist. Kavon's eyes narrowed as he watched the intimate gesture. "My father will

make you miserable for this. I've done everything I can to
hold him back, but there will be no stopping him this
time."

"If Karl so much as looks at Alexis the wrong way he'll
answer to me."

Kavon smirked. "Just what do you think you're going to
do, Malcolm? You can't stand up to us."

"If you do anything at all to Alexis I will spend the rest of
my life making sure you pay. I refuse to let you hurt her any
more than you already have. Stay away from her or I'll see
you in court."

"I don't respond to idle threats."

Malcolm smiled. "Whoever said it was idle? You treated
Alexis like a possession you could put up on a shelf and take
down whenever the mood struck. She is a beautiful, intelligent young woman with her whole life ahead of her." He
looked at her tenderly. "A life I'm hoping she'll consent to
spending with me."

She felt a huge lump settle in her throat as she looked up
at him. He got down on one knee in front of her and pulled
the ring from his pocket. "I was going to ask you this
tonight, but I think the time has come to do this now. Alexis,
will you marry me?"

She stared down at him in disbelief as he opened the
box to reveal a beautiful diamond ring. Never in a million
years would she have expected him to do something like
that. Her eyes filled with tears and her heart nearly burst
open. "Yes," she whispered softly as a tear slid down her
cheek.

Kavon stared at them wordlessly as Malcolm slid the ring
on her finger. She looked up at that instant and saw the look
in his eyes. He knew he'd lost her. No amount of apology on
his part would do a bit of good.

He'd lost her to the one man he despised more than anyone else. He'd lost the woman he loved, because of his own
stupidity. His father had cost him everything he thought he'd
wanted in Sydney.

"I can see I'm no longer welcome here," he said as he

picked up his jacket. "You'll be sorry, Alexis. Malcolm will never love you the way I do."

She smiled softly as Malcolm held her in his strong embrace. "You're right, Kavon. He loves me more than you ever did." Kavon threw one last look of disgust her way before he headed out the door.

Epilogue

Alexis smoothed imaginary wrinkles from her ivory silk dress. There were a million butterflies in her stomach that refused to settle down. She couldn't keep her hands still as she stood up to check her reflection in the mirror one last time.

She'd often heard her mother talk about the glow on a bride's face on her wedding day and often wondered if she would wear that glow when she decided to get married. As she studied her image in the mirror she saw the joy her mother promised reflecting back at her. The only sadness she felt was that her mother hadn't lived to see this day. A soft knock on the door interrupted her thoughts.

"Come in." To her surprise, Kavon walked in the door. She hadn't seen him since the day he showed up on her doorstep to threaten her. "What are you doing here?" she questioned as she stood up.

"I had to see you before the wedding." He paused. "I had to see if there was still a chance we could work this out. I know we've been through a lot the past few months, but . . ." His voice trailed off.

As she stared at him she felt sympathy for everything he'd been through, but sympathy wasn't enough. "There was a time when I thought you were the man I was destined to spend the rest of my life with, but now I know that's not true. I love Malcolm."

"You once loved me."

She shook her head. "I hung on to you because you were my safety net. You came along at a time when I needed you, and I clung to that. There is nothing left for us. It's over."

"My father is no longer in the picture, Alexis."

"Karl has nothing to do with this. I'm happier with Malcolm than I've ever been. He completes me in a way I never knew existed."

"You're really going to go through with this?"

"Yes."

"For what it's worth, I do love you, Alexis. I didn't realize that until it was too late, and now I've lost you to someone else." His smile was sad. "He is a very lucky man. You're a wonderful woman."

"Thank you, Kavon." She touched his arm. "I love you, Kavon, but not in that way."

He nodded. "I had to try." He smiled one final time before he kissed her gently on the forehead and closed the door behind him.

Alexis felt a serenity she'd never felt before as she sat there staring at her reflection. Kavon was in the past. It was time for her to start her future with a man who truly loved her. She looked up as Cecile opened the door and stepped inside. She smiled. If it hadn't been for Cecile, she never would have met Malcolm. She thanked God every day that Cecile intervened when she did.

"Nervous?"

"A little."

"Malcolm will make a wonderful husband." She picked up the veil from the table. "I hope the two of you live happily ever after."

"I hope so too."

Cecile placed the veil over her head. "For some reason I always imagined you marrying Kavon on your wedding day. Now I know that will never happen."

"Believe it or not, I always imagined the same thing." She

turned to face the mirror. "Until a certain waiter handed me a glass of champagne."

"I'm glad everything worked out between you and Malcolm. Lord only knows how many times people have tried to set Malcolm up with someone and failed."

"Who knew I would be the one?" She laughed.

"It's show time," Reverend Adkins stated as he stuck his head in the door.

"Ready?" Cecile questioned as she finished smoothing the back of the gown.

"As ready as I'll ever be."

"Let's go."

Alexis followed her out the door. As she approached the main hall she heard the music begin to play. From her viewpoint she could see Malcolm standing at the altar with a huge smile on his face. Darryl, standing beside him, mirrored his smile. She saw Sonya standing on the right with tears glistening in her eyes. To Sonya's right was Courtney. They were almost friends now that they were about to be sisters-in-law. Darryl and Courtney had eloped two months before, to the surprise of everyone.

Malcolm's parents were sitting on the front row. Despite her nervousness over meeting them, they'd welcomed her into their home as if she were one of the family. His mother had even given her the dress she wore on her wedding day.

As if he sensed her presence, Malcolm turned around to face her with a joyful expression that took her breath away. Here was the man she'd been searching for her whole life. A man she'd met at the most troublesome time in her life. Other than the music from the organ, the huge church was silent as she continued her walk down the aisle. She finally reached her destination and stood in front of the man she loved. The reverend smiled as he picked up his Bible.

"Dearly beloved, we are gathered here today in the sight of God," he began. Alexis listened as he spoke of God and true love. She smiled up at Malcolm. The reverend finished his short sermon and turned to Alexis. She felt tears moisten her eyes as they locked with Malcolm's and she began to recite the vows she'd memorized.

"Today I give you my heart. I never thought love could be so beautiful and so pure, but now as I stand here before you today I realize that it's not just love that makes the world go around. It's the people that you love. I love you, Malcolm, with all of my heart. I take you as my husband and my mate because of the love you have given me and for the joy that you continue to bring to me each and every day. I pray that God will bless this union forever till death do us part."

The reverend turned to Malcolm.

"My darling, Alexis. I never thought I would ever stand before God again to join in holy matrimony, but you changed that for me. You were the light at the end of the tunnel. You brought something to life in me I didn't even realize was missing. You gave me back my ability to trust and love someone. I will be eternally grateful for everything you've done for me." He looked deeply into her eyes. "I promise to love you forever as much as I love you today. I stand before you today in the sight of God and recite my vows, because it is only by His blessing that I found you. I will spend the rest of my life making sure I show you exactly how much you mean to me and how much I love you."

The reverend smiled. "By the power vested in me by the state of Florida I now pronounce you man and wife. Malcolm, you may kiss the bride."

Alexis felt tears of joy slide down her face as Malcolm kissed her gently with the promise of a love that would last a lifetime. Dreams did come true after all.

A FATEFUL POSSIBILITY

LaShell Shawnte Stratton

A writer writes, but staying at the keyboard is a trial in itself, so I want to thank my family for kicking my behind and making sure that I keep typing. So, Mom and Dad, though I didn't say it at the time, I appreciate it. I also want to thank my English teachers from grade school and onward (Ms. Duffy, Ms. Haviland, Mr. Hill, and Ms. Liorel) for believing in my writing and encouraging me to pursue it professionally. And as always, I want to thank my Aunt Debra. That remains consistent . . .

One

"Why you standing out here?" the old man asked. "Your mama and I was looking all over for you."

Christina Saunders turned her gaze from the driveway and smiled at her father, who stood behind her as she leaned against one of the columns below the veranda. After the best man's toast, the young woman had crept out of the reception hall, hoping that her absence would go unnoticed. But from the worried expression on her father's face, she guessed it hadn't.

Christina looked down at the small bouquet of lilies of the valley and baby's breath gathered in her hands and shrugged.

"You out here waiting for him?" her father asked.

"Yes," she said. "He told me yesterday he wouldn't be able to make it to the wedding. He said he would meet me for the reception afterward. I thought if I stood out here I might see him driving up. I hope everything's okay. He's not usually late like this."

Her father smiled and shook his head. "I'm sure he's all right. I wouldn't worry about it none."

The older man turned back toward the French doors at the

entrance but snapped his fingers as if he had just remembered something.

"By the way, you left this inside, sitting on your chair, baby," he said as he pulled open his lapel.

Christina laughed. Her father had tucked it haphazardly into his cummerbund. She didn't know why she hadn't noticed it trailing from the bottom of his jacket.

Mr. Saunders handed the blue satin shawl to his daughter and chuckled. "It *is* getting a little chilly out here. You'll probably gonna need it anyway."

"Thanks, Dad," she said as she kissed him on the cheek.

Her father hugged her before opening the door. He winked as he walked back inside.

Christina turned and gazed into the night. With only the flicker of candles along the driveway, the world in front of her was pitch-black with the exception of the stars that shined above. They dotted the heavens and twinkled brazenly while not even the silhouettes of hundred-year-old trees could make themselves visible against the darkness.

Summers were always warm in Loundon County, Virginia, but as of late a cool, nightly breeze managed to sweep from nearby ponds to the country club and the homes around it. Christina rubbed her arms against the growing chill and gathered her shawl tightly around her.

A romantic serenade could be heard from the reception through nearby windows. Christina walked back, leaned over a banister, and peeked through an opening in the curtains. She could see her brother and his bride dancing slowly in the center of a crowd. He leaned down and gently kissed her. Christina sighed. She had to admit it. They made a nice couple.

She smiled whimsically. Life was definitely unpredictable. It was hard to believe that a little over three years ago she had been planning for a similar night of her own.

Three years earlier . . .

"Chris? Chris? What on earth are you doing in there?" her mother exclaimed.

The voice drifted to her from the other side of the lilac-patterned curtains. When Christina heard it, she lifted her head, sighed, and scribbled the last of her brief journal entry.

April 25, 1999
Decisions. Decisions. I'm writing to you from the depths of bridal hell trying to choose between a poofy dress, a poofier dress, and the poofiest dress that God ever created. I don't care how expensive they are—I don't like any of them. But I am drowning in taffeta, and my mother could not be happier. To see me dressed like a fairy-tale princess has always been her dream. Now she wants me to rush outside to show off the latest gown chosen by popular vote of mother of the bride and mother of the groom. My vote didn't count, mind you. So what do you think? Should I step through the curtains or hightail it out the window two stalls over? No, I guess I'll brave another audience rather than make a quick escape.
I'll finish this entry later . . .
                                                    Christina

She rose from the macramé-covered bench on which she sat. Christina began to gather the fabric of the wedding gown that she could conceivably wear in six months that now pooled around her ankles. It bubbled as she pulled it upward. Her legs were engulfed in a cloud of white as she dragged the bodice back to her waist and shoved her arms into the satin sleeves.

"I'm trying to get this dress on," Christina lied as she rolled her eyes and shoved her journal into her polka-dotted shoulder bag. "But you need four years of calculus to figure out how to snap these cuffs."

"Do you need me to come in there?"

"No, thanks, Mom. I know how to dress myself, thank you," she said as she raised a zipper.

Her mother replied with a sigh that bristled with irritation. Beneath the hem of the curtains, Christina could see the brown toe of her mother's shoe tapping against the hardwood floor. The tap grew louder the longer the impatient woman waited.

"Well, speed it up, Chris. Everyone is waiting to see the dress."

"Why?" she mumbled as she ran her fingers over the crystal beading and then the tulle skirt. "It looks like the last six dresses."

"What did you say?"

"Nothing," Christina sang as pushed back the curtains and pasted on a smile. The dress barely fit through the dressing stall. The gown symbolized her future wedding, all fluff, pomp, and circumstance and totally unlike her personal style. She wearily eyed a simple silk gown that hung from a satin hanger on a faraway rack. That was more her taste. She could imagine herself feeling more comfortable in a dress like that. Her hair pulled back. She would do her face in soft tones. One calla lily would don her hair instead of a six-foot-long veil.

But then again, she thought ruefully, *what I feel and want is of little importance.*

Christina stepped into the midday light that showered the bridal salon and forced herself to parade, once again, for the women in front of her. Christina's mother and future mother-in-law beamed from the comfort of a white, embroidered couch while Christina's future maid of honor, Shauna Maxwell, tried her best not to look amused. Her best friend shook her bottle of chilled coffee and muffled a laugh by biting down on her lower lip as she stared at the strained grin plastered to Christina's face.

Shauna knew Christina was finding the moment unbearably painful. Christina hated primping and preening more than anything.

"Doesn't she look beautiful, Claire?" Christina's mother whispered.

"Yes," Mrs. Emory replied, "just beautiful." The auburn-haired woman sniffed as she searched frantically for a Kleenex in her tote bag. "She looks like a fairy princess. She reminds me of myself at her age."

"Like a fairy princess." Christina's mother grinned before nodding in agreement. "David will cry when he sees her."

Shauna could hold in her laughter no longer. She released a loud snort that broke the solemn moment, and covered her mouth, drawing scathing glares from Christina's mother and Mrs. Emory. Stifled giggles then started to erupt from Christina. The two older women rolled their eyes as the younger women continue to laugh.

Christina gasped for breath as she walked toward a series of full-length mirrors in the back of the salon. She gazed at her reflection and frowned.

Shauna raised the bottle to her lips to stifle her laughter.

"I'm sorry. You can't drink that in here," a crimson-lipped redhead said primly as she walked past Shauna in midsip. Shauna glanced at the now forgotten teacups that sat on a nearby silver tray. Mrs. Saunders and Mrs. Emory had drunk out of them less than five minutes earlier—compliments of the salon. Shauna seethed and then sighed before screwing the cap back onto her bottle. She chose not to point this out, and for one of the few times in her life, to keep quiet.

"You know, it *is* a beautiful dress," Christina's mother proclaimed.

She walked behind her daughter and gently placed a pearl-capped veil atop Christina's head before molding her hands around the younger woman's shoulders. She stopped and gazed at the image they created in the full-length mirror, smiling as she saw a younger version of herself peer back at her. (Though, to her great sadness, it was admittedly three shades darker than her *café con leche* complexion.) Mother's and daughter's heart-shaped faces were the same for the most part, though the deep dimple in her left cheek made Christina's face somewhat different. Both noses were upturned, giving them an air of superiority. Their eyebrows arched at sharp angles, making them seem constantly knowing and alert, and a pronounced widow's peak was at their brows. Mrs. Saunders's hair was in a stylish bob while Christina's sun-kissed locks brushed past her shoulders. Their lower bottom lips pouted slightly, imitating the curves of their petite bodies. Seeing herself in her fitting, two-piece tan suit and her daughter in her gown, Mrs. Saunders quietly tried to envision herself as a regal queen and Christina as her beautiful princess. Unfortunately, her daughter was marring her daydream by frowning constantly and tugging at her skirt.

"Don't make that face, Christina. Its not attractive."

Christina raised her chin and smiled primly.

"That's better," her mother reassured her before turning to face the women behind them. She clasped her hands together just as Christina rolled her eyes and removed the veil from her head. The young woman winced as she tried to remove a lock of hair from the headpiece.

"Well, I think this is definitely the best dress we've seen so far."

"And the most expensive," Christina muttered sullenly.

"I was partial to the other Vera Wang," Mrs. Emory volunteered with eyebrows raised. "Though I will admit the Badgley Mischka was a gorgeous sight."

"Potato, tomato," Christina mumbled.

"What do you think, Chris?"

She glanced down at the bridal gown and shrugged her brown shoulders with disinterest. "This one is fine."

"Fine?"

She nodded as she walked toward the dressing rooms.

"Are you feeling all right, Chris?"

"I'm fine," she answered before pulling the curtains closed.

"It's fine. I'm fine." The older woman's dim shadow wavered back and forth among the lilacs. "I suggest you get out of this mood you've been in lately, Christina," her mother's voice ordered sternly in a throaty whisper. (Her mother always gave orders in whispers. She said shouting was undignified.) "I've been trying to chalk it up to prewedding jitters—I know about these things, it comes with my line of work—but God help me, I seem to be more interested in the details of your wedding than you do. And any question I ask you, you act as if I'm bothering you!"

She sighed gruffly. "Do you know what my mother did for me for my wedding? She gave me thirty dollars to put toward my wedding dress, two food vouchers, and told me she was sorry she couldn't help me with anything else but she had 'more important things to do.' And here I am, helping you choose your wedding gown, the reception hall, and table linens. . . . I even know the name of the florist and you don't! Are you listening to me?"

"Yes, Mom," Christina answered quickly, though she could not hear her mother after that point. Her mind drifted off as she tried to remember the remaining lines she would write in her journal.

"You were kind of hard on her, weren't you?" Shauna asked.

They had stopped at a red light long enough for Shauna to check the redness of her lips in the visor mirror, long enough for her to stop her curses at bungling drivers.

Christina blinked while turning away from her reflection in the tinted window of her best friend's Volkswagen Beetle. She squinted and stared at the woman beside her with confusion. "What? A bit hard on who?"

"Your mother. Who else would I be talking about?"

"Shauna, I wasn't aware of the fact that we were talking at all. Consequently, I would not assume you were talking about my mother."

Shauna rolled her doelike eyes. "Speak English," she spat.

"What?"

"You know what I mean." She tugged her shoulder-length braids out of the collar of her cotton T-shirt. "I hate it when you give me that BUM talk."

BUM talk. *B*lack *U*pper *M*iddle class talk. The language of the black upper middle class that urban, "take no bull" Shauna found both patronizing and irritating. Shauna said it was too uppity for its social standing. It, like the people who used it, seemed richer than it actually was.

"Okay, Shauna, what did you mean when you said I was being hard on my mom?"

Shauna flipped up the driver's-side visor, pressed her foot down on the accelerator, and shrugged.

"You were raining on her parade, Chris. You know how much she likes that stuff, and you wouldn't even fake like you were having fun."

"Hey, I was playing along even though I was thinking the entire time, 'Why should I?'"

Christina sighed gruffly as she turned her attention back to the tinted window.

"It's not my wedding, Shauna. It's *her* wedding, *her* extravaganza created so that she can show off for the members of the country club and the Stafford Manor community." She frowned. "Why should I keep pretending it's anything else? Besides, I wanted something small and intimate. I wanted to wear a simple, white dress. She's the one who turned it into the biggest event since the White House Inaugural Ball."

Shauna chuckled.

"And she keeps haggling me about her decorating and catering business."

"That again? Doesn't she know that you hate it?"

"No, she doesn't seem to know even though I keep telling her. And it's not just that I don't like it," Christina argued. "I'm just not good at it. I can't get the staff to do anything. I hate bossing people around. My mother may do it well but I didn't inherit her bossy gene. I'm a horrible cook, so when she keeps telling me to keep an eye on the chef I have no idea what I'm 'keeping an eye' on! What? Whether or not he's going to run off with one of the salt and pepper shakers? I have no idea what the food is supposed to look like or taste like!"

Shauna chuckled. "Remember the time when she put you in charge of the music for the Winthrop barbecue shindig?"

Christina covered her face and shook her head. "Please don't remind me!"

"Mrs. Winthrop said she wanted a calypso band from Martinique to go with the Caribbean theme of the party, and you thought she said mariachi band." Shauna paused. She could barely stop laughing.

"She did say mariachi!"

"So here they were in their backyard with palm trees and jerky listening to these guys with sombreros! It looked like some retarded *Cinco de Mayo* celebration!"

Shauna was now laughing so hard, tears were streaming down her eyes.

"Well, my point was," Christina continued, trying to ignore her friend's laughter, "I did get a degree in business administration but it wasn't just so that I could ease into a position in *her* business. But she keeps saying, 'Oh, you'll come around.' She just doesn't understand that there are other things I want to do. I have my own aspirations."

"Its tough being a rich girl," Shauna said in a high, squeaky voice. She batted her eyelashes and sighed whimsically.

Christina quickly rolled one of the bridal magazines that were stacked on her lap and thumped Shauna's crown.

"Hey, girl, I'm driving here!"

"And making fun of me."

"Yeah, that too," Shauna admitted before sticking out her tongue.

Christina grinned though she could feel her smile teetering on the brink of a frown. She shrugged helplessly.

"Well, I'm glad you can find the humor in all this, Shauna. I wish I could."

Shauna rolled her eyes heavenward and shook her head. "You can't find the humor, Chris, only because you have to realize things could always be worse. So your mother can be a bit much at times. So your wedding's going to be a little bigger than what you expected. It's not the end of the world! Hell, at least your parents are paying for it!" She raised a bottle of chilled coffee to her lips and swallowed. "I'm trying to feel for you, girl, but me being low on cash and not a decade close to getting married makes me less than sympathetic, if you know what I mean."

Even as she listened, Christina opened one of the magazines on her lap and gazed at the pages in front of her. She gazed at a blond bride. A bouquet of irises was cradled in her arms. A knowing smile painted her peach-hued face. The bride's head tilted slightly. Christina wondered what the woman in the picture was thinking when she took the photo.

"See it this way," Shauna said as she pressed a radio button. "Whenever you think your life is crappy, just remember my small apartment that I share with my five-year-old cat. Remember my student loans and my mother who cares more about *Wheel of Fortune, Jeopardy,* and reruns of *Good Times* than she does about me. Whenever you feel low, think of my life."

Christina silently nodded, making her soft brown curls sway back and forth. Christina would not tell Shauna that it was the freedom of her best friend's life in comparison to her own that made her feel so depressed. She wished sometimes her mother would try to not be so *involved.*

"And if it gets too bad," Shauna continued, "just say it and stop acting like a little kid. Sulking. Refusing to say anything. You'll never get your point across that way."

Christina nodded silently. She knew her friend was right but Christina could feel a thought tugging at her, a worry that her unhappiness wasn't due to just her mother. Maybe it was the marriage itself. Was Christina really ready to get married now? She had just graduated from college a couple of years ago. She still hadn't lived away from her family. She'd never been on her own . . .

No, that's not it, Christina thought, second-guessing herself. *David and I are meant to be together.*

"You need to learn how to stand up for yourself, Christina. This passive-aggressive stuff just is not working for you. You need to tell your mother and everyone else what you really, really want! You can't keep . . ."

Shauna's voice faded as she turned left. She focused her concentration on angling her car into one of the numbered parking spaces in front of a quaint row of condominiums. They simultaneously glanced at the black Mercedes-Benz sedan that was parked four spaces over.

"Looks like he's home already," Shauna said.

"Yeah, looks like it."

"Well, at least you don't have to get out your key. He can buzz you up."

"He's probably studying," Christina said while shaking her head. "He won't hear the buzz."

Shauna smiled.

"That will be ten dollars, miss," she said, mimicking an Indian accent while holding out her hand.

"Put it on my tab," Christina replied with a laugh before opening her car door. "Drive carefully, Shauna, and for God's sake, slow down!"

"I drive fine. It's everyone else on the highway that's the problem," Shauna yelled through her open window before pulling out of the parking space and pressing the accelerator as her Beetle scuttled down a vacant street.

Christina stood on the sidewalk and watched until her best friend's Barney-purple Volkswagen disappeared behind a neat line of pine trees.

She turned and walked up a tulip-bordered pathway until she reached glass doors. Christina scanned the wall panel and pressed a black button alongside a nameplate that read EMORY, DAVID. She leaned forward, her lips almost brushing the wire mesh of the speaker.

"Hello?" a deep voice answered.

"David, it's Christina."

Her words were quickly followed by a buzz and then a click as the front door sprung open.

She regretfully allowed the lines of her journal entry to melt away knowing that with David upstairs, she would have little or no time to write them. Her confusion would have to linger for a bit longer with no means to see her thoughts on paper.

TWO

The moment she stepped inside his building, she was assaulted by the pungent smell of the blooming potted hyacinth that perched on windowsills. Christina's eyes were greeted with high cathedral ceilings and a skylight that splashed the complex's lobby with the orange glow of mid-afternoon. She walked up a series of wrought-iron staircases, pausing to tug her bag farther up her shoulder. She turned right and walked past a few doorways. When she reached his door she turned the gold knob and pushed, knowing it would be unlocked.

"So how'd it go?" she heard David call out from the kitchen.

She smiled at him before locking the door behind her.

"Fine. Your mother and my mother decided on a dress and I tried my best not to look bored."

David laughed. He put the finishing touches on his sandwich before slicing the monstrosity down its center. Pieces of salami coated with mayonnaise slid onto the counter from the edges of wheat bread. Slices of tomato fought for space among hunks of Swiss cheese.

Barefoot with jeans nestled around his hips and a taut, white T-shirt straining across his chest, David seemed handsomely, almost effortlessly charming. His six-foot, two-inch frame was lean and solid from years of athleticism. He had inherited the green flecks at the center of his eyes from his mother. The curly hair that he had also gotten from her tended to get unruly when he missed a cut, so he went to a family barber once every two weeks so that his mane was as neat as the man who wore it.

"You're mighty lucky you're studying for the bar, my boy," she lamented as she kicked off her shoes. "If that wasn't the case, I'd make you come on these wedding trips with me. You'd learn to *love* it as much as I do. The differences between off-white, cream white, and antique white are truly fascinating."

"Are you hungry?" he asked. He opened the refrigerator door and loudly thumped a two-liter soda on the kitchen island. David then opened one of his cabinets and pulled out a jumbo bag of rippled potato chips.

She peered over his shoulder before wrinkling her nose at his king-size sandwich.

"No, I'm fine. Don't worry about me," Christina said while patting him on the back. "I don't know what your mother would say to a meal like that though. It's so unseemly."

She shook her head and laughed, making David shrug.

"Canapés are for garden parties," he said before chomping a huge chunk of his sandwich. Mayonnaise lingered at the corners of his mouth.

"I see," she murmured, before wiping the edge of his lips with her thumb.

Christina frowned. "I thought you were going to study at the library today."

"I was. I mean . . . I did." David shrugged. "I'm just taking a break. I'm heading back in a few hours."

"Wanted to eat lunch at home, huh?"

"Yeah, that," he said between bites of his sandwich. "Among other things."

"Among other things?"

"Yep," he said before popping a potato chip into his mouth. His eyes glinted wickedly.

Christina sighed before removing her sweater. "Are you telling me you came home for lunch and sex?"

David laughed before nodding. "Don't say it like that! It helps me clear my head after staring at law books and case profiles all day."

Christina laughed. "We just started about half a year ago, David. Remember? It's great that it clears your head and all but I haven't mastered quickies yet. I just got my learner's permit and you're telling me to drive the Daytona," she joked before flopping onto his sofa.

"Practice makes perfect," he sang.

"How did you know I'd be here when you came home? I could have been at my house."

He raised an eyebrow.

"I figured that if you were out most of the day, going over tableware patterns and champagne glasses with your mother, the last thing you would want to do is go home. You'd run to my place in search for some peace, quiet, and solitude, thinking that I wouldn't be here," he explained as he finished the last of his sandwich. "I'd catch you off guard. I'd offer you some lunch and maybe a back rub or a foot massage. Finally, out of deep thanks for my gentlemanly kindness, you'd offer me gold-medal-worthy sex."

She laughed so hard her stomach ached. "So that was your whole plan?"

He nodded as he dumped the remains of his lunch into the trash can. David pulled his T-shirt over his head as he walked toward her.

"That was the gist of it," he muttered before leaning down and kissing her earlobe.

His mouth wandered to her neck and then her shoulder. She laughed as he fumbled with the buttons of her shirt.

"There's no stop clock, David. If we slow down I can un-button my own clothes."

He rolled his eyes and slumped backward, watching her as she fiddled with her bra clasp.

"All right, let's take this into the bedroom," he said before leaning forward and throwing her over his shoulder. Christina squealed as he carried her down the hallway. Her head bobbed helplessly, missing the corner of his bedroom door by half an inch.

"Me, Tarzan. You, Jane," he grunted before dropping her to the bed.

Christina giggled as she watched David finish undressing. She leaned over and opened his night table drawer and noticed that with the exception of a nearly empty bottle of cologne and single cuff link, the drawer was empty.

"Did Tarzan remember to buy condoms like I asked him to?"

David's shoulders slumped as his jeans fell to his ankles.

"Tarzan thought Jane was on the pill," he said. He sat on the edge of the bed and began to remove his Ralph Lauren boxer briefs. "When did you tell me to buy condoms?"

"David," she began before rolling her eyes, "I told you that last week. The same day I said my doctor was putting me on antibiotics for my ear infection. Do you ever listen to me?"

"What do condoms have to do with ear infections?"

"The pill doesn't work when you're taking antibiotic medication!"

"Says who?"

"People."

"People? What people?"

She tossed a pillow at the back of his head. "The people who know this stuff: doctors and pharmacists. The people who write the labels on medications."

"Don't be so worried. We'll be fine," he assured her as he rose from the edge of the bed and climbed beneath the covers.

"Oh, do you think so, Dr. Emory?" She laughed as she kicked her shorts to the bottom of the bed.

"Sure," he said. He kissed her gently as he eased her panties past her hips and then her knees. "It's like how they tell you not to take an antihistamine before driving. You might get drowsy and cause a six-car pile up. Then again, you might not have an accident at all and be perfectly fine. More than likely, you'll get home safely."

She laughed.

* * *

She could hear his heartbeat through his chest. The rhythmic thudding was more soothing than a lullaby. Christina raised her head slightly, resisting the urge to fall asleep. She wondered if she had done everything right and hoped she had pleased David. At least she could take comfort in the fact that they were both ingenues fumbling beneath the sheets, trying to extract some morsel of pleasure from an activity that was completely new for the both of them. If they both weren't so new at it, she would be embarrassed. Her timidity would probably be irritating to a more experienced man. Thank God both of them had agreed to wait this long.

Sex had been hard for them at first. Though mentally Christina realized the act was only bringing two people in love closer physically, her body had fought against it at every turn. Her nervousness and anticipation had given way to discomfort. Discomfort had given way to pain. *Excruciating* pain, to be exact. But David assured her with whispered promises that the more they did it, the more it would feel better and become easier. One day, he promised her, she would like having sex with him. Christina speculated aloud that maybe she didn't like having sex with him because he wasn't doing it correctly.

She had been resentful at first. Neither one of them had any experience at this, but from the noises he was making and the expressions of ecstasy on his face, he seemed to be enjoying himself. Why couldn't *he* feel any pain? Why didn't *she* share in his pleasure?

It had been an uphill battle. It had required a lot of patience on David's part and a lot of perseverance on hers—not to mention a lot of practice for the both of them. Now having David inside her body was almost familiar for Christina. Sometimes, she even found the experience enjoyable.

"The phone's ringing," David mumbled drowsily. He wiped his eyes.

Christina sighed. "It's your phone."

"But it's on your side of the bed."

The ringing stopped only to begin again.

"You know who it is, Chris. She's going to keep calling back until you answer. Just pick it up."

"It could be *your* mother."

"My mother's too polite to let the phone ring that long."

Christina pinched his shoulder before rolling her eyes and removing the phone from the night table. "Hello?"

"Where have you been?" her mother asked heatedly.

Christina yawned. "I've been here."

"Do you know what time it is?"

She lifted the edge of the bedsheet and checked her wristwatch. "Five o'clock."

"And where were we supposed to meet at four-thirty, Christina?"

She suddenly remembered. The young woman squeezed her eyes shut and grimaced. "At the church."

"Exactly, at the church. Did you write it in your appointment book like I asked you to?"

"Yes," Christina lied.

"Well, I guess we're going to have to reschedule. That's if Reverend Nixon can work us in this week."

Christina closed her eyes and nodded.

"Will David drive you home?"

"Sure, I guess."

"Well, remind *him* to remind *you* to finish the wedding invitations. I won't be home until seven o'clock."

"Okay."

The phone call ended with an abrupt click from her mother's end.

"I'm in trouble," Christina muttered before lowering the phone back into its cradle.

"So what else is new?" David asked with a laugh.

"I was supposed to meet her at four-thirty." She buried her face in her hands. "God, how could I have forgotten that?"

David glanced at the digital clock on his dresser before slowly rubbing her back.

"Maybe it clears your head too," he said.

He dropped his arm back to his side as she swung her legs over the edge of the bed, stood up, and walked toward the bathroom.

"I have to take a shower," she mumbled.

"Save some hot water for me," David called out as he attempted to turn on his wide-screen television. He had to pause to remember which remote was for the bedroom television and which was for the entertainment center in the living room.

"Better yet," he yelled over the blare of the sports cable network, "you want any company in there?"

Christina glared at him before shutting the bathroom door firmly behind her.

"Guess not," he muttered with a chuckle.

"Do you have everything?" David asked as they walked toward his car. He unlocked the door with a loud beep and held it open for her as she slipped inside.

"I think I do," Christina mumbled as she buckled her seat belt. She pulled down the visor mirror and quickly reapplied her lipstick. She hastily began to brush her tussled hair back into a ponytail and pushed her shirttail back into her shorts.

As he shifted the car into drive, David brushed a finger across Christina's chin and smiled. "What are you getting all dolled up for? Meeting another guy later on?"

Christina rolled her eyes at him. He knew very well why she was rushing to fix herself before she arrived back home. She hated returning to her parents' house with that "I've been in bed with my boyfriend all afternoon" look.

The fifteen-minute drive was carried out in relative silence, but that silence was interrupted when David's sedan turned the corner of her block. Christina could hear the thudding music through the passenger-side window.

She surmised that Ronald, or Ronny G as he preferred his friends to call him, was back from Virginia and obviously her mother hadn't arrived home yet.

The music was so loud and she could determine the volume level with more than just her ears. She could tell it was too loud from the way David's car windows vibrated and then nearly pulsated the closer they drew to her family's two-story, redbrick home. (With this much vibration, the Ionic columns that held up their veranda could probably buckle at any moment.)

Christina's older brother, Ronald, was probably in his

beloved basement studio, remixing one of the songs he had produced with a crew of aspiring rappers. Ronny G was always sure that fame was only a good remix away.

Christina had had little knowledge of this type of music before Ronald introduced it to her. (It had been banned from their household.) Like Ronald, she liked the music form, though not as openly as her brother did, for fear of offending her family. Ronald never seemed to care about other people's opinions of him though in all aspects of his life.

Her father deemed her brother's career choice as "a waste of a college degree." Her mother had given up on Ronald long before that, when he used his high school graduation fund and decided to buy, of all things, a Hummer rather than one of the many luxury automobiles young men in their neighborhood usually bought.

"With that car," she had remarked, "he looks like a common drug dealer."

"It's actually very fashionable, Mom," Christina had said, trying to defend her brother.

"It's not fashionable, Christina," her mother had chided. "It's a passing fad like bell-bottoms or platform shoes. It will seem ridiculous years from now."

Christina had opened her mouth to protest that bell-bottoms and platform shoes had become fashionable again but she figured, what was the point? Her mother would never admit she was wrong anyway. Ronny had stopped arguing his point with her years ago. It was one of the many reasons why Christina adored her brother. He was able to rid himself of the family pressure to be perfect and had simply followed his own lead.

"He's going to go deaf in there!" David exclaimed. "Doesn't he at least care that he's embarrassing his family with that loud, hood rat music?"

Christina rolled her eyes.

Despite David's fondness for hoagie sandwiches and his kinship with the sports channel, his well-bred upbringing always found a way to rear its ugly head. He could definitely be a snob when he wanted to. It was one of David's less than endearing qualities.

"He's not going to go deaf," Christina shouted over the noise with a laugh. She kissed David's cheek. "Ronald's used to it."

Christina gathered her things and slowly began to climb out of David's Mercedes.

"I will see you tomorrow," he said.

"What?"

"I'll see you tomorrow!" he yelled, visibly exasperated by all the shouting.

She smiled and waved good-bye in reply before shutting the car door firmly behind her.

Christina walked calmly up their driveway and the small flight of stairs that led to their front door, peering over her shoulder as she waited for the Mercedes to turn the corner. But the instant she stepped into their foyer with its mahogany staircase, crystal chandelier, marble floors, and Rembrandt reproductions and closed the front door behind her, she dropped her bags and started to imitate one of the video dancers she had seen on television earlier that week.

She became so lost in her "rump shaking," she hadn't noticed the opening of the basement door.

"Go, Chris! Go, Chris! It's your birthday! It's your birthday," her brother yelled as he stood at the top of the stairs leading to his humble, secluded abode.

Ronald's shirt looked nearly three sizes too big for him. A silver-studded belt that fell at his hips held up the jeans he wore, while the rest of the denim bagged around his ankles. A fire-engine-red cell phone stuck out of his front pocket, and a black doo-rag was tied around his head.

Christina laughed, clutching her chest as she caught her breath.

"Don't tell Mom, okay?" she said between gasps.

Ronald shook his head and chuckled. "Why the hell would I tell her? She'll probably think I'm corrupting you or something and kick my ass out." He leaned his head toward the stairwell. "Come downstairs though if you're going to dance like that. She's not here, but if Pops catches you she'll probably read his mind and find out."

They laughed and walked down the dimly lit stairwell.

Christina prepared her nose for yet another assault of the day. Thanks to Ronald, the Saunderses' basement always had a strange mix of smells, as if it were a musk-filled wine cellar and an aerobics gym wrapped all into one with the slightest aroma of an illegal substance wafting from the ashtrays.

The music was loud upstairs but it was even louder now that she was twenty feet from Ronald's booming speakers. She motioned for him to turn the music down. He went five steps better and turned the music off completely.

"So what's up with ya'?" he asked as he pushed aside magazines from his couch that promptly landed on the floor. He gestured toward the newly made seat and Christina sat down.

"Nothing," she murmured.

Ronald raised an eyebrow. "Nothin'? Nothin'? Man, somethin's up." He eyed her carefully. "It got anything to do with David?"

She frowned. "No, everything's perfect with him. We're fine. Really, there is *nothing* wrong with me, Ronny. At most, I'm a little tired. That's all."

Ronald slowly nodded and fiddled with the buttons on one of the many gadgets that were attached to his stereo system.

"Anyway," he began, "how's that wedding stuff going? Mom told me a few days ago on the phone that you got a party coming up in a couple of weeks—"

Christina shook her head. "Let's not talk about weddings, please?" She smiled. "I talk about weddings and caterers and registries all day. Tell me about Virginia."

Ronald squinted and stared at her face as if he was trying to decipher the blank expression she now gave him. He then shrugged before inspecting one of his compact disc covers.

"All right, whatever you say, sis. Well, Virginia was all right," he murmured. "We got a couple of tracks laid down. They sounded tight—for the most part. They could use some tweakin' but there's no rush. We'll keep working on it until we get it right." He glanced at her slyly. "Plus, I met a girl."

"A girl?" Christina exclaimed with a laugh. "A girl? I hope you mean you met a *woman!*"

"Yeah, I mean a woman. A *nice* woman. She's smart. She's

funny and sexy as hell!" He shrugged. "I think I kinda like her."

Christina smirked as his words faded and he stared into nowhere, starry-eyed.

"Hmmm," she said. "If my intuition serves me correctly, dear brother, it sounds as if you more than just, 'kinda like her.' It sounds as if you like her a lot!"

He grinned, turning his back to her, pretending to stack magazines on his bookshelf as he allowed himself a few seconds to blush freely.

"What is her name?" she persisted.

Ronald shrugged. "Sheila. Sheila Macintosh."

Christina laughed. She was suddenly filled with the impishness of her youth. "Ronald and Sheila sitting in a tree. K-I-S-S-I-N-G. First comes love, then comes marriage, then comes—"

"Man, get out of here! I don't have time to be messin' with you," he barked with a grin. "Go upstairs before I throw you up there!"

She rose from the couch, clutching her stomach as she giggled. "—Sheila with the baby carriage."

Christina slowly walked up the staircase, leaving her brother to his solitude. As she closed the door behind her, she smiled whimsically, reflecting on the pleasant reverie that overcame Ronald when he talked about this woman named Sheila, someone with whom he had unwittingly fallen in love.

Christina then frowned, contemplating whether the same feeling overcame David when he talked about her. Did the same expression cross his face when he thought about his fiancée, his future wife? She hoped it did.

She then gazed at the yellow, three-karat diamond that adorned her ring finger, hoping that the same expression crossed her face when she talked about him. That's how people act when they are in love, correct?

"I love him. I love him. I love him," she chanted as she slung her bag over her shoulder and climbed the stairs to her bedroom. She stopped in her doorway as a feeling of nausea overcame her.

"Oh, God," Christina muttered. The room started to swirl around her as she grabbed for the edge of her bed. Her heart was thudding in her chest and her ears, and beads of sweat dotted her forehead. The world around her began to darken. She was going to faint.

She was caught in the throes of a panic attack.

Christina collapsed against her comforter, gasping for air. She rolled onto her back and stared at the ceiling. The twirling of the room started to slow down as she cried silently.

"I can't do this," she whispered to her empty room.

You can and you will, a voice answered. It was strong and resolute. Christina was surprised it had come from inside her head.

She sighed and slowly nodded. Her heartbeat began to slow and she could feel a cool breeze coming from her window.

She rose slowly from her bed and pulled her journal from her bag. In a mad rush, she wrote the words that had popped in her head before she forgot them.

April 25, 1999
  I can and I will marry David. I love him and he loves me. We were meant to be together. I can't doubt that.

                                          Christina

She wouldn't doubt anymore.

Three

One week later, on a sunny weekend afternoon, she found herself running up the crisp green lawn of the Stanford Manor Country Club. Christina saw David leaning against a column at the entrance, staring at nothing in particular until he noticed her gulping for air. He slowly smiled.

"I know. I'm late," she grumbled while tidying her hair. The neat ponytail she had brushed earlier that morning was now closer to a flopping pompom. Christina straightened the front of her capri pants that had twisted askew, and smoothed the nonexistent wrinkles in her polo shirt. "I would have been here fifteen minutes earlier but I couldn't find a parking space. Is there a luncheon today?"

"Why didn't you just have one of the attendants handle it for you?" he asked as he wrapped an arm around her waist.

She glanced up at David, smiled weakly, and shrugged. Christina did not want to tell him that the very idea of having someone else do something for her that she was fully capable of doing herself made her uncomfortable. Instead, she chose to say nothing as he held the door open.

"Good morning, Miss Saunders. Mr. Emory," one of the club's caretakers said as she stepped onto the foyer's oriental rug. He had been working there as long as Christina could remember.

"Good morning, Otis," she replied with a smile. David merely nodded in acknowledgment. Christina gritted her teeth when she noticed.

As they walked across the foyer, David held out a hand to her and she took it begrudgingly. She guessed he couldn't help it. Perhaps his mannerisms, his expectations, and his view of people simply came with the old money. She guessed she and David would always be different in that way. They ran in the same circles, but their backgrounds were quite dissimilar.

The differences between their families would always be glaring. Even with the equal presence of money, these differences could not be erased. When their lists of achievements and pedigrees were compared, the scales would always lean toward the Emory side.

The Emory line boasted to be nearly a hundred and fifty years old. They were a family of black lawyers and circuit court judges that began in the South during the Reconstruction Era and gravitated to the North when the South no longer wanted them. Occasionally, one of the Emorys would break the old mold and become an obstetrician or a neurosurgeon—to the great angst of everyone else in the family. Only in the Emory pack could an offspring who became a doctor be considered a disappointment.

One of their younger generation, Jacob Emory, became a partner in a black-owned law firm in the mid-1980s. Years earlier, Jacob had married Azalea Rousseau, the reigning beauty queen at his alma mater, and on October 1, 1977, Azalea—the light-skinned, green-eyed, auburn-haired Louisiana debutante—gave Jacob a green-eyed son whom they would name, David, after his great-grandfather.

He would be their only child. The hope and future of their line of the Emory clan would always rest upon his broad shoulders.

In contrast, the Saunders family was a lot more humble. Very few clear lines pointed from descendant to forefather in their family tree.

Gerald Saunders, Christina's dad, didn't know who his father was. He couldn't point him out in a crowd and, frankly, didn't care one way or the other. Gerald was a self-made man in every sense of the word. At twelve, he went door to door selling newspapers. "Without a bike," he often boasted. At seventeen, he worked nights to make extra money, cleaning the high school that he attended during the day. When he turned twenty-three, he started a septic-tank drainage business, ringing doorbells in his overalls and work gloves, selling his service in neighborhoods within a fifty-mile radius. He then expanded it to a chain of septic-tank businesses, then dry-cleaning locales, and finally, mom-and-pop-themed chicken joints in the poor district. By the end of the decade, he had accumulated a small fortune that only ballooned with each new venture he made.

But his wife, Wilhelmina—now known as Helen by friends and clients—never seemed to be pleased. She had been born poor and raised poor and so had her mother before her. Wilhelmina always thought this was a grave injustice. She fastened herself onto Gerald when she was nineteen because she realized he had drive and skill, but she was dismayed these traits only led him to menial business enterprises. A chain of septic-tank businesses? Chicken joints? Both were unlike her catering and decorating, which, she often boasted, epitomized sophistication. When she finally convinced him to retire his overalls and his work gloves, to manage operations from the comfort of a downtown office rather than knee deep in the muck, she sighed with relief both for her sake and his. The embarrassment could end. At least the money he had amassed could afford a proper lifestyle for her and their two children. From that point, she would try her best to align their family with the proper social connections—starting with Christina.

Christina Saunders and David Emory first met as toddlers at a catered luncheon at the Stanford Manor Country Club held by an auxiliary committee to which both their mothers belonged. Well, to be more accurate, Mrs. Emory chaired the committee that year while Mrs. Saunders was still vying for membership. David wore his baby-blue knickerbockers.

Christina wore a pastel yellow and pink Easter dress. Neither one remembered that day well, though their mothers insisted they "hit it off famously." Christina often found that an odd way to describe her first meeting with David considering that, as she had often been told, he spilled his punch on her, lobbed a canapé at her head, and yanked one of her pigtails.

They would cross paths from time to time throughout the years, though not really forming a friendship until he was fourteen years old and she was eleven. By then David would be tall, handsome, athletic, and popular. He was a boy who matured faster than the others. He had grown facial hair that he trimmed daily and his voice had dropped several octaves the year before. In contrast, Christina was bookish, quiet, and gangly. Her features had not caught up with one another. Her nose was too big for her face, and her teeth seemed too large for her head. To her disappointment, her breasts were still no more than barely visible nubs. To not draw attention to her appearance, she said little, keeping her thoughts inside her, becoming lost in paperbacks and her journal. Christina was a social outcast in many ways, so nerdy that the boys had no problems making fun of her, and many of the girls had no problem picking on her. She supposed David had pitied her or seen in her something the others did not see. In many ways he kept her teenage years from being completely unbearable. David stood up for her when the guys made fun of her and even found a way to keep the popular girls of their crowd in check.

A relationship developed between the two that often develops between the "blessed" and "unblessed." He was her lord and protector. She was the president of his fan club. Christina adored David, and David watched over Christina. The arrangement suited them just fine until the fall of her sixteenth year when Christina's mother became involved.

For a long time, Wilhelmina Saunders had silently watched their friendship forming—to her great surprise—and wondered just how far it would go and how long it would last. Though her daughter's interest was always first and foremost, Mrs. Saunders was a social climber at heart. She saw a connection between Christina and the Emory boy as an opportunity to climb more than just a few rungs on the ladder. So two days before the annual winter ball, Mrs. Saunders decided it would be a good idea for her and her daughter to take an impromptu trip to New York. "To see the skyscrapers and museums," she said, knowing that her daughter would never miss an opportunity to look at a building or a painting. (So help her, Lord.)

When they arrived in New York City, they veered past the Empire State Building, the Museum of Modern Art, the Rockefeller Center, and pulled up in front of a posh salon. The bespectacled Christina was surprised, confused, and then angry, slowly realizing that she had been tricked. At first she refused the makeover, poking out her lower lip and putting her foot down. She only agreed when her mother promised they would go to a museum afterward.

Two days later, after the salon and several boutiques, Christina arrived at the Stanford Manor Country Club soiree, sullen but beautiful, radiant but uncomfortable in her new lavender ball gown and ill-fitting high heels. Her eyes were downcast. She had wanted to hide in a dark corner and would have had it not been for her mother firmly holding her arm and keeping her in place.

"Mom, I want to go home," Christina had whimpered.

"You won't do any such thing."

"I look ridiculous!"

"No, you don't," her mother had argued through clenched teeth. "You look beautiful, now straighten your shoulders!"

David quickly spotted Christina from across the room, though not as fast as Mrs. Saunders spotted him. From the look in his eyes, the calculating woman knew instantly that despite the odds against it, she had made a successful match between her daughter and an Emory.

And here the couple was, back on the grounds where the whole thing started, standing on the golf green of the country club, waiting for Christina to putt her ball.

"Just concentrate," David said. He grinned as he held his

putter behind his neck with both of his arms draped over each end.

"This game is so stupid," she muttered through gritted teeth. Christina's eyes wavered from the ball to the hole in front of her and back again. "I hate golf."

"You just hate it because you're not good at it." David chuckled as he slowly walked toward her. "Here, I'll help you."

He stood behind her, stooping slightly so his chin did not rest on her crown but grazed her cheek instead. He wrapped his hands around her hands and extended his arms so that any slight movement he made, she would move accordingly.

"Now pull your wrist back gently," he whispered, guiding her movements as he said it. "Gently. Gently. Now . . . tap."

She followed his command and the ball rolled forward, veering off course by only a few centimeters though returning within seconds to land quickly in its hole.

Christina grinned.

"It worked!" she shouted, bouncing gleefully.

"You're right. It did," he whispered as he nuzzled her neck.

"Okay," she said, pushing up the brim of her visor. "Where's my driver? Let's move on to the next hole and have this baby over and done with before sundown."

"Why? I think we're fine just the way we are," he murmured, linking his arms around her waist.

"Oh, really?"

"Really," he said, pushing her hair aside so that he could lightly kiss the back of her ear.

"Get a room!" someone yelled.

David peered over his shoulder. He turned and waved to his best friend, Julian Hightower, who rode toward them in a white and blue golf cart. Julian stopped and jumped out with a bounce, gesturing to the long-legged, ebony beauty that sat in the passenger's seat.

"Sorry, David," Julian said, patting his much taller friend on the shoulder. "I had to stop to harass you. I was taking Constance to the clubhouse when I noticed you guys standing over here. Couldn't miss the opportunity to spoil your fun."

He grinned.

"Hello, David," Constance McHenry said with a wave, smiling as if she had been rescued from the pits of boredom. She gingerly bounced her sparklingly white golf shoes as she crossed her legs. She then nodded. "Christina," she said. Her eyes withered slightly.

Christina forced herself to smile. "Hi, Constance."

"So what are you guys up to this evening?" Julian asked. "Want to join Constance and me for dinner? We're trying out a new site downtown. It's reservation only, but I know the maitre d'. I think I could work in two more people."

David smiled, wrapping his arm around Christina's shoulder. "No, that's okay, Julian. I have to be up early tomorrow to make up for the studying I missed today."

"Really? Are you sure?"

David nodded.

"All right. Well, I guess I'll catch you two later," Julian said with a wave as he bounced back into the golf cart.

He quickly drove off while Constance gazed at them over her shoulder until the cart disappeared from sight.

"Hmmm, do you think we should call it a day, sweetheart? Christina? Christina?"

Christina frowned.

"What's the matter?" David asked as he loaded their bags unto his family's golf cart.

"I don't know, maybe I'm just overly sensitive," she muttered, shrugging absently. "But did you see how Constance looked at me? Like I was dog pooh-pooh. I don't know what it is, but that girl has never liked me, David. She's been like that since we were in fourth grade. I have no idea why she acts like that toward me."

He chuckled. "I wouldn't take it personally, sweetheart. She's not a likable person anyway."

"That's not true," Christina argued as she climbed inside the golf cart. "Julian seems to like her, for some inconceivable reason though." She shrugged. "I don't know why."

David rolled his eyes. "Julian is merely waiting his turn, Chris."

"What? What does that mean?"

"What do you think it means?" he asked as their cart lurched forward.

For several seconds, Christina frowned and then her eyes widened with awareness.

She squinted. "Are you saying—"

"What I am saying," he said dryly, "is that you have to be the most innocent and naive person I've ever known."

"I'm not naive," she exclaimed, pointing her finger at him. "I see the way Constance looks at you. I *know* she has a thing for you."

"I wouldn't put too much into it. She likes a lot of guys. Besides, a lot of women have a thing for me," he said with a sly grin.

Christina laughed. "And it's good to know you're so humble about that."

"Look, if it's really worrying you, the only reason why Constance would have anything to do with me, Christina," he said as the cart came to an abrupt stop, "is that she knows I belong to someone else."

He slowly took her left hand, pointed at the ring on her finger, and gently kissed the inside of her palm before kissing her mouth firmly. If this was David's way of reassuring her that she belonged to him and he belonged to her, it was very successful. As David kissed her deeply, thoughts of Constance quickly disappeared.

After their golf game, David had dropped Christina off at her parents' house so that she could go through the drudgery of completing their wedding invitations alone because, as David claimed with many apologies, he was "really behind on his studying." Even though Christina objected to doing it all by her lonesome, her mother had been pestering her for the past month to complete them, and the invitations *did* have to be done. But after an hour, Christina soon figured out there was no need to suffer through the hard labor alone. She quickly dialed her future maid-of-honor's number, and Shauna pulled up in front of her house within minutes.

Now while sitting on the plush, pure white carpet in her bedroom, Christina pasted another address label onto an envelope, checking the name off on the list beside her. She was waist high in stationery. Her arms were aching, her chest was pounding, and her throat was dry, but she could see victory in the distance. Unfortunately, something or, more accurately put, *someone* was holding her back.

"Would you slow down?" Shauna grumbled as she licked another stamp and placed it on the right corner of an ivory-colored envelope. "My tongue is numb."

Christina sighed and rolled her eyes heavenward.

"I swear," Shauna exclaimed. "I literally can no longer feel my tongue in my mouth. You got a sponge or something for these stamps?"

"Shauna, it is not that bad."

"The hell it ain't! You try doing it!" Shauna said as she pushed the stamps toward her. "All you have to do is just put those little sticky things on the envelope and check it off. I've got to lick it and stick it on the envelope *and* place it in the little box for mailing. I'm recording two steps for you, dear. Mine is a three-step process."

"What are you talking about?"

"I don't know!" Shauna yelled as she tossed the parchment into the air. "I told you my mouth has malfunctioned!"

Christina and Shauna laughed heartily, becoming teary eyed. They slowly began to regain their senses.

"Okay, we'll switch places but make sure you record it correctly, please. We can't afford for someone to be missed," Christina said as she walked to the other side of the bed and landed on the floor with a thud. She then crossed her legs Indian style. "It will be our necks if we mess up."

She illustrated her words by running her finger across her throat.

Shauna shrugged. "Girl, I'm not scared of your mother. That's just you."

"I am not *scared* of my mother, Shauna."

Shauna raised an eyebrow.

"No, I am not scared. I simply respect her. There is a difference between fear and respect. Plus, in order to avoid conflict, I agree with most of the things she says. I just don't have a thing for confrontation. I never have."

"I know."

Christina furrowed her eyebrows. "You know? What is that supposed to mean?"

"It means I know you don't like confrontation. You don't like to confront your mother. You don't like to confront David. You don't like to make any waves."

Christina lowered the pen she was holding to the floor. Her mouth gaped slightly. "How did David get into this?"

"Chris," Shauna began, huffing and rolling her eyes, "why am I here doing these wedding invitations and not David? Why is your mom helping you do all this wedding stuff and David hasn't gone to one, not to *one* appointment with you?"

"Because he has his juris doctorate and now he has to prepare for his bar exam. He doesn't have time for stuff like this right now."

Shauna silently placed an address label on an envelope.

"It's not that it's not important to him," Christina continued. "It's just that he's preoccupied, and I understand. I'm not going to ask him to give up something he worked for for his entire life just so that he can help me chose a china pattern."

Shauna checked the name off Christina's list.

"Besides, it's not just wedding details that he's put off, Shauna. He hasn't set aside any real time to enjoy himself either. With the exception of a few hours here and there, he's always in the library studying case profiles and—"

"Thank God for Saint David," Shauna mocked.

"What?"

"Look, forget it," Shauna proclaimed, throwing up her hands. "Forget it! Forget I said anything, okay?"

"No, I can't just forget it!" Christina nearly shouted. "You've accused me in the past three minutes of being terrified of my mother and a doormat to my boyfriend . . . I mean, fiancé. What is this about, Shauna? A few weeks ago, you accused me of being too hard on her. What are you trying to say?"

Shauna opened one of the invitations and read it quietly. She then turned to her best friend. "I'm just saying, don't be afraid to make waves. That's all."

Four

Another week had passed and yet Shauna's words still lingered in Christina's head. Earlier that day she had tried to write a journal entry to tame her thoughts, but it hadn't worked. She couldn't focus them into comprehensive sentences. They came out all muddled and confused. Christina now tried to push them aside as she mounted the steps to Julian's house with her arm linked through David's. She could hear the music from inside as they rang the doorbell. It would be a festive occasion and one of many engagement parties thrown in their honor that Christina would have to attend in the next few weeks. This would be the only party held for the thirty-and-under set though.

The door sprang open and Julian quickly took their coats, ushering them into the skylight foyer crowded with people. Christina gazed in amazement through the glass tiles beneath her feet at the bar in Julian's basement.

"Nice touch, huh?" he said as he followed her eyes to the floor. "I installed it about a month ago."

She smiled and nodded.

Julian was a minimalist at heart though he allowed a splash of color to enter his home through artwork. Cubist paintings hung from the walls of his foyer. A Lichtenstein his parents had bought him as a housewarming gift hung in his living room. His furniture was expensive and Scandinavian. Everything was made of either chrome or Norwegian wood. The pieces looked so delicate. Christina was afraid to sit on them.

"You two go downstairs. It's a free bar. I decided to be benevolent and not charge for drinks," Julian said with a chuckle as he pointed to an open doorway. David took Christina's hand as they walked down a winding staircase of steel and wires. He said, "Excuse me" to whomever they bumped along the way.

The good cheer around her did little to alleviate the slight frown that seemed firmly fixed to Christina's face.

"Are you okay?" David asked.

"I'm fine," Christina said with a forced smile.

"I'll get us something to drink. A white wine spritzer, right?"

Christina slowly nodded. David disappeared into the crowd.

Though her thoughts were far, far away, she stood by the winding staircase at a party held in honor of their upcoming nuptials, trying her best to look as if she were enjoying herself.

Christina glanced around her.

Fashionable black couples were scattered around the room. Some danced to the music that surrounded them, though most talked listlessly in groups of four. The talking was so constant the room seemed to be filled with the murmur of chatter, a literal "buzz" of conversation.

Christina rubbed her forehead, feeling a pain surge across her brow.

"Perk up, soon-to-be married lady," one of the female party goers said, jarring Christina from her thoughts. "You're supposed to be enjoying yourself!"

Christina forced a smile and waved her hand absently at the woman who wore horn-rimmed glasses with a Fendi purse slung over her shoulder. "No, I'm fine. I think I need get an aspirin though."

The woman frowned. "What's wrong, honey?"

"Nothing, nothing. Just a slight headache. You wouldn't happen to have an aspirin, would you?"

The woman shook her head.

"It's okay, I'll just ask Julian if he has some in his medicine cabinet."

Christina smiled good-bye and waited for David to return. When the pain in her temple increased she decided to search for Julian instead. She weaved her way through the throng of people. Occasionally, someone kissed her cheek or gave her a hug while giving her well-wishes on her future marriage. It made the walk a lot longer. By the time she finally spotted Julian among a group of men, her head was pounding.

"Hi, Chris. I was looking for your other half but I haven't spotted him anywhere. I wanted to show him my new golf clubs," he said, tipping a beer bottle to his lips. "Do you know where he is?"

She smiled. "He went off five minutes ago to get drinks and I haven't seen him since. I guess he stopped to talk to someone."

Julian nodded and then tilted his head. "Hey, are you feeling okay?"

"Not really. My head is killing me and I need an aspirin."

He quickly stood. "Sure, no problem. I'll get one for you."

Christina smiled and waved her hand. "No, no. Sit down. I didn't want to interrupt your conversation. If you could just tell me where you keep your medicine, I can get it myself. I'll be fine."

"Well, if you're sure you're okay," Julian said as he frowned. "It's in my bathroom, in the cabinet, upstairs two floors, second door to your left."

"Thanks, Julian."

She slowly made her way up the flights of stairs, holding her head as she did so. She quickly found his bathroom and the bottle of aspirin, though her headache was quickly disappearing now that she was on the relatively silent second floor. The murmur from downstairs was still audible. She turned on the faucet and ran water into one of the disposable cups on his bathroom counter. Christina swallowed the aspirin tablet along with the water and breathed a sigh of relief. She turned and switched off the bathroom light just as she heard a muffled voice in the next room. It was then followed by another voice. It sounded like a couple, she presumed, who seemed to be in a heated argument. The voices slowly became louder.

Christina stood in Julian's bathroom silently, frozen in the spot where she stood. After some deliberation, she quietly walked out of the bathroom but then jumped back into the darkness when the door farther down the hallway swung open.

"You're drunk. Sleep it off," a familiar male voice said in hushed, angry tones.

"I'm not drunk! I am not drunk and I don't have to take this from you," Constance yelled as she stomped into the corridor. Her brown eyes flashed with anger as her purse swung in her hands.

"Shut up! Someone is going to hear you."

"I don't care! I don't care if someone hears me," she screamed. Her eyes started to well with tears. Constance's furious gaze withered. She lowered her eyes, seeming almost apologetic.

"Yes, you do," the voice answered. "Your boyfriend is downstairs and so is my fiancée. Lest we forget! I don't want an audience."

"How could you do this to me?" Constance whispered hoarsely. "How could you treat me like this? Like I don't mean anything to you, like—"

"I'm not doing anything to you. I explained everything in the beginning. You just didn't listen."

The fury returned to her eyes as her brow lowered. "Well, you don't have to worry about me ever calling you again! No more late-night rendezvous in your car, David! Do you hear me? I hope you and that bitch are happy together!"

David slowly walked through the doorway, glaring as he pointed his finger at Constance.

"Look, I don't care how drunk you are, I told you not to call her that," he said through clenched teeth. He slowly shook his head before throwing up his hands helplessly. "To hell with this. I told you ten months ago that it was over. For some reason, you don't seem to get that."

"Go to hell, David," she spat.

"You're with Julian now and I'm with Christina," he continued. David was undeterred by Constance's rage. "Do you understand that? Not you, Constance!"

David ducked as she threw her purse at his head. It landed against the wall behind him, and the contents rolled down the hallway. A bottle of perfume clattered near the bathroom entrance.

"Fuck you," Constance muttered as tears streamed down her cheeks.

She turned and ran to the opposite end of the hallway, disappearing down the staircase.

David watched her silently, not making a move to stop her. He then sighed and rubbed his face. He turned to look at the mess in the room behind him and shook his head. He waited a few minutes before slowly making his way downstairs.

Christina continued to stand in the darkness of the bathroom, too stunned to move.

The rest of the party went by for Christina as if she were stuck in a daze. She managed to avoid David (though barely) for the rest of the night, not knowing what to say to him. What could she say? How could she possibly confront him now without embarrassing the hell out of *herself*? She was angry, seething with anger, but she was also too well bred for calling him out in front of a group of mutual friends.

Feeling stifled by the atmosphere around her, Christina finally managed to escape the party by walking into Julian's backyard. She could feel a panic attack about to emerge. Her legs were wobbly and the world was starting to spin around her like a crazy circus of lights and trees, people and music. She stumbled to a wooden bench and sat down to catch her breath. The feeling of nausea became less overwhelming as she held her head in her hands.

When she felt strong enough to do so, Christina nursed a glass of red wine.

"Just get through tonight," she quietly told herself as she sipped from her glass. "Get through tonight, and we'll think this out in the morning. Okay?"

She looked up at the moon. It was full tonight and beautiful with a lovely blue hue. A rare, blue moon . . .

"There you are," David said, grinning as he peeked his head through a crack in the sliding glass door. "They're about to do the toast soon, sweetheart. You should come inside."

It was amazing. He had just broken off an affair with another woman less than an hour ago and yet he acted perfectly normal.

"No, thanks. I'm fine out here," Christina muttered, refusing to look at him.

"What?"

"I'm fine out here!"

David frowned.

"Is something wrong?" he asked, as he closed the sliding door behind him. He walked over to the bench and sat down beside her. "Julian told me you had a headache earlier but you took an aspirin. I guess it hasn't kicked in yet, huh?"

He reached out to push a lock of hair out of her eyes and she flinched visibly.

"Don't . . . do that," she said, pushing his hand away.

David's shoulders squared and he narrowed his eyes. "Tell me what's wrong. You've been acting strange all night."

She turned and stared at him quietly for several seconds, memorizing every line and crevice of his face. Christina had known David for what seemed to be her entire life, but he now seemed so alien to her, as if he were a total stranger.

"I don't think we should talk about this now. It's not appropriate here," she finally said, making sure to keep her voice evenly toned.

He stared back at her and she could almost see his mind silently working, trying to figure out how much she knew—and how much she didn't know.

"Why don't you want to talk about it now?"

"Because I don't."

"But why?" he insisted.

"Let it go, David. Trust me. Let it go."

"Why don't you want to—"

"Because you're fooling around," she said, her blood now warmed with wine and anger, "is an inappropriate topic of conversation for our engagement party, don't you agree?"

David closed his eyes and slowly exhaled.

"You heard us," he muttered.

"Yes," she nearly yelled. Christina tossed her wineglass into the yard in front of her. "Yes, I heard you! How could I not hear you? I'm surprised the whole damn party didn't hear you two upstairs."

"Chris, I can explain. Just calm down."

"What is there to explain, David?"

"I ended it with her nearly a year ago," he pleaded. "We haven't been together since then."

"Oh, thank you. That's a relief. That's a good thing to know," Christina said as she rose from the bench. "Considering that I thought we had been dating exclusively since I was sixteen years old, it's very nice to know this relationship—or whatever it was—with Constance ended over a year ago!"

He lowered his head as she clenched her fists. Her chest heaved. "I cannot believe this! I cannot believe this, David! Here you were, demeaning Constance McHenry as the biggest slut Stanford Manor has ever seen, when you had been sleeping with her! 'Julian's simply waiting his turn, Chris,'" Christina said, mimicking David's baritone voice. "Well, I guess you would know about that, wouldn't you?"

"Christina," David slowly said, glancing over his shoulder, "you were right. This is not the best place to talk about this. We'll get in my car. We can even go back to my place and you can scream at me all you want. Just not here, sweetheart. Not here."

"I want to know one thing, David," she continued, undeterred by his words. "Since I know now that you have been *involved* with another woman while we were together, how many women have you been with exactly? If I wasn't your first, I'm sure Constance wasn't either!"

"Christina, I don't—"

"Hey, you two," Julian said with a wave. The cacophony

of sounds from the party came through the sliding door as he opened it. "We've been looking all over for you. We need you in here to do the toast."

David smiled weakly. "We'll be right in, Julian. Just a few more minutes, please. We're—we're looking at the stars."

Julian nodded and grinned.

"You can get a nice view from out here, can't you? Okay, just come inside when you're done," he said as he firmly closed the door behind him.

Christina gritted her teeth. "Just tell me how many, David. That's the least you could do. Can you count them on one hand? Two hands? Your fingers and your toes?"

David finally stood while shaking his head.

"This is ridiculous," he muttered. "Look, I told you I'm not going to talk about this here! I'll explain everything to you after the party is over! You can then decide whether you love me or hate me! Until that time comes, I'm not going to go into details about whom I've dated or slept with in the last twenty years right now, okay? *Okay?* Now let's go inside. They're waiting for us."

Christina glared at David silently.

"Come on, Christina! I've had enough of this for one night!"

He grabbed her arm and pulled her toward the sliding glass doors, but she wrestled it away from him.

"Stop it! Stop it! Get off of me," she screamed.

Christina could feel her eyes brimming with tears.

"You've got some damn nerve," she yelled as she stepped away from him. "So that's it? I'm just supposed to shut up and go back inside and pretend that everything is perfect? Why should I, David?"

"Don't do this, Christina."

"Don't do this? Don't do this?" She squinted her eyes in disbelief. "David, I thought you loved me. I wanted to marry you because I thought you loved me."

Seconds passed in silence as David softened.

"I *do* love you." He sighed. "Now listen to me. That stuff with Constance doesn't change anything. It doesn't mean anything."

Christina slowly walked over to him. He extended his arms to welcome her into an embrace but she stopped just short of his touch and removed her engagement ring from her finger.

"It does to me," she murmured as she put the ring in his hand.

Christina turned and then ran across the thicket of the yard, heading to the street below.

News of the Saunders-Emory breakup spread like wildfire in their small community. After merely one day, a chain of gossip ran from chuckles among the men at the country club, to bored lunchtime conversations, to slightly envious women who sat under blow-dryers at the local black hair salon, and back again. Tales of David's embarrassment and his apologies to Julian's party guests and Christina's less than dignified exit—in a rented cab, no less—were retold and exaggerated ten times over. Some said they heard that someone at the party had seen her slap him before she left. Some said he had slapped her. It was hard to tell which story was the right one or if it was a combination of the two.

Many people in their community felt justified in their malicious gossip. They had always thought it presumptuous of anyone with a background like Christina's to try to marry an esteemed member of the Emory clan. She had been lucky to get a man like David Emory. If their engagement dissolved, it was probably her fault. Many of the very same people who had attended the engagement party last night and who had received invites to the upcoming parties were happy to hear the two had split up.

Thankfully, Christina was oblivious of all this. After tearfully explaining everything to her father, she spent most of Saturday in bed, crying softly, surrounded by a sea of pillows and Kleenex. She managed to write a few lines in her journal:

May 17, 2000
   David is not the person I thought he was. I feel

betrayed. I don't know what to do. I'll write when things make sense.

Christina

That was all she could muster.

Her phone rang constantly. At first she simply picked up the receiver and quickly hung it up before she could hear the voice on the other line, but even that grew tiresome after a while. Finally, she unplugged the phone from her wall and hid it in her closet.

Her father ventured into her room around noon with a tray of graham crackers and apple juice. He had offered the same meal to her when she was five years old and came down with chicken pox.

"You okay, sweetheart?" the round man asked softly, peeking his head through the doorway.

Christina wiped her red eyes and swollen nose. She nodded. "I'll be okay, Daddy. Thanks for checking on me though."

He stood in the center of her bedroom, smiling weakly. He sat the tray on her night table. The folds near his eyes crinkled.

Her father was visibly uncomfortable, not knowing what to do. When she was a little girl and something or someone had made her sad, he would take her to the park or buy her a new toy. Mr. Saunders figured that method wouldn't work too well now. A toy couldn't heal a broken heart.

"You've been getting calls on the phone downstairs all morning," he said, hesitating before sitting on the foot of her bed. "Your friend Shauna called. She said she keeps trying to call you but the phone keeps clicking off. And Ronald gave you a ring. I—I told him what happened." Mr. Saunders looked down. "He said he'll be home from Virginia as soon as he can. I haven't heard from your mother. I guess she's busy with that event she's supposed to cater today. Oh, and David called."

The older man paused and shrugged. "That boy has called damn near about twenty times, but I told him . . . I told him I don't think you want to talk to him right now. I said, 'If she didn't answer the phone in her room, she did it for a good reason.' I would have given him a lot more of my mind but I figured . . . it wasn't in my place. Unless you want me to?"

Christina smiled and slowly shook her head.

"I can fight my own battles, Daddy," she said softly and then sniffed.

He nodded, sighed, and rose from her bed with creaking knees.

"Well," he called out with a wave, "just yell downstairs if you need anything, baby. I'll just tell everybody you're not feeling well and you'll give them a call when you're up to it."

Her father silently closed her door behind him.

Christina sipped some of her apple juice before she climbed beneath her sheets and turned over on her stomach. Within minutes she was fast asleep.

She woke up abruptly nearly two hours later when she felt her sheets being pulled off her. Someone's hands shook her—hard.

"Wake up," the voice ordered.

Christina, still groggy, yawned and peered over her shoulders.

Her mother stood inches away from her bed with her hands fisted at her sides. A pink hat perched on her head but it sat at a strange angle, as if the wind had knocked it out of place. The older woman's nostrils flared angrily and her delicate eyebrows furrowed.

"Tell me what happened," her mother said.

Christina sat up.

"What are you talking about?" she asked, slowly regaining her senses.

"What am I talking about? What am *I* talking about?" The older woman stepped back and shook her head as she paced back and forth. "I received a call from Mrs. Emory this morning, Christina. I was up to my elbows in pâté and watercress and I was told by one of my workers that there was a phone call for me. It was an emergency. I answer the phone and Mrs. Emory then proceeds to tell me how you broke off the engagement with her son and how he is at his wits' end because you refuse to even talk to him! And here you are lying in bed asking me what I'm talking about! What happened?"

Christina leaned back against her headboard and looked down at her hands.

"You have really done it this time, Christina. I should have known from the way you were behaving about the wedding preparations that something like this was going to happen. Are you doing this just to spite me, because if you are I—"

"I found out David cheated on me," Christina whispered. "I think he's been doing it for years. I don't know." She balled up one of her tissues and tossed it in a nearby wastebasket. "I found out about it last night—at Julian's party. I overheard him arguing with her."

Christina waited patiently for her mother's response, though the steely woman no longer showed any facial expression. She simply gazed down at her silently, now removing the hat from her head.

"Oh," her mother finally uttered.

"*Oh?*"

"Well, Christina, what do you expect me to say?"

Christina's eyes widened comically. She stared at her mother with disbelief. "I don't know, Mom. How about, 'Baby, I'm sorry that I barged into your room and yelled at you'? How about, 'I had no idea he had done that to you and I'm sorry for instantly taking his side'? Or how about just, 'I'm sorry'?"

Her mother rolled her eyes heavenward. "Now you're just being dramatic, Christina."

"*I'm* being dramatic? Mom, you are the queen of drama!"

"Don't you dare yell at me! Don't you forget who I am, girl!" her mother barked, momentarily showing her roots.

Her "take no bull" upbringing reared its ugly head.

The older woman took calming breaths and cleared her throat. She flattened the lapels of her blushing pink suit.

"Now . . . let's stick to the subject at hand, Christina," she said, regaining her composure. "Does he want to be with this girl? Is he in love with her?"

Christina shook her head, slightly dazed.

"I cannot believe this," she mumbled.

"Well," her mother continued, not hearing her, "then I can safely assume the answer is no. He's not in love with this girl and he doesn't want to be with her. He wants to be with you. He has stated this plainly. So there's no reason why you two can't reconcile your differences. By not talking to him, you're simply aggravating a very delicate situation."

"Mom, he cheated on me! He lied to me! He's been doing it for a long time and I just can't—"

"Christina," her mother began sternly, "there is no, and I repeat *no*, perfect man in this world—your father included. You are twenty-three years old. You are therefore an adult, and an adult has to deal with reality and make the best of it. David Emory is a good man. He's a smart man. He comes from a good family. He loves you and he will take care of you! What more could you want? So what if he messes up . . . occasionally? Who could fault him? Everyone has imperfections!"

"Then why don't you marry him?" Christina challenged.

Her mother narrowed her eyes. "Cute, Christina. But I'll have you know I probably would have married him if I had met someone like him thirty years ago."

She walked briskly toward Christina's door. "I would have been thankful to have a man like David Emory. But I didn't have the good luck to meet him. I just made sure my daughter would, and this is how she shows her gratefulness."

"What should I be grateful about, Mom, huh? That you had a life planned out for me that I didn't want? That I felt like you were pushing me into marrying David from the very beginning—long before he even *asked* me to marry him—and now I know the reason why? It had nothing to do with me! It had everything to do with what you wanted! With what plans you made!"

Christina's mother turned on her heels. "I have no patience for the rants of small children! We'll talk, Christina, when you've proven you're ready to be an adult!"

Mrs. Saunders slammed the bedroom door behind her.

Christina gazed at the door and climbed out of her bed, seething with anger. She had expected her mother to be surprised, even a little dismayed by the ending of the engagement, but she hadn't expected her to react like this. Screaming? Bullying her to make up with David? Instead of comforting her own daughter, she yelled at Christina as if *she* had been wrong. To make matters worse, when her mother finally figured out what had really happened, she still showed no pity or even remorse. She still insisted that it was up to Christina to make things right, to "act like an adult."

Christina's heart pounded as she tried her best to calm herself down.

After a few minutes, she resolved to indeed show her mother that she was an adult. Just not in a way Mrs. Saunders would expect.

Five

"Is this the last box?" Ronald asked, smoothing masking tape across the lid.

Christina frowned. "I hope it is. Anyway, all my clothes are already packed. I guess we can finish loading this stuff into your Hummer."

She rose from her knees and swiped at the dust on the front of her sweatpants. "Whatever doesn't fit into the back of your truck, Shauna offered to bring in her car." Christina frowned. "Though I don't know how much will fit into her Beetle."

Ronald gritted his teeth as he heaved the heavy box unto one shoulder.

"Okay. I'll meet you downstairs," he said as he took a few precarious steps through her doorway and then down the winding staircase.

Christina turned around and gazed at her bedroom. Even after three days of packing, it still was not empty. The cherry-wood, four-poster bed and other boudoir furniture still dominated most of the room. Varsity banners from high school and college still hung from the walls. But her bedroom seemed lifeless now for some reason. There would no longer be a young woman occupying the space, making noises, and cluttering it with the essence that transformed it into more than just a room. Just gazing at it flooded Christina with sadness. Before she became too emotional she decided to walk out and firmly close the door behind her in more ways than one.

On her way downstairs, while looking over the side of the banister, Christina could see her mother sitting in her small office with her door open. The older woman was fingering linen samples, pretending to take notes, and trying her best to ignore her daughter's exit.

Shauna cracked open the front door and peered into the foyer. "You ready, girl?" she asked.

"Just a second," Christina said. She walked toward her mother's office and hesitated, not knowing what to say to the woman who had raised her.

As Christina had expected, her decision to move out and live on her own hadn't been readily accepted by either her mother or father. But while Mr. Saunders had reacted with worry, asking how their youngest child could manage to live by herself with little money and no job, Mrs. Saunders chose to show anger instead.

"Fine, Christina," she had said with withering severity, "you may decide to leave this house but you aren't taking everything we've ever given you with you. When I left my mother's home I did it with just the clothes on my back. But I will be a lot kinder to you than my mother was to me. You can take your clothes, your mattress, your mementos, and a few pieces of furniture, but the *bulk* of all those things upstairs stays in this house. Your Lexus stays in the driveway."

"Fine," Christina had said firmly, though the moment she uttered the word, she was struck with panic.

Clothes, a mattress, old teddy bears, a few CDs, her collection of books, her night table, and her writing desk—this was all she could take with her according to their agreement. Christina tried desperately to convince herself that it wasn't the end of the world (her wardrobe alone could fill two average-size closets), but having everything she could ever want at her fingertips for the last twenty-three years had made her more than just a little jaded. For Christina, this would be the closest she would ever come to subsistence living.

As she packed her things during the wee hours of night, she did the math. Currently, in her expense account, she had a little over two thousand dollars. It wasn't a small sum by any means, but in no way imaginable would it last an entire year. Nor would she be able to count on her trust fund, credit cards, stocks, or bonds for extra money. (Another one of her mother's stipulations.) Christina's entire existence now depended on that two thousand dollars—at least until she found a job.

Merely scanning through the housing classifieds convinced Christina that if she moved into a condo or loft and bought the bare amount of furniture, her savings could be used up within a month or two. If she wanted her money to stretch the furthest distance, she would have to set her sights a lot lower. Thank God, she had a frugal friend. Shauna said she knew a place where Christina could move. It was ten blocks from Shauna's apartment building, and the landlord's wife was a friend of her family. She might be able to get Christina a reasonable deal. Shauna estimated that the apartment would probably cost her a little over five hundred a month, not including utilities.

Christina, though desperate with worry, did not ask Shauna what the apartment looked like. She did not ask about the neighborhood or the closest means of transportation to the building. She simply handed over one month's rent and a security deposit to Shauna and hoped for the best. Christina was just relieved that at least she did not have to live in a cardboard box two months from now. She just hoped her new home would not be the five hundred-dollar equivalent of a cardboard box.

"Mom," Christina now said as she stood in front of her mother's door. "Mom, I'm leaving now."

"I gathered that," her mother said, not looking up from her notepad. "Good-bye, Christina. Oh, and tell Ronald to drive carefully. There's no need for him to be pulled over and harassed in that car by the police if he doesn't have to be."

Christina's shoulders slumped.

"Yes, mother." She sighed.

Christina turned and headed toward the front door, rolling her eyes heavenward. She should have known it wouldn't be a scene to remember. Her mother wouldn't tearfully tell her good-bye, nor would she take the time to wish her well. In the end, the only words she would share with her daughter were for Ronald not to get pulled over by the cops on the way to Christina's new apartment building.

Warm attitude, Mom, Christina thought sarcastically. *Very warm, indeed.*

She closed the front door behind her and walked toward Shauna's Beetle.

"You can take the lead. Ronny's going to follow behind us," she said.

Shauna nodded as Christina closed the car door. She turned her key in the ignition and shifted gears. Just as she began to pull out of the driveway, the front door to the house swung open and Christina's father ran toward the driveway, stumbling slightly as he carried her bedroom television in his arms with the cord dragging behind him.

"You forgot this," he yelled.

Christina frowned and slowly opened the car door. She walked back onto the sidewalk and closed the car door behind her.

"You forgot this," he said again, now slightly out of breath.

"No, Dad." Christina shook her head. "I left that in my room purposely. I'm not supposed to take that. Mom and I agreed—"

"You forgot this and your stereo." He turned toward Ronald's car. "Help me bring the stereo down for your sister, son. I can't carry that damn thing by myself without throwing my back out!"

Christina frowned. "Are you sure you want to do this, Dad? Mom is going to be really mad when she finds out I took this stuff. We agreed—"

"I'll handle your mama," he said with a wink as he placed the TV between two boxes in the back of Ronald's Hummer and tightened the television's cord into a knot. "Besides, it's my money that paid for most of this stuff. If I've got to have it out with her, I just will. If you can fight your own battles, I can certainly fight mine."

He reached into his jean pocket and pulled out his wallet. He then placed three fifty-dollar bills into his daughter's hand. "Now, this is all the money I have on me right now. I know it ain't a lot, but if you need anything else—and I mean *anything*—you just give your daddy a call, you hear? I don't care what your mother said."

Christina frowned. She became overwhelmed with a myriad of emotions: sadness, happiness, nostalgia, longing, and confusion. With no other means to express them, she quickly wrapped her arms around her father's neck and loudly kissed his cheek. Tears stung her eyes.

He patted her back as he held her tightly. "You be careful now. You do what you got to do, but you be careful."

"I will, Daddy," Christina said as she wiped the tears away with the back of her hand. "Don't worry."

As he continued to hold her, Christina quietly slipped the money he had handed her back into his pocket. She sighed as she realized that if she was really going to do this, she had to do it on her own.

As they pulled in front of the apartment building in a poor, glass-littered neighborhood, Christina hoped Shauna had stopped the car merely to take a break. *Maybe she wants to stretch her arms and her legs and let out a yawn,* Christina thought. When Shauna took the key out of the ignition, Christina hoped her friend would look up at the building before turning to her and nudging her shoulder. She would then say, "Scared you, didn't I? I was just joking with you, girl. This ain't the place."

But as Shauna slowly climbed out of the car, Christina realized her best friend hadn't stopped the car to rest and this was no joke. This building would be the place where Christina would have to live for the next several months.

"So what do you think?" Shauna asked while closing the car door behind her.

Christina instantly planted a smile on her face, trying her best to mask her disappointment. "It's fine."

Shauna frowned. "You don't like it, do you?"

"It's a place to live, Shauna, that's all that's important." Christina walked around the car and gave Shauna a quick hug. "Thank you for finding it for me."

Christina then peered up at the building with twenty-year-old graffiti fading on its edifice and a drunken man napping in a lawn chair with his legs spread-eagled on the front stoop.

Fortunately, she thought, *I will now have a roof over my head.* Unfortunately, from initial impressions, it seemed as if there wouldn't be much else.

"Let's start taking the boxes upstairs," Christina said. "Does it have an elevator, Shauna?"

"Yes, it has an elevator."

"That's good because I wasn't carrying this stuff up a lot steps if I didn't have to. But who's going to stay here?" Ronny asked as he leaned his head out his car window.

Christina frowned. "Why would anyone have to stay here? We could get it done a lot faster if we all take it upstairs at the same time."

Ronny raised his eyebrows in disbelief. He and Shauna exchanged a look that could only have been interpreted as, *From what planet is this girl?*

"Are you out of your damn mind?" he sputtered. "You can't leave this stuff sitting down here while we go upstairs! When we come back fifteen minutes from now, the boxes *and* maybe even the cars will be gone!" He shook his head. "And I'll tell you what. I don't plan on walking back home tonight, Chris."

Christina turned to Shauna with a confused expression on her face. Perhaps her good friend could explain the situation to her, because Ronald certainly wasn't making any sense.

Shauna vigorously nodded. "He's right. One of us should stand here and watch your things while the other two carry the boxes upstairs. I would ask one of the dope heads or ragamuffins around the corner to keep an eye on the cars, but they could very well steal your stuff themselves. You'd see them selling your Dolce Gabanna blouse on a street corner two weeks from now for twenty dollars."

Shauna wrapped an arm around Christina's shoulder when she noticed the stunned look on her friend's face. Shauna chuckled. "I guess we should have put up the 'Welcome to the Ghetto' banner, Chris, but we didn't have enough time. Consider this your official greeting . . . and learn the rules quickly."

Christina gulped loudly.

"I'll stay downstairs. You can go up with Ronny and look around the place while you're setting up your things," Shauna said.

Within twenty minutes, Christina was turning the key to her new apartment. She then pushed the door open with her hip as she and Ronny carried the night table into her living room.

Thankfully, the apartment building on the inside was not as bad in appearance as it was on the exterior. Christina had entered the structure expecting to find a place one step up from a homeless shelter but instead she discovered that the landlord had managed to treat the interior rather nicely. True, pea green wouldn't have been her choice of color for a lobby. True, the elevator did make a sound as if the cords that dragged it from floor to floor could snap at any moment. True, the lighting fixtures did look as if they had been installed in 1943, and the exit signs that led to the stairwells at the end of the hallways flashed like strobe lights, but the building still had a comforting feel to it.

One of the janitors greeted them as they walked toward the elevator. She could hear the sounds of children on the other side of apartment doors. She could smell family dinners cooking as she walked down the hallway. She could not identify with the place just yet, but at least it had the potential of becoming a home.

Christina and Ronny slowly set the night table on the floor and closed the door behind them. She gazed around the apartment while her brother quietly watched her.

"It's going to need some paint," she said aloud as she looked at the water-stained ceilings. Christina then glanced down at her feet.

"The carpet needs cleaning. It looks like I'll have to mop the kitchen floor quite a few times too."

She walked over to the window and blew on the blinds. A cloud of dust rose and made her sneeze. "I'm going to need a feather duster."

Ronny shrugged. "Besides that?"

"Besides that," Christina said with a smile, "I like it."

For the entire first night Christina spent alone in her apartment, it rained. It pelted her bedroom and living room windows with fat droplets the size of her fingertips. With all the lightning and thunder outside, Christina was thankful that she had her television to keep her company. The drone of commercials and late-night programming kept the few empty rooms from being filled with only the sound of the storm. Plus, the continuous noise helped her push back her fears that came with being alone.

She quietly ate a tuna sandwich as she sat Indian style on her living room carpet and flipped through a magazine. Christina glanced over at the cell phone Ronny had loaned her until her phone service was installed. She then sighed. Christina supposed she would only have to use it in case of emergencies, because at this moment there weren't too many people she could call. Shauna had a hot date for the evening and, with luck, wouldn't be able to answer the phone until the next morning. (Shauna said her date was smart, funny, and bore a striking resemblance to the actor Morris Chestnut. He would have to mess up horribly on this date—their fifth—in order not to get an invite back to her apartment.) Ronny had driven back onto the highway hours ago after he unloaded the last of Christina's boxes and headed to Virginia to be with his new girlfriend, Sheila, so calling him was out of the question. Christina had phoned her father less than half an hour earlier, informing him that she was fine and, once again, that he shouldn't worry. It would be silly to call him back again now.

After staring blankly at the television for several minutes, Christina could feel her thoughts wandering back to David.

Now that Christina had made it plain that she had no intention of marrying him, had he felt free to rekindle his relationship with Constance? While Christina was sitting alone, eating a tuna sandwich on a dirty carpet and watching television, was Constance "comforting" David?

She swallowed.

Shauna had questioned her earlier that week on how it had been possible for Christina not to notice that David was experienced in bed, or at least too experienced to qualify as a virgin.

"Was he *that* bad, girl?" her friend had asked.

On the contrary, Christina said, David was *very* good, but then again, she didn't have much to go on. Remember, she said, she hadn't slept with anyone before him. There was no litmus test against which she could compare him.

Also, truth be told, Christina had trusted David. She hadn't known or even wondered if David's abilities in bed were due more to experience rather than just his love and his eagerness to please her. When he tried to coach her and coax her into doing things, she had always assumed, naively, he had read about it somewhere or seen it in a film or something. She had no idea he may have practiced the move on someone else before her.

Christina had trusted her fiancé completely and foolishly. She hadn't felt the need to question him. She hadn't considered the possibility that he would cheat on her. She hadn't thought it was in his character.

A vision of David rolling around beneath his sheets with some random, beautiful woman suddenly popped into Christina's head and ignited her fury all over again. She nearly choked on the food she was eating before she clutched at her throat and gulped down a glass of water.

When she could breathe again, Christina inhaled deeply and sighed.

"I hope it falls off," she muttered.

A boom of thunder soon followed.

Six

On Tuesday, in the wee hours of morning, Christina ventured to her local corner store to purchase a newspaper. The ground was still wet from the rain that had sprinkled the neighborhood for several nights, and the leaves on the trees were weighed down with the same wetness. An older woman, who was wearing a bouquet of flowers on a hat only worthy of a Holy Roller church, said hello to Christina and smiled. Christina, more than just a little intimidated by her new surroundings, was happy to come upon such a kind face. She responded with a greeting and waved as she walked away. But she frowned when the older woman continued to say hello, over and over again, in a bellowing voice.

"Good morning! Hello! Hello! Hello!"

Christina turned to look over her shoulder. The woman was still standing on the street corner. She smiled and waved wildly as if a huge crowd of people were in front of her. But save for her and Christina, there was not a person in sight.

"Don't pay her no mind," a raspy voice said. Christina jumped before she looked up to find an elderly man standing in the doorway of the corner store with a lit cigarette quivering at his lip as he spoke. One of his shoulders jutted upward as he leaned against a metal cane and its rubber handle. "She says hi to everybody—even if nobody's standing there. Been doing it since 1986. I see her morning and night and that's all she does."

Christina smiled nervously. "I suppose she's just friendly."

He shrugged as he waved Christina inside the store. "Most people would call it crazy. You new to the neighborhood?"

Christina hesitated before climbing up the small steps. She pulled her pocketbook toward her. "Yes, I just moved in a few days ago."

He smiled. "Yeah, you look it—and sound it too. You definitely aren't from around here. That's for sure. You ain't no city girl. So what can I get you? We got all kinds of stuff. Candy bars. Sodas. Luncheon meat. Jamaican pies. You ever tasted a Jamaican pie?"

"Actually, I just wanted to purchase a paper."

"A paper? That's all you wanted?"

Two children ran past her and she stepped back with surprise.

"Well, yes." Christina paused. "Though I guess it wouldn't hurt to buy more bread and water."

The old man frowned. "Bread and water? You fasting or something, girl? A little thing like you? Don't think I like that. A woman always looks better with a little meat on her."

Christina shook her head and laughed. "No, I'm not fasting. I'm just on a limited budget at the moment."

His cigarette tipped upward. "I see."

He quickly rang up her three items (a newspaper, a loaf of bread, and bottled water) and handed the bag to Christina.

She reached into her wallet but he shook his head. "Don't worry about it. The stuff you bought didn't cost no more than three dollars. It ain't worth opening the cash register for."

Christina smiled and thanked him.

"Now remember, sweetness," he said as she turned and walked toward the entrance. "If you ever need anything you just call on Mr. Davis. I'll get you anything you need. I got a bad hip but a heart of a young man, if you know what I mean. Come down and see me sometime."

He looked her up and down, letting his gaze linger a little too long on certain regions.

Christina smiled weakly as she waved good-bye but frowned as she walked back toward her apartment building, wondering if she should have just paid the three dollars.

When she returned to her apartment, Christina quickly opened her newspaper to the job classifieds. She left the paper splayed on her living room floor as she proceeded to make another tuna sandwich. After a few minutes she knelt in front of the paper with a red Magic Marker. While eating quietly, she began to circle the jobs that looked promising.

Christina noticed a few listings for business analysts. She circled these though she knew in her heart that years of studying business management had yet to prepare her for a life of wearing a shoulder-padded suit forty hours a week and attending meetings once or twice a day. Christina then came upon a few positions as a proofreader. If there was one thing she could rely on, it was her aptitude in English. She circled these listings and put a star next to them. She noticed a few openings for a librarian but frowned when she noticed in bold type, *Must have 3 years of experience as library personnel. Degree in library science desired.* Christina circled these hesitantly and put a question mark over them. After an hour had passed, she had nearly six pages of circles, question marks, and stars. She resolved that this jumbled mess that would decide her future needed order.

Christina searched frantically for a blank sheet of paper but found none. While burrowing through one of her boxes, she found her journal and opened it. She had done it initially to make a list, to figure out what jobs she really preferred and what jobs she actually had the chance of getting. But she stopped when she came upon an old journal entry. She had written it years ago. After a while, she found herself skimming her journal, mesmerized by thoughts and feelings she once had as she pieced together her past:

October 3, 1994
    It is my second month in college and things are going pretty well. My classes aren't very challenging

but I'm meeting some nice people. One in particular is totally unlike any of the girls I've ever met in Stanford Manor. Her name is Shauna Maxwell and she is my freshmen roommate. She's confident, smart, and funny. We do everything together. Shopping. Going to the movies. She's introduced me to a few people on campus and showed me how to do the reggae dances that are popular at parties. When I told Mom about her, Mom instantly asked me about Shauna's family. "What are they like? Where on earth do they come from?" I told my mom that I had no idea. I hadn't asked Shauna for her pedigree card! After Mom kept pressing me for details, I decided to be a smart-ass and told her I suspected Shauna's father was a West Indian drug dealer and her mother collected unemployment checks. Mom practically fainted! God, I'm so bad. Oh, well. Gotta go. Shauna's experimenting with a new hair color and she wants my evaluation.

Christina

May 25, 1999

I graduated from college today . . . summa cum laude, to Dad's great pride. I have the leather-encased certificate to show it, which is a good thing since the entire moment seems surreal.

I am the first in my family to get one. I guess that's why Dad and Mom seemed so proud.

I beat out my brother by a semester or two. He decided to take off a year ago to explore the "music business."

When the dean handed the certificate to me, I had no idea what to do with it. I smiled at the auditorium filled with people even though I was totally baffled. I was silently asking myself, "Well, where can I go with this?"

David said that's completely normal. He said he felt the same way for a split second when he got his bachelor's three years ago. I don't see how that's possible. It always seemed to me as if he had his future

*neatly lined up in front of him. Shauna said she didn't
have time to be confused. She starts her new job in two
weeks. She has to start paying back her student loans.*
Christina

October 18, 1999

*Last night, I am ashamed to say, I hid in the bath-
room for at least an hour. I was at David's place and I
tried to calm myself with a few glasses of white wine
but it just made me light-headed and nauseated. He
coaxed me out of the bathroom after some pleading. I
tried to convince him that I wasn't hiding, that I was
fixing myself up, but David knew the truth. I felt bad.
We had both agreed that the timing was right. I've already started taking the pill. I guess I got scared at the
last minute . . .*

*David said there was no need to be nervous. That
he wouldn't do anything to hurt me. That it would only
go as far as I wanted. He said all this with perfect patience (more than I had expected from a guy who had
put off sex for that many years), and that's when I realized how silly I was behaving and how stupid he must
feel talking to me through a closed bathroom door
with me barricaded on the other side. That's when I
opened it.*

*It's hard to describe what it was like to be with him.
I don't know if I can put it into words without sounding
like a dribbling idiot, but I'll just say it was . . . unreal.
Both better than I had hoped and more intimidating
than I had anticipated, but I would do it again. I trust
him now.*
Christina

February 28, 2000

*I am twirling my engagement ring on my finger.
Every now and then, I'm tempted to slip it off and hide
it in my jewelry box. I told David I wished he hadn't
bought such a large one. It's pretty bold for my taste
and makes me a little uncomfortable. He says that's*

*the point. He wants everyone to know we're getting
married. He said if it were up to him he'd staple a bill-
board sign to my finger. I told him if that were the case,
I'm definitely glad it's not up to him.*

*I guess I am looking forward to the wedding, but
my mother seems a lot more excited than I am. We both
composed our lists of people whom we wanted to invite. I combined both David's and mine and our list
equaled to about 80 people roughly. My mother's was
230 people (!) with only 20 repeats from our list. We
had the same argument about "overdoing it," but she
keeps assuring me "the more the merrier."*

*She seems to be pulling out all the stops. She wants
flowers imported from Asia and cloth woven in Italy.
The cost of the thing will probably bankrupt Dad, but
we're all leaving it up to her. That's what she wants.
Mom is very confident about her plans for the wedding—that is, until she speaks to Mrs. Emory. I have a
feeling David's mom has always intimidated her.*

                                          Christina

May 17, 2000
*David is not the person I thought he was. I feel be-
trayed. I don't know what to do. I'll write when things
make sense.*

                                          Christina

It was, indeed, her last entry to date. Christina read it and
sighed. She then straightened her shoulders and wrote a new
entry in her journal:

May 25, 2000
*Things still aren't quite right but I'm wading my
way through them. I'm proud of myself. I won't think
of what I've lost. I'll just remember what I've gained.
Life didn't end.*

                                      Until next time,
                                          Christina

Seven

Christina nervously tugged at her teal jacket that was quickly becoming dampened by her perspiration as she clutched the folder that contained her résumé. She bounced the folder on her lap unconsciously as she sat on an uncomfortable chair. The sitting area was deserted for the most part save for Christina and the secretary that sat at a waist-high cubicle with a shelf around its rim. The Hispanic woman had only spoken to Christina to tell her to sit down and wait. She was now speaking into her headset while pressing buttons on her switchboard. Christina could hear that she was entrenched in a serious conversation with the person on the other end about yesterday's *telenovelas*.

Christina sighed. She had been waiting for several minutes and the fluorescent lights overhead were hurting her eyes. She had to force herself not to bite her nails as she fended off her edginess by reading her résumé. This was her second interview in the past week and the fifth in the past month, and so far Christina had yet to hear from any of the people who had interviewed her. She hoped this one would turn out differently.

"Miss Saunders?"

Christina looked up to find a middle-aged black woman

smiling down at her. Her brown eyes crinkled. She was dressed simply in a cream-colored blouse and tweed skirt. Her hair was pulled back into a bun with an ivory comb.

"Hi, I'm Margaret Smith. We spoke on the phone. I'll be your interviewer today."

Christina stood as she nervously smiled at the woman with the warm southern accent.

"Yes. It's nice to meet you, Ms. Smith," she said as she shook her hand.

The woman nodded and continued to smile warmly. "Sorry for the wait. I had an important call and I tried to make it as short as possible but . . . some people. Honestly, I swear they try to run me crazy." She left it at that and shrugged. She then clapped her hands. "Would you follow me to my office? Did you have trouble getting here?"

Christina smiled again. She shook her head as she followed Ms. Smith down a corridor. "No, I didn't have any problems."

"That's good," she said as she closed the door behind Christina and gestured for her to sit down in one of the chairs facing her desk. "Now you are applying for a position in data entry, is that right?"

"Yes." Christina flashed a smile yet again. Her cheeks hurt from the strain of her constant grin.

"So I see you're from this area. That's rare. For some reason, I seem to get a lot of people from New Jersey. I was hoping to run into a few people from North Carolina—that's where I'm from—but no luck."

"No, I was born and raised here."

"Yes. And you once held a job as an assistant to a . . . caterer?"

Christina gritted her teeth. She wished she hadn't put that on her résumé. She preferred not to be reminded of her mother at this moment.

"Yes, I . . . worked for her for a long time. She handled catering for weddings mostly."

"Uh-huh. So if you don't mind me asking, why are you applying for a job in data entry?"

Christina blinked, slightly taken off guard by the woman's

question. She hadn't expected it. Why did most people apply for jobs?

Christina wanted to say, "I'm applying for a job in data entry because I want to keep food on the table and a roof over my head and I'm quickly running out of money. Because I tried to apply for positions that I would like better but they didn't call me for an interview and instead I'm left with jobs I know I will hate. Because I'm quickly approaching my last resort, which is begging Mr. Davis at the corner store for a job at his sales counter. Because I refuse to give in to my mother and go back home!"

Instead, she smiled and said, "I guess I'm applying for a position in data entry because I admire the fiscal capabilities of Corps Industries, and what better way to learn good business than in an entry-level position where you can observe the managerial efforts of people who make the day-to-day workings of the company so great? I could potentially apply the skills I learn here to future endeavors."

Ms. Smith nodded and slowly smiled. "Good answer, honey. But I wasn't testing you. I was asking my question because you seem overqualified for the position. Now I will admit . . . you don't have a lot of job experience." She glanced down at Christina's résumé and scanned it quietly. She then leaned forward in her chair. "But you went to a very good school with a wonderful business program and did well. Your recommendations from your teachers checked out fine and they spoke nicely of you. But quite frankly, honey, when someone with your credentials applies for an entry-level position, it tends to make the people in management"—she pointed up at the ceiling—"a little nervous. They're wondering if they have an upstart on their hands . . . if this is somebody who's going to take their jobs away in a few years. My job, as a personnel officer, is to interview you and figure you out. Ease any potential worries." She laughed.

Christina gaped. Now she was definitely shocked by the woman's candidness. Was Christina delusional or was this woman spilling all her secrets? But Ms. Smith's words explained a lot. Christina hadn't thought the other interviews had gone badly, or at least not so badly for *no one* to call her back. Did the interviewers see her as a potential challenger or troublemaker? All Christina wanted was a job!

"So are you saying you aren't interested in hiring me?" Christina asked with a frown.

Ms. Smith shook her head. "Not at all, but I just give them my recommendations for the job. The final decision isn't mine, honey."

Christina slumped back and sighed.

"Look," the kind woman began, "I've already spoken to most of the other applicants I would even consider for this job, and trust me, girl, you're in the lead. If it were up to me, you'd have the job. I'll make the recommendation to the people upstairs, but like I said, the decision isn't mine. I see young black folks coming in here all the time looking for a job. I try not to get their hopes up if I don't have to. Besides, are you sure this is a job you would really want?"

Christina bit her lower lip, not sure exactly what she should say. Was this some bizarre employment test? Human Resources Reverse Psychology 101?

"The job market is bad but I don't think it's that bad," Ms. Smith said with a chuckle as she glanced at the flashing button on her phone. "Why didn't you get a job in marketing and development or something when you graduated from school?"

Christina looked down at her hands. She could not tell Ms. Smith that many employers had vied to get Christina on their payroll but she had turned the jobs down, partially because she had convinced herself that she needed a little break after she received her degree, and secondly because she wasn't sure if she really saw business in her future.

"Have you ever tried smaller businesses? They have lots of young people like you. They aren't scared of someone with smarts either."

The woman stood up and extended her hand to Christina. After Christina rose from her chair, Ms. Smith patted the young woman's hand gently and smiled.

"I wish you the best of luck either way, dear. If you get the job, I'll definitely give you a call."

Christina sighed, smiled weakly, and then nodded.

* * *

More than just a little crestfallen, Christina decided to walk around the city after her interview, hoping that a stroll would make her feel better. She unbuttoned her jacket and hiked through the business district, carrying her purse and her résumé folder as she glanced into shop windows and gazed at the bustle of midday traffic. *This is too much,* she thought. She just couldn't win. How was she going to convince someone that she was more than qualified for a job but also not interested in taking his or her job? More importantly, how was she going to be able to pay for her apartment two months from now?

Christina walked and walked and eventually sat on a park bench when she became tired and stared at the marble water fountain in front of her. The water lapped softly and pigeons dipped their heads into the pool sprinkled with pennies and nickels, cooling themselves in the increasingly warm weather of May. Christina stared at them and eventually returned to her thoughts.

She really wanted to prove herself—to her parents for the most part and to her mother particularly. She wanted to show that she could take care of herself, that she could be a *real* adult. Unfortunately, so far she wasn't having much success in her attempt. In fact, she felt as if she was failing miserably.

Christina sighed, removed her jacket and tossed it over her arm. Her stomach grumbled. She supposed she should buy lunch. She hadn't eaten anything that morning because she was too nervous about the impending interview to even down a bowl of cereal. She spotted a vendor several feet away selling a wide array of foods, including hot dogs, hamburgers, and gyros. Her mother had always warned her not to buy anything from the stands in the city. "Have you ever seen the things they do to their food? It's absolutely nauseating," she would sniff. But Christina was starving and was not in the mood to hike back to any of the local restaurants. Besides, they were too expensive and as always, she was on a limited budget.

Christina walked across the park and smiled at the vendor. Not paying attention, she tripped slightly over a crack in the sidewalk and her résumé folder fell from her hands. Just as she leaned down to pick it up, a tall man stepped in front of her. Christina's eyes widened and she put a hand on her hip, fuming at his impoliteness.

"I'll have the usual, Ahmed," the tall man said as he reached into his pocket and pulled out his wallet.

"No problem, Mr. Neeson. I'll have my wife get it for you." The vendor turned and spoke to the woman who stood behind him, leaning against a freezer. "Get our favorite customer, Mr. Neeson, his special gyro, Fatima. Just a few minutes, sir. No problem. Can I get you anything, miss?"

The man called Mr. Neeson turned around to look at Christina after the vendor acknowledged her, and he smiled apologetically. "Oh, I'm sorry. Were you trying to order something? I didn't know you were standing there."

Christina wiped the front of her folder and slowly nodded. "That's . . . that's okay."

The mocha-hued man with the lanky build was handsome by most standards. Unobservant Mr. Neeson, who was probably in his late twenties or early thirties pushed his pencil-width dreads out of his eyes, revealing piercing black pupils and dark brows. He smiled, flashing gleaming white teeth. A trim goatee curved around his pink mouth, and wire-rimmed sunglasses were perched at the top of his head. But the clothes he wore negated his bohemian look. His white shirt and tan pants were simple though barely businesslike.

The edges of his eyes crinkled as he continued to smile. "That was very rude of me to get in front of you. Let me make it up to you by buying your lunch. It's the least I could do."

Christina sighed and shook her head. "Thank you but no, thanks." She looked up at the vendor. "I'll have a gyro too, please, and a Coke."

The vendor nodded. "Seven-fifty."

Christina reached into her purse and handed him her only ten-dollar bill.

The vendor the looked down at it and frowned. "Miss, it is seven-fifty. This is a five."

He handed the bill back to her. It was indeed a five-dollar bill. Why hadn't she noticed that? Christina blushed slightly and dug into her purse. She rifled through her wallet and all the side pockets but all she had was the five dollars. She couldn't even uncover any change.

The tall man observed this quietly after he was handed his gyro, and pursed his lips to keep from smiling. He looked up at the vendor and waved his hand. "Ahmed, don't worry. I'll cover it."

Christina profusely shook her head. "No, really, I—"

"It's nothing. Just think of it as an apology for my rudeness," he said as he dug back into his wallet and handed the vendor the money.

She tucked her hair behind her ear and closed her purse. Christina was now more than just a little embarrassed. "Thank you," she murmured.

"No problem." He handed Christina her meal and gestured toward a nearby bench. "My name is Jason Neeson, by the way."

He held out his hand and she shook it.

"I'm Christina."

"Christina. That's lovely. Does it come with a last name?"

She gave a lopsided smile. "Yes, Saunders. Christina Saunders. Thank you for the lunch, Jason. It was very nice of you and very nice meeting you."

Christina turned and began to walk away but he jogged after her and grinned as he bounced in front of her, blocking her path.

"Hey, what's the hurry? You know, if you really feel uncomfortable about accepting a free lunch from me, you could pay me back by eating with me."

She opened her mouth to say no but he interrupted her before she could utter the word.

"I'm on a break from work," he continued. "Things were pretty busy today and I could use some nice conversation and company from a beautiful lady with a lovely name."

Christina sighed and smiled weakly. She squinted against the afternoon sun that blazed down on them through the park's trees. How could she turn down a perfect stranger who had just forked over ten dollars for her? It was just lunch and he seemed like the persistent type. He probably wouldn't just take a quick no for an answer anyway.

"Okay," she said quietly. "Sure."

They sat on a bench in front of the fountains. He handed her a napkin as she opened her soda can.

"So, Miss Saunders," he said as he removed the aluminum foil from his gyro, "tell me about yourself. Do you work on this block?"

He fixed her with a steady gaze as she shook her head and rolled her eyes.

"I wish."

"Excuse me?"

Christina laughed, bit into her gyro, and wiped her mouth with a napkin. "Sorry. No, I don't work here. I was just at an office building a few blocks away for a job interview."

"Really, for what job?"

She cleared her throat.

"A data-entry technician," she said with great formality.

Jason raised an eyebrow. "Data entry, huh? So how'd it go?"

Christina shrugged and sipped from her soda can. "Not too good, actually. The personnel officer said I was both overqualified and underqualified. I guess that just means it's not likely that I'll get a call back."

Jason smiled with an expression of puzzlement. "How are you both overqualified and underqualified?"

"I have no idea. But I was just told about an hour ago that most of my interviewers probably make up their mind about me long before I even get there. It's all in my résumé."

"Really? Do you have your résumé with you? I'd be interested in seeing it."

Christina frowned. This guy was smooth. Was this some sneaky way to get her address and phone number? She scrutinized him silently. After a month of living in her neighborhood, she had quickly learned whom she could talk to, whom she shouldn't talk to, and what was just the right amount of information to share with a stranger. Her girlfriend would be proud. This guy was slowly pushing her borders.

If Christina were observing this scene from afar, she would probably give Jason points for cleverness, but since she wasn't observing it and was instead participating, she had to be careful. Did she really want this guy calling her? She figured, after some deliberation, that the chances of him actually memorizing her personal information permanently in a matter of seconds were pretty slim. She reached over and handed Jason her folder, resolving to take it away from him after a few minutes. She then shrugged.

"Okay," she said. "Maybe you can figure it out."

Jason opened her blue folder and pulled out the cream-colored parchment on which her résumé was printed. With narrowed eyes, he scanned her job objectives and her achievements. After a few minutes he raised his eyes to stare at her openly and cocked his head sideways. "If someone were to offer you a job today, how soon could you start?"

Christina frowned. "What do you mean?"

"I mean exactly what I said. If someone were to offer you a job today, how soon could you start?"

She laughed. "Why? Are you offering me a job?"

He nodded, making his dreads swing gently. "Pretty much. Of course, I'd have to check out your references and talk to my associates, but I'm doing this with the assumption that all the things you have typed on here are legit."

Christina, for the second time that day, gaped openly.

"Let me explain." Jason smiled. "You see, my partners and I help design grant proposals for nonprofit organizations, mostly social advocacy groups. Stuff for kids, minorities, and immigrants a lot of times. It's not your typical business thing. Sometimes we try to work the organizations through the process of getting these grants. We help them to make the money work the best way it can."

He handed Christina's résumé back to her. "My partners and I have been looking for someone for quite a few months who knows a lot about business strategy. We prefer someone with a history in management, but most of the people who fit the bill aren't willing to work for what we're offering, but we're willing to pay twenty-eight thousand a year with benefits. About the same you would get if you were in data entry, right?"

She slowly nodded.

"So you think you'd be interested in working with us?"

Christina grinned. She nearly screamed out loud from excitement. She had been dragging herself from office to office for the past month trying to get a job, and now she was being offered one out of the blue on a park bench from a perfect stranger. This was incredible! This was unbelievable! She never would have expected this to happen.

Her smile quickly faded.

Christina momentarily paused from her excitement and assessed the situation. Okay . . . she was being offered a job—not just a job, but a *great* job that paid—out of nowhere by the same guy who had bought her lunch and flirted with her openly for the past half an hour. Was this for real? She studied the man in front of her carefully.

"I am interested but I would have to see your business, of course," she said.

He nodded. "Of course. I'd have you meet everyone on the staff, and everyone would fill you in. But besides that, does it sound good to you?"

She gazed at him silently and he sighed.

"Look, I know what you're thinking, but believe me, I'm not that type of guy. You're cute, *very* cute, but I wouldn't hand out a position like this to a pretty face that didn't know her stuff. It's not my style. Besides, my partners, Jay and Robert, wouldn't let me do something like that even if I wanted to."

Christina laughed. "That's good to know." She tossed her empty soda can into a nearby trash can. "Okay, Mr. Neeson, if you are tentatively offering me a job, I tentatively accept it."

He raised an eyebrow. "Well, thank you, Miss Saunders, and call me Jason, please."

She nodded. "Okay . . . Jason."

Eight

Shauna waved her hands frantically. "Over here!" she yelled over the noise of the throng of people who walked throughout the mall.

Christina rolled her eyes. She had been searching for Shauna for at least fifteen minutes with her hour lunch break quickly dwindling away. She wasn't happy about that. Now three months into her job as a grant consultant, Christina found herself daily with towers of paperwork waiting for her at her office. Today wasn't a day when she could dawdle around in search of Shauna in a crowded mall.

"I thought you said to meet you in the food court at twelve-thirty, Shauna," Christina exclaimed as she walked over to her friend. "This is not the food court. This is you standing in front of a clothing store."

Shauna pursed her lips. "Well, excuse me, Miss Punctual. I was expecting you to be fifteen minutes late. The dress in the window caught my eye and I went inside to check on the price to give you time. Besides, I saw you, didn't I?"

Christina slowly smiled and shook her head while Shauna's face clouded in an expression that could only be described as shock. Her mouth twisted.

"Are you off from work today or is it casual Friday and

someone forgot to tell me?" Shauna asked, as she looked Christina up and down.

Christina glanced down at her khaki skirt, white T-shirt, and low-heeled sandals and then at Shauna's two-piece black suit and the Gucci knockoff purse she carried. A headband held Christina's hair back, while Shauna's new hairstyle consisted of a complex cascade of tendrils and curls.

"I did go to work today, thank you. We just have a relaxed work environment at our office, that's all. The people who come in for our help are usually wearing the same thing as us. It intimidates them to see us in business suits."

Shauna raised an eyebrow. "Is that so?"

"Yes, it is so," Christina said firmly, letting her friend know subtly that it was better to drop the subject. "So why did you ask me to meet you down here anyway? If we're not going to eat, what did you want to do?"

Shauna rubbed her hands together and grinned wickedly. "Darryl's coming over tonight and you're going to help me pick out lingerie to wear. It needs just a hint of sophistication and just a smidgen of naughtiness."

"No! No!" Christina whined as her friend tugged her in the direction of a lingerie boutique.

"Oh, come on, Chris! It'll be fun!"

"How is me watching you leaf over garters, panties, and bras supposed to be fun? Shauna, if you had told me this on the phone I would have told you no." She rolled her eyes and crossed her arms over her chest. "Damn it, I'm hungry and I could be eating a chef's salad right now."

"Oh, listen to you. 'I'm hungry. I want a chef's salad.'" Shauna smiled and winked as they walked into the scented salon. Headless mannequins decked in lace and satin hung from the lavender walls around them. "You know, if you bothered to look around maybe you'd find something for yourself," Shauna muttered. "Something you could wear for . . . what's his name?"

Christina frowned. "What are you talking about?"

"You know. The guy you work with."

"What guy? I'm not going out with anyone from work." Christina squinted with confusion as she tried to figure out whom Shauna was referring to. After a few seconds, her brown eyes widened. "You mean my *boss,* Jason Neeson?"

Shauna shrugged as she held up a black lace bra embroidered with silver thread. "Why are you saying it like that? What does it matter that he's your boss?"

"Nothing . . . besides the fact that it's completely unprofessional to date your superior."

Shauna threw the bra back into the pile in front of her and rolled her eyes. "Oh, come on, Christina! Don't even fake like that. You've gone out with him plenty of times!"

"Excuse me, those were business dinners. Besides, most of the time someone else from the office was there with us. We always talked about stuff related to work."

"He's driven you home," Shauna countered.

"I don't have a car! He offered me a ride home so I wouldn't have to take the bus."

"He bought you that nice gift a month ago."

Christina fisted her hands at her hips. "No, *Jay and Robert* bought me that gift. They gave it to me for the good job I've done so far with our new clients. It wasn't anything personal. They did it in front of the whole office!"

A gray-haired woman two racks away from them frowned and turned around to look at the arguing pair. Shauna raised her eyebrows, silently challenging the woman to say something to her. The woman placed her silk chemise back on the rack and walked away. Shauna then returned her attention to Christina. She shook her head.

"All right, Chris, you know he likes you. How long are you going to pretend that he doesn't?" she asked.

Christina took a deep breath and sighed. She ran her fingers threw her hair and flapped her arms helplessly. "As long as I can."

They said nothing as they crossed to the other side of the store. The two slowly made their way to a bin filled with thongs.

Christina glanced at a display of corsets hanging on the wall just as Shauna began to dig through a pile in front of her of Lycra, lace, satin, and silk.

"Are you sure you're not dating this Jason guy just because he's your boss?" Shauna asked. "Are you sure it has nothing to do with David?"

Christina blinked and had to force herself not to flinch. She hadn't heard that name in quite a while. "Why would it have anything to do with . . . David?"

Shauna looked over at her with narrowed eyes and pursed lips. "I don't know, Chris. You tell me. You just happened to go out with the man for seven years and you were engaged to him. That's all."

"Shauna, I haven't seen or heard from David in almost four months. Who I date or don't date has nothing to do with him. I don't care what he thinks. I guess you could even say . . . " She paused. "You could even say I don't care about him anymore."

"You don't care about him anymore, huh?"

"No, not really."

"Well, that's good to know."

"Why is that good to know?"

Shauna raised a pair of pink panties to look at their price tag. She kept noticeably silent.

"Come on, Shauna. What did you mean by that? Why is it good to know that I don't care anymore?"

Shauna put down the pair of panties she was holding and gazed at Christina silently. She looked as if she wanted to say something but wasn't sure if she should. Christina steeled herself. Shauna was probably was going to tell her that David was already starting to see other people and that he was involved in a relationship. And only after four months since she had broken off the engagement . . . Christina was surprised it had taken him that long.

"Look," Shauna finally said, "I don't know all the details. This is just hearsay, all right? A he said/she said type of thing."

"I understand. Go ahead and tell me."

"Well, I just heard that David's not . . . doing too well."

"What do you mean? Is he sick?"

Shauna took a deep breath and shook her head. "No, not sick. Well, not sick like sick in a hospital with an IV in his arm kind of sick." She shrugged. "He couldn't focus after

the stuff that happened between you two. He failed his bar
exam and some people are saying that failing like that and
you leaving him, I mean breaking up with him, made David
kind of depressed. Well, no. I guess you could say *really* depressed."

Shauna looked down and sighed. "The people who have
seen him in the past couple of months said he isn't at his best
right now. His father told him to come back to work at the
firm when he gets his shit together. Until then, he doesn't
want David there. I heard that after his father said that to
him," she continued, "he just lost it. David didn't get out of
bed for a couple of days. Some of his buddies check up on
him every now and then to see if he needs anything, if he's
okay, but he hasn't gone out of his house in weeks. He doesn't
want to go out."

Christina stared at her blankly, not knowing what to say.
She was totally shocked by Shauna's words.

"Chris. Chris, are you okay?"

Christina blinked before ardently nodding. "Oh, yeah. Of
course, I'm okay. I'm just a little surprised, that's all. I wasn't
expecting . . . that."

"Look, don't feel bad, all right? I know you." Shauna
rubbed her friend's shoulder reassuringly. "Whatever
David's going through right now he brought on himself. He
only has himself to blame. Remember that."

Christina cleared her throat and nodded again. "You're
right. You're absolutely right. I won't feel bad. Whatever
David's going through no longer deals with me. Separate
lives. Separate people." She forced a smile before holding
up a pair of sequined thongs. "So. How about *these* for
tonight? You think Darryl would like them?"

Shauna raised her eyebrows and frowned as Christina
handed the thong to her. "Yeah, right. I'll tell you what. I'll
wear them if you wear them. Until then, let's leave them for
the strippers."

Later on that day, Christina found herself leaning back in
her desk chair, saying good night to the people in her office

who were gathering their things and preparing to head out the front door for the evening.

"Working late again, huh?" one of them asked. Her coworker, Ahn Lee, pulled the strap of her leather bag onto her shoulder.

Christina nodded before typing off a few computer keys. She glanced at the darkening skyline outside the office's windows and smiled. "Yeah, I have a couple of things to do before I head out. I'll probably leave in about an hour or two though."

"Okay then. Be careful on your way home."

"I will."

"Bye, Christina."

"Good-bye, Ahn. See you tomorrow."

Christina closed her eyes when the office door closed. She dropped her face into her hands, listening to the silence of the now empty room that surrounded her. After a few minutes, she pulled her headband from her head and tossed it on her desk. It landed by her coffee mug.

It was going to be a long night.

She was staying late to finish the work she hadn't completed today, because all afternoon she had found it hard to concentrate. Every time she looked at her computer monitor, every time she took a phone call, every time she made a trip to the photocopier, her eyes would glaze over and her mind would drift back to what Shauna had told her. Even though she had tried to put up a noble front, the news had been devastating. Was David really that bad off or had the stories Shauna heard through the gossip grapevine been exaggerated? More importantly, why did Christina care either way?

Yes, David had broken Christina's heart. This was definitely true. But she had slowly gotten over the hurt his betrayal had inflicted upon her. She had had no choice but to move on. The concerns of day-to-day survival had pushed thoughts of David, her mother, and other past pains and nuisances into the back of her mind. But hearing about *his* pain, hearing about how *he* was now hurting was bringing it to the forefront for Christina all over again. She had imagined him in that type of situation. She had even dreamed about it. But now that it was actually happening, it didn't seem so great anymore.

"What are you thinking about?" Christina heard someone ask.

She turned around and looked up to find Jason's smiling face. He had been standing over her shoulder with a stack of manila folders in his hand. Christina quickly pulled the pencil she had been gnawing away on out of her mouth and tossed it into her trash, looking more than just a little unnerved.

"Sorry," he said. "Didn't mean to sneak up on you. I called you from the other side of the room when I realized I wasn't the only person here. I thought everyone had gone home."

"Everyone except me," she said with a weak smile.

He nodded. "Yeah, well, I walked over when it didn't seem like you heard me. You looked like you were floating in outer space somewhere."

"I guess I was a little preoccupied," Christina agreed as she placed her headband back on her head.

Jason frowned. "Nothing to do with work, I'm assuming. You want to talk about it?"

She shook her head. "No, not really. It's not . . . it's not anything serious. I'll be fine."

Jason continued to frown. He opened his mouth before closing it abruptly. He rightly figured out that it was better to drop the subject. "Okay. No problem. Well, I was just about to head downstairs. So what do you say to us taking a little break? Why don't we go across the street and pick up dinner and bring it back here?"

Christina leaned back in her chair and smiled nervously. Shauna had made it glaringly obvious that Jason's interest in Christina would probably never be limited to just a professional basis. This was a very sticky situation for her. She liked Jason. She really did and she had no intention of alienating him, but he was her boss. Nothing could change that. She didn't want to alienate the other people in her office no matter how attractive she found him.

"I don't know," she murmured. "Besides, I don't think

anything's open. I thought most places downtown close at the end of the business day."

"Most of them do but a few serve dinner because they understand the economic benefits of workaholics with no lives. We're always in the office and we need nourishment too." He chuckled and tapped Christina on the shoulder. "I could use a sandwich and you could too. Come on, Chris, a little walk could do you some good."

"I don't know. I really should get some work done."

Jason slowly nodded and though she could tell he was trying his best to mask it, he looked more than just a little disappointed. "No problem," he said. "I won't twist your arm. I'll be back in about an hour or so. Do you want me to bring back something?"

She shook her head.

Jason set his stack of manila folders on a nearby file cabinet and walked toward the front door. Christina gazed at him silently before rolling her eyes. She sighed.

"Wait," she called out as he opened the door. "I'll go with you. Just let me get my purse."

Jason paused, turned, and grinned. "Take your time," he said.

The diner was mostly deserted. Jason held the door open for her as she walked inside and sauntered to the glass-encased counter and absently patted her stomach that grumbled loudly. Nearly empty trays of salads, meat, imported cheeses, and piles of vegetables were underneath the glass. The glare of overhead halogen lights reflected off of them and further brightened a room that seemed starkly bare without the bustle of a business crowd coming in and out the front door. Christina looked up at the menu on the wall and frowned, not knowing what to order.

"A roast beef, please," Jason said as he stepped toward the counter. The glare of the overhead lights also reflected off his glasses and hid his dark eyes. "What will you have, Christina?"

She squinted and shrugged. "I guess a tomato with pesto would be good. I think I'll order that."

The young woman behind the sales counter nodded and quickly typed the order into her cash register.

"Oh," Christina said quickly, "I'm sorry. Those sandwiches weren't together. They're separate orders. I was just thinking out loud."

Jason smiled and shook his head. "No, they aren't. Don't be difficult, girl. Let the woman do her job." He smiled at the woman behind the counter and winked. "She never lets me pay for anything. She thinks she's liberated."

The cashier giggled and Christina rolled her eyes heavenward and sighed.

With the absence of a line of customers, the two were quickly able to get their orders done. They were handed their sandwiches within seconds. Christina tried to pass money to Jason as they started to leave, but he pushed her hand away absently, shaking his head.

"Take it," she insisted.

He laughed. "Do we have to go through this every time? Look, I'm not going to take your money. Okay?"

Frustrated and obviously not thinking clearly, Christina glared at him and shoved her money into his pocket as he turned to walk toward the door. Jason stopped and looked down with wide eyes to find Christina's soft hand wrist-deep in his pants pocket. She looked down, realized what she had done, and yanked her hand away as if she had touched a stove burner.

"I just don't like you paying for me, Jason," she mumbled, refusing to meet his eyes.

Jason smiled wickedly. "I wouldn't worry about it. If you'd moved your hand a little more to the left, I think I would have had to pay you."

He laughed again. Christina's face was now painted with the pink hue of embarrassment.

"Looks like it's about to rain," he said, mercifully changing the subject. "Did you bring an umbrella?"

She shook her head.

"No problem. I got it." He walked over to one of the diner's tables and removed a newspaper that had been left there earlier that day. "I'll hold it while you walk under it."

She nodded. Christina wasn't in the mood to argue.

Christina and Jason began the long walk back to their office building. After a few steps it indeed started to rain and as he promised, Jason held the newspaper over her head the entire way. When he realized there wasn't enough room for the both of them underneath it, he stepped from under the newspaper and walked beside her with drops splattering his face and clothes. Finally, they reached the building. She stepped into the lobby bone dry, while he looked as if he had taken a shower while still wearing his clothes. Jason removed his glasses and shook his head with his dreadlocks swinging every which way. When he was done, he looked over at her and smiled.

"Did I get you?" he asked.

"No," she said as the elevator doors opened. "I'm sorry you're so wet. You didn't have to—"

He waved his hand and shook his head as they walked inside the elevator.

Christina sighed and leaned back against the elevator's metal walls. "Why don't you let me apologize for anything?"

"I don't know, Christina. Why do *you* keep insisting on apologizing?"

"Because, Jason, you're being really nice to me . . . unnecessarily, all the time, and it makes me feel a little . . . uncomfortable."

He stopped wiping his glasses and gazed at her silently. "It makes you feel uncomfortable. I see. Do you want me to be mean to you then?"

"No, you know that's not what I mean."

With the beep of the elevator in the background as they climbed from floor to floor, Jason slowly walked over to Christina, towering over her.

"Well, if that's the case," he said softly, "then I think you need to tell me exactly what you mean." He pressed himself against her, letting the moistness of his clothes dampen her own. "So is this the type of thing that makes you uncomfortable?"

She gulped loudly. His mouth was inches away from hers. "Yes, frankly," she whispered.

"Why? Because you just don't like it or because I'm doing it?"

Christina labored to catch her breath. "Because you're doing it."

"Well, what's wrong with me? What's wrong with me doing it?"

The warmness of Jason's breath brushed her lips as he spoke. Christina peered up at him, struggling to find an answer. She blurted the first one that came to mind, the truest one.

"Because you remind me too much of my ex-fiancé," she said.

He blinked and leaned back slightly, surprised by her answer. Within seconds, the elevator doors sprang open.

"I'm sorry, Jason," she said as she pushed her way past him. "I'm sorry. I just can't."

Nine

The weeks following their encounter in the elevator were awkward for Christina and for Jason as well. They avoided each other's eyes and spoke to one another only when they had to during group meetings and when he had work to give her. Christina took the change between them hard because things had turned out just as she had feared. She may not have wanted to have a relationship with Jason, but she had always liked him as a person. Unfortunately for her a hint of romance with her boss hadn't worked out for the best, so it left a sense of discomfort that was hard for both of them to ignore. She should have followed her first instinct and simply decided not to go to dinner with him.

"Christina," Ahn said.

Christina looked at Ahn and held up one finger, motioning for her office mate to wait a second as she listened to the person who was speaking to her on her phone.

"Okay, thanks and good-bye," she said quickly and then hung up the receiver. "Sorry. I had to take that. What's up, Ahn?"

"First, let me say that I like your hair."

Christina laughed. "Thanks," she said as she twirled one of the ropes of hair around her finger. Shauna had talked her into trying something new. Christina had gone to one of the women who lived in her building and gotten shoulder-length twists at a decent price. It had been her first introduction into "urban styling" and it had been a relatively good experience with the exception of the children who kept running in and out of the kitchen, screaming and throwing objects at one another as their mother styled Christina's hair near the kitchen sink.

"Secondly," Ahn said sheepishly as she looked down at her feet. Her jet-black bangs flopped over her eyes. "Jason asked me to tell you to come to his office. He said he needed to speak with you."

Christina frowned. "Is something wrong?"

"I have no idea . . . but he didn't sound like he was in a good mood. I don't know if it has anything to do with what he has to talk to you about or if it's due to something else, but I would just say, tread carefully."

Christina slowly stood up from her chair and smoothed the front of her gray pants. "Thanks for the advice."

She walked across the office and swallowed before gently knocking on Jason's door.

"Come in," he said curtly.

Christina breathed deeply before opening it.

Jason was standing behind his desk, biting down on his lower lip as he leafed through a stack of papers. There was practically no place for her to sit down. His office was in its usual state of disarray.

"Close the door, please," he said.

Christina hesitated before doing as he asked. After he heard the door click, he removed his glasses and looked up at her. "I got a complaint from one of our nonprofit groups. They said they wanted to make a few changes to our grant proposal. They had questions. They've called you for weeks and you haven't gotten back to them. One of their reps said your treatment of her is very rude. I want to know what the problem is."

Christina frowned. "Rude? Rude to whom? I don't know what you're talking about."

He sighed before sitting down in his chair. "I'm talking

about Jessica Peters over at Safe Kids International. Does that ring a bell?"

"Jessica Peters? No, I wasn't aware that I had any problems with her until now. She never spoke to me about it."

He shrugged. "Maybe because she's had a problem getting you on the phone."

Christina gritted her teeth. "Jason, come on, that is not fair. This is the first complaint I've ever had against me in the months I've been working here and I don't even know what the woman is talking about. Yes, I know she's had to leave messages on my answering machine. But I also left messages on hers. We've each been away from our desks when the other has called. I didn't know it was upsetting her that much. Did you ever consider that she complained to you just to complain?"

Jason gazed at her quietly. "No, I didn't consider that, Christina. Did you ever consider that any suggestion of unprofessionalism by one of our employees looks bad as a whole for our organization?" She opened her mouth to reply but he turned around to his computer before she could answer. "Just make sure it doesn't happen again," he said abruptly. "That's all I had to say. You can get back to your work now."

Christina stared at the back of his head, completely flabbergasted. She shook her head as if in a daze and turned to walk toward his office door. It was force of habit not to act unladylike and not to yell. But force of habit hadn't gotten her anywhere in her life so far. Christina decided to, for once, let anger be her guide. She turned back around.

"No," she said with hands fisted at her hips.

Jason eased back in his chair and faced her. "Excuse me."

"No, I will not go back to work, because this is a bunch of crap! Up until now you've been praising the work I've done. Some chick calls you on the phone and tells you I pissed her off with my 'rudeness' and I'm fussed at and dismissed back to my desk like some little kid? No, I'm not going back to work! I want to talk about this, Jason."

Now it was his turn to act surprised. His mouth gaped openly but he quickly regained his control.

"Christina," he said quietly, "I think you're out of line."

"No, *you're* out of line. And *you're* the one acting unprofessionally, because you know why you're acting like this!"

His gaze instantly turned disdainfully cold. "I don't like what you're suggesting, Christina."

"And I don't like the way I'm being treated, Jason. If you're mad at me because of what happened that night we worked late, just say it! But don't use Jessica Peters at Safe Kids International as an excuse to put me down!"

Jason slowly stood up from his desk and leaned against it. He fumed as he glared down at her. "Christina Saunders, do *not* raise your voice to me ever again. I've always addressed you with respect and I suggest you do the same or you can find yourself a job somewhere else. I am your boss and you will damn well treat me as such and that's regardless of what chip on my shoulder you *think* I may have! And for the record, I told you I don't mix my personal life with business and what happened that night has nothing to do with what I'm saying to you now!" He leaned back and breathed deeply. Jason realized that he was also shouting and without a doubt, the entire office was now listening to their argument. "I say we drop this. This is not the appropriate time or place to talk about it."

Christina shook her head furiously. "No. No, I want to talk about this now because I'm being penalized for acting like a professional. I'm being punished because I refused to date my boss."

His lip twitched as he fought back a smile. "The reason why you wouldn't kiss me that night has little to do with me being your boss, or don't you remember?"

And with that, the wind was taken out of her sails. Christina looked down and cleared her throat. "Well, whatever it was, I'm glad nothing happened," she said, hoping her words would hurt him. "I can tell from the way you're acting now that it just would have caused more problems."

He shrugged. "Maybe it would have but I wouldn't be the reason why it wouldn't work out."

She raised her chin and turned to walk toward Jason's door.

"Why is he your ex-fiancé?"

She stopped as she reached for the handle. "What?"

"Why is he your ex-fiancé?" Jason questioned as he put back on his glasses. "The guy you said who I remind you of. Why is Mr. Wonderful in the doghouse?"

Christina narrowed her eyes and leaned against the door frame. "Because I found out he was cheating on me, if you must know."

Jason rolled his eyes and sat back in his chair. "You'll go back to him."

Her lip twisted with disgust. "Pardon me?"

"You're obviously still in love with him. You'll go back to him. Women always do."

Christina clenched her teeth before walking out of his office and slamming the door loudly behind her.

She was surprised that Jason didn't fire her after their argument. The next day Christina brought a large cardboard box to work, preparing to pack her things at a second's notice, but neither Jason nor Jay nor Robert said anything to her about what had happened in Jason's office. With the exception of a few whispers she overheard near the coffee machine, no one in the office said a word about it.

Christina resolved that keeping her job was definitely a good thing. She had gotten used to the regular income and had started purchasing things for her apartment. Her dining room was nearly complete. Her living room was completely furnished. She hoped to be able to afford a bedroom set in a month or two. One weekend she purchased a bookshelf for her living room wall. One of the janitors in her building who flirted with her regularly, Tyrone Douglas, said he would hang it for her.

He arrived at her apartment around lunchtime with ketchup stains on his overalls. Within seconds, he was at work on her bookshelf.

"Hand me the screwdriver, would you, baby?" Tyrone said over his shoulder. He held up the small bookshelf compartment with both hands as Christina knelt down and fished through his paint-splattered black toolbox.

"Which one?" she asked as she frowned, pushing the hair out of her eyes as she gazed at the haphazard pile of carpenter tools in front of her. "There are at least four screwdrivers in here."

Tyrone chuckled. "The one with the four-prong head."

She frowned and shrugged, picking one of the screwdrivers according to his description.

"Okay," he said, "you hold the other end and I'll put the screws in and then go over it again with my drill when we see this baby is level."

Christina followed his orders as Tyrone wiped his brow and meticulously inserted the screws.

"So why you putting this thing up anyway?" he asked.

Christina grinned. "Because all my books have been scattered on my bedroom floor for the past month and I figured I could save space by actually putting them away."

Tyrone glanced over his shoulder at the pile of hardbacks that were spread across her couch.

"You really read all them things?" he asked, frowning slightly.

She laughed. "When I can find the time, yes, I read them."

Tyrone shrugged as he removed the last screw from his overalls' front pocket with his gnarled fingers. He inserted the screw through a hole in the bookshelf and then a hole in the wall he had made with a hammer and nail a half hour earlier.

"Shoot," he muttered as he stepped back and pulled a leveler from his toolbox. "I take cable TV and a VCR over them books any day. Don't have to hurt your eyes like you would reading a book."

Christina shook her head, brushing her now damp palms against the front of her jeans. "Your eyes can be equally damaged watching television, Tyrone. Even more so than they could by reading a book."

Tyrone grinned, revealing the gap between his two front teeth and a gold incisor. "Not when you got a cold beer to ease the pain, baby."

Christina laughed.

Within the next twenty minutes, the bookshelf was erected and Christina escorted Tyrone to her door, politely brushing off an invitation to watch a new movie on cable with him later on that evening.

"Maybe some other time though, all right?" Christina said, patting him on the shoulder.

She then closed the door behind her and assembled the books on her new shelf. Christina finished a glass of water and smiled at the finished product that now adorned her wall. She then flopped back onto her sofa but quickly jumped up when she felt something hard and metallic prick her in the behind.

"Oww," she yelped, rubbing her now bruised posterior. Christina turned and rolled her eyes when she realized the culprit was one of Tyrone's screwdrivers. As if on cue, she soon heard a knock at her door.

"I thought you'd come back," she said, smiling as she walked toward her door. She quickly removed the lock. "Tyrone, I'll have you know I found your screwdriver with my—"

Her words instantly faded as the door opened.

"Hi, Chris," David said, in a barely audible voice, forcing a smile.

Ten

David gazed at her. Christina breathed in sharply, startled by how differently David looked.

He had lost weight evidently. She could tell from his gaunt cheeks and prominent cheekbones. Neither had been that pronounced a few months ago. Even his sweater hung limply from his broad shoulders. Dark circles were underneath his eyes, and frown lines decorated his mouth. Christina gazed with bewilderment at the man who had shaved every morning religiously since he was fourteen years old, until his chin was as smooth as a baby's bottom. He now had a full beard. A shaggy mane of hair also haloed his head.

She leaned her forehead against the door frame and sighed.

"David," she said breathlessly, "you look—different. You don't . . . you don't look too good."

His eyebrows shot up in amusement.

"Uh, thanks for the candidness," he said with a laugh, blushing slightly.

She shook her head. "I'm sorry. It's just . . . It's just—"

"You look different too. I like your hair." He smiled. "I would never have envisioned you wearing braids."

Christina patted her head self-consciously. "They're twists, actually." She looked down at the blue vase he held in front of him, filled with an array of colorful flowers.

"What are those for?" she asked with a frown.

"They're a housewarming gift," he said weakly. "Your mother told me about your moving here. She gave me your address."

Christina fought the urge to roll her eyes. She should have known her mother would be behind something like this.

"I knew you liked wildflowers and the color blue. I thought they would be a nice touch for your new place." David peered over her shoulder. "Is it okay if I come inside?"

Christina paused. It was strange. What sympathy she had managed to build up for him weeks ago quickly faded the instant she saw him. Now she remembered why she had hated him. Now she wanted to instantly tell him, *No. Hell, no, and go away! What the hell do you think this is?*

But he looked so . . . so . . . pitiful, she thought, and just as bad as Shauna had described. Fifteen minutes. Fifteen minutes at most and then Christina would ask him to leave. *What difference does it make?* she thought. Seeing him now, she could happily say, *I'm over you.*

She silently opened her door and waved him inside. Christina then closed it behind him. She walked into her living room with David mere steps behind her. When she glanced over her shoulder, she found him gazing at the room. He turned in a small circle. A slight frown marred his face. He had set his vase in the center of her kitchen table.

"It's . . . It's . . . nice, I guess. Very—homey."

Christina shrugged.

"It suits me," she said, shoving her hands into the back pockets of her jeans.

"Is the neighborhood safe? You haven't had any problems, have you? A few of the characters I saw standing around outside looked a little—"

"The neighborhood's fine. Look, David, this may sound blunt but, why are you here exactly?"

He slowly sat down on her couch and reached over to toy with the screwdriver that lay at his side.

"Is this yours?" he asked with a smile, staring down at the tool as if it were a rare coin.

She shook her head. "No, I'm not much of a handyman. It's Tyrone's."

He placed the screwdriver on the coffee table in front of him.

"Is Tyrone a friend of yours?" David's voice was strained at the back of his throat.

Christina closed her eyes and sighed, now pushed to the brink of patience.

"*Why* are you here, David?" she asked.

"I just wanted to see you," he muttered before staring down at his hands. "I wanted to see how you were doing." David looked up and smiled. "It's good to find you much better off than I am. I haven't been doing too well."

She gazed at him silently and crossed her arms over her chest while he cleared his throat.

"Things have kind of gone . . . downhill, suffice it to say, since I last saw you. I didn't pass the bar exam—"

"I know," she said quietly. "I heard."

He nodded. "I figured you might have. But I didn't come to talk about that and I'm not trying to make you feel sorry for me."

"Don't worry. I don't," she answered quickly, making David heave a heavy sigh. "I was hoping," he continued, "we could talk, or if we didn't talk, I mean, have a conversation about, what happened . . . I wanted to say a few things to you before I had to leave. Because I knew you would want me to leave. I knew that when I decided to come here. Who wouldn't? But I just wanted to have a chance to explain why I did the things I did. I guess." He gritted his teeth.

"Yes, I think that's what I'm trying to say."

"David, you don't have to explain."

"No, I do."

She shook her head. "Well, you may feel that you have to explain, but I really don't want to hear it. So if that's what you came all the way here to do, you wasted a trip."

He gazed at her silently.

"You've changed," he said.

"You told me that already."

"No, not just physically. I mean you've really *changed*."

"More than you know," she replied.

David sighed, rubbing his face with his hands. "When we first started going out, you were quiet and timid. You wouldn't say anything to anyone unless they spoke to you first, but you were also the kindest person I knew. That was the quality I admired in you. That's what I liked about you."

"No," she said, "I was a pushover. That's what you liked about me."

"That's not true," he persisted. "Don't put yourself down like that! Everyone else, all the other girls seemed to be completely involved in themselves, totally dependent on money and status and connections, but you were different. You legitimately liked people. You legitimately liked—me. Your heart was pure and I admired that."

"Yeah, and you had a really unique way of showing it," Christina said as she strolled from her living room into the hallway, preparing to open her front door. "Look, David, I think—"

"I know I'm the reason why you changed."

"That's great, David. Now I'm going to have to ask you to leave."

"I've messed up a lot of things in the past few months, Chris, and I've had a lot of time to think about this, so hear me out. Okay? Just hear me out. My father, my perfect father, has been married to my mother for over twenty years," David began, raising his voice slightly. The expression on his face was one of desperation. "But he's had a mistress as long as I can remember. My mother knows. She's known since the beginning but it doesn't bother her because she's always had men on the side."

Christina frowned. "David, you're not making any sense. What are you talking about?"

"Whenever my mother gets mad at my dad for cheating on her," he continued, "she just goes on a shopping spree. A new car. A new mink. Once she took a trip to Europe for an entire year just to avoid him. Most of the people at the country club know about my father's affairs. Hell, I've known since I was nine years old, but no one talks about it. Everyone just . . . accepts it. Because that's what people like us do."

"People like us?"

"It's just accepted."

"Okay, I get it. This elaborate story is supposed to have a moral. So what are you saying?" Christina asked with furrowed eyebrows. "That I didn't get the elite, screwed up marriage itinerary? That infidelity is the status quo among 'people like us' and I should have just dealt with it?"

"No," he insisted while rising from the couch, "I'm not saying you should have dealt with it. The affair with Constance was wrong. Cheating on you with all those other girls while we were together—though there weren't as many girls as you think—was wrong too. Look, I'm just trying to explain that I've seen this stuff my entire life! That I know it's not the right thing to do, but it's the accepted thing to do and I fell into the trap along with everyone else! I thought I wouldn't do the same thing, but I did and I hurt you in the process and I never meant that to happen! I made you change!"

Christina breathed deeply and closed her eyes. When she opened them again he stood inches away from her.

"David," she said quietly while taking a step back from him, feeling uncomfortable as he now towered over her. "That's all well and fine. I'm glad you figured it out. All right? But why you cheated on me for nearly a decade with several people and why you lied to me for that same amount of time doesn't mean anything. Not to me." She pushed strands of hair over her shoulder. "You were right. I *have* changed. I'm not the same person I was a few months ago. I'm not listening to the same crap I would have listened to then. I'm sorry your father isn't faithful to your mother and she gets back at him by going on crazy shopping sprees, David. I'm sorry that they've taught you to be this way, but their screwed-up marriage has nothing to do with me. I really . . . I really think you should leave. I'm asking you nicely to leave."

She believed her words, or at least she believed most of them. As she said them, Christina simultaneously felt empowered and heartbroken.

While she gave her speech, David did no more than stare

down at his shoes. After a few minutes, he slowly worked up the courage to look her in the eyes.

The green flecks in his iris dimmed slightly. What happened next happened quickly, catching Christina off guard and leaving her with little chance to respond.

Within seconds, David had her pressed against the wall behind her with his arms wrapped firmly around her waist and he lifted her so that she had to stand on the balls of her feet. She pushed at his shoulders and tried to pull her mouth away from his but found that even though he had lost a considerable amount of weight, he still had the advantage over her by at least sixty pounds, not to mention that he was nearly a foot taller. There was little she could do as far as might was concerned.

When she felt his hand creep beneath the fabric of her T-shirt, her first instinct was to scream. Christina's fight-or-flight mechanism kicked into overdrive.

The way he held her and kissed her now brought back no recollections of the tender caresses he had given her months ago or the polite kisses. His demeanor at this moment was both forceful and imperative. The look on his face and in his eyes was totally unfamiliar, almost ravenous. She had not made love to this person before. Finally, she managed to wrestle an arm from his grasp and struck him. A red welt appeared on the side of his face.

David pulled back abruptly and glared down at her.

She wasn't sure what would happen next. Was he going to force her against her will? Was he going to hit her back? Christina braced herself against the wall and silently cursed herself for inviting him inside her apartment. She waited, prepared for anything and now fully aware of the many advantages he had over her.

"Go on. Do it. Make me lose what little respect I have left for you," she growled angrily.

His eyes widened. He hadn't expected that. A look of horror slowly crept across David's face. He gazed down at Christina. Her tussled clothes. Her swollen lips. He staggered away from her and tripped over the coffee table before falling across the couch.

She took calming breaths as she stared across the room at David. It was then that she realized that while he was holding her, there had been a struggle from his side also. As hard as she had fought to gain her footing, for months he had found it equally hard to regain his.

David lowered his head in his hands, refusing to look up. She hesitated, hearing the whistle of the pounding of her heart in her ears, before she slowly rose and walked over to him. When she stood a mere foot away from him, he reached out and pulled her toward him, burying his face against her stomach. Muffled apologizes escaped his lips as he held her.

Christina swallowed hard, not knowing what to do next. The moment seemed surreal, not a scene she would have imagined in a thousand years: David huddled against her stomach, crouched down, begging for her forgiveness. Instinctively, she lowered her hands to his head and rubbed it gently, only wanting to comfort him.

It was then that Christina realized she hadn't gotten over David as she had claimed for the past several weeks. Shauna had been right. Even Jason could see it. Christina hadn't "moved on" and left David and her old life behind. Instead of healing her wounds, she had allowed them to fester by ignoring them. She still had not accepted all that had happened and what he had done to her, how her mother had treated her. It had hurt . . . it had hurt so much she could not put it into words. Because of all this, her wounds were now achingly sore.

Having David hold her now was only a grave reminder.

She began to cry. Softly at first, until the warm tears she could push away with the back of her hand multiplied tenfold.

David gently pulled his arms away and stood up to console her. He cradled her against him, still apologizing, and she slowly pulled her head back, stood on her toes, and raised her mouth to his.

Christina didn't know why she did it. Hadn't she been fighting *him* off of *her* just minutes earlier? Perhaps it was loneliness. Maybe it was the memory of what she believed they once were. Either way, Christina found herself with her lips firmly planted against David's, feeling his whiskers rub against her chin.

She could sense him hesitating, not knowing how to react though impulsively wanting to immediately kiss her back. He slowly closed his eyes and mechanically parted his lips, returning her kiss with his own.

They fell back against the couch and removed their clothes in a fevered rush. Both drowned in sensations of the familiar: the smell of one another, the taste of each other's skin, and the feel of fingertips. Before they knew it or cared, they were naked and tumbling from the couch to the floor below with the coffee table inches from their heads and Tyrone's screwdriver at their feet. Christina's world was turned upside down again.

David venerated her, with each kiss, suckle, and caress. When he pulled back the folds between her legs and tenderly kissed the pulsating center, she gasped for air. Her sight dimmed slightly as the blood rushed from her head. David eased her onto her stomach, smoothing her braids out of the way. He then gently kissed her between her shoulder blades. Christina's tremors started seconds before he raised her hips and inserted himself. He thrust rhythmically while she fought to gain her balance, frantically clutching the edge of the coffee table with one hand, fisting the fibers of her living room carpet in the other.

Early the next morning Christina awoke in her bedroom, gazing up at the ceiling, with David's head buried into the crook of her neck. He was still asleep.

They had made love several times that night, sometimes tenderly and sometimes with a hurried desperation, as if the world would end at any second. She had said little. David had done most of the talking as they huddled together beneath her sheets, holding one another. He had said emphatically that he loved her. This she believed, though with a slight hesitation. He asked her to forgive him. For this she would not offer a yes or a no. He said he would make things right again . . . .

With his flood of assurances and promises, that night felt eerily just like old times. But in the back of Christina's mind, she wondered if David's last profession was possible. Could he really make things "right again"? And if he could, did she really want to go back to the way things were months ago before her ideals and perceptions had been pulverized into nothing? Did she really want to return to Oz? The pain of changing to a new life had been great (now she would happily admit this), but she had learned a great deal over the past several months. She wasn't sure if the woman who was now emerging from the other side was ready to shrink back into her shell.

The warmth of his body soothed her. It was like burrowing deep into a dark, warm cave. It was comforting to be in David's arms again, but she wondered if that was reason enough to reunite with her ex-fiancé.

A lethargic ache now spanned Christina's body but she still managed to rise from her mattress. David stirred a little as she walked toward her bathroom, but he did not awaken.

She firmly closed the door behind her, turned on the faucet, and gazed at her reflection in the bathroom mirror. She did this for several minutes, leaning against the linoleum sink, staring at her face, every detail, every crevice. She asked herself, point-blank, if she should restart a relationship with David simply because being with him had always held a familiarity for her. What was more comforting than familiar? After a while, the answer to her question came. She lowered her head, realizing what she had to do.

Christina took her shower, quietly and quickly got dressed, and scribbled a note to David on a pad that was stacked among the clutter of her night table.

She chose her words carefully though she didn't know what would really be adequate in a situation like this. She prayed he would understand. With deliberate strokes, she wrote:

David,
   This isn't right for me. I'm not ready for this and I won't say that I ever will be. Please understand that

I'm not angry anymore. Resentment has become too painful—but I think we both should admit that things couldn't go back to the way they were. I care for you and I always will, but when I come back a few hours from now I don't want to find you here. Take care of yourself. I've learned that if you don't, no one else will.

Christina

She left and walked around her neighborhood, doing her weekend errands as if the night before hadn't happened. She said hello to the cashier at the corner store. She smiled when she picked up her clothes from the Asian family at the dry cleaners down the street. She purchased the morning paper for thirty-five cents. All the while Christina felt as if she were being held together loosely, as if her insides were stitched carelessly with tape and glue and she could burst at any moment.

When she returned to her apartment in the early afternoon, she hesitated as she turned the lock of her front door, not knowing if David would still be on the other side. She finally opened it, lowered her bags to the floor, and slowly walked into her bedroom with her eyes partially closed. She opened them and sighed with relief. It was empty.

Christina then looked at her night table. David had crumpled the note she had written into a tight, angry ball. Her old engagement ring was perched carelessly at its side.

Eleven

David didn't call Christina the next day, nor did he make another impromptu visit to her apartment in the weeks that followed. She had expected as much, considering the letter she had written to him, but forever the nostalgic one, Christina had mixed feelings about David's absence. She had enjoyed the night they shared together but did not anticipate that it would be repeated any time soon. Christina decided perhaps it was for the best anyway. She came to that sorrowful conclusion while on the bus riding to work one day, gazing out the window as she watched the people milling about on the sidewalk.

Mentally she steeled herself and was prepared to move on, but it seemed physically her body would not. It rebelled. As the month of September neared to an end, Christina noticed that she had not gotten her period and she had reason to worry. During the night she and David spent together, she hadn't been on the pill. The moment had been so rushed; neither had suggested they use anything. But David had come to her house empty-handed. No wallet. No bag. She doubted that he had even brought any condoms with him. It would have been useless to ask. Besides, who would have expected that night to go the way it did? She doubted he had planned it.

Christina now vaguely remembered months ago that she had warned David to be careful. She had brought up the idea of them having an unexpected pregnancy when they *had* been using something. Now her words were comically coming back to haunt her. At least then they had been engaged! Now something like her getting pregnant could lead to more than just a slightly awkward situation of her walking down the aisle in an empire-waist gown with a barreled belly. Now she had to deal with the possibility of being a single mom.

It was a nail-biting scenario, one that threw her into another tailspin of guilt and worry. Her lateness could very well be a false alarm, but what if it wasn't? Should she tell David? And if she did tell him, would he urge her to keep the baby? He might even use it as an argument for them to become engaged again.

"Emorys don't father illegitimate children, Christina," David would say. Or at least, they *claimed* they didn't.

Hold it together, she told herself while sitting at her office desk and leafing through a pile of papers. Christina didn't have leeway to stare off into space all day worrying. She was already falling behind on her work as it was.

"Christina," Ahn said as she walked toward her desk. Christina looked up form her manila folder. "Yes?"

Ahn smiled brightly . . . maybe a little too brightly. "First," Ahn said, "let me say that I love that turtleneck you're wearing. Green looks very nice on you. It complements your skin tone."

Christina frowned. "Jason wants to see me, doesn't he?"

Ahn looked down at her feet, shrugged, and nodded.

Christina closed her folder and sighed. She slowly made her way to Jason's office. What had she done now? This time he would definitely fire her. She knocked and pushed the door open when he called out for her to do so. When Christina stepped inside, she found Jason standing near his file cabinet, coffee mug in hand, scanning the multicolored tabs that earmarked his folders.

"Could you close the door, please?" he asked.

She did as he requested, trembling slightly.

Jason glanced at Christina and smiled. "Stop acting like that. You look like I'm about to bite your head off. I didn't ask you in here to fuss at you."

She loudly breathed a sigh of relief. She then pushed her braids over her shoulder.

"You wanted . . . you wanted me to give you a progress report on my work with Safe Kids International, right? I got in touch with Jessica about a week ago. We talked and cleared the air and I apologized for the misunderstanding. She said—"

He closed the file drawer and shook his head. "No, I've already spoken with Jessica. She explained everything to me. That's not what I wanted to talk to you about. I brought you in here because I wanted . . . I wanted to apologize."

"You wanted to apologize?" she asked. Christina said it as if Jason were speaking another language.

He stuck his hands into his pants pockets and raised his eyebrows. "Yes, to apologize. I *can* do that from time to time, you know."

She smiled weakly. "I know. I know, it's just . . . I hadn't expected you to say that."

"I want to apologize to you," he continued, "because you were right. I can admit now that I was very unprofessional and I let my anger over . . . something not related to work affect how I treated you . . . as my employee. It was wrong of me and I owe you an apology." He removed his glasses and cleared his throat. "That's all."

Christina looked down at her feet and nodded. "Thanks. And I apologize for yelling at you in the office. That wasn't a good way to handle it. It's just . . . I was so—"

Jason held up his hand. "It's okay. I know."

She smiled and walked back to his door.

"Christina," Jason said.

She paused when he called her name. She then slowly turned back to face him.

"If you do end up with this guy again—you know, Prince Charming—just make sure that he treats you right this time around. If he can't give you what you're asking for, then whatever else he's offering isn't worth anything. That's all I had to say." Jason looked down at his desk and within seconds shifted gears back into business mode. "Okay, you can go back to work now."

She gazed at him silently before opening the door and walking back to her desk.

Christina sat back in her chair and started her work again.

"How'd it go?" Ahn asked with a worried expression on her face an hour later.

Christina gave Ahn the thumbs-up sign. Ahn grinned.

"Oh, by the way," she said, "before you went to Jason's office I forgot to tell you, you got a fax this morning. I didn't want to pick it up. I didn't know if it was confidential or something."

Christina laughed as she stood up to head to the copy room. "Ahn, nothing in this office is confidential. Thanks for telling me though."

She walked a few steps before clutching her stomach as she felt a sharp pain spread against her abdomen. *Could it be?* she wondered.

Christina took a detour from the copy room and walked toward the ladies' room. She pushed one of the stall doors open.

She had gotten her period.

After work, Christina stopped at the corner store on her way home that evening to pick up a few things to fill her cabinets and refrigerator. She arrived at her apartment building around dusk with bags in her arms. Christina's eyes widened as she noticed her mother's BMW parked along the sidewalk. She frowned slightly, wondering if dear Mrs. Saunders had recently gone insane and allowed Ronald to borrow her car. Maybe he had decided to pay Christina an early visit. But she wasn't expecting him to come over until Saturday. He said, cryptically, that he had something important to tell her.

The car door swung open as Christina neared it, and her

mother leaped out. The older woman tugged her wool coat around her, fluffing the fur near the collar.

"Thank God you finally showed up, Christina," she exclaimed, shutting the car door and locking it behind her with a loud beep. "I had no idea when you would arrive back home. The instant the sun began to set I decided to leave before it reached nightfall. I was counting down the seconds. I didn't want to get robbed! If I go inside for a few, do you think my car will be okay out here?"

Christina hoisted one of the bags unto her hips as she dug into her wool coat pocket for her keys.

"Hi, Mom," she said flatly. She walked past her mother and headed toward the front door.

"I don't know how you could live in a place like this, Christina. Your father and I raised you for much better. This is an absolute hovel," her mother said as she followed Christina inside the building. She sniffed as she looked around the lobby, narrowing her eyes at the sixties decor. Mrs. Saunders sighed. "I'm surprised you managed to live here this long without getting raped or mugged."

Christina chuckled as the elevator doors opened. "People around here rape only on holidays, Mother."

"What?"

Christina shook her head and laughed. "Nothing. Never mind."

They rode to the fourth floor in silence and Christina was thankful for the quiet. Unfortunately, when the elevator doors opened again, Mrs. Saunders repeated her nitpicking.

"The lighting in this hallway is very dark," she commented. "You would think the janitor would know how to install a lightbulb."

Christina walked to her apartment door with her mother trailing behind her. "Tyrone knows how to install a lightbulb, Mom. He knows how to do a lot of things. But the wiring in this building is very old. He has nothing to do with that."

Mrs. Saunders rolled her eyes heavenward.

Christina pushed the door open and gestured for her mother sit down on the couch.

"I'll stand," Mrs. Saunders said as she began to unbutton her coat.

Christina shrugged. She carried her bags over to her kitchen counter and began to open the cabinets.

"I gave David your address," her mother said as she looked around Christina's living room.

"I know," Christina replied as she pushed aside a box of cereal and placed two boxes of rice beside it.

"Did he come to visit you?"

"You know he did, Mom."

Her mother shrugged. "Yes, I do but David won't talk about it. He won't tell anyone, not even his friends or Mr. and Mrs. Emory. He won't tell anyone whether or not you two made up. He said that's between you and him. I was hoping . . . maybe you could tell me."

Christina slammed the cabinet door closed before turning to her mother.

"We're still not engaged," Christina said, "if that's what you mean."

"Yes, but are you moving toward it? Did you talk about to him about it?"

"I told him I didn't know if I wanted to be with him again."

"You don't know. Why did you tell him that? How could you—"

"Mom," Christina said, slamming down a can of peas. "What David and I talk about is none of your business. It has nothing to do with you!" She threw up her hands. "God, why can't you just get a life of your *own?* Why are you always involved in mine? I'm a grown woman! I chose where I want to live! I chose where I want to work and I *will* choose who I want to marry! I don't have to clear my decisions with you before I make them!"

Mrs. Saunders steeled her shoulders and her gaze. "Have you lost your mind, Christina? How dare you talk to me like this? Your father always spoiled you—"

"No, how dare I stand here and listen to this! I can't believe I had to listen to you talk, talk, talk, talk, talk for twenty-three years!"

Her mother fisted her hands at her hips. "You are a disrespectful, ungrateful, mean-spirited little girl and I don't have time to—"

"Mom, I haven't been a little girl in over ten years." Christina shook her head and sighed. "Just . . . just let it go. Let me go! Look, I thank you and Dad for your sacrifices and your hard work and even—your love. But you obviously have a life planned for me that I don't want. We both know it. Why do you keep forcing it?"

Her mother stared at her silently for several moments. Finally, the older woman turned and slowly walked toward Christina's living room window. She looked down at the sidewalk below.

"Did you know I lived in a building worse than this with my mother and my sisters and brothers?" she asked softly.

Christina sighed, crossed her arms over her chest, and shook her head. "No, I didn't."

"A one-bedroom apartment. Six kids and one bathroom. She always had men coming in and out. We never had any food in the refrigerator, and what little we had she would save it for them . . . her men, our 'uncles.'" Christina's mother turned to face her with tears brimming at the corners of her eyes. "When I finally left that apartment, she didn't give me anything. Not a dime. Your father married me when I had nothing. I swore my children wouldn't end up the same way. The sky would be the limit."

"I know, Mom," Christina said quietly as she quickly walked toward her mother. She then gently rubbed the woman's arm and smiled. "I know."

"Well," her mother said with a sniff as she wiped her nose with a handkerchief from her skirt pocket, "you can lead a horse to water but you can't make it drink. I guess neither you nor your brother can help the way you are."

Christina grinned. "And neither can you."

Mrs. Saunders raised an eyebrow and opened her mouth to say something but thought better of it.

"Speaking of your brother." She cleared her throat. "He told me today he got engaged. It happened a few days ago."

"Oh, my God! Really?" Christina frowned. "Hmmm,

maybe that's what he wanted to come down to tell me about this weekend."

Mrs. Saunders nodded. "Yes, he's getting married to some Sheila Macintosh person. I don't know her. I've never met her family. He says they plan to make it a long engagement because she's studying to be a nurse. He wants her to 'finish her education.' I suppose that's a good thing. At least they're thinking about the future."

Christina smiled as she wrapped her arm around her mother's shoulder. "So . . . how did you take the news, Mom?"

The older woman rolled her eyes and sighed. "Oh, not well. But he seems bent on marrying her. Why should I try to convince him differently? It didn't work with you. I *know* it won't work with your brother."

Christina laughed.

Epilogue

The present . . .

Christina gathered her shawl tightly around her. She tried to remember the young woman who she was several years ago. That Christina seemed like a total stranger now.

The sound of a car's engine brought her out of her reverie. She looked up to see a valet walking swiftly to the driveway as David's car abruptly pulled up. The valet opened the door and David stepped outside. His face brightened and slowly broke into a smile as he looked up at Christina.

"Hi," he said to her as he handed the valet his car keys. David's green eyes twinkled with amusement.

"Hey," Christina said with a smile and a wave of her fingers.

"You look gorgeous," he said breathlessly.

"You look nice too."

It wasn't a false compliment. Gone was the wan, sickly thing that had shown up at her apartment building one night three years ago. He had long ago regained the weight he had lost and had gotten rid of the beard that shadowed his face. David filed out nicely the navy blue suit he was wearing. His lean yet muscular frame made a fetching silhouette.

Christina looked over David's shoulder and noticed the valet circling to the other side of the car. Just as he pulled the handle to open the door, it quickly swung open, nearly knocking him off his feet. A set of brown legs leaped out of it. As David climbed the steps to the Stanford Manor Country Club with his gaze firmly fixed on Christina, Constance McHenry practically had to run in her four-inch heels to catch up to him. When she finally did, she linked her arm in his own possessively and smiled.

"I haven't seen you around here in a long time, stranger," he said, as he stood in front of Christina and looked her up and down. "Now that is definitely a beautiful ensemble you're wearing, but what's with the getup? Is there a formal today I didn't know about? I've been out of town."

Christina shook her head. "No, my brother just got married. They're holding the reception here. I was a bridesmaid."

"Always the bridesmaid, never the bride, huh, Christina?" Constance piped, thrusting her way into the conversation. "It's been ages since I've seen you. By the way, did anyone tell you David and I are engaged?"

Constance shoved her long, slender fingers into Christina's face and Christina had to lean back slightly to keep from getting hit in the eye. It's good she did. She was sure the "Hope Diamond" on Constance's finger would have blinded her.

Christina looked over at David, whose face had paled slightly. Christina smiled before returning her eyes to Constance. "Congratulations," she said flatly.

"Our parents are absolutely elated," Constance said with a wave of her hand, making sure that a light hanging from the veranda shined on the ring and made it sparkle. "They're just beside themselves with joy."

"Constance," David said quietly, "I'm sure Christina doesn't want to hear the details of your wedding plans. We haven't even set the date yet."

"Oh, David, I wasn't going to tell her *everything*. We have to leave something for a surprise! I was just going to say that

I told my mother just yesterday that she had to get hold of herself so she could help me with everything. But I'm just so deliriously happy nowadays, I haven't been able to plan anything."

"I know what you mean," Christina said with a nod. "I'm engaged too."

"Oh," Constance uttered, now visibly disappointed. "Well, congratulations . . . to you, Christina." She glanced at David. "Hopefully, this engagement will actually make it to the trip down the aisle. Well, I suppose my wonderful fiancé and I should get inside. We have a table waiting for us in one of the dining rooms." She walked toward the door, tugging her cashmere shawl around her shoulders, but paused to turn around. David hadn't budged. "Are you coming, sweetheart?"

"Just a second."

Both women raised their eyebrows in surprise. A scowl marred Constance's beautiful face as she waited for her "wonderful fiancé" near the front door.

"I didn't know you were getting married," David said.

Christina tilted her head sideways and smiled. She then shrugged. "Not too many people know. He just asked me a few days ago. We haven't set a date either."

"Really. Is that so? So who is he? I want to shake his hand."

Christina shook her head. "I don't think you'll have the chance to. You wouldn't know him."

David slowly nodded. "He's a very lucky man, whoever he is."

"Yeah . . . and I'm a very lucky girl."

"David," Constance said with one hand firmly planted on her hip. Her voice prickled with irritation. "Are you coming?"

"I've got to go." He hesitated before lightly kissing Christina on the cheek. "Look, good luck to the both of you."

"Good luck to you too."

Christina watched as he walked away and took Constance's elbow. Even though she hated to admit it, they made a fetching sight: David with his dark good looks and Constance with her beautiful yet sometimes over-the-top persona. Both of their families were equally old and affluent. Maybe they made a good match after all, Christina conceded.

"I don't believe you! Were you going to leave me standing here the whole night while you make lovey-dovey eyes at your ex-girlfriend?" Constance whispered through clenched teeth as he opened the door.

David rolled his eyes heavenward and sighed. "Just shut up and go inside. I don't feel like hearing your crap tonight," he muttered as they walked into the foyer.

Christina's eyes widened. And then again, maybe they didn't, she thought.

"So was that Prince Charming?"

Christina turned to the driveway and smiled. Jason slowly mounted the steps.

"Not my Prince Charming, if that's what you mean," Christina said as she straightened his necktie and stood on her toes to kiss his lips. She frowned. "Where were you? You're a half hour late."

He shook his head, making his dreads swing gently. "No, I was *fifteen* minutes late. It took me that long to get here. It then took me another fifteen minutes to find a parking space."

"They have valets. You know, the guys in the red jackets and the black bow ties?"

Jason raised an eyebrow. "Why would I use a valet? I know how to drive a car."

Christina linked her arm into his and laughed.

He held the door open for her as they stepped into the foyer. Thumping music burst from a reception hall. It sounded like one of her brother's new rap albums. Christina could just imagine what her mother was now doing. She was probably hiding in the ladies' room, waiting for the song to end. Christina gathered her skirts and began to walk toward the entrance of the hall, but Jason grabbed her hand and tugged her back to his side.

"I have to get back to the reception," she said with a giggle as he wrapped his arms around her waist. She peered up at him and smiled. "I'm with the wedding party, remember?"

"Just a second. Just a second. I have to do this," he said as he leaned down and kissed her again.

THE ART OF SELFISHNESS

Kori Nicole Brown

One

I live outside myself. At least I used to. That's what my therapist told me . . . Well, actually she's the woman who does my hair, but I guess they are one and the same. Before anyone starts getting any ideas, I'm not crazy. I'm the last person on this earth that would think about going to see a therapist. But my friend suggested it so I took her advice and, well . . . That's what she told me; and she's right. I've lived outside myself for a long, long time now, because it's easier. I guess when you just decide you don't want to feel pain anymore you kinda decide to watch what happens to you like a movie. You can shake your head and suck your teeth and think about how sad the story is.

Most of my family is proud of Jasmyn Renai Perry, because I'm nineteen and I'm in college. That is a great accomplishment in some people's eyes, and in others' it may not be a big deal. To me it's a big deal. When I think about the way I was raised it's a wonder I'm not some type of crack head or serial killer.

I suppose everything started with my mother. I think that's where *everyone's* story starts. My mother is beautiful. One of the most beautiful people I've ever seen. She's tall, with creamy caramel skin, silky black hair, and beautiful green eyes. You know, the whole package. I look more like my dad, I'm more brown-skinned, my hair is nowhere near silky, and I'm short (petite, if you will). My mother's name is Renai Marie DeWitt.

My first memory of Renai Marie DeWitt was watching her sleep. She had me when she was only eighteen years old and we lived with my grandmother and her husband (my mother's stepfather) in this little brick house on Zamora Street in south central Los Angeles. I can still remember my mother's room to this day . . . decorated in pink and white like a little girl's. My mother always seemed so out of place in that room, even though she's the picture of femininity. I think when she *was* a little girl she was probably out of place in that room. My mother is not a pink person.

Anyway, I remember I had a little pallet on the floor. I couldn't sleep in the bed because she said I slept too wild. My grandmother didn't like me sleeping on the floor, but she didn't say anything. My mother kept saying she would buy me a bed but it never happened. I slept amid six huge comforters on the floor. It wasn't that bad. But sometimes at night when I'd wake up and it was dark, only the light from my mother's little TV lighting the room, I would sneak into bed with her. I had to be about three then. I remember waking up and putting my face close to hers. Feeling her warm breath on my face as she snored. She snored, something so utterly human, and not necessarily feminine and attractive. She slept with her hair back in a ponytail. It was black and thick and hung to the middle of her back like a bolt of silk. I remember studying in awe the little tendrils that had escaped the ponytail while she slept. My hair was thick and always braided up by my grandmother. I didn't have "good hair" like my mama. I would compare my cinnamon-brown skin to her creamy lemon complexion and wonder if mine would ever look as pretty and smooth with that slight glow underneath, and would my lips ever have that slight cherry-red hue to them? I was only three and I knew that my mother was extraordinarily beautiful. She had to be the most beautiful thing I'd ever seen.

I scooted into bed with her and laid my head against her

back. I was careful not to wake her up. Her skin was so warm, and she smelled like Ivory soap. This was the closest I ever got to being held by her.

The only person that had actually held me or hugged me at that point was my grandmother Ma Belle. She was this dark rich ebony color. Her hair was thick and nappy like mine and she wore it pressed. She was the total opposite of my mother, but I knew at three that she was just as beautiful, just in a more realistic way. She and my mother never really got along even though Ma Belle would swear "the sun rose and set on Renai." My mother was her youngest girl and she was the "spittin' image of her daddy's kin," Ma Belle would say with pride.

When I was almost four my stepfather's nephew came to stay with us in the little house on Zamora. My mother was hardly ever home, as she worked as a secretary. She would come home and change her clothes and go right back out. I used to sit on the frilly pink canopy bed and watch her sort through mountains of clothes to find just the perfect outfit. She rarely said anything to me while she got ready, but I knew that just her tolerating my presence was something to be valued. My mama didn't play games with me or do my hair, and she certainly didn't bake cookies or read bedtime stories. I knew I had to take what I could get.

When Matthew Linton Hughes moved into our house, my little world changed. I remember studying him in curiosity. Everyone was a giant to me then, but he seemed larger than life. He was dark, and looked just like my Mr. Hughes (that's what I called Ma Belle's husband). I remember staring at his hair because it was braided somewhat like mine. He wore all blue (I remember that vividly because I was just learning my colors) and he never seemed to smile. He didn't really pay me much mind and that was okay because I was used to being ignored.

Ma Belle didn't work, and she would stay home and take care of me. We would clean the house, and I would get to watch Nickelodeon in my mother's room while she watched her stories in the living room. When Matthew moved in, Ma Belle didn't take me with her all the time the way she used to. She would leave me with him for a couple of hours in the afternoon while she ran errands. She'd always put me down for a nap so that I wouldn't be too much trouble.

I remember one afternoon. I woke up from my nap. I don't know what made me wake up but I knew something wasn't right. Matthew was lying on the bed next to me. He looked at me as I woke up, and I can still feel his hands on me to this day. I couldn't breathe. I just lay there looking at him with my scared eyes and wondering why he was doing what he was doing.

"Look what you did! You peed in the bed!" he yelled at me.

"Uh-uhh. I dinna pee!" I screamed. Peeing on myself was something I had mastered control over. Ma Belle and I had been working on my getting up and going to the bathroom when I was asleep for a few months, and I hadn't wetted the bed in a while.

"Yes, you did. Go get washed up," he yelled at me.

I jumped off the bed and went into the bathroom. I stood on the toilet to reach the sink and soap and washed myself the way Ma Belle had taught me. I went back into my mother's room and pulled some new underwear from the bottom drawer that held all of my clothes. I hadn't peed on myself. I had started to speculate on who actually did wet the bed as I resnapped my overalls when Matthew came back into the room. He held a black belt in his hand.

"Lie across the bed, Jasmyn," he said gravely.

"I dinna pee! I promise . . ." I said, realizing I was about to get a spanking.

He grabbed me by my arm and made me lie across the bed. He let loose on my little pink-corduroy-clad behind for a good ten minutes. I don't know when I stopped screaming, but I did. When Ma Belle or my mother spanked me, it was only a few swats, but Matthew wasn't stopping.

When he finally did stop I remember rolling up in a ball. I was whimpering, but the tears were more silent than anything. I grasped the comforter and wished Ma Belle were home.

Every Monday afternoon Ma Belle would run errands. I

would be left with Matthew, and there would be a repeat performance of what had happened *that* afternoon, beating included. I used to hate it. . . . I hated staying alone, and my little behind was getting welts on it from constantly being spanked. I finally decided to tell Ma Belle.

She was sitting in the living room watching her stories. I climbed onto the couch and she pulled me into her lap as always. It was a Tuesday, so my behind was still a little tender. I winced as she adjusted me on her lap.

"What's the matter, Jazzy?" she asked me, watching me shift in discomfort on her lap. She was the only one that called me Jazzy. I liked it.

"I got a spankin'," I said quietly.

"Why?" she asked.

"I pee in the bed. Matthew said I been peein' again. But, Ma Belle, I dinna pee in the bed. Him pee in the bed," I said earnestly.

"Go on, finish," she said in her gentle voice.

She wasn't getting mad, so I was feeling a little bit more comfortable in telling her.

"Let me see ya behind, Jazzy. Show Ma Belle where you got spanked," she said carefully.

I jumped off her lap and bared my little bottom to her. I heard her gasp, "Sweet Jesus," but then she just had me pull my pants up and she gave me a cookie.

"I in trouble?" I asked her, enjoying my cookie.

"No, Jazzy, you not in trouble," she murmured as she dialed the phone.

After that I'm not sure what happened. I just remember her telling my mother that it was time she found a place for herself and me, and my mother telling me we had to find somewhere else to live because Mr. Hughes paid the bills in Ma Belle's house and Matthew was his family. She was angry and I remember her packing our clothes. I didn't say anything, I just cried. I was scared. I didn't want to leave Ma Belle.

When we got into my mother's car I remember kissing Ma Belle good-bye. She had tears in her eyes. I felt as if it were all my fault.

After that we went to stay in a nice condo. It was bigger than Ma Belle's house, and my mother didn't have to go to work. Her friend Mr. DeWitt would come and visit almost every night and I would have to stay in my room when he came. He was white, and my mother told me she was going to marry him one day.

I started going to school after that and I liked it. My favorite subject was math because I loved numbers. I would wake up every morning and be quiet because my mother hated to be wakened early. I would climb onto a chair to get my cereal and carefully pour myself some milk. I would eat while I watched cartoons. I had to turn the volume down low though. It was okay, I didn't mind watching cartoons with no sound. I would make up the words the characters would say.

My mother always left a dollar on the kitchen counter for my lunch. I would slip it into my sock so I wouldn't lose it and close the door as I left for school. The bus would come and pick me and two other little kids up by the mailboxes at our condo complex. I was the youngest. I know the bus driver thought it was a little strange that no one actually walked me to the bus stop, but he never said anything.

My life was pretty simple back then. My mother never really discussed the situation with Matthew with me. Ma Belle would call and talk to me every so often, but as time went on she called less and less.

Mr. DeWitt came around more often. My mother always made me stay in my room when he came. He didn't really say much to me. I don't know when I noticed when my mama started to drink. I remember getting up for school and she would be on the couch passed out in the pretty dress I'd seen her in the night before. I would just lay a cover over her and be extra quiet.

By the time I was eight I was pretty self-sufficient. I was really content with my little life too. I had a few friends whom I played with at school, and I could cook about anything a person would want to eat. My mother always made sure there was food to eat and she would sign anything that needed her signature for school.

Then one day my world changed. It was the last day of

school. I can still see myself lugging a huge black trash bag filled with the contents of my desk. I walked into the house and was a little shocked to discover my mother up and ready to go somewhere. There were two suitcases by the door.

"Jasmyn . . . go to the bathroom. We're about to go somewhere," she said, quickly hanging up the phone. I was a little excited. We were both going somewhere together.

We drove well into the night. I fell asleep not sure where we were going. I only knew that my mother had this look on her face as if she was hiding a special secret. It made me smile, because if she was happy I was happy.

I will never forget my first true glimpse of Colorado. I remember vaguely seeing shadows on the horizon, and I wasn't quite sure what they were. Eventually as we got closer I realized they were mountains. Purplish blue with some gray mixed in for flavor. My little mouth dropped and I looked quickly at my mother, who seemed oblivious of the scenery. I decided not to mention the mountains to her. The afternoon sun seemed brighter as it beat through the windshield of my mother's Lincoln.

As we entered Denver it began to feel a little bit more familiar. . . . Even though it didn't seem as busy as Los Angeles, there were tall buildings, and highways. The streets seemed narrower to me, but things weren't as crowded. I read the names of the streets in interest. Colfax, Colorado Boulevard, and many others that seemed odd to me. I didn't dare ask where our destination was.

The digital clock on my mother's dash board read 2:00 P.M. as we pulled into the driveway of an older brick house. It was bigger than any house I'd ever lived in. It boasted a huge porch that hugged the front of the house. I noticed the yard was well kept, with a green snake of a garden hose nestled in marigolds. My mother turned to me and spoke the first words that I'd heard in the past twenty or so hours, beyond asking me if I had to use the bathroom.

"Jasmyn, listen to me very closely. I'm getting married to Mr. DeWitt. He doesn't want any children right now and neither do I. So this is your daddy's house, where you're going to live from now on," she said carefully.

I looked at her in shock. In a few sentences she had as much as told me that she didn't want me anymore.

"But, Mama, I want to stay with you," I said, trying not to cry.

The look in her eyes will forever haunt me. I saw my mother for what she really was. At that moment it dawned on me that she had *never* really wanted me. I was just there, and at this point in my life and in hers it was going to be convenient for her to get rid of me. I knew that no amount of pleading was going to convince her to let me stay with her. I *knew* at eight years old that the next time I saw my mother wouldn't be any time in the near future. But for self-preservation's sake I had to make some type of effort to get her to keep me. If only for the fact that I had no idea where I was and the word *daddy* was so foreign to me I had no way of comprehending what it could mean.

"No, you need to be with him. I've had you on my back for eight years. Let him have the next eight," she said bitterly.

"Please, I won't be any trouble. I'm sorry. I won't make any more noise or anything. Please take me with you." I was pleading at this point. I was trying to think of everything in my eight years of life that had irritated her.

She ignored me and got out of the car. She popped the trunk and unloaded my two suitcases. I got out of the car too. I realized that pleading with her was a lost cause. She knocked on the door, but no one answered. She shrugged and turned to me.

"Sit on the porch," she said crisply, without so much as a backward glance. She sauntered to her car and got in and drove off.

I watched in shock and amazement as the only parent I'd ever known drove away. At that point I decided to cry, because I figured holding my tears back hadn't gotten me anything, so why not let it out? I cried until probably three o'clock, then went to sleep. It was springtime so I wasn't too cold. I woke up at around 3:30, hungry as I'd never felt before, and I had to pee. I waited. I'd never met my father.

At approximately 3:45 P.M. I met my first brother, who

was a year older than I. He narrowed his deep brown eyes in inspection as he studied me.

"Who is you?" he said, eyeing me incredulously.

"Jasmyn Renai Perry," I said, eyeing him with equal suspicion.

We studied each other for a minute. I couldn't help staring at him because he looked so much like me. I'd never seen anyone that looked like me before. All the other family members I'd encountered up until that point had looked nothing like me. But this little brown child had my eyes. Deep and brown, his eyes were serious just like mine, and his nose and even his ears appeared to be mine. He wore a pair of black spandex shorts with a yellow stripe running down the side (I clown with him to this day about those shorts) and a Nike T-shirt that had three blue ribbons and a red one pinned to it with *Sunnyvale Elementary Field Day, 1st Place* embossed on them, except the red one said *2nd Place*. He carried a plastic bag bulging with what looked like papers, and a GI-Joe backpack hung dejectedly from one shoulder. It was obvious that it was his last day of school, just as mine had been the day before. It made me feel a little more comfortable; this boy could easily have been one of my schoolmates . . . except he had my face. I couldn't help gawking at him. He didn't seem to mind, because he gave me an equivalent scrutiny.

"Why you on our porch?" he said, probing. He reached into his backpack after dropping the bag at our feet and pulled out a fireball, stuck it in his mouth, and sucked on it thoughtfully.

"This my daddy's house," I said proudly. I stared longingly at the fireball. I was hungry.

Before he could reply, another boy, older, the spitting image of the smaller one, appeared. I looked at him cautiously. I had been cautious of older boys ever since Matthew.

"Who is this?" he said, asking the younger boy.

"She say her name is Jasmyn Renai Perry. And she say her daddy is our daddy," the little boy said, shaking his head.

The older boy studied me for a minute. Before he could

say anything, another boy joined him. He seemed to be even older. I watched in amazement as yet another mirror image of myself appeared to join the group that was pondering me on the porch.

"She say she our sister, man," the older boy said, shaking his head. The other one gave me a double take, and I knew he was shocked.

"Hey . . . little girl, are you hungry?" the smallest one said. He seemed to have recovered first.

I nodded yes. He motioned for me to follow him into the house. I followed him regally, trying to walk the way I'd seen my mother walk when Mr. DeWitt was around.

"What yo name?" I asked, sitting at a table that had seen cleaner days.

The little brown boy was making a mess fixing me a peanut butter and jelly sandwich. He put it on a napkin, then opened up a monstrous bag of Lays and set it in the middle of the table. He poured himself and me a cup of Kool-Aid, then sat down at the table.

"My name is Jordan," he said, grabbing a handful of chips and crunching on them.

"Oh . . . this sandwich is good," I said, gobbling it down.

"I won first place in all the events at field day . . . except one," he said, smiling proudly and poking out his chest to show me his ribbons.

I smiled and gave him the respect he'd earned. Every eight-year-old knew that if you placed first at field day, you were on the level of an honest-to-goodness Michael Jordan of your grade. He'd have bragging rights the whole summer.

"So why you say your daddy is our daddy?" he asked with a mouthful of chips.

" 'Cause . . . my mama said so," I said, munching on a chip.

"Who yo mama? My mama died," he said to me. He didn't seem to be fazed by that fact.

"Oh . . . um, my mama's name is Renai. She brought me here to live this morning," I informed him.

"How old are you?" he asked, obviously bored with learning about my mother.

"I just turned eight in May," I said.

"I'm nine and a half," he said, smirking at his obvious superiority in age.

Before we could continue our conversation the older boys came into the room. The one that was a little bit older than Jordan was shaking his head. The older one just stared at me.

"Man, she can't be our sister. Mama never had any more kids after Jordan," the medium-size one said.

"That doesn't mean anything. Look at her, she *looks* just like the rest of us. Which means she looks like daddy," the bigger one said.

"Jaleel, she's eight. Just turned. Now I ain't the baby no more. I think we should keep her," Jordan said, interjecting. He smiled at me.

Jaleel, the medium-sized one, raised an eyebrow and looked to the bigger one, who just shook his head.

"Little girl, when did you get here?" the biggest one asked me. I got a little nervous.

"Th-this morning," I stuttered.

"See, Jamie? You scarin' her. Leave her alone. Let's go watch cartoons," Jordan said, obviously upset at the fact that his two older brothers didn't accept me as readily as he did.

I decided I liked Jordan, and I followed him to a back room that looked to be made for just watching TV. There was a huge TV against one wall, and Jordan pulled pillows from behind an old couch and tossed one to me. We settled down to watch the *Cartoon Express*.

"Daddy be home in a little while," Jordan muttered as we watched the Smurfs defeat Gargamel once again. I just nodded. I wasn't quite sure what to think about a daddy since I'd never had one before.

I must have fallen asleep, because when I woke up it was dark and I couldn't remember where I was. Then the light clicked on. I sat up to be faced by seven male figures. I wanted to scream but I thought better of it. I recognized Jordan and the ones named Jaleel and Jamie. The other five were strangers to me.

Then I recognized my father almost immediately. He was

standing in the middle of the bunch. He was tall. Two of the
other boys were slightly taller than he but not bigger. My
daddy had muscles, while the other two were skinny. His
skin was a little darker than mine with more of a reddish
hue. But his eyes were just like mine. Deep and brown. He
was wearing a suit. And I knew that when he spoke, his
voice would be deep and would command whomever he directed it at to listen. I was a little scared, but not quite. He
didn't seem mean. But I already knew that looks could be
deceiving.

"Jasmyn." He said my name. I knew at that moment he
was the one that had named me. I stood up.

"You my daddy," I said, more as a statement of fact than a
question.

"Yes," he said simply. I didn't know what to say or think.
I just stared at him.

Then I started to cry. I wanted my mother, or even more
so I wanted Ma Belle. I needed to see some type of familiar
face. There were just too many of them. All of them looked
at me helplessly. I didn't know what to do when my daddy
picked me up as if I weighed nothing and started patting me
on my back. I froze. I'd hardly ever been hugged after we left
Ma Belle's.

"Shhh, princess, you don't have to cry," he said in a soft
voice. He sat down on the couch with me. I rubbed my eyes
and looked at him. I was sitting on his lap. I laid my head on
his shoulder. I was exhausted. It had been a rough day.

All of my brothers gathered around. I looked as some
took seats on the couch or chairs. Jordan and Jaleel sat on
the floor.

"These are all your brothers. You have six of them. Boys,
introduce yourself to your sister, and tell her your ages," my
father said carefully.

I watched as the introductions began. The oldest one, who
looked the least like the rest of them, stood up.

"I'm Jonathan . . . I'm nineteen," he said, smiling at me. I
smiled back.

"I'm Jared . . . eighteen," the other grown one said. He
was lighter, like the other old one.

"I'm Jayson and I'm fifteen," another one said. I was a bit confused until I realized that the other one, Jamie, was his twin.

"I'm Jamieson. I'm fifteen too," he said. He was sitting next to my dad on the couch.

"I'm Jaleel and I'm twelve," the other one murmured from the floor.

"I'm Jordan and I'm nine." Jordan smiled at me.

"I'm Jasmyn Renai Perry, and I'm eight," I said, joining in. I couldn't believe it. I had six brothers!

I looked at them all very carefully. None of them had that look that Matthew had. They were all quietly looking at me.

"You want some pizza, baby girl?" my father said, rubbing my head.

I looked at him and for some reason I knew I was safe. That had to be the first time in my life that I felt as though I fit.

"What yo name, Daddy?" I asked carefully.

"James Perry," he said, smiling at me.

I smiled back. We all had *J* names.

TWO

When I awoke the next morning, it was to a very loud house. I was sleeping in the extra bed in Jordan's room. He was jumping on my bed.

"Wake up, wake up! We goin' to Elitche's today! Hurry up and get in the bathroom. Daddy said you get to use the bathroom by yourself." He was bouncing around the room, going through his drawers.

I was a bit stunned. But I knew enough about Elitche's to know it was a place I wanted to go. I had never been to an amusement park before. I slid out of bed and opened one of the suitcases that Jamie had brought up to my room the night before. I found a pair of jean overall shorts and a T-shirt, I collected my underwear and toothbrush, and was promptly directed to the bathroom. I closed the door and locked it. I did my business and was ready in about fifteen minutes. My mother had gotten my hair braided on a regular basis by one of her cousins, and now my fresh cornrows decorated my head in an intricate pattern that grazed my shoulders. I stepped out of the bathroom smelling like Keri lotion and returned my pajamas to my suitcase. Before I could do anything I felt myself being lifted into the air by a strong pair of hands. I was startled when I turned to see who had picked me up. I was surprised to see my big brother Jared.

"You want a piggyback ride downstairs?" he asked me.

I nodded and climbed on. He deposited me in the kitchen and scrambled out the back door to go and wash the car, he said.

I was in the kitchen alone. It was a big kitchen but it was messy. I loaded the dirty dishes in the dishwasher and swept the floor. Then I wiped all the counters and the table. I found some pancake mix and quickly located the eggs and bacon in the refrigerator. I pulled the chair up to the stove as I'd done since I was five and began cooking breakfast. I didn't know how much to cook, so I just cooked it all. My father came into the kitchen as I was expertly removing some bacon from the skillet.

"You know how to cook, baby girl?" he asked me. He seemed a little surprised.

I smiled shyly and nodded. I didn't know why he would be surprised. For as long as I could remember, I'd been cooking for myself when my mama didn't go and buy something. Ma Belle had shown me a lot and I was always careful with the stove.

"You always cook when you with your mama?" he asked.

"Yep . . . I cook all the time. I know how to make lots of stuff," I said proudly. I had just finished the eggs.

"You sure are smart, Jasmyn," he said quietly.

I beamed.

Jordan insisted we eat on the front porch, so we did. We sat on the cement edge of the porch, our legs swinging, faces sticky with syrup. I watched as three cars pulled into the driveway. The first one was a blue minivan, the second a bright red Cadillac, and the third a Volvo station wagon. Three men got out of the driver's seats, all of them looking like copies of my daddy except that they were in three different shades. I watched in interest as females of three varying shades stepped out of the cars, followed by a stampede of children. Some were too small to walk and were being carried. I looked at Jordan in question.

"That's our uncles and our cousins. The light one is Uncle Jordan . . . I'm named after him. He's younger than daddy. The medium-colored one is Uncle Jamieson. That's who Jamie is named after. And the chocolate-chip-colored one is Uncle Lewis. We call him Uncle Lew. He's older than daddy."

"Wow, it sure is a lot of them."

I watched as everyone finally made it to the porch. Jordan had finished his breakfast and so had I. I got glances from all the adults, but they retreated into the house. The older cousins walked into the house as well, but the younger ones stayed outside.

"Who is you?" one of them asked, stepping so close to me that I could smell the cherry Blow-Pop on her breath. I appraised her swiftly. She was a little taller than I and the identical chocolate-chip color as Uncle Lew. Her hair was braided similarly to mine. She held the hand of a little boy who looked just like Jordan, and I thought he had to be about two. He looked at me with the same curiosity.

"Latiana! Get out of her face, that's my new sister," Jordan said, pushing the girl back.

"My name is Jasmyn," I said, trying not to sound intimidated.

"My mama said that you ain't really our kin. She said yo mama a high-yella ho!" Latiana shot back, smirking.

I didn't know what a high-yella ho was, but I knew it wasn't a compliment. Before I knew what I was doing, I reached back and slapped Latiana across her face so hard a few of her beads flew off and all of them clicked against the side of her head. The little boy started to laugh and so did Jordan and the five others who had gathered around. In a few seconds, Latiana and I were rolling around on the ground. I was trying to punch my cousin in the nose when I felt strong arms lift me off her. I was kicking and clawing when I heard my daddy say, "Jasmyn, stop it!"

I ceased immediately, my breath was coming in huge gasps. I looked up and saw that Latiana's daddy had her in a similar restraining hold.

THE ART OF SELFISHNESS

"What happened?" my daddy asked me. I was scared, and I knew that I shouldn't have slapped the girl.

"Did you say something mean, Latiana? Because if you did you're going over to your aunt's house and you can forget Elitche's," Latiana's daddy said gravely. All of the kids on the porch got reverentially silent. Not going to Elitche's was as serious as capital punishment. Tears welled in her eyes. She looked at her shoes.

"We was just playin', Daddy," I said, looking at my shoes.

He looked at me closely, his eyes narrowing. I knew he could tell I was lying. Latiana's head snapped up in amazement; then she looked at her daddy.

"Ya'll better not play-fight anymore, because then somebody gets hurt and it turns serious," Uncle Lew said gravely. We nodded.

"Now ya'll go in there and have your auntie fix your hair," my daddy said, sending us both into the house. Latiana looked at me and smiled shyly. I smiled back.

The aunts were sitting in the kitchen around the table. Two of them were holding babies. Latiana's mother was the one doing most of the talking. She had the same Hershey-toned skin as her husband and children. Her hair was braided, but not like mine; it looked as though she had a million little braids on her head. She had pretty, light brown eyes and the straightest, whitest teeth I'd ever seen in my life. I listened to her voice. It was very melodic and she had an accent that sounded soft and breezy. I later learned from Latiana that she was from Jamaica.

"Now I know that I ain't got no business being judgmental, but we all know her mother was a lil' freak. James just automatically assumed that baby was his. He ain't never had a blood test done to prove it. Then she just go drop her on the doorstep? Please, I tell you what, something ain't right 'bout it."

Latiana and I paused. We knew we were listening to grown-folks' business, but it was *oh so interesting*.

"You know what, Hera? You need to quit. James says it's his, and you know, you haven't even seen the child up close yet. You shouldn't say things like that about her mama, because she might hear you. How you think she's going to feel hearing you talk like that!" A light-skinned woman who sat across from her said this. She held a brown baby on her lap, who was fast asleep.

"All I'm saying, Katie, is that you never know. I just don't want dere to be any drama," Hera returned with less venom.

"There always is some type of drama with the Perry boys. Whether it be good, bad, or just plain wild. That's why ya'll married them," the brown-skinned woman said smoothly, giving both women a look. Her accent was straight out of the South. From Louisiana, I later learned.

"Oh, yeah, and, India, why did you marry one?" Hera asked.

" 'Cause they make pretty babies!" she said, kissing the fat little boy on her lap, who was playing with a plastic key ring.

With that the women erupted in giggles.

"I know that's right!" Hera said, smiling as she noticed us standing in the doorway.

"Good Lord, child, what happened to ya beads?" she asked Latiana.

"We was wrestlin'. . . ." Latiana began sheepishly.

"Go get my purse from the living room," her mother muttered.

Latiana scampered off. I stood for inspection as the women quietly appraised me.

"Well, she look just like her daddy! And she look just like your Langston, Hera!" the brown-skinned woman proclaimed, giving me a huge smile.

Hera's mouth dropped open in surprise, then quickly closed. She was obviously miffed.

"I guess we don't need no test after all," the lighter one named Katie said with a wink.

"Well, child, I'm your Auntie Hera." She gestured for me to come near, and she began repairing the damage to my braids. Latiana had returned with the purse, and her mother pulled out a little plastic bag of beads. She slipped them onto my braids.

"I'm your Auntie Katie, and this lil' man right here is Kamden," she said and smiled warmly.

"I'm your Auntie India, and this is Benjamin." She smiled.

That was my first introduction to my aunts. They never spoke of my mother again, and they treated me as their own. I later learned that the house we lived in used to be my grandmother's. She had died a year before I got there. She had been a very determined woman. According to my daddy she had owned three prosperous hair salons in the Denver area, one of which was in Cherry Creek. All three of my aunts had come to work in the salon or had been clients, and that's how they'd met my uncles. To this day I wish I could have met her. Jordan always said she was amazing.

There is something about amusement parks and children that's just extra special. I don't know. Now when my friends and I go to amusement parks I have to prepare myself for the long wait in line and the expensive admission fee. It's fun, yes, but it's something you have to prepare yourself for.

That Sunday I went with my family I can't seem to remember anything except waiting anxiously in the car and playing the "that's my car" game with my cousin Jordan as I rode with Latiana and her little brother, Langston. We were so anxious we almost killed ourselves getting out of the car. Beautiful memories are locked in my heart of how dizzy I got when Jordan and I rode the Spider. Or how Jayson won me three stuffed animals playing carnival games. I remember eating pizza and funnel cake and ice cream until I thought I would burst. I remember sitting on my daddy's shoulder while he navigated the huge crowd of people looking for my older brothers. I remember sitting on the carousel and laughing when Jordan and Jaleel tried to switch horses even though the attendant told them not to. I remember standing on the bridge that was over the ride Amazon Falls and getting drenched as a boat full of people plunged into the water below. I remember my girl cousins spending that night with me and all of us playing hide-and-seek with Jordan and the boy cousins until we got so tired we fell asleep in front of the television in the family room watching cartoons. I remember going to picnics and movies. I remember falling asleep in my cousins' basement while the grown folks played bid whist late into the night listening to Parliament and Al Green.

For the first time in my life I was a child. A real child. Not only did I have six brothers, I had aunts and uncles and so many cousins I forgot their names when I first met them. I learned things about my family too. My father was an accountant, and both of my older brothers were in college and only lived with the rest of us during the summer.

Jordan became my best friend. We continued to share a room through the summer and rarely fell asleep until one or two in the morning. He had a flashlight, which he hid under his underwear in his drawer. Why he hid it I really don't know, but he did. I bought my own flashlight at the dollar store that was around the corner from our house, and Jordan and I would signal through the window to the kids that lived in back of our house.

My daddy gave all of us an allowance every week if we did our chores. Jordan had to attempt to keep his room clean. I actually had to do less than what I'd done while living with my mother. I had to clean the kitchen twice a week and the bathroom. Sometimes I cooked but my daddy told me I was only to cook when I wanted to.

So I suppose one would say I had settled into a normal life. I never questioned the absence of a woman in the house. I knew my daddy had been married to my brother's mother for a long time and that she had died. My daddy never really talked bad about my mother, and two weeks after I'd been there a box containing all of my toys and the remainder of my clothing arrived at the house. I knew then that my stay there would be permanent.

Three

The first eight years of my life faded into the background of my existence with such subtlety and with so much ease that many times the only time I thought about it was if I dreamed. Yes, I dreamed of Matthew and what he'd done to me. I dreamed of my mother and Ma Belle mostly. I dreamed of my mother so much I used to look forward to going to bed at night, because that would be the time I'd get to visit her. No judge on earth could have granted the type of visitation I had with Renai Marie DeWitt. Every time I saw her in my dreams she was so different than the reality that I began to realize that the person I dreamed of at night wasn't really my mother, but the mother I wanted.

Every dream would always end the same way though. She'd leave me. At first I would wake up crying. Silently, careful not to disrupt the gentle snoring of my little brown partner in crime in the next bed. They all seemed so happy and I didn't want to change that with my tears. After a few tears though I'd realize I could always wait to dream about her the next night. So as long as I could dream about her . . . it didn't matter.

School started for us and I was surprised to see how the atmosphere in our house changed. No more staying up late at night watching cartoons, or playing hide-and-seek in the backyard. No more sleep-overs with my girl cousins, and no more eating at McDonald's and Pizza Hut on a regular basis. There were no more trips to the amusement park and movies every week. James Perry was all business when it came to school. First of all, we had to go to bed at 9:30. No if, ands, or buts. Jordan and I didn't play anymore, due to the fact that my father would be right in the room telling us to go to sleep. I noticed my daddy never used a belt when we were bad. All it took was a *look*. Secondly, when we got home from school we had to do homework. No waiting. He said it was better to get it out of the way and completed while it was fresh in our minds. So we all would find a spot at the kitchen table or on the floor in the family room to complete our work. For the first time in my life an adult created structure. I liked it, and I knew that my father loved me just as dearly as he did the boys.

My story is a nice one isn't it? I guess this is the part in the movie where everyone sighs and says, "Awww." I made it through grade school and middle school without any problems. Of course with older brothers and the endless number of cousins I had, school went smoothly. We stuck together and no one really messed with me. I was still quiet. I think that is just a feature of my personality, though I can't help wondering, if the first eight years of my time on this earth had started in the house of James Perry instead of my mother's, would I still be as quiet? It's one of those things in life I will never know.

All of the love and nurturing I received in my daddy's house couldn't have prepared me for my first meeting with Anthony Jacob Michaels. I was in my junior year of high school, and though Jordan still lived at home he went to college. He was transferring to a college out of state for his sophomore year, and I think the only reason he went to a local college was that he didn't want to leave me by myself completely. My daddy was proud and by this time he was a grandfather. My older brothers had been married and I had four nephews but no nieces. I still had my cousins, who were the same age as I and attended the same school with me.

By my junior year I was somewhat popular by association. I hadn't fallen in love yet though. I'd been on a couple of dates and had a couple of boyfriends, none that lasted over a month, and I didn't really give love much mind. I was determined to go to college and be an accountant like my dad. Jordan wanted to be an engineer like my older brother Jayson. Jamieson was studying law. Jared was a lawyer. My oldest brother, then twenty-seven, was completing his residency and was a doctor.

As I said before, my father was proud. I'd never put too much thought into guys, because my father and all of my brothers had basically laid out for me the thinking pattern of the male species at my age.

"They all after the nana, Jasmyn . . . don't forget that. No matter how nice they are," Jonathan had told me one night at a barbecue. I had nodded, wondering what his other doctor friends would think about him using the word *nana*.

"They don't care about anything but knocking the boots." That had been Jared. I raised my eyebrow at the old school term "knocking the boots," but he was as serious as a heart attack as he warned me about this when he'd come over to visit us from school one year.

I got numerous warnings from all the males in my family, including Jordan, who knew everything about me anyway. When I turned fifteen my Aunt India showed up at the house and disappeared into my father's study for an hour and a half. The next day she took me to the doctor's office and I left with a prescription for birth control pills.

"Now, honey, this ain't nuthin' but a precaution, all right? I know you ain't out there yet, but I know what they do in high school nowadays . . . Shoot, I know what *I* did in high school. Take these religiously," she said with a smile as she pulled into Chilli's parking lot for lunch.

Needless to say, at seventeen, almost eighteen, I was a virgin in high school. It didn't bother me what other people thought, because I figured it was none of their business anyway. That's what my dad had told me. "Don't mind what people say about sex. Women who have class don't discuss their sex life with anyone," was how he'd put it to me. I'd used that line a time or two with some girls who thought I should be giving it up by now.

So you'd think with all this preparation by my family that meeting Anthony Jacob Michaels wouldn't affect me the way it did. Life is funny like that. I changed schools in my senior year. My father bought a bigger house, in the Westminster area, for reasons unknown to me since almost all of my brothers had moved out. The house we lived in was huge and took me out of the school district I'd gone to since I was eight. My cousin Latiana was the only one that attended the school I went to and she had just graduated the previous year. She'd gotten a scholarship to Howard. It was a little hard for me starting at a new school and not being able to graduate with my cousins.

I learned two very important things about St. Matthew's High School. First of all, basketball was life. Second, there were two star basketball players at the school who were rumored to be going pro right after they graduated. They were slated as first and second in first-round draft picks, something that had never happened in the history of the school until that time. The school had an air about it. It was a very nice high school, and never let it be said that I didn't get a quality education. The parking lot was filled with SUVs, sports cars, and your occasional used Mercedes or Lexus. Students had pagers attached to their hips and cell phones to their ears even though the rules forbade them. FILA sponsored the basketball team's jerseys and shoes all because Anthony Michaels, who was said to be going number one in the draft. My brothers even knew who Anthony was! I wasn't really a basketball person though, so I wasn't too aware of who he was. I'd seen him a couple of times, but my focus was that of every other senior . . . graduation. Then I met him.

I was standing in line in the cafeteria of our school, being inconspicuous since I was new. I was as hungry as a hostage waiting to get a slice of pizza and a milkshake. Well, here came Anthony and three of his friends.

"Hey, love, can I please get in front of you?" he said, stepping in front of me and leaving me little to no choice.

Honestly, I felt that old elementary school rage well up in

me, you know, that uncontrollable urge to pop somebody in the back of the head so hard they forget where they are, for even thinking of cutting (everyone has felt it). I should have told him to take his black butt right to the back of the seventy-five-person line along with his stupid friends. But for some reason I didn't. First of all, I am a nonconfrontational person. I always have been. Second, Anthony Jordan Michaels was the most popular person in our school. I'd already figured that out. He was treated like the Second Coming because of his skills on the basketball court. He could have made it very hard for me at that school. So I just nodded, and watched as he and three of his friends got their food before I did. The girl behind looked as if she was about to take off her expensive Nine-West boot and knock the taste out of my mouth, so I just stared at my shoes.

"Hey, shorty, let me borrow two dolla's," came a familiar voice in front of me.

I stopped examining my shoes long enough to realize Anthony Jacob Michaels was talking to me again.

"I only have three," I said carefully.

"Come on now, I'll hit you back, I haven't eaten all day. Please. I only have my credit card," he said pleadingly.

Neither have I, I thought to myself.

But I was holding up the line, and Ms. Thang behind me looked as if she was about to turn Shaft on my butt if I kept her from her lunch a second longer. Taking a deep breath I kissed my pizza good-bye and handed him two one-dollar bills.

"Thanks, boo, what's your name?" he asked grabbing his food.

"Jasmyn," I said, paying for my milkshake and wishing I had some food to eat.

"Straight. Good looking out Jasmyn," he muttered as he caught up to his loud friends.

"You are dumber than a Mike Tyson interview," came Ms. Thang's voice behind me.

I turned around and looked at her. She was one of the prettiest girls I'd ever seen. She was at least five-ten (six feet, to be exact), she had this crazy hair that was natural and ebony black, and she had the most startling green eyes that were a deep contrast against her chocolate skin. I knew she had to be a model. I simply shrugged. I really didn't feel like having my cowardice thrown in my face. I couldn't quite comprehend why I had given him my money.

"I bet you're hungry too. You goin' to let that wanna-be Michael Jordan take your lunch money?" she said, sucking her teeth and rolling her eyes.

Without another word she grabbed a slice of pizza and a salad and paid for it and my milkshake.

"Come on, let's find a seat," she said, rolling her eyes.

I followed her, dazed. Why was she being so nice to me?

"I'm Chayenne Janine Martin. I just moved here, and I'm rich, so don't worry about paying me back," she said, handing me the pizza and digging into her salad.

Chayenne and I have been tight ever since.

I couldn't get him off my mind. Later that night after I'd given Anthony my money and let him cut in line I dreamed about him. To this day I will always remember that dream. We were standing in the cafeteria, and he was talking to me. I couldn't hear his voice, but I could feel his words. I didn't know what he was saying to me, and it didn't matter. I was just studying him. He was tall. Very tall. Taller than my brothers. Six feet six. He had this smooth skin. Reminded me of Ma Belle's and it seemed to flow over his high cheekbones and full lips with the consistency of milk. He wore his hair closely faded and had the most beautiful smile I'd ever seen. In my dream all I did was look at him. I woke up sweating . . . and smiling. I knew then that I was going to experience my first love . . . or obsession . . . whichever way you want to look at it.

Four

Anthony, I soon learned, wasn't just the star basketball player. He was amazing. His nickname was "Prodigy" for a reason. You could tell when he played that it was as much mental as it was physical. He didn't showboat all the time either. People said he passed like Magic Johnson. As the season began, there was no doubt that he was going to the NBA. It was only a question of when. It was rumored that NBA scouts were talking to him already. I really didn't put much credence in this since it was a rumor.

The next time we met was in the library at school. It was study hall and I was completing the research on some boring paper I had for English. I was sitting at my favorite table at the back of the library. I hadn't had an encounter with Anthony for two weeks and I was beginning to focus on other things. I looked up as someone sat down at my table. There he was in all his ebony glory. He had a stack of books in his hands that he unceremoniously unloaded on the table.

"Hey, shorty, what's poppin'? Jacqueline, right?" he murmured, sitting next to me.

I looked at him thoughtfully. I had to wonder about the butterflies that automatically just appeared in my stomach.

"Hmmm, think you have me confused with someone else," I said nonchalantly, looking down at my books.

"Nah . . . you the shorty that let me cut and lent me money, right? I remember you," he returned.

"Yeah, that would be me. Do you have my money?" I smiled back

"Uhh, nah, but, umm, I was wondering if you wanted to hit up this party with me after the game tonight," he said, smiling at me.

"Nah, that's cool . . . I have plans."

I knew I didn't have definite plans but I wasn't about to let it go that easily. I had to play a little hard to get. Besides, Anthony was with a different female every week. I wasn't about to be added to the list.

"Oh, you have a man? It's cool, my bad," he murmured, backing down.

"Tell you what, Mr. Prodigy, you find me after the game, and I'll go with you. My girl Chayenne and I," I returned, using the nickname everyone in school gave him.

He looked at me a moment, and for a second I thought he was going to tell me never mind. He didn't, he said, "You straight, Jacqueline . . . you straight."

I smiled at him as I gathered my books and stuffed them in my red Jansport.

"My name is Jasmyn." And with that statement I sauntered off, switching my hips, knowing he was watching me.

I had to practically threaten bodily harm to Chayenne to get her to accompany me to the party.

"Why do you want to go to this stupid party? Anthony just wants to get some anyway! If you go give it up you don't have to do it at the party. Make him get a hotel and . . ." Chayenne argued as we slipped into her Lexus after the game.

"You're crazy! I'm not given anything up! It's just a party! Please, Chayenne, girl, you know I can't roll by myself!"

"A'ight," she relented.

We went to the party, and Anthony was with me all night. He didn't drink and he didn't pressure me to. It was cool, really, and Chayenne danced a little bit, so she was satisfied it wasn't a waste of an evening. Anthony decided that he wanted to take me on a real date. I turned him down. I told him he could come over and chill out to meet my family if he liked.

I was a nervous wreck. It was a Friday night and my father was staying home just for the purpose of meeting Anthony. Jordan was a little suspicious because they'd never seen me act that way about a guy. Chayenne came over to help me prepare.

"I don't know why you're working yourself into a tizzy, Jasmyn. Anthony is a playa. Pure and simple. You're better than that," Chayenne scolded as she went through my closet to find me something to wear. She still didn't like Anthony, due to the fact that he still hadn't given me my two dollars back.

I rolled my eyes and continued painting my toes.

"Girl . . . he was cool at the party, and he was the perfect gentlemen. Why shouldn't I spend a little quality social time with him? Ain't like I'm marrying him."

Chayenne stepped out of my closet with a pair of blue jeans and a white wife beater. She wore her hair in Afro puffs and was rocking a long festive purple skirt and a stylish black top that was somewhat reminiscent of a Gypsy. She looked exotic as usual.

"Don't try to fake the funk . . . I can tell you like him. I'm not going to hate. Maybe he likes you too. Just be careful, Jazz, ya know?" She was going through my top drawer looking for something.

"I'll be fine." I really believed that too. I had butterflies fighting a battle in my stomach though.

Five

Anthony came over after practice. I had changed into the outfit Chayenne had personally approved. I was in the kitchen making the dinner that I knew was going to blow him away. I heard my father answer the door.

A few minutes later Anthony appeared in the doorway of the kitchen. He was smiling.

"I didn't know you could burn, girl!" he exclaimed, taking a seat at the table.

"There's a lot of stuff you don't know about me," I returned coyly. I'd already figured out Anthony got bored really quickly when it came to females. I kept up the games with him to keep him on his toes. I knew that eventually he'd be caught though.

My father came in and gave me a hug, told me he was going to step out for a little while and head over to my uncle's house to play cards. I gave him a kiss on the cheek and tried to gauge his reaction to Anthony. My father is very good at masking his feelings. I knew he would give me his opinion sooner or later.

After Anthony had finished devouring the dinner of collard greens, candied yams, homemade biscuits, and golden fried chicken, we sat on the floor in the family room to talk. I pulled out some huge throw pillows and turned the lights off. I got a little nervous so I kept my distance. He didn't seem to want to do anything but talk though.

"I wish my mama cooked like you, Jasmyn," he began. He was lying on his back looking at the ceiling.

"Your mama doesn't cook?"

"Nah, she into clothes and stuff. She says that when I go pro I can hire her a cook that will do all the cooking."

I didn't want to bring it up but the rumors at my school were running rampant. I had to know if it was true what everyone was saying about him going straight to the pros from high school, so I asked, "So you think you're going to the pros?"

"Girl, if you only knew. I want to go to college. But then I figure, what can college give me but an education to fall back on if I get injured? I could live off my signing bonus alone, and go to school if something happens. It's so much drama, Jasmyn," he murmured more to himself than to me. I could tell he was torn, and I felt sympathy for him. I didn't say anything for a moment. We just sat there in silence. Me lounging back on my pillow, not quite as relaxed as he was, and him lying on his back staring at the ceiling. I couldn't see his eyes because I had turned off the lights. We were just lying there in the dark.

I scooted closer to him. I stared down at him. His eyes were closed. I studied the intricate shadows that now made up his features in the dark. I don't know what motivated me to do it, but I reached down and caressed the corner of his eye. A warm tear greeted me. Then without warning it turned into a steady stream. I leaned down and gingerly tasted the saltiness of his sorrow. Tears are funny things. They ease out of us like liquid pain, and allow us a little relief if we are fortunate. Sometimes shedding tears is too little too late. I thought about the tears I had cried years before when Matthew was spanking me for peeing in the bed. I thought about the tears I cried when I watched my mother pull her car away from my father's house, abandoning me on a doorstep.

He turned toward my warm mouth. He faced me. I wrapped my arms around his body. He smelled like male deodorant and a touch of sweat. I had smelled it so many times before on my brothers. I held him as if he were my baby. As I wished my mother would have held me so many times before when I would sneak into bed with her in the middle of the night. I held him the way my brothers and my father had done all my years growing up. He began to cry in earnest then. Tears shaking his body.

"I just love to play, Jasmyn. I just want to play. Ever since I was little that's all I wanted. I don't care if I play for college or NBA . . . or just wit' my boys . . . I just want to play. My mama says that I better sign with a team if they offer it. She's raised me. I haven't seen my father since I was two. I think he's locked up. I feel like I owe her, but I want to go to school too. I want to be an architect. I've always wanted to . . ." he gushed. He pressed his head into my chest. I rubbed his back.

"I don't know what to do anymore. I feel like just offin' myself sometimes," he said, his voice hauntingly low.

"Anthony . . . what do you want?" I asked, my voice so quiet I didn't see how he heard me.

"I want to play . . . that's it. I want to go to school. I want the money too. I want it all," he said.

"You'll play if you go to the pros and you'll play if you go to school. Don't worry about the NBA. If they want you now, they'll want you later. Don't give up everything you've worked for because of your mother. She'll always be your mother. You're not trying to hurt her," I murmured, wishing I could tell him I knew because of experience. My own mother didn't want me.

"So much pressure. I mean, do you know how many females have been trying to get with me? I had a couple dudes try to hook up with me too. I couldn't believe it. Everybody hears about money and they start doing the craziest things. I just need somewhere I can forget about it all." His voice was mildly amused. His tears were no longer flowing. I kissed the top of his head and he tightened his hold on me. We were like the only people on earth. Safe in my daddy's family room cuddled on throw pillows.

"I need you," came his whisper.

"I know," I returned. That was the beginning and the end.

Six

I never told anyone about that night with Anthony. After we'd spoken those words to each other, it was as if everything was cemented. No other words were needed. No game to be kicked, no phone tag, no flirting. We were together. He needed me. I knew that, and I would never leave him alone.

"So how did your evening go?" Chayenne asked me later that night after he'd left. I'd slipped into my pajamas and gotten into bed. She was trying to sound nonchalant but I knew she was champing at the bit to find out what happened.

"It was fabulous," I said simply.

"You didn't give him any, did you?" she asked incredulously.

"Of course not . . . you think I'm crazy!"

"Just making sure. You have that smug tone in your voice like you have a secret or something," she clarified.

"Nah, all we did was talk and chill. We're going to the movies tomorrow night." I smiled.

"Oh, my goodness, my girl has fallen for a jock. You know it's gonna be some major drama. All of those skoochies at the school are gonna be muggin'. Then his boys are gonna be muggin'. Imma have to put on my ho-stompin' boots and

regulate. Because I know you are just too nonconfrontational for words."

I could hear her getting riled up as usual. I couldn't help
laughing. But I knew she had a point. How much drama
would Anthony and me being together cause?

I got my answer a week later in PE. Our PE class was run
by Mrs. Wrigley. When I first met her I thought gym would
be a breeze. Mrs. Wrigley was about five-one and weighed
about 115 pounds. She was as old as dirt. She wore khaki
shorts in assorted pastel colors with little matching polo
shirts. She had to be at least sixty. How hard could a senior
citizen make gym class? She always carried a clipboard and
a whistle.

Along with 90 percent of our class, I underestimated her.
She could run laps with the best of the male gym teachers
and she showed no mercy. I absolutely loathed gym but I
needed the credit to graduate. It was torture at its best.

Every Monday, Wednesday, and Friday we had to do circuit training in addition to our normal schedule. We had
partners whom we used every week. My partner was Sherina
Davies. Sherina was a pretty, butterscotch-colored girl with
long silky hair that could only be rivaled by my mother's and
a booty that made a Hype Williams video extra look lacking.
Sherina was dating Marcus Wells, one of Anthony's best
friends. If everything went the way people were saying, he
would be the number-two-draft pick.

"So, you and Anthony kickin' it now, huh?" she asked
while I labored my way through seventy-five sit-ups. She
held my feet down.

"We're talking," I said, hoping she wasn't losing count.

"Oh, word. Anthony told Marcus he's been feeling you,"
she said her light hazel eyes twinkling.

I kept my expression bland. It wasn't very difficult since I
felt that I was about to pass out due to the sit-ups. Anthony
had told me he didn't want everybody to know we were together. He knew how things got started at the school. He
said everybody would figure it out for himself or herself.

"I like him too," I said nonchalantly.

"Just for your info, me and Anthony got busy a couple of times. Before I was with Marcus. He doesn't care nothing about anything but basketball. He may act all cool now, but he'll have changed flavors within a month." She smiled maliciously.

"He hasn't tasted any of this flavor, so I'm not worried about it," I said smugly. If she thought her little revelation was going to make me run to Anthony and demand an explanation, she was crazy. I knew he'd slept with tons of girls. It came with the territory. He hadn't gotten any from me though, and I had made a determination that it would be a long time before *that* even became an issue.

She shrugged and continued counting my sit-ups.

That night with my phone tucked under one ear and my other ear kissing my pillow I spoke with Anthony. He called me every night before he went to bed. We usually didn't talk about anything in particular. I just listened to him go on and on about practice and his coach, his mother, whatever was on his mind.

"You mad at me, boo?" he asked after a few seconds of silence.

"No, why?" I said, surprised.

" 'Cause Marcus said that his girl told him you were pissed off at me. Something about me cheating on you or you thinking I was talking to somebody else."

"Huh?" I was in shock now. That was a complete lie. I really didn't know what to say. I mean, I felt I would be keeping stuff going if I told him about what Sherina had told me in gym. Then I felt I would be saying it was true if I didn't bring it up.

"It's cool. She must have been thinking about something else. So we're together now, huh? Not just talking?" I decided to switch the direction of the conversation.

"No doubt. I mean, Jasmyn, right now I feel like you're the only one in my corner. You ain't asked me for anything. You listen. You definitely my lady. I'll tell anyone who asks, too. I ain't gonna be all on the low about it anymore," he said seriously.

I smiled. Jasmyn Renai Perry had a man.

Seven

I guess I started acting a little differently. My daddy didn't notice too much. He'd met Anthony and he liked him. My daddy had started dating again. He was seeing some woman who was an attorney. I had met her once before and she seemed pretty nice. I think he was living a little since there was practically no one left at home. I couldn't hide my being in love from Jordan though. He and I share everything, and he was a little more wary when it came to Anthony.

One Saturday he took me out to lunch at Chilli's. That was our spot. They had the best food ever. He and I had been going there since we had our own money.

We sat in a booth. I had my hair back in a bun and was wearing a blue Nike sweat suit. He had on a matching gray one. I don't think we matched on purpose, that was just the way it ended up. I studied him for a moment. I couldn't help my memory from slipping back to the first day I'd met him. Those huge, serious chocolate eyes, so much like mine, and that smile that lit up his face like a spotlight. Now he just looked handsome.

Skin that was so smooth and taut it looked as though it had been created by some fine sculptor who used genetics as his medium, and those eyes that had captivated me with their similarity to my own years ago were now those of a full-grown man. Jordan had tons of girlfriends. He just wasn't ready to settle down. I wondered who would be the lucky woman who would somehow capture his heart. I wondered if he could tell I was in love already.

"So, you feelin' Anthony, huh?" Jordan mumbled as he devoured a mozzarella stick. We always started with that appetizer.

"Yes. It's weird, Jordan. It's like he's the only guy I really have felt. You know? I mean I've had my crushes, but this is so much more," I heard myself say. I really hadn't shared how deeply my feelings for Anthony ran. I was still trying to figure out why they ran so deep.

"I guess my baby sis has fallen in love. I don't know about him though. I've seen him play ball. He's nasty on the court. I know that fool is going to go pro. I just hope he don't hurt you."

I grabbed a mozzarella stick and dipped it into the marinara sauce in front of me.

"His feelings for me are just as deep," I said seriously.

Jordan knew when to back off a subject with me. So he did. We were silent for a moment. I watched him study one of the pretty waitresses that had walked by our table for the fourth time. Some females are so obvious.

"Jordan . . . you ever been in love?" I couldn't keep myself from asking.

"Nah . . . never have. I mean I've been real attracted to some females, but not like love. I guess I'm not ready yet. I mean I think it has something to do with my mom." He had this thoughtful look on his face, and for some reason his eyes couldn't hold mine. I took a deep breath. I had never heard him talk about his mother. I'd seen a picture of her one time. He had it in a shoe box under his bed. She was pretty. Not beautiful like my mother, but definitely pretty. Her genes had somehow dominated a little in my older brothers. Jordan, like the rest of us, was just a carbon copy of my daddy.

"Why do you think it has something to do with your mom?"

"They say the first woman in your life is your mom, and that's how you learn about relationships with women and stuff. I never knew my mom. She died having me. I think maybe I don't know how to get close with women, because the closet ones to me, other than you, are like our aunts and grandmother?" He was playing with the skinny white paper that had come with his straw. I felt a lump in my throat form, he looked so sad.

"What all do you know about your mama?" I probed.

"A'ight. I guess it's time that I run you down the whole story of Daddy and my mom. Nobody else will tell you. Daddy might if you catch him on a good day, but I doubt it." He leaned back and stretched. I braced myself for a long story.

"Daddy is all proper and stuff. But everybody got their nasty drawers in the back of the closet, you know? Daddy and our uncles liked to go into strip clubs. That's where he met my mama. She was like fifteen, dancing for cash. Daddy was like eighteen about to be nineteen. They hooked up that night, and she turned up at Grammy's door two months later pregnant with Jonathan. You know Grammy had mad money because of her businesses or whatever, and she felt like she couldn't turn her away. Daddy married her. And it seemed like after that she kept having babies. She was faithful to Daddy. But he left her to go to college. He'd come back and visit on the holidays, but Jonathan and them stayed at home at Grammy's.

"Jasmyn, Grammy told me my mother could barely read. She wanted to go to school so much but Daddy wouldn't let her. He wanted her to raise the kids. Grammy said she wasn't that happy. By the time Daddy got out of school and they moved out of Grammy's house, my mother was depressed.

"There were complications when she had me, and she died before she even got to see me. I never knew her. We moved back with Grammy after that, and Daddy started working a lot. He would travel a lot. I think that's how he met your mom. I just never was that close to a woman except for Grammy. It's like I don't need to be. And after Grammy died, then that was it. Then, I look at Jonathan and Jaleel and see what they have with their ladies, and I wish that I could be that happy." He finished his story with his eyes. Sadness.

"Jordan, love will come, trust me. I mean your mama died, but she wanted you and your brothers. My mama never wanted me in the first place. I don't know which is worse." I returned.

"We sound like an Oprah special, you know that?" he said after a moment of silence.

"I know." I laughed.

The conversation changed instantly, and we went back to goofing off the way we normally did when we spent time together.

That night after I had hung up the phone with Anthony, and right before I slid into a contented sleep, I realized something. That was the first time I'd spoken about my mother since I'd come to live with my brothers and my daddy.

Eight

Your first fight with the man you love is always something you remember. Anthony and I had been going strong for two months. I was at the height of popularity at my school. Which really didn't faze me. The only person I chilled with was Chayenne, because I knew she was the only genuine person in the school. I had changed though.

Anthony had convinced me to get rid of the braids I had taken to wearing and wear my hair straight. He paid for me to have it done every week. I loved my braids, and my hair really didn't do well with a press, but I endured it because he wanted a girl that had that "good hair." Anthony also convinced me to dress a little bit more provocatively.

"Baby, you should wear your stomach out a little more. It's sexy," he told me one afternoon when he picked me up for a date. He bought me clothes that I personally would never have chosen to wear. Some of the outfits I wore to games and on dates were flat-out hoochie, but that's how my man liked it.

"Anthony, where are you getting the money for all this mess?" I said one day when he picked me up at the nail shop. He'd spent over five hundred dollars on me that weekend, counting the restaurants, movies, hair, nails, and cloth-ing.

"Don't worry about that, baby, when I go pro you won't ever have to worry about anything," he said, giving me a kiss. I knew the subject was closed for discussion and I never really asked him again about his money.

Chayenne didn't say anything. She was diplomatically keeping her mouth shut. At least that's what she told me, but her expressions spoke for themselves. Chayenne always had an opinion about fashion. My daddy didn't really notice, be-cause all of my girl cousins dressed a little more provoca-tively, so I think he figured it was normal. As long as my grades were good he didn't care. Jordan was immersed in his schoolwork and only gave me the occasional reprimand for my change in attire.

We didn't fight about the clothes though. That would have been way too simple. We fought about another man.

Going to the mall as a couple was something I was new at. I rarely went at all, only if Chayenne dragged me there, really. Anthony loved to go. He and his friends always made a weekly appearance on Saturdays and he wanted me to come with him. I finally gave in.

I wore a pair of skintight black flared-leg pants that made my booty look out of this world and a skintight shirt that stopped right above my belly button. It was a cute outfit but it wasn't me. It was a part of the "hoochie wear" Anthony wanted me to wear.

We held hands and made our way around the food court to his favorite store, Babbage's. I like electronic things, but I couldn't spend two hours immersed in a conversation about a video game the way Anthony could. After about twenty minutes I became bored. I started glancing at different things in the store, leaving him and the salesperson to dis-cuss their video game. Dressed as I was, I wasn't surprised when a man came up to me and tried to flirt.

The brutha was cute, no doubt about that. Six-one, hazel eyes, and skin the color of Ma Belle's lemon pound cake. He smiled at me.

THE ART OF SELFISHNESS 279

"You look nice in those pants, ma," he said, flashing a smile that showed his player status. The boy even had dimples.

I couldn't help smiling back. That's a natural reaction when a handsome member of the opposite sex smiles at you.

"Yeah, my boyfriend thinks so too," I returned.

"Oh . . . my bad, I should have known a fine woman like you was taken," he said, letting his expression imitate regret. I knew if I gave him any type of reason to believe I was anything less than 100 percent faithful to my man, he would be on me like a pit bull on a piece of meat.

"Thanks for the compliment though," I said, flashing him a smile of my own. I turned to find Anthony, and he was right there. He had this look on his face that I'd never seen before and I really didn't know what to say to him.

"Let's go," he said gravely.

"Okay," I murmured, trying to smile. I was shocked when his iron grip enclosed itself around my wrist. That made me angry and I tried to yank my wrist away. I was unable to loosen my wrist from his grip and I almost tripped as he yanked me out of the store like some naughty child. The cute guy just watched. He looked as if he was about to say something, but I glanced back at him and shook my head.

We got into the car, and Anthony didn't say anything to me. I rubbed my wrists and decided to wait until we got to my house to bring up his scene in the mall. He was silent. His jaw was tight with tension. I took deep breaths and just stared out the window. I was seething. I wasn't used to being manhandled. My own brothers didn't grab me like that. In addition to that I was humiliated. He had dragged me through the mall and parking lot like some three-year-old.

No one was home at my house. I walked into the living room first. I jumped as he slammed the door. The next thing I knew I felt the back of his hand across my cheek. It felt as though the side of my face had exploded. I reeled back and fell to the floor, grabbing the side of my face. Before I could react to being knocked senseless he had dragged me to my feet and wound his hands in my hair. I lashed out with my knee but he deflected my blow and took a knee in the hip. His breathing was labored. He pulled my face so close to his, it was as if I could feel the heat of his anger pulsing under his skin like lava under the surface of the ground right before a volcano erupts.

"Let me catch you talkin' to some dude when I'm standing right there again. I will knock your teeth down your throat. Do you hear me?" he screamed into my face.

I flinched. I was very still. I was afraid, but more than that, I was frozen in shock. How could the man I loved be like this?

"I told him I had a man. He tried to talk to me. Girls try to talk to you all the time, and it's not an issue," I said, my voice trembling. He still had his hand in my hair.

"I'm going to be in the NBA. Hoe's come with the territory. You are my lady. And the way you were flaunting it all in his face I'm not surprised he was trying to spit game," he shot back, pulling on my hair.

I winced.

"Flaunting! Look, if you don't want me to be just one of your hoe's stop trying to make me dress like them. I hate the stuff you like me to wear. It's tacky and it's not me. How you go yell at me about flaunting myself and you make me dress like a hoochie in a cheap rap video?" I returned.

"You dress for me. I mean it ain't like you're giving me anything else. It's cool though. Don't let it happen again, Jasmyn," he said, shoving me away from him and releasing my hair. I fell to the floor again. Tears began falling down my cheeks in two streams that I knew would be only the beginning of tears I would cry for Anthony.

He slammed out of my house. I went to my room, after I got some ice for my face. If it still showed by the time my daddy got home I could always cover it up with makeup.

So that's how it began.

He tried to call me later that night. I wouldn't take his phone call. At school that Monday I ignored him and avoided him. My face didn't bruise all that much and I decide not to tell anyone about what happened. It just got added to the list of things people have done to hurt me that I kept locked in some dark room inside me.

Finally, Wednesday afternoon after school, Anthony approached me. He was looking fine as ever in crisp, ironed jeans and an FILA T-shirt. I glanced at him carefully as he approached my locker. I tried to convince myself that I wasn't scared of him, but when someone flips on you the way he'd done you have no choice but to be a little scared.

"Jasmyn, we need to talk," he said, his voice low and smooth.

"About what?" I said, trying to force coldness into my voice. I began loading books into my locker. I didn't want to look him in the eye.

"About what happened at the mall. Baby, I'm sorry. I was out of line. It's just that when I see other dudes looking at you like that, it drive me crazy. I know what they want and I just don't know what I would do if you left me." The painful resonance in his voice seemed to force my eyes to his. He looked sad and regretful.

"That's not an excuse for hitting me, Anthony. It was no big deal. A guy tried to talk to me, and I told him I had a boyfriend, end of story. Think about it. If I was really trying to play you, would I do it right in front of your face? I've never been like that. I'm not like the other scandalous females at this school. I would never cheat on you." I sighed.

"I know I was out of line for hitting you. I've been talking to my coach about ways I can handle my anger. I have a really bad temper and sometimes I just snap. I know I was way out of line, baby. I just need to know that you forgive me. I mean I know that you may not want me to be your man anymore, but at least say you forgive me for acting like that. I should respect you as a woman. What I did wasn't respectful at all and I know that."

"I forgive you."

When I heard my voice say those words it was as if I were dreaming. Every part of me screamed that what he had done was unforgivable, and he didn't deserve a second chance. But I knew that my forgiveness held in it the hope of reconciliation, and he knew that as well. I watched him breathe a sigh of relief.

"Does this mean that we can try to make this work again?" Anthony asked me after a pause.

"Yes," I murmured.

He pulled me into his arms for a huge hug that made it apparent to anyone passing by that we were together.

Nine

It seemed that the longer Anthony and I stayed together, the more drama seemed to erupt in my life. PE class became more of a chore because my good ole partner, Sherina Davies, had decided to hate me. Her prediction about Anthony and me had not come true, and it obviously bothered her.

It was an enigma to me why she was so upset that we were still together. I knew *she* didn't want Anthony. Rumor had it that she was hopelessly in love with Marcus, her boyfriend. He was hopelessly in love with her as well. All of Sherina's friends dated athletes. It was a prerequisite to be considered part of their clique. They ran the school like a group of seasoned divas. They infiltrated every part of every student organization, focusing their monopoly on the cheerleading squad and drill team, as well as student government. I simply ignored them and continued to focus on school. I was determined to get a scholarship to go to a good school. I already knew I wanted to be a CPA like my daddy. Sherina had backed off since the little incident in PE when she blatantly lied to her boyfriend about my reaction to her little attempt to break up my relationship. She simply ignored me, although we saw quite a bit of each other.

Anthony and Marcus were best friends, and usually if we weren't going out alone we were double- or triple-dating with members of the clique.

It was in the locker room after PE when she started some more drama.

"Jasmyn, are you going with us to the lake this weekend?" Sherina had cornered me by my locker as I was trying to efficiently use the ten-minute changing period we were allowed. She had raised her voice to an almost scream. I merely rolled my eyes at the girl's poor attempt at putting me on the spot and putting my business in the streets.

"Lake?" I said.

"Oh, Anthony didn't tell you? We are all going to spend the weekend at Marcus's parents' cabin in the mountains. It's just for couples. I wonder why Anthony didn't tell you."

If I could have slapped the smug look she sported off her face, I would have. But I didn't need to get suspended for getting into a fight in my senior year of high school. I shrugged indifferently.

"I hadn't heard about it," I returned.

"Oh . . . hope I haven't opened a can of worms. I didn't mean to get Anthony in trouble," she said with an attempt at embarrassment that was laughable.

"Don't worry, you didn't," I returned, shooting her a cold look. She walked off.

"Oh, I can't stand that heifer! She thinks she is so cute!" Chayenne hissed at lunch that afternoon. I had just finished telling her about the incident.

"I can't stand her either . . . but I don't major in the minor ya heard. She's always trying to start something between Anthony and me. It's so obvious when she does it too. She's just mad I don't want to be down with her stupid little clique," I said, rolling my eyes.

"Watch your back, Jasmyn. Females like Sherina have fangs," Chayenne said, shaking her head.

I heard what my friend told me . . . but I didn't really listen. If I had, I probably could have avoided the impending disaster that would finally make me stop watching my life like a movie, and actually participate in the terror.

Anthony told me about the lake that night. He said that he planned to go, but he didn't want to invite me because he knew my father would say no. He was right and I had no intention of hiking my black butt up a mountain for a weekend. I was strictly a city girl and I didn't care how modern the cabin was.

"So, um, you're going to go," I said, burrowing deeper into my pillow. My hair itched around the edges. I made a mental note to have Chayenne break out her pressing comb and touch up my edges.

"Yes. Why?"

"Who are you taking with you? Sherina said it was going to be for couples only."

"Oh, so it's like that, Jasmyn? You're going to listen to ya little friend and accuse me of cheating?" he snapped.

"First of all, Sherina is not my friend by any stretch of the imagination. Trust me on that one. She came up to me and asked me if *I* was going. It seems ya'll have been planning this little getaway for a minute. Second of all, I didn't accuse you of cheating. But you sound like you have a confession to make. Go ahead and get it off your chest if you do," I shot back.

"Who do you think you're talking to like that? You better watch your tone. Besides, ain't no rule that it's couples only. You just have to be invited. Marcus is my boy and I need a minute from all the pressure and drama. I'd think you'd understand that." His tone was menacing to say the least.

I took a deep breath and suddenly felt a little guilty. I knew how the pressure was getting to him. His coaches were seeing dollar signs, because everyone knew he was probably going to go pro and forgo college for the time being. I was pretty sure his mother was on his back. I hadn't met her yet and really didn't plan on meeting her either, but she was definitely an issue with Anthony. I knew he was going to be looking for an agent soon. There I was grilling him about a stupid weekend with his boy. I had let Sherina's little attempt to come between us succeed.

"I'm sorry, baby. I know it's been hard for you lately. I wasn't trying to say you were cheating on me . . . I just . . . never mind. You have a good time," I said soothingly.

"Thank you."

Anthony left that Friday morning, skipping school to go to the cabin. I knew none of the teachers would care.

I spent the night at Chayenne's house. She lived in Westminster too, but her house was way bigger. Some of the Broncos were her neighbors'. We settled in her room, which was really a suite complete with a kitchenette and a small sitting room with a big-screen TV. We watched *Mystic Pizza, Pretty Woman,* and *Coming to America.* We love Julia Roberts, and, well, *Coming to America* is one of the funniest movies ever made.

I lay on her plush cream carpet wrapped in one of her down comforters and watched her locate the *Coming to America* tape. She was placing tape after tape into the VCR. Chayenne never bought videos, she taped them bootleg off of cable. The thing I never could figure out is why her crazy behind never labeled the videos!

"You really need to start labeling your videos, geek," I said, shaking my head as she inserted another tape. I munched on a Twizzler.

"Don't worry about my video skills. There is a method to my madness, trust me. Anyway, let's talk about why you're mad that Anthony is in some freakin' mountain hideaway with Sherina and her crew probably doing Lord knows what." She stopped going through tapes and turned her attention toward me.

"Uh, what makes you think I'm upset?" I said, avoiding eye contact. I unwrapped myself from the comforter and went to her mini-refrigerator and grabbed a strawberry soda.

"I can tell you're upset. I'm your best friend," she said, simply catching the orange soda I knew she would want.

"I love him so much, Chayenne," I said, keeping the tears out of my voice.

"Then you should be able to trust him. Look, girl, Anthony is about to be a professional athlete. Do you know

what that means? Do you know how many females throw
themselves at athletes? It's sickening. They think it's their
opportunity to be a millionaire. Shoot, you are a potential
millionaire, girl, you know how people act when money
comes in the picture. They get ignorant. Don't let him put a
price on your feelings, Jasmyn. You deserve somebody who
ain't a player," she said, looking me in the eye.

I just nodded. I was beyond words. I think she knew that I
would never leave him.

I spent Saturday with my brother and daddy watching TV
and we eventually went to dinner with his lady friend. I was
good and tired when I went to sleep. Dreams are funny
things. They just creep up on you, and you have no control
over whether you have them or not. You don't know what
triggers them or even if they can help or harm you.

The only meaningful dreams I'd ever had in my life were
about my mother. I hadn't breathed her name since she had
left me at my father's door. I had simply added her to the
things in my life that had hurt me and I wanted to forget. My
father never mentioned her either. He never spoke badly
about her, he just considered her a nonentity. In our household, Renai DeWitt didn't exist. The only thing I had received from her was the box containing the rest of my
belongings a couple of weeks after I had arrived at my
daddy's. There was no note, and there was no further corre-
spondence. I never missed her either. How can you miss
someone that hates your very existence? How can you
mourn for the loss of someone you never knew? No calls on
my birthdays, no inquiries through my father or other
sources. Nothing. She faded from my life, like a ghost, and
in the stream of time of a person's life, nine years really isn't
all that long, is it?

So that Saturday night when I crawled into bed, I never
would have guessed I'd have to prepare myself for seeing
Renai DeWitt again. But I did.

She was wearing a wedding dress. It was all white. She

looked like an angel. She was standing in front of a preacher. She was the perfect bride. I could feel myself approach her, and I must have been small, because I was looking up at her.

"Mama?" I heard my voice ask.

She turned to me and there was such a look of disgust and disdain on her face that I could feel myself flinch. Then without a second's thought she slapped me. I felt my body jerk with the force of the blow.

"I hate you! *I hate you!*" she screamed.

I started to cry. There was nothing else I could do. I knew she hated me. It seemed that I had been born with that knowledge. It just hurt to hear it verbalized. I turned and started to run. I felt myself trip and fall. Suddenly I looked up and there was Matthew, belt in hand. I knew what was about to happen. I didn't fight it. I didn't scream or cry. Or try to cover myself with my hands the way I had done when I was four. I just lay there and waited for the punishment that I knew would be unjustly meted out. Then I woke up.

I was sweating, and it seemed that it took me a good two minutes to begin breathing normally. I immediately flipped on the light next to my bed. My cheeks were wet with tears. I was shaking. I didn't know what to do. I had never woken this scared before, not even when I was eight. I could hear my heart beating in my chest. I got out of my bed and walked to Jordan's room. I slipped into the darkened room illuminated by the light from his computer. He was sitting at his desk in some sweats pecking away at the keys. His smooth brown face was knotted in intense concentration as he worked.

"Jordan . . . can I sleep with you tonight?" I asked. My voice was a hoarse whisper, and fear dripped from it like rain down the eaves of a house.

"What's the matter, Jasmyn? You all right? You look scared," he said, looking up at me curiously.

"I just had a bad dream. Tripped me out."

"Yeah, you can sleep in here. I still have to finish this essay for school though. If you don't mind my typing." He turned back to his computer.

"Thanks." I had already slipped under his covers and snuggled into his pillow.

"Don't forget to save it, Jordan," I said before I slipped off into a relieving sleep.

"Oh, dang, girl, I'm glad you told me!" he said, accompanying his exclamation by a few meaningful clicks of the mouse. That was my Jordan. Always saving things till the last minute.

The next morning I woke up and Jordan was lying over his keyboard. I woke him up and told him to get into bed, which he did reluctantly. I saved his essay again on his computer and shut it down. It was eleven o'clock on a Sunday, which meant my father probably wouldn't be home that afternoon. He had taken to spending the weekends with his new lady friend.

I decided to make my brother a big breakfast and invite Chayenne over to share it. I gave her a call and told her to get her lazy butt out of bed and began making breakfast.

"Wake up!" I said cheerily into the phone as I harassed Chayenne.

"Negro, do you know what time it is?"

"Yes, I do, it's only nine-thirty. It's a beautiful morning and you need to come over and enjoy some of my light-as-air pancakes." I smiled as I got down the ingredients for my world-famous pancakes.

I listened as Chayenne fumbled with her phone. She dropped it.

"Okay, okay, okay. I'll be over in like, hmmm . . . an hour." I could hear her drifting back to sleep.

"Make it thirty minutes. Oh, yeah, and bring some orange juice," I said, opening the refrigerator and taking out milk.

Ten

Chayenne arrived forty-five minutes later. It was a ten-minute drive from what I called "the Mansion." She would get mad when I referred to her house that way, but I mean it was a mansion. She did bring a gallon of orange juice, so I forgave her tardiness.

"I can't believe you are going to eat and run. That is so ghetto. You know what? I can't believe you would do us like that," Chayenne exclaimed as Jordan wolfed down a plate of food and found his basketball.

"I know I'm ghetto. Chayenne, I would stay if I knew there was a chance that you'd grace me with your regal attention." My brother thought he was such a player.

I swear I have only seen my friend Chayenne blush a handful of times. She blushed under her pretty chocolate skin.

"Negro, please, you better go play some ball and quit playing around," she murmured, sipping her orange juice regally.

I could only giggle. My brother flirted with anyone of the female persuasion. It was in his nature, he couldn't help it. Chayenne knew this, and I knew they only joked around with each other. He was definitely not her type. My brother shrugged and grabbed his ball and headed out the door.

"So what do you want to do?" Chayenne asked after we had finished cleaning the kitchen.

"I don't know. I had this weird dream last night." I found myself telling my best friend in the whole world about something I'd never mentioned to anyone. Not even my brothers knew about my mother. I think my father had given them a vague story, but nobody really knew about the details. I told Chayenne about my dream.

She settled herself on the kitchen counter and crossed her long model legs in front of her and just listened. She wore gray sweatpants and a St. Thomas T-shirt that I knew she had gotten on a vacation with her parents. Her Afro was meticulously combed out and patted down and held back from her scrubbed face with a black headband. She smelled of Sunflower perfume, and I knew she hadn't just jumped out of bed and rushed over to my house. Chayenne was always together, even when she was just relaxing. It was her. I studied my friend casually, searching her body language for anything that would give me a clue about how she was taking my story of my dream. It was interesting. She just looked at me and listened. No judgment when I had finished.

"Girl, that's pretty interesting. . . . Jazz, can I ask you a question?" She was swinging her feet like a little girl.

"Sure." I was obsessively wiping the kitchen table.

"What's the story with your mama? You hardly ever talk about her. I thought she was dead or something." Chayenne was always to the point. That was one of the things I liked about her.

"Okay . . . how can I explain this? It's a long story," I said, my voice quivering.

"I got time." Chayenne slipped off the counter and sat at the table.

"I guess you can say my mama didn't really want me. She was eighteen when she had me. We lived with my grandmother until I was like four. Then, um, we moved out and she got married. She married this rich old white guy. He didn't want children either. So she brought me here to live with my father when I was eight. And here I am." My voice was a whisper. It was the first time I'd ever told anyone about the time line of my life. It didn't seem real when I told her. It seemed so far away from the reality I was living in.

"Whoa. That's pretty heavy. Have you talked to her since she left?" Chayenne probed.

I was staring at the multicolored dishrag in my hands.

"Nope. Not a phone call . . . not a letter . . . or a card. She got what she wanted when she left me here. It was good though. Because my daddy's family gives me all the love that I'd ever need." I sighed.

"Have you talked to your grandmother?"

"Actually no. I haven't seen her since I was six. When my mother and I left her house we didn't really have a lot of contact with her. Ma Belle really raised me though, but I don't have a way of contacting her," I said wistfully. I'd been thinking a lot lately about the only maternal influence I'd had in my life.

"Jasmyn, you should try to contact her. Do you think your dad might have a contact number?"

"I don't know and I don't want to hurt him by asking," I said, dismissing the thought.

"You won't hurt him. He loves you and would understand you wanting to talk to your grandmother. You should ask him."

"Yeah . . . maybe." I sighed.

"Okay, enough reminiscing, let's go to the mall or something," she said, smiling at me.

I could only smile back.

The thought of my mother was heavy on my mind as Chayenne and I navigated the mall and snacked on Chic-fil-A and ice cream. When I got home and saw my father's Range Rover in the driveway, I decided to talk to him.

That Sunday night my father came home for a few hours. He was going out again with his friend (I couldn't get myself to say girlfriend when it came to my daddy). He was in his room putting on his tie. I sat down on the huge oak bed that Jordan and I had hidden under while playing hide-and-seek.

"Hey, Jasmyn, what's going on, baby girl?" My daddy had this smile that he used just for me. I had been seeing that smile since I was eight.

I smiled back. "Daddy, can I ask you a question?"

"Please do," he said, turning back to the mirror and straightening his tie.

"How did you meet my mother?" The words eased out of my mouth without an ounce of difficulty. I guess words that you have been keeping inside for so long free themselves easily when you get up enough nerve to finally speak them.

He was silent, and he got a very serious look on his face. I hadn't seen that look since he'd heard that Jonathan had gotten into a car accident and the hospital had called our house. He sat by me on the bed and he looked me straight in the eye.

"I knew, Jasmyn, there would come a time when I would have to explain some things to you. I told the boys. I didn't want to tell you because you were so little. I'm going to be honest with you though.

"When the boys' mother died, I was really a mess. I let my job send me anywhere they wanted. I was just running from the pain, and my children. I was a young man who had sons to raise and no wife. I was selfish, Jasmyn. I never really took care of the boys up until then. Their mother and my mother had always taken care of them. I just went to school and pursued my career. Then she died and I didn't know what to do. So I became more of a workaholic. The firm I worked for needed me to go to California to help them get ready for an audit. I was at a McDonald's one day and the most beautiful woman I had ever seen walked in and ordered a strawberry milkshake. I started talking to her. I could tell that she was out of my league. But needless to say I didn't care. We were together for the month and a half that I was down there, and then I left.

"She called me a few months later to tell me she was pregnant. I asked her to marry me, because I thought that would be the right thing to do. She never told me she was only seventeen. Your grandmother told me that after she got pregnant. I didn't know what to say. I felt like I had messed up again. I was just learning how to raise my boys. When I had told her about my sons, she had made it obvious she would never be a stepmother. I asked her to send me the baby. She said no. She was going to give it up for adoption since it was too late for an abortion. I begged her not to. So then your grandmother said she would take care of the baby, if I sent her money every month. If I missed one payment, then she would give the baby to a foster home and have me put into jail for statutory rape. She said I could come and get you when you turned five. But for some reason you guys moved when you were four and your mother said I needed to send the checks to her, so I did. I had my lawyer send her a letter two weeks before she dropped you off at my house. I was going to take her to court, but I didn't have to." He let his story trickle out with the same ease as my question.

I sat and absorbed what he told me. Ma Belle had been getting money for me the whole time I lived in her house. I was a foster child in the home of my own grandmother.

"How much?" I said, my voice steel.

"Baby girl—" my daddy began.

"I want to know, Daddy. How much did you pay them a month?" I persisted.

"Two thousand. I had some investments, and you know your grammy was very wealthy. . . . She made most of the payments. It was the only way until I got you back," he said gravely.

"Do you have my grandmother's phone number?" I said, controlling the tears of rage that threatened to make trails down my cheeks.

"No, I don't. It was changed after your mother moved out. I do have a contact number for your mother though."

"Can I have it?"

"Of course."

It was that simple. My daddy had eased the tension that had been weighing on his heart for seventeen years. He was relieved, and yet it seemed that my load had increased and made me wearier. But I suppose that's how life is. We exchange loads with those we love. Some things we all just have to take turns carrying. He wrote the number on a piece of paper and handed it to me with a kiss on the forehead and a hug. He didn't tell me what to do with it.

I watched as he went to meet his friend Terry. She was an

attorney, and kind of reminded me of Lynn Whitfield. I supposed she was nice.

I placed my mother's number in front of me on my bed and dialed.

"Hello?" a masculine voice answered.

I felt the phone freeze in my hand as a voice I would never forget echoed in my ear.

"Look what you did! You peed in the bed!"

"Lie across the bed, Jasmyn."

"Jasmyn, if you tell anybody about you peein' in the bed you're going to get it worse. Do you understand?"

My hands began to shake and soon I was just listening to a dial tone. I don't know how long I sat there staring at the phone in my hand and wondering. Why was Matthew Linton Hughes answering my mother's phone?

It took me a minute to get a hold on reality. I had fought so hard to be successful in forgetting I'd ever met him. I'd worked so hard to pretend that those afternoons I spent alone with him weren't enough to affect me permanently. I had never told anyone but Ma Belle. I don't know if she told my mother. All I knew was I didn't ever want to visit that place in my memories where I was a defenseless four-year-old.

I immediately took a shower. I let the warm needles of water pound into my back until it became numb. I had to feel some type of numbness. I slipped into some pajamas and even though it was only eight in the evening I let myself slip into a black sleep.

Eleven

The next time I saw Anthony was on Monday in the school library. I knew the only reason he was there was to talk to me. For some miraculous reason he was able to breeze through his classes. I think he rarely did homework, but he was smart. He'd actually helped me with some homework, and I was on the honor roll.

He was wearing a wrinkled gray and blue Karl Kani shirt, a pair of equally wrinkled dark blue jeans, and some Jordans. His eyes were strained and red as if he'd been up all night. In the few months that I had known him I'd never seen him look this broken down. He approached my usual table in the back of the library.

"What's wrong with you?" I asked as he placed his head on his hands on the table.

"I'm just tired. It was a rough weekend. I tried to call you Friday night. Where were you?" he returned.

"I was out."

"What's that supposed to mean? Where were you?" He glared at me.

Before I could reply he had grabbed my hand and was holding it in a death grip.

"Owww . . . let go, Anthony. I was out with a friend," I murmured.

"What friend? You think you're going to play me, Jasmyn? I know how you hoes are . . . as soon as a brotha leave, you start trippin'. Don't think you can play me," he whispered in my ear. His voice was pure venom and the grip on my hand got tighter. I felt my eyes start to tear.

"I spent the night over Chayenne's, okay? I am not trying to play you. How can you call me a hoe?" My voice was shaking a little. He had that crazy look in his eye that he had before when he had hit me.

He looked me in the eye and with a more menacing squeeze he released my hand.

"I'm sorry, baby. I just have a lot on my mind. The season is about to start, and I've been under a lot of pressure. My mama is trippin', my coach is trippin'. I couldn't take it if you weren't in my corner."

"When have I ever *not* been in your corner, Anthony? Why do you keep hurting me? I overlooked the last time, but if you put your hands on me again, this will not work." I heard my voice coming from somewhere deep inside me. It was as if I was trying to sound strong. I knew I wasn't though. I knew that it was me just saying the mandatory thing. I knew that I would stay with him no matter what.

"You know what? It seems like every time you hang out with that rich freak Chayenne you get this little attitude and forget who you're talking to. You need to check that, Jasmyn. I don't have time for that. You my lady. Do you know how many women want that position? You need to be grateful. I told you I was sorry but you have to get an attitude with me." He sounded so weary and disgusted that I didn't say anything.

"I want you to meet my mama," he muttered finally.

I couldn't help smiling. I knew that he was trying to make things right between us.

"Okay." I sighed.

"I'm going to invite you over Friday. Are you sure you won't have plans with your little friend then?"

"I'll be there."

"Good, give me some sugar," he said, gracing my lips with what I think to this day are the softest lips on earth.

When I made it to gym that day I was tired. It takes a lot of work to forget about something, and I had been using all of my energy to forget about calling my mother and hearing Matthew answering the phone. In addition to that, Anthony's little display in the library didn't help. I changed quickly and actually tried to look forward to working away some of the emotional stress that had piled up on me that weekend. I rolled my eyes and braced myself when Sherina approached me in the locker room after class. I was just slipping into my jeans.

"I need to talk to you," she said, her voice sounding a little different than the overly smug tone she seemed to reserve just for me.

I studied her for a moment. She was already dressed and though she was her usual high-polish, perfect-ten self, something just didn't mesh right. Her eyes weren't as alert, and did she have just a little more makeup than usual?

"What?" I said after I had slipped on my Timberlands. I was a little interested to hear what she would tell me. Anthony hadn't mentioned anything about the weekend at the cabin, and I was a little curious as to what happened.

"Look, I don't want to talk here, okay? Is there any way I can come to your house after school?" she asked.

I almost told her no, I didn't want her in my house, but something stopped me. Was that a look of desperation in her eye?

"Okay." I gave her my address. I knew there wouldn't be anyone home. My dad would be at the office, and Jordan was always in and out of the house.

I don't know why I felt I had to prepare for Sherina coming over my house. I vacuumed and lit one of my vanilla candles. I made sure we had something to drink, and made sure the bathroom was straight.

The doorbell rang just as I had slipped out of my school clothes and into some sweats.

Sherina was at the door looking nervous and out of place. Which I couldn't blame her for. She knew that I was aware of her attempts to come between Anthony and me.

I invited her to sit down in the family room. It wasn't as homey as the one at our old house, but it was the most comfortable room in the house.

"You must have a tight family," she said as she surveyed the pictures that cluttered every open place in the room.

"Yes, we're very close. Do you want something to drink?" I asked, trying to sound polite.

"Okay," she murmured.

"Lemonade?"

"Sure."

I retrieved two glasses of lemonade and some oatmeal cookies. I offered her a glass. Then I sat down on the couch.

"Sit down, Sherina. You don't have to keep standing in the middle of the room like I'm going to jump on you or something," I finally said, exasperated.

"I guess you have a reason to be mad at me, huh?" she said sheepishly as she sat down.

"What would give you that impression?" I returned.

"Look, Jasmyn. I know I've done my share of mess when it comes to you and Anthony. I really love Marcus though. I just don't want Anthony to get hurt. It takes a special kind of woman to be in our position," she said, sitting on the edge of the couch.

"Position?" I said warily.

"Yes. I mean don't front, Jasmyn. You know that Anthony is going pro. Mark is too. We are the females that men like them marry. We're the Juanita Jordans of the world. It takes a lot to be that. Not everyone has what it takes," she continued.

"Okay, well, I'm sure you didn't come over here in the name of basketball sisterhood. Don't front with me, Sherina, I know you don't think I'm quality enough to be with Anthony, and I also know one of the girls in your little clique is champing at the bit to get Anthony. Why are you here?" I said, my head throbbing. It was taking all I had not to let the pressure of what had happened that weekend get to me.

"Cool. I'm not going to beat around the bush anymore. Money. We need money."

I looked at her for a good minute. "Huh?" It was the only appropriate reply I could get out.

"The weekend at the cabin was a setup. They have Mark and Anthony on tape doing things that they shouldn't be doing with some strippers. They want ten grand apiece to stay quiet," she shot out.

"Who is they? What do you mean setup?" I was lost.

"Okay, some strippers just showed up at the cabin this weekend. I don't know who called them. I just went to bed. They must have planted some cameras in the cabin. Your man and mine got a little freaky while we were up there, and they got it on tape."

"Let me get this straight. Anthony and Marcus went on this little weekend in the mountains. You went too and some of your friends, and they got freaky with some *strippers,* and somebody has it on *tape,* and they want *twenty* g's to hand over the tape?"

It all sounded so crazy that I half expected her to start laughing. She didn't though. Her face was serious.

"Yes," she said finally.

"You let your man be with another girl?" I said.

"Yes . . . Marcus has his moments. I don't say anything normally as long as he remembers who his woman is. That's how it is, Jasmyn. Men like them get it thrown at them all the time. They don't know how to say no," she explained, sitting down in frustration.

"Yeah, well, if Anthony is getting freaky with some stripper while I was here all by myself bein' faithful, oh, well. I don't care *who* blackmails him." I was shaking. I'd never been so angry in my life.

"Jasmyn, I know you're hurt. I'm hurt too. I love him though. I know that you love Anthony, and sometimes they can't help what they do. You'll understand. You will, I swear you will, once you've been with him longer and see how it is. Think about it. Something like this could ruin their careers," she pleaded.

"So what? They should have thought about that before they did it."

"There's more. I saw the tape. Those girls put something in their drinks, Jasmyn. They were knocked out. Those girls . . . put them in certain positions that would really mess them up. You can tell they are knocked out on the video, but that doesn't matter. The press isn't going to care." She was pacing my floor now.

"Positions?" I croaked.

"Look, they gave me a copy of the tape," she said, pulling a videotape out of her bag.

I didn't say anything when she handed it to me. I walked over to the television and slipped it in. As an afterthought I locked the front door and closed all of the windows.

I wanted to throw up. The first ten minutes of the video was harmless. Them getting drunk and the strippers dancing around taking off their clothes. After that it just got worse. Worse than a porno, worse than anything I'd ever seen. You could tell when they passed out. But the things those girls did with them when they were passed out . . . well, suffice it to say they would ruin their careers. Both Mark and Anthony were well respected in the community. Just the other week the local news had done specials on them volunteering at an after-school intramural basketball program. Flashes of both of them surrounded by awestruck, admiring children floated briefly through my mind. I pushed stop and rewound the tape. I handed it back to Sherina.

"How do you know they won't put it out on the Internet, Sherina? Twenty thousand is not a lot of money. People who blackmail people usually don't stop," I said thoughtfully.

"I thought of that. They won't. There is only one other copy, the original. I did some checking. They're probably on drugs. They just want some money; besides, after they get their money I can hire someone to scare them into not talking. That's not a problem. They just want some hush money so they can get high," she said carefully.

"Okay, where are we getting twenty thousand?" I shot back.

"Oh, they have the money. Trust me. Mark has been getting money under the table from certain scouts for a while. I know Anthony has at least fifty thousand from a couple of teams. We just have to get it from them," she said, sighing.

"Wait, are you sayin' they don't know that they are on this tape?" I said incredulously.

"No, they don't. I'm not telling them either," she said.

"Why not?"

"Insurance, Jasmyn. Mark will marry me. I will be an NBA wife. There is no doubt about it. I'm the best thing that has ever happened to him. He needs me to survive. I have to have my insurance though. There are too many wives getting screwed in prenups and that kind of mess. It isn't happening to me. There are two tapes, and only two. You get ten from Anthony and you get the other insurance policy." She was all business.

I didn't say anything. I kept my mouth shut. There was such determination and seriousness in her voice. I knew she loved Mark, but she was as serious as a heart attack when she spoke about getting an "insurance policy." Sherina was from a different world than I was. I knew her parents were wealthy enough since she lived by Chayenne, but I never guessed she was so money hungry. Mark's parents were paid too. I didn't understand this money situation at all. Anthony just bought me things, and occasionally he'd give me a hundred dollars here or there.

"How am I supposed to ask him for ten thousand dollars? I've never asked him for twenty dollars, let alone ten thousand!" I said.

"How much do you think that herringbone around your neck cost? Tell him you want money to buy a car or something. Look, you see that car I'm driving now? That was twenty thousand. Everybody thinks my parents bought it for me. News flash: Mark bought that car. It's in my parents' and my name. He gave me the cash. The car he rolls now, his parents bought for him. He can't look like he's getting money under the table, but he has it. I asked him for three grand the other day to go shopping. He didn't even blink when he gave it to me. I just need seven more. I'm going to tell him my grandmother needs help paying some of her bills. He'll come off with that money without blinking. It's nothing compared to what he knows he's going to get," she said, breaking it down to me as if I were a child.

I thought about it for a moment. I fingered the herringbone around my neck. I had been shocked when Anthony presented it to me on a teddy bear, but I never thought twice about it.

"Okay, let me think. I'll get the money. Set up a meeting with the blackmailers for the tape," I said.

"I knew I could count on you, Jasmyn. I knew you were NBA wife material."

I didn't say anything. I didn't even know if I was NBA girlfriend material at that point. I just had this feeling that I needed to take care of this.

Twelve

"What you want ten g's for, baby?" he asked me.

It was Tuesday night, and Anthony was laid out on my bed with his shirt off. I was rubbing his back down. I did it every Tuesday night for him after he got home from practicing. Even though the season hadn't officially started, he practiced every day. My dad was out of town, and Jordan didn't care what I did. He was the only one of my brothers that viewed me as an adult.

I had lit my aromatherapy candles, and my favorite Jodeci CD was playing. Anthony was spending the night. We hadn't taken *that* step yet and I was still a card-carrying member of the "V" club. Which was strange to me, because I knew most guys expected their girlfriends to be giving up the drawers within two weeks of them being together. Anthony seemed to be satisfied with some kissing, and he loved for me to hold him until he fell asleep, so that's what I did. I worked some peppermint-scented oil into his shoulders.

"I want to buy a car," I said carefully.

"I'll buy you a car. My boy has the hookup, what kind do you want?" he said absently.

"I want to buy it, baby. My daddy thinks I've saved up

enough money to get a car on my own. He doesn't know I spent some of it. So he expects me to buy a car by the end of this month. It has to look like I have the cash in the bank," I whispered in his ear. I slowly worked the muscles in his neck. I felt his body tense, then relax. He was drowsy.

"Okay, I'll give it to you tomorrow. What kind of car you getting?" he inquired, slipping into sleep.

I didn't answer, because he was knocked out. I sat there for a minute and thought about what I'd just done. I had just hustled ten g's from my boyfriend. I thought about that for a long time before I slipped into sleep.

A week later Anthony left an old FILA bag in my closet after a visit. It was ten thousand exactly.

It was Friday and I was going to meet his mother.

"What should I wear, Chy? I'm trippin' over her, girl. I mean I've never met his mama, and the way he talks about her, she ain't no joke," I said into my cordless. It was the afternoon and I was feverishly going through my closet.

"Look, wear something cute but simple. Don't try to impress the heffa, because if she's all that he says she is, she won't like you anyway. Women like that view other women as a threat. Trust me. I wouldn't sweat it."

"That's easy for you to say, Ms. Cool, Calm, and Collected. First of all, I don't look like an *Ebony* model like you. Second, I don't have the wardrobe of an *Ebony* model like you. Third, I do actually want to look nice when I meet my man's mother. I want him to be proud of me," I retorted.

"Okay, okay, okay. Hmm, what are you all going to be doing?" she murmured.

"We're going to Tony Roma's for ribs."

"Laid-back and yet slightly dressy. Wear your black slacks and that silver and gray pin-striped button-down shirt. Curl your hair and wear it down. Little to no jewelry, and a little lipstick. If she's half as nuts as he says she is, you don't want to outshine her. But you still want to look nice for your 'man,' as you put it." I could see Chayenne squinting her eyes in concentration.

"Thanks. I'll call you when I get home."

"Oh, please do. I want to hear about the hen that laid the golden egg," she said sarcastically.

I could only laugh.

I was proud of the outfit I chose to meet Anthony's mama in. I wore exactly what Chayenne suggested. I put on a dab of the Chanel Number 5 perfume my father had bought for me as a gift, and I slipped on a touch of cinnamon lipstick. I surveyed myself in the mirror. For some reason it didn't feel as though I was looking at me. I was looking at someone else. I'd never felt that way before. The girl/woman in the mirror looked somewhat like my mother. Just a little of the shape of the face, and the hair that I had to press almost daily to keep bone straight hung a little past my shoulders. I could see myself on Anthony's arm. Going from place to place, his arm candy. Perfection. I saw all of this when I looked in the mirror, and I wanted to ask the girl standing there, "Girl, why you put yourself through all of this?"

I shook the feeling in a split second. I'm good at that. Putting on the face that I knew Anthony expected to me to wear. I went to sit in the living room. Ten minutes later he pulled into my driveway.

"Is your mother coming?" I said, slipping into the passenger's seat and buckling my seat belt.

"Oh, so no hi for your man. You know you've been forgetting who I am to you lately. Jasmyn, you need to show the proper respect," he said bitterly.

"I'm sorry . . . hi, baby, how was the rest of your day?" I quickly murmured.

"Okay. Give me some sugar," he said smiling at me.

I leaned over and kissed him on the cheek.

"Oh, you're funny. Open your mouth, I want some tongue," he demanded, grabbing me by the back of my head and forcing my mouth to his. I didn't have a chance to respond as he immediately put his tongue in my mouth. For a moment I contemplated biting it, but I didn't want to start something before I'd even met his mother. I just let him finish and then fixed my makeup.

"I'm going to pick up my mama, right now. She's still at home getting ready," he murmured as he pulled into the street.

I felt my eyes begin to burn with tears. I guess they were the kind of tears that you don't know exactly why you are crying them, but they just need to get out. I had so many reasons for tears. The last tears I'd cried were because of something he'd done to me. I couldn't blame the tears that stung my eyes in the car totally on him though. My mother. The fact that the only woman I'd ever respected as an authority figure in my life had blackmailed the only man who had given me unconditional love, instead of her giving me to him. It all just hit me. My tears stung my eyes. But I bit my lip, and held them back. I was skilled at holding back. Very skilled. I watched as the rain made trails down the car window. I watched them, and envied them. They flowed so easily. Letting chance determine their path and where they fell. My tears had so many constraints on them. I sighed.

In the time we had been together I'd never seen Anthony's house. It was some unspoken rule that we spend most of our time at my house if we weren't out somewhere. I was a little shocked to see it was ten minutes from mine. It wasn't as large as mine, but it was a nice brick house with a beautiful yard. Rosebushes in the front. I noticed a Mercedes in the garage. Anthony pulled his Jeep Cherokee next to it.

I didn't say anything as he helped me out of the car. He smiled at me. I found the strength to smile.

We entered the house through the garage, which put us in a family room. There was a glass case to my left that filled the whole wall. It held all types of trophies and awards. I didn't have to look to see that they belonged to Anthony. The furniture was forest green, Italian leather. A big-screen TV occupied a wall along with a stereo. I smiled as I noticed a wall full of pictures of Anthony. There were his baby pictures, showing him all fat and chubby. A picture of him no older than three holding a basketball. There was elementary and middle school. A picture of him sporting a box haircut that I knew I was going to have to clown him about later and an assortment of others filled the basement. It was cute but for some reason it gave me this strange feeling . . . as if I were looking at a shrine.

I wasn't prepared for the entrance of Ms. Tanya Braxton Michaels. She was not what I had expected at all. First of all, she was only about five feet tall. She was petite. And she had her hair cut like Halle Berry's. She had a beautiful shade of skin that reminded me of this antique dresser I had seen at Chayenne's house. The wood was so rich and deep that I couldn't resist running my fingers over it. Red and brown. Not extremely dark or light, just floating in that happy medium of color that many races can claim.

It's funny how people package themselves. Chayenne always says that clothes are merely packages people come in. They usually tell a lot about the gift. Ms. Tanya was packaged all wrong. She wore a red suit that was way too loud for her beautiful skin tone. And an equally loud and flamboyant gold and red scarf. Her hair was expertly curled and I could smell the fresh relaxer that a hairdresser had obviously applied earlier that day. Her lipstick matched her suit and she overdid it by adding blush and gold eye shadow. She reeked of perfume that I knew was expensive. Her nails were red talons. That's the only way I could describe them. She wore a ring on every finger but her thumb, and the ice that was on them was definitely real. Her shoes completed the outfit, spike heels. Red. She held on to a mink coat. And her purse proudly boasted the Chanel label. Basically she looked like what she was. A woman who was trying to appear rich. Everything about her was overstated.

She eyed me with the same inspection. I held my head high. Not too high, but high enough to let her know that I wasn't intimidated by her display of wanna-be wealth.

Chayenne always told me you can distinguish the difference between the wealthy people of the world and those who want to look wealthy. She said the wealthy don't have an obligation to look rich. They know they are. You won't see them flaunting the huge diamonds and gaudy jewelry. The wanna-be rich, as she called them, were easy to spot: everything they wore (most of the time at the expense of good taste) just screamed *money*. I looked Tanya in the eye and smiled.

"So this is Jacqueline, is it?" I knew she knew my real name. There was no way she couldn't. I let that little barb pass.

"Um, Mama, this is Jasmyn. My girlfriend," Anthony stuttered.

"Oh, Anthony, she is so cute," she exclaimed.

I wanted to slap her. But of course I didn't, I just stared at her. Smiled again.

"Hello. I'm pleased to finally meet you," I said, giving her eye contact.

Oh, I was not going out like a punk. It was on. I could already tell. We walked out to the car after a few seconds of awkward silence, and Tanya was very vocal about being driven to the restaurant in the Mercedes. She, however, didn't want to drive it.

"Jamie, dear, you don't mind if I sit up front, do you?" she said in a sugary-sweet voice that I was beginning to hate.

"No, not at all, and it's Jasmyn. Just think of the princess in *Aladdin*," I returned. Score some points for me with that one. I don't think she liked the idea of me putting my name and *princess* in the same sentence.

"How cute."

Anthony was unusually quiet. Normally, when we were in a social setting he was the center of attention. All of the charm and finesse that he was known for on and off the basketball court was gone. He was sweating, and I could tell he was nervous for some reason. I felt sorry for him. I slipped into the seat behind him, and before I buckled my seat belt I gave him a reassuring rub on the shoulder. He smiled at me in the rearview mirror, and his mother sucked her teeth in disgust. I prepared myself for a long evening.

By the time he dropped me off at home that night I was more than exhausted. His mother hadn't stopped with the insults and petty little barbs. They went on and on and on. She called me every *J* name she could possibly think of and I was beginning to wonder if she had purposely studied a name book just for that purpose. In addition to that, she was extremely rude to everyone else around us.

She called the waiter an incompetent imbecile twice, and sent her food back three times. I never sent my food back and neither did Anthony. I can only imagine what happened to the food after she sent it back. She actually told a woman sitting across from us to leave, since her baby was "absolutely disgusting," and the list went on and on. She basically ignored me and spoke to Anthony about what he needed to do as far as his basketball career was concerned. I interjected something into the conversation a couple of times, but on the whole I was quiet and just waiting to go home.

I slipped into bed and was two seconds away from drooling on my pillow when my daddy knocked on my door.

"Come in," I called.

"Hey, baby girl, how was your dinner?"

"Daddy, you don't even want to know. Anthony's mother brings new meaning to the word *evil*."

"Well, sweetheart, I got a call today at work. It was . . . It was from your mother, Jasmyn. She said that your grandmother has died. She wanted you to know and she wanted to know if you were coming to the funeral." He rubbed my hand that was laying on top of my comforter.

It felt as if I were standing in a tunnel and someone yelled something to me. It wasn't quite clear what he was saying. It seemed to echo through my mind like words in a tunnel. But it got to me. I bit back my tears. I didn't want to cry anymore. I'd already had to avoid tears earlier with Anthony. Ma Belle was gone. I didn't know what to say or to think. I didn't know how to act. All I knew was that a piece of me was gone, forever. A sense of loss consumed me with a ferociousness that left me aching. Memories flooded my head like a tidal wave. I pushed them back.

"I'll call her," I said.

"Baby, I didn't want to tell you before you went to bed, but I felt that news like that should be told immediately. If you want to go, let me know, I'll make your travel arrangements." My father hugged me and rubbed my back. And suddenly I was a scared eight-year-old little girl who was meeting seven males with names all beginning with *J* and promising me pizza.

Thirteen

I knew I had to go to Ma Belle's funeral. I actually thought about not going. I thought about just sending flowers and a card. It would be easier that way. I wanted to remember my grandmother with my four-year-old eyes and heart. I wanted to remember the woman who had made me peanut butter and jelly sandwiches with chicken soup every day for lunch.

The funeral was to be held that Friday, and I decided I just wanted to fly in on Thursday and leave Sunday. That gave me more than enough time to see my cousins and visit Ma Belle's family, who hadn't seen me since I was a baby. I had an older great-aunt and great-uncle whom I hadn't seen since I was four as well. I had cousins whom I barely kept in touch with, and I knew the funeral would be as good a time as any to spend time with my family. I told Jordan he just had to drop me off at the check-in. I didn't need him to wait with me. He was hesitant, but I insisted. I needed to be alone with my thoughts. I checked in and got a waffle cone while I waited for my flight. I hadn't even talked to Anthony, but speaking to him didn't seem all that important at that point. So many other things were taking priority. Like a zombie I got on the plane when they called my row number.

I stared out the window of the airplane. It's funny when

you're flying, it's as if you are only a few feet above a blanket of cotton balls. I'd flown twice before that, to visit my daddy's family in New York. I had been about nine. Jordan and I had fought over the window seat, so my father put us on a rotating schedule. Every thirty minutes we had to change seats, taking turns. I had loved it. Now looking out of the window I just felt empty. Usually memories of my brother and me growing up made me smile, no matter how upset I was. Now it seemed as though even that brief snapshot of the happier moment in my childhood no longer brought me joy. It was sad. Was there anything that could make me happy anymore?

My cousin Sonya picked me up at LAX. We climbed into her cherry-red Mercedes and drove to her apartment. On the way to her spot she told me how she was dating a "balla" who had no problem with keeping her laced. Which basically equated to her dating a drug dealer. No big deal there. Her father had been a drug dealer. The apple doesn't fall too far from the tree.

I took a shower and slipped into a pair of shorts and a T-shirt. Nothing fancy. I was going to enjoy my time away from Anthony's appraising eye. I was going to attempt to be myself for the few days I was there. If I could remember who Jasmyn was, that is.

"We're supposed to go over to Ma Belle's house for dinner tonight. All of the family is going to be there," Sonya told me as she plugged in her curling iron in her miniscule bathroom.

"Come, sit in here and talk to me while I curl my hair. . . . I know we were cool when we were kids, but I haven't seen you since we were babies," she said, giving me a shy smile.

I maneuvered my way into the bathroom and sat on the toilet. I surveyed my cousin for a minute.

She had the same ebony skin that Ma Belle had worn so proudly. Sonya barely reached five-one, and was all curves. Her hair (what percentage of it was actually hers was debatable) was up in a ponytail that grazed her shoulders. She had strategically placed red tracks in it, so I assumed she was wearing something red to Ma Belle's. Her nails were artfully done, boasting the initials J.P. in gold glitter. I guessed those were her man's initials. I wondered what Anthony would say if I got his initials on my nails. Rings on every single finger, diamonds shining and twinkling. She was wearing a pair of Nike sweatpants with a matching T-shirt. Her toes were air-brushed in a similar pattern as her nails. Ghetto fabulous. We didn't look related at all. Sonya was the only girl cousin I could really remember when I lived in LA. Her mother used to braid my hair.

"Tell me about yourself, girl." The curling iron sizzled as she applied it to a section of her ponytail.

"What do you want to know?" I murmured.

"Okay . . . hmm, where do you stay?"

"I live with my daddy, and my brother," I said, watching her expertly grab another piece to curl.

"Oh, for real. You just have one brother then?" she probed.

"Actually I have six. They're all grown, but Jordan is not much older than me."

"You got a boyfriend?" Sizzle.

"Yes. His name is Anthony." It felt strange saying I had a boyfriend. Back home in Denver everyone in my world knew I was with Anthony. Los Angeles wasn't my world though. I could just as easily have lied and said I didn't have a boyfriend.

"Coo. My man, Jasaan, will be there tonight. You'll meet him. He ain't much to look at but he real sweet." She smiled.

I considered myself warned. I mean if a female admits her man is ugly, then he really must be *ugly*.

We arrived at Ma Belle's around six o'clock. I decided to dress sharp, simply because I knew my mother might be there. I seriously doubted it though. Renai rarely associated herself with the ghetto side of her family. It was as if she'd used them for genetic material only. There were numerous cars parked along the street in front of the house. Children played in the yard. I vaguely remembered being one of those children. Not a care in the world.

I stepped inside the little brick house and prepared myself to smile and look equally as mournful. My aunts and uncles

sat crammed into whatever chairs they could find. An assortment of cousins was there as well. The smell emanating
from the kitchen was rich and warm, reminding me of the
meals Ma Belle had cooked every night. I noticed not much
had changed. Beyond a few new appliances and a new sofa,
everything was the same.

Mr. Hughes, Ma Belle's husband, had died years ago, I
was informed. Everyone hugged me and kissed me and
oohed and *aahed* over how I'd grown up, and how pretty I
had gotten. Numerous aunts discreetly gave my hair a polite
pull or tug, verifying if I was wearing a weave or not. I found
a place at the kitchen table and swiftly finished my mandatory plate of food and watched as everyone proceeded to get
drunk and mourn my grandmother. My aunt Sharon, Sonya's
mother, placed food in the refrigerator and washed dishes. I
quickly got up to help her. She was a mirror image of Sonya.
Or I guess Sonya was a mirror image of her. She wore her
hair in a short bob, and for some reason her eyes looked a lot
younger than her daughter's did.

"I am so glad you were able to make it, Jasmyn. Mama
talked a lot about you after your mother moved out," she said
as I dried the dishes she had finished washing.

Why didn't she contact me then? I wanted to ask so badly,
but the words just wouldn't come. It really didn't matter at
that point.

"Your mother didn't really want much else do with us.
You know that Renai has always been one to isolate herself.
Mama always put her on a throne," my aunt said wistfully.
Did I detect a note of bitterness?

"Is my mother coming tonight?" I said carefully.

"Probably not. I told her we were having dinner. She said
she'd drop in if she could. She seems to be so busy these
days. I don't know why. She doesn't work. I guess she has
better things to do than come down to south central though.
She lives in Beverly Hills, you know."

"No, I didn't know. I guess I will see her tomorrow at the
funeral."

"Matthew might come by though. He's been such a help."
My aunt was wiping the counter down.

I dropped the knife I'd been drying but quickly recovered it from the counter.

"Matthew?" I croaked.

"Yes, you remember Mr. Hughes's nephew. He lived with ya'll for a while. You were only four then, so you probably don't remember that much. He's been really helpful. He and your mother are dating . . . go figure, right? He's a very successful businessman. He's in the real estate business. He turned his life around. When he was living here he was a thug. In a gang and everything. But Ma Belle worked with him and sent him to college, Lord knows where she got the money, and he did good for himself."

I felt my heart stop beating for a moment. I wanted to scream. Just scream. I guessed I had thought that Matthew would disappear just because my little four-year-old mind wished it to happen at the time.

I knew where Ma Belle had gotten the money to send him to college too. I guess my daddy had contributed to the re-formation of a thug without knowing it. I excused myself and found myself going into the bedroom that used to belong to my mother.

It hadn't changed much. The bed was still the same, and the pink chenille bedspread had been replaced by a softer mauve comforter. The white furniture scarred in many places was still there, and the television that had rocked me to sleep many nights was still on the dresser. I wanted to throw up. If I looked hard enough I could see a four-year-old pressing herself against an ice princess while she slept soundly. I could hear my voice begging and pleading with him, trying to convince him I didn't wet the bed. I could taste the fear that was forced upon my almost toddler mind week after week. It made me sick and I wanted to throw up.

"Matthew, I am so glad you came. I saved you a plate. Let me go warm it up."

I heard my aunt's voice in the kitchen, and I knew that *he* was in the house. Suddenly, I had to leave.

I rushed out of the bedroom. If I hurried I could be sitting in Sonya's car and waiting without having to see him. I didn't make it. I bumped into a steel chest that smelled faintly of

Escape. I knew it was him. I backed up a little and looked at him.

He hadn't changed much. He was still tall, and instead of the sagging pants and blue flannel, he was wearing an Armani business suit. He had gotten rid of the cornrows and now had little locks, which were neat and groomed. The eyes were the same. I just stared at him.

"Excuse me, I'm sorry for bumping into you. I was coming back here to make a phone call." He smiled apologetically. Gone was the ghetto slang that I distinctly remembered him using. It was replaced by a rich, classy eloquence. I realized he didn't recognize who I was.

I just stared at him. There were no words I could speak at that point that would do justice to what I felt.

"I'm Matthew. Ma Belle saved my life. She was married to my uncle. Are you one of Sonya's friends?"

"No," I said coldly.

"Okay . . . are you related to the family?"

"Yes," I returned. I really couldn't believe he didn't remember me.

"Hmm . . . you must excuse me, I really am not familiar with everyone in the family, but most . . . people I know. What's your name?" He was sounding a tad awkward.

"Jasmyn Renai Perry," I said, enunciating every word. *I bet you remember me now . . . child molester,* I thought to myself.

I know that it is virtually impossible for someone as dark as he is to turn pale. But he did. Very pale. His eyes widened in surprise and narrowed. He was shaken, I could tell.

"Um . . . oh. You're her granddaughter. I didn't recognize you. I don't know if you lived here at the same time I did," he said shakily.

"Oh, I was living here when you first moved in. I *remember,*" I said quietly. I stressed the word *remember.* I didn't want him to think that I forgot anything. I squeezed past him careful not to touch him, more than necessary. Sonya was sitting on the couch next to her boyfriend, who true to her word looked like a mud duck with gold teeth.

"You ready to go, Jasmyn?" she asked, yawning.

"Yes," I said, sighing.

For some reason I felt a little empowered. I realized that my being there made Matthew more uncomfortable than he made me uncomfortable. I hadn't seen my mother yet. That would be the real test.

Fourteen

I woke up around 4:30 that next morning. I was nervous. I lay awake on my cousin's sofa sleeper and tried to prepare myself for seeing my mother. I didn't know why it was such a huge event. I mean if I really thought about it, my mother didn't have such a monumental role in my life growing up. The only time she really interacted with me was out of necessity. I was a nonentity to her. She got rid of me as soon as she could. I think I just wanted her to see what I'd become. I wanted her to acknowledge my existence. At eight I couldn't demand much of her. I didn't know what exactly a mother was supposed to do. But lying there staring, listening to the clock my cousin had in her kitchen tick the seconds away, I knew that she owed me something. Whether she thought so or not.

I didn't know what I was going to wear either. I knew Ma Belle would have wanted me to wear bright colors. Nothing too dark and somber. She always told me God let us see colors for a reason. I had brought a couple of outfits just in case I came to the point where I didn't know what to wear. Now I *really* didn't know what I should wear. I had no choice but to call my fashion adviser. I located the phone card my father

320 Kori Nicole Brown

had given me and picked up the phone and called Chayenne. She answered on the eighth ring.

"Somebody better be dead or dying."

"Chayenne . . . " I said, my voice shaking a little. I gulped for air and tried to calm my nerves.

"Jasmyn? What's the matter?" I could hear her sitting up.

"I, um, sorry to call so early. I know it's five-thirty there, but I just . . . I'm seeing her today and I have no idea what to put on. I don't want to wear what I planned," I stammered.

"Go look in your suit bag," she said smugly.

"Huh?" I was confused.

"Now, see? Did Cinderella question her fairy godmother when she hooked her up? Nope, she just did as she was told. But you know Negros have to question. Go look in your suit bag," she said.

I got up and found my suit bag hanging in the hall closet. I opened it. On top was the most beautiful suit I'd ever seen. It was cream, and the cut was sharp. But what made it stand out were these unusual rose accents around the collar and through the middle. It was in fact a work of art. Very feminine yet very sophisticated. I knew Chayenne had spent a mint on it. I opened up my suitcase and found the matching shoes and purse.

I rushed back to the phone.

"When did you have time to?" I breathed.

"Look in the purse," Chayenne said.

I opened up the purse and dumped out four jewelry boxes. I opened them. I'd seen jewelry before. Chayenne wore enough of it, and to see some of the jewelry her mother wore at times would make anyone's mouth drop. But never had I had jewelry of my own. Now it seemed that I would be wearing diamonds to Ma Belle's funeral.

"Don't say anything. Don't even attempt to cry or get all sentimental. Save it for the funeral. My mother just thought you should go into battle with the correct gear. If you need anything, girl, I'm here," Chayenne said with a yawn when she heard me pick the phone back up.

"I love you, Chayenne Janine Martin," I said, trying to hold back tears.

"Ditto."

"Oh, how should I wear my—" I began.

"You can wear it down. I would wear it loose. Wear it however you think she will wear hers. You want people to know that you are related. She won't have any choice but to acknowledge you," Chayenne said gravely.

"Thank you."

"Good night, girl." And with that she hung up the phone. I felt a little better.

"Oh, girl, where did you get that suit!" Sonya exclaimed as we climbed into her Mercedes. She was dressed in a fire-engine-red suit, and her hair was no longer in the ponytail, but was back in a French roll. She had on minimal makeup, and other than her nails she looked very classy. She had taken off some of her jewelry. Her boyfriend was meeting us at the funeral home. The rest of the family had opted for squeezing into the limousines that would be leaving from Ma Belle's house. I found a pair of Chanel sunglasses in the purse, with a note from Chayenne that read:

Hey, J, wear these when you first walk into the service. They will make you look mysterious, and they will hide your red eyes when you start to cry. Renai will probably be wearing a pair too.

Love you
C

"Why aren't they having it at a church?" I inquired of my cousin as she zipped through traffic.

"Ma Belle knew too many people, girl. There's not enough room at the church. Don't worry though. There will be more than enough preaching. Trust me."

When we pulled into the funeral home it was packed. We found somewhere to park, and I slipped on the sunglasses. Sonya smiled at me and we both took deep breaths.

There's something eerie about entering a funeral home. No matter how comforting and cheery they try to make it, it's still a place of death. My stomach seemed to do cartwheels as I followed my cousin like a robot to the front section of seats that had been reserved for the family. There were tons and tons of flowers. And there was Ma Belle, resplendent in a beautiful flowered dress lying in a lavender casket. I sat down. I couldn't bring myself to look at her up close. All of my aunts and uncles were there as well as my cousins. People looked at me questioningly. Some whispered. I sat still and listened to the organ music being piped into the spacious room. Then I saw my mother.

I didn't quite know what I had expected to see. Maybe I thought that she would be uglier to my more mature seventeen-year-old eyes. Or maybe I thought I would see some flaw that I hadn't seen when I was four. But Renai Marie DeWitt was as perfect as ever. She wore a gray suit that was cut in such a simple and unimposing way you knew it was designer. Her hair was down and soft around her face. It looked as if ink had been poured over her shoulders. Curves perfect. Feminine. She also wore a pair of sunglasses. Composed yet solemn. I could only stare. I watched in horror as Mathew Hughes placed his hand on her shoulder and rubbed her arm intimately as she went to view the body.

I guess my seeing Renai was a little anticlimactic. I didn't know what I had expected, really. But somehow I felt there was some vital emotion absent from my psyche that I should have been feeling at that moment.

I got up. I decided it was time for me to face Ma Belle one last time.

I walked the ten feet to the casket that would be her final resting place, and I peered in. Her skin was as smooth as ever, very few wrinkles or creases. Just around the eyes because she had laughed and smiled a lot. Her hands were folded carefully over her chest, and her hair was curled simply. I saw her and I wanted to hug her. I wanted to hear her laugh and call me Jazzy, and tell me how much she had missed me. I wanted her to braid my hair. I wanted to tell her about my brothers and my father. I wanted to tell her about

Anthony. I wanted to ask her why she'd kept me away from my father. I wanted to ask her about why my mother was so cold to me. There were so many things that I wanted from her, but they all required that she be alive. I felt a few tears collect in the corners of my eyes. It had come to this. It was too late. What's more, I wanted to tell her how much I loved her. I wanted to tell her I forgave her for what she'd done. I heard my mother gasp. I looked over my shoulder, and though our eyes were both hidden behind our designer glasses we saw each other. I knew hers was a look of shock, and mine was a look of contempt. She lowered her head as I approached her.

"Hello . . . " I said, my voice unusually strong. Or maybe it was just void of feeling. I didn't know what to call her. When I was younger I had called her Mommy, but every time I did I could see how much it irritated her so I just stopped addressing her all together.

"Hello, Jasmyn," she said smoothly. She had regained her composure.

"I'm leaving on Sunday. Can you take me to the airport?" I asked.

"Sure. I'll be there early," she acquiesced. I knew she wanted to decline, but she couldn't since all of her brothers and sisters were sitting right there.

"That girl looks a little like you, Renai," I heard one of my uncles murmur.

"Oh, my goodness, she's beautiful, Renai." That was one of my aunts.

"All that's her real hair too." That was my great-aunt.

I gave each one of them a kiss and a smile and I sat down next to Sonya.

I really can't describe the next few hours. They were heart-wrenching. It's scary watching a family say good-bye to someone that they've known for so long. When you bury family it's as if a part of you dies. For some reason I held my tears in though. I knew that if I let them flow I might not be able to stop them. I resigned myself to cry them by myself.

My mother pulled up at three o'clock to take me to my 5:30 flight. I wore a pair of blue jeans and a red quarter-length cotton shirt. I had a sweater tied around my neck, and I had put my hair in a simple twist. I had mastered the "classic look," as Chayenne had termed it. My mother had on a flowered dress that exposed her beautiful shoulders. She looked perfectly at home in her Mercedes.

"Okay, so let's cut the niceties, Jasmyn. You're old enough to condemn me for how I messed up your life or traumatized you or whatever . . . so why don't you get it out of the way?" she said after we had gotten on the freeway.

I was a little surprised at the bitterness in her voice. "Why Matthew?"

"Look, he has nothing to do with this. This is between me and you," she returned. I knew she hadn't expected me to go to there.

"You know what? I have made excuses my whole life as to why you were such a failure as a mother. That was easy. There are a lot of people who have mothers that really didn't want them. I mean believe it or not I had enough of a mother in Ma Belle, and my father has given me more than enough love. I haven't dwelled on the fact that you weren't there with me growing up. What I don't understand is, why would you want a man that likes little girls?" I said coldly.

I felt the car swerve slightly. I watched her perfectly manicured hands grip the steering wheel. She was fighting for her composure.

"That is a filthy lie," she said coldly.

"I thought we were cutting the niceties. You know why we moved out of Ma Belle's house. You knew what he did to me. You knew before you married Mr. DeWitt you needed me out of the way just in case it happened again. So you left me at Daddy's. But why do you want him now? What's the angle? What can he do for you? I mean you're rich enough, aren't you? I know Matthew is paid, but I don't know if he can quite yet compare to what your husband left you. Why him?"

"Jasmyn, don't try to understand, okay? Matthew and I have an understanding. I've been with him for a long time, and we will probably get married. As for you, my dear, you can stay right where you are. Away from me. That way you don't complicate things. If you ever try to come back into our lives with those filthy lies again I will make sure your life and your father's are miserable. I have the money to do it too." I had never heard so much ice in a person's voice.

"Don't worry about me. I'm going to be paid. You know that high school student basketball player everybody is raving about?" I shot back.

"Anthony something or other. I've heard of him. They're comparing him to Michael Jordan. . . . A friend of mine is a sports agent." She shrugged nonchalantly.

"Well, that's my boyfriend. He's in love with me. And I don't have to worry about money. If you ever try to do anything to my family, I'll make sure that *your* life is miserable. And *I will* have the money to do it." The iciness in my voice matched hers perfectly.

She was silent a moment. She glanced over at me and I could feel her measuring the truthfulness of my statement. "Okay. So maybe you are ready to play with the big girls. I mean you are my daughter, after all, and don't think I didn't notice that suit you had on yesterday. It was almost something to be proud of. You'll never be a beauty like me, but you are pretty enough to get a millionaire. Just remember this, sweet child of mine. You have a conscience, I don't. And, um, your little boyfriend doesn't have money yet, now, does he?"

"He does have money. I just asked him for ten thousand dollars the other day. He's getting paid already," I said smugly.

"By who?" She raised an eyebrow in disbelief.

"He won't tell me."

"Sounds like he's definitely going pro. You know they pay players all the time." she said, smiling.

"No, he's not doing anything illegal!" I insisted.

"Jasmyn, let me explain something to you. Pro teams do a lot of things to get the players they want. I'm sure he drives a nice car, doesn't he? He probably buys you all kinds of gifts. Word is he wants to play for a western division team. Probably right here in Los Angeles, matter of fact. Watch my words," she murmured. Her voice wasn't cold at all. It held a slight measure of sympathy. I thought about it for a minute and I knew she knew what she was talking about.

"Why did you need ten grand?" she asked after a brief silence.

For some strange reason I decided to trust her. I knew I was in over my head, and if anyone knew about the cutthroat world of money and power, it was she. I told her the whole story about the tape and Sherina.

"First thing, Sherina isn't your friend. As a matter of fact, don't trust her at all. You give her the money and you get the tape. Let your involvement end there. Second, I'm going to do some checking on your boyfriend. I'll find out where he and his friend are getting their money, and then I'll call you and let you know," she said matter-of-factly.

I didn't know what to say. She was giving me advice. "Thank you."

"Don't thank me. Jasmyn, I don't know how to love anyone but myself. That's the personality flaw I've been given. I can help you with this though. I'm going to give you some money so that you can get a car, and you can just tell your father it's my gift to you." Her voice was flat.

"Okay."

"Ma Belle left you money, Jasmyn. She left me money as well. I don't need it, so I'm splitting it and giving it to your cousin Sonya because I like her and she has a nut ball for a mother. I'm going to give the other half to you. It's over one hundred thousand dollars. I want you to give me your bank account number so that I can have my accountant transfer the funds as soon as I receive them. I'm going to give you a check for thirty thousand now."

That's exactly what she did. I sat on the plane that afternoon with a check for thirty thousand dollars in my purse and a headache. But for some reason I felt a little lighter. Or maybe my grasp on reality was slipping.

Fifteen

Jordan picked me up at the airport, and asked me how everything went. I didn't tell him about Matthew. I told him about seeing my mother and about the money she was giving me. We went straight to the bank, and I deposited my check. They told me it would be a while before it would clear and I said that was fine.

I called Chayenne and told her about the money I was getting. She told me I should look into investing it. I told her that I had thought about it and she said she would talk to her mother and father and see what they could do in the way of helping me start using my money.

I didn't call Anthony. I couldn't. I was afraid to. I wanted to know how he made his money. I called Sherina instead.

"Where have you been!" she hissed.

"There was a death in my family and I had to go to California. Anyway, I have the money," I said, ignoring her attitude.

"You know it's almost too late. I had to give them my money and then promise the rest in a week. The week is up tomorrow, Jasmyn. I hope you have the money," she said.

"I have it. It's cash. I want the second tape though," I murmured.

"Bring the money to school tomorrow and put it in the trunk of my car and I'll bring you the tape when they give them to me."

"No. I'll go with you to get the tapes, and *I'll* give them the money."

"Oh, so I see you're getting a little hip to the game. Well, that's fine. I'm going to meet them at a restaurant for dinner tomorrow evening."

"Fine." I hung up the phone not quite sure what to expect the next day. I knew I was in way over my head . . . Renai had made that evident. I was just curious to see how well I'd be able to play the game.

Anthony found me at school the next morning right after my first class. I had wanted to avoid him until my mother had given me the breakdown on exactly how he was able to give me a duffel bag filled with money at my request.

"Hi," I said, smiling sweetly and giving the requisite kiss.

He pushed me away. "Why didn't you call me last night?"

I felt my smile disappear. He had that angry look in his eye again, and I could hear the bitterness in his voice.

"I was tired. I knew I would see you today. You know I did just come back from my grandmother's funeral, Anthony. You could give me a little sympathy before you start giving me the third degree," I returned. My patience was at its limit. Besides that, my nerves were shot since I'd placed the cash in Sherina's trunk.

He didn't say anything, he just grabbed me by my hair and pushed me into my locker. My head made a resounding ring that caused the busy hallway to quiet and everyone to look in our direction. I felt my face flush, with humiliation.

"Let go of my hair." My voice was barely a whisper.

"Get your stuff," he yelled, gesturing to my backpack.

"Let go of—" I began again.

"Get your stuff and come on!"

A few people jumped and a teacher poked her head out of a classroom. She surveyed the scene in the hallway quickly and seeing that Anthony was the one causing the commotion, she promptly closed the door to her classroom. I decided I didn't want a scene, and for the sake of peace I would grab my books and pretend to follow him. His grip on my scalp was beginning to hurt. When he saw me attempt to get my books he released my hair and gripped the back of my neck and pulled me by the arm through the nearest exit.

I didn't say anything as he pushed me into his car. As soon as he slammed the door I erupted.

"We're through! I don't want anything to do with you," I shouted as he pulled the car out of the school parking lot.

"Shut up, Jasmyn." He was unusually quiet.

Five minutes later we had pulled into his driveway. I didn't think his mother was home.

"Get out of the car!" He was yelling now.

"Take me back to school, Anthony. I really don't have time for this."

He opened the car door and yanked me out. I stumbled to the ground and would have fallen if he hadn't been holding my arms. He pulled me into the house.

I can honestly say that I did fight him back. I think I slapped him once. But in the end I basically ended up on the floor of his living room shielding my body as best I could from his blows. I really don't remember the physical beating as much as I remember my thoughts.

First of all, I wasn't shocked. I knew Anthony had it in him to beat me senseless. I'd seen that side of him numerous times. He had a temper. But up until that morning, I'd never thought he'd hurt me at the risk of losing me. Secondly, I felt helpless. There was nothing I could do to stop him. I didn't like that feeling. So because of these two facts, I began to cry. Tears so hot that I thought they would burn my face slid down my cheeks, and I lay there helplessly as he lit into me. I don't know when he stopped. I know my head hurt, and my mouth was a little salty because he had caused it to bleed when he first slapped me. The majority of his blows had landed on my back, arms, and thighs. He had taken care to avoid my face. He'd only slapped me there once.

I remember the feel of my tears and the carpet that his mother had no doubt paid an arm and a leg for, creating the strangest scratching sensation against my cheek. I could smell his mother's overpowering perfume as well as a hint of his own aftershave and sweat. I heard him breathing heavily as he dropped to his knees beside me. I rolled over. Blood has the strangest taste. Almost metallic. I slowly sat up. The tears rolled uncontrollably. But it was almost like a natural reaction. Like the blood. I wasn't really sobbing. There was little hurt in my tears. They were not cleansing at all.

I couldn't look at him. I just sat there and held my lip so that my blood wouldn't drip on his mother's carpet.

"Look what you made me do, Jasmyn! Why do you make me do this to you? You are the only one I have in my corner, don't you know that! All they want is money! You're the only one who isn't out for money. Don't you understand?" He pulled me into his arms. I winced.

"I don't want you anymore," I said calmly.

"What?"

"I don't want you anymore. I can't be your punching bag when you need to vent, because everything is messed up in your life, Anthony," I said, grabbing a tissue from an ornate box on the coffee table. I wiped my lip. It had stopped bleeding.

"You can't leave me," he said woodenly.

"I just did."

"Jasmyn . . . don't you love me? If you left me now . . . Jasmyn, I couldn't take it," and with that he shot to his feet. He ran upstairs and before I could say anything he came down with a nine-millimeter in his hand.

The first time you see a gun is one you always remember. You'd think it wouldn't be such a big deal with as many guns as you see in movies or on television. But when you see a gun in real life for the first time, the only thing you can do is contemplate how powerful that little piece of steel is. Anthony held the gun so easily. I watched as he loaded the clip and placed it to my head. I felt the surprisingly warm metal against my temple.

"See, Jasmyn? I can't have you leave me. If you left me I'd have to hurt you . . . then I'd hurt myself. You are *all I have.*" His voice was shaking.

I began to shake again.

"Please, Anthony—" I began.

"No, no, no! See? Now you're scared. You don't think I'm serious, do you? You think I'm just trying to scare you! I will kill you, do you understand me? I will kill you if you leave me. I'll kill myself too, but I know you don't care about that. I'm going pro and I need to have everything straight before I get to the NBA. I don't want to deal with a whole lot of females, and STDs and all that. I just want you. You're pure. I know you a virgin, I checked around to see if you'd been giving it up to anyone. I'm the only fool you've ever *kissed*. You know how many girls can say that? Somebody like you is too hard to find. You are not leaving me. Tell me that you're not leaving me." His voice was perfectly rational.

One would think that with a gun to one's head a person would suddenly come to some conclusions. I've heard some say that in a moment such as the one I found myself in, their whole life flashed before their eyes. They might say that they came to appreciate life more and realized how fragile it was. I guess at that point I was so detached that I just didn't care. The only thing I could really think about was the mess my brains would make on Anthony's mother's floor. I wondered if he accidentally pulled the trigger if I'd finally find some type of release from the unending pressure that seemed to be building in my life. See, that's why I acquiesced. That's why I decided to stay. Not because I was afraid that he *might* kill me. There was this part of me that reasoned that if I stayed with him long enough . . . he actually *would* kill me. Put me out of my misery.

"Okay. I'll never leave you." I was crying now. Trying my best to sound scared. I knew that if he had any idea of how calm I *really* was at that moment he wouldn't be able to handle it.

"Say it again. Say, 'Anthony, I'll never leave you.'" His voice was smug now.

"Anthony, I'll never leave you."

"Get up and clean yourself up. We need to go back to school," he said in the most normal voice imaginable.

What could I do but follow directions?

* * *

I had to tell someone about what had happened. I was so scared. I didn't know what exactly he was capable of, and I didn't want to die. I told Chayenne.

"Jazz . . . you have to go to the police, girl. There is no question. If that fool pulled a gun on you? Think about it, he could have killed you accidentally while trying to scare you. If he really loved you he wouldn't have taken a chance like that," she said, her voice low, almost a whisper.

"Chayenne, I can't just go to the police. You know that mess will be covered up. I'll look like the bad guy. He's about to go into the NBA! You know when you first tried to tell me about money and fame and all that I didn't get it. But now I'm starting to see how crazy people start acting when they think they are close to someone with money. His teachers don't hold him to anything, his mother is a complete snake, all the coaches, everyone is on his side!" I was crying. We were sitting in her car during lunchtime.

"Okay . . . so we play the game his way. We know that Anthony does care about himself, so we find a way to put his career in danger. He'll leave you alone then, 'cause no female is going to be worth his basketball career." Chayenne smirked. Lawyer mind at work.

I sighed. My ribs ached from being kicked, and I hoped there wasn't any damage I'd have to go to the hospital for. Usually Anthony knew when to stop . . . right at the point before I needed hospital attention. He'd hit me a couple of other times before, but nothing as bad as when he pulled out the gun.

"Okay, I can get something. I need to borrow your car though."

Chayenne gave me the keys to her car that afternoon after school.

"Just don't wreck it. My mama would be very upset with me," she said as she jumped out of the car and ran up to her front door. I laughed and shook my head. Chayenne was the only junior at our high school pushing a Lexus.

I decided to dress for dinner with Sherina that night with care. For some reason I didn't want her to know that I didn't trust her. I slid into a denim skirt that reached my knees and a multipatterned pink shirt. I looked very high school and very harmless.

"Do you have it?" she asked me when I pulled up in front of her house.

"Yes, I do," I murmured to her.

"I'll drive."

"I can follow you then." I could tell she was a bit miffed about the fact that I wasn't about to give her complete control of the situation. I followed her to I-25 and we made our way to Colorado Springs. About an hour and fifteen minutes later we made it to the Broadmoor Hotel. I was a little impressed. The Broadmoor was swank to say the least. I tried to act nonchalant as I gave the valet my keys, and I discreetly removed the huge red shopping bag from the trunk. Wrapped very neatly among some tissue paper was the money.

"We're meeting them at the grill," Sherina said, giving my outfit a look of distaste. She wore a simple pin-striped black suit that was anything but cheap.

I shrugged and tried to look unassuming. The grill was on the first floor and it seemed we had reservations as we were shown quickly to our seats.

"Okay, let me do all the talking. The couple doesn't deal directly with us. They have a spokesperson. I'm not sure who he is. We'll have dinner, and then we'll leave. Leave the money under the table. Understand?" she muttered, peering at the menu. I nodded.

He was a tall white man. He wore a business suit and looked very ordinary.

"How are you, Sherina?" he asked, smiling as he was seated.

"I'm breathing. I hope this is our last meeting." She grinned.

"Oh, it will be. They just want to settle down. I think that's what we all want. This whole thing will be taken care of this time tomorrow," he said easily.

"Whatever. It would really bother me if there were more than two tapes out there, Ken. I mean *really* bother me. I get a little paranoid when I think people are trying to screw me."

"Sherina, trust me, there are only the two tapes. . . . This must be Jasmyn. You didn't introduce me." He turned his attention toward me.

I looked him in the eye, and something wasn't quite right. I couldn't put my finger on it, but I knew there was more to the dinner meeting than was being said.

"Hi," I murmured shyly. I then took a big gulp of my water.

Sherina rolled her eyes in disgust.

Dinner went smoothly, and we left before Ken did, as planned. Sherina handed me a plain paper bag. To the passersby it would appear to be a doggy bag. It contained my copy of the tape.

"Jasmyn, I hope we don't have to do something like this again," she said before the valet brought her red Camaro around. I could only shake my head.

Sixteen

When I got home my father was up. Very rarely did he stay up past midnight on a weekday. He'd never given me a curfew, because I'd never really stayed out late. I usually went to sleep before he did. I knew he wasn't worried, because I'd told him I was going to dinner with a friend, but still he seemed a little troubled.

He was sitting at the kitchen table with Jordan. They were both engrossed in a game of dominoes. I could see the concentration on both of their faces. I walked into the kitchen and sat on the counter, and watched them for a minute.

My daddy was wearing a Hard Rock Café London shirt, and a pair of run-over sweatpants. Jordan had on a wife beater and some basketball shorts. For some reason both of them showed a fear of lotion when it came to their feet, and the looks of concentration were so identical I couldn't help laughing. They looked up at me in unison.

"What?" they said in chorus.

I laughed harder.

"What's so funny? How was your little dinner date? Why are you dressed like Punky Brewster?" my brother said, shaking his head at my outfit.

"I know you ain't clownin', when your heels look like you were dragged behind a car," I returned.

My daddy busted up laughing.

"Your mother called you, Jasmyn. She told me to have you call her. She left her cell number. I was thinking, maybe we should go look for a car Friday. What do you think?" my daddy said, plopping down a domino.

"Okay," I said, careful not to let my enthusiasm show. I was curious to see what my mother had uncovered about the source of Anthony's money.

I glanced at my watch. It was almost one o'clock in the morning, her time. I decided to call anyway. I went into my bedroom and locked the door. I picked up my phone and dialed the number that my father had given to me.

She answered on the third ring.

"Yes," she said simply. She didn't sound tired at all.

"Hi, this is Jasmyn. You have some information for me?"

"Oh, yes. Well, my dear, it appears as though your boyfriend has a very interesting past. First, I want to ask you about some things . . . you've met his mother."

"Unfortunately."

She laughed with understanding.

"I'll assume that you don't like her. I'll also assume that you have just reason too. She's a wanna-be lady. She has the money, but lacks the style and class. She's made it her goal to be accepted into 'higher society,' as one might put it, and has been shut out at every corner. She's actually from LA. She's still married to Anthony's father."

"What! Anthony told me his father was locked up. He made him sound like a deadbeat." My mouth was wide open at this point.

"Not very accurate. Apparently, Ms. Tanya Reeves Carrington has taken to going by her maiden name. However, she is very married. They've been separated for the past ten years. A very tidy relationship, it appears. He pays for the house and gives her a monthly allowance that's just enough to keep her from working, and she pretends to be a struggling single mother. It's quite pathetic. Anyway, his father was a big-time drug dealer. When I say big time, I'm not talking about someone selling on the corner, or even their supplier. He has connections. He eventually went legit when Anthony was born, and figured out Tanya wasn't the one for him. He owns quite a few businesses that are doing very well. He lives in New York. Tanya can't wait for her son to become a star so that she can live in the manner to which she had become accustomed when she was with his dad."

I think I had stopped breathing when I heard the words *drug dealer,* but I'm really not sure. All I knew was that Anthony had lied to me.

"What is Anthony's relationship with his father?" My voice was shaking.

"They talk, occasionally. Anthony's father is a very smart man. He seems to love his son. If it weren't for Anthony, Tanya wouldn't be getting any type of money."

"How is Anthony getting paid?"

"It appears that the wonderful coach at your high school has graciously agreed to act as a go-between for someone who's interested in Anthony in the NBA. He's getting paid a nice sum of money if he can convince Anthony to 'persuade' the team that gets him in the draft to trade him. It's all planned, Jasmyn, he'll definitely end up playing for the team he wants."

My mother was very matter-of-fact as she delivered this information.

It only convinced me that breaking up with Anthony was essential for my well-being.

"Jasmyn, you have the tape, correct?"

Her words snapped me out of my thoughts. "Yes. I got it tonight."

"Okay, you're in the game. You can marry Anthony if you want at this point. But the thing is, if you do that, you have to know what you're getting into. And once you get into the game . . . you're in," she said softly. I could almost detect a hint of regret in her voice.

I had to think about what she said for a moment. I'd never considered myself a person that knew how to play *any* game, and I definitely didn't want to be with Anthony for his money only. The fact of the matter was at that point I *couldn't* leave him without losing a part of myself. I had lost too many pieces of myself already. Ma Belle dying had taken a piece, Matthew Linton Hughes had a piece, as had my mother. If I wasn't careful, there would be none left for me.

"Thank you for your information." I was ready to end the call.

"Dear girl, I will be keeping in touch," and with that she disconnected the call.

I sat in the darkness for a moment, a little numb from the information I'd received.

I picked up the phone again and gave Anthony my mandatory call for the night. He would probably not pick up the phone, but if he didn't have a message on his voice mail, that was going to be a smack in the face at least when I saw him.

"Hi, baby, this is Jasmyn. Just calling to tell you I love you and I was thinking about you. See you tomorrow at school." I used the soft, sweet, innocent voice he liked, and made sure I said, "I love you."

I listened to the message three times before I finally pressed one to send it. I don't know why. I think I was just reaffirming my decision to be with him no matter what. But the scary thing was that the message was so fake, and the only reason I'd left it was that I knew he'd demand it.

Seventeen

The next day at school was a normal day. Chayenne didn't mention the situation with Sherina, and neither did I. At lunchtime she took me to the bank to get a safety deposit box. I placed the videotape in it. I told her about Anthony's father.

She couldn't believe it. "So, let a sista get this straight. Not only does Anthony have a father, but he's not locked up like he claimed," she exclaimed as she pulled into the drive-through at McDonald's.

I nodded.

"Wow . . . I mean just wow. This is soap opera material, you know that, right?"

"I hope not. I just can't believe he lied to me like that. He made it sound like he was struggling and he had to play basketball, to keep some of the burden off of his mother. Now I'm finding out he's got a father who probably loves him and his mother is a styleless, gold-digging troll," I muttered, munching on a fry.

"I could have told you his mother was a styleless, gold-digging troll."

We broke up into laughter.

"But seriously . . . I have everything I need to get

this. That ESPN game is in a week. He can't afford to have anything happen this close to the end of the season to mess up his image. Anyway if he doesn't see it that way, I'm sure his coach will," I said, wiping the tears out of the corner of my eyes.

"Okay, I'm feeling that. You have to be careful though if he pulls out that gun again, girl . . . " Her voice trailed off.

I was already thinking along those lines. "I know but I'm going to see him tonight, and I'm going to break it off. I feel like the longer I've known him the less I know about him. What's wrong with me, Chayenne, how could I even want somebody like him?" I was trying to control the tears in my voice.

"Jasmyn, people rarely make drastic changes in a short period of time. You're probably seeing what was already there. Anthony is comfortable with you now. He knows that ya'll are going to be together, so maybe that's why he's acting so comfortable with you. Think about it. Everyone knows he's going pro. What female in her right mind would give up an opportunity to be the wife of a professional ballplayer? It's like winning the lottery. He knows that. He thinks that fact alone will keep you with him."

"You know what, girl? You're probably right. He probably thinks that the money is the main reason why I'm with him. If he only knew the thing that's keeping me with him is that he has something I can't live without."

"What?" She paused to look at me. We had pulled into the school parking lot, and were about to get out of her car.

"My heart," I said simply.

Anthony had practice after school, which gave me a few seconds to breathe. My father decided I should go and purchase my car. So he and my brother Jordan and I got into his Range Rover and drove to a dealership. The owner of the 'ership was one of my father's clients, so he gave us a 'eal. I was the proud owner of an Acura, champagne, accents and tinted windows. It was used, which me because I didn't want to use all of my money on a car. My brother insisted I get some custom wheels, but my father said wheels weren't very professional. My brother pointed out that I was only a junior in high school. My father insisted I would eventually take the car to college, and wheels weren't going to give it class. My brother just shook his head.

"If you want to get some fifteens, my friend Tyrell has the hookup. Just let a brother know," he whispered to me conspiratorially as we left the dealership office.

I shook my head.

I called Anthony at 8:00 that night and told him I was coming over.

"Why, what's the matter?" he murmured.

"I need to see you. I'll be over there in thirty minutes."

"A'ight then, Mom's gone, so it's cool." I knew what he was thinking. Little did he know I had something for his lying behind.

I called Chayenne as we had planned and she followed me to his house. I had my daddy's cell phone in my pocket and I called her number.

"Okay, I'm not going to hang up from this call. When I go in there, you'll be able to hear everything," I said after dialing her phone.

"Got you," she said.

I got out of my car, making sure my phone was clipped to my hip. . . . I prayed it worked.

Anthony answered the door in a pair of basketball shorts and that's it. I sat down on the coach in the living room. He stood and just looked at me expectantly.

"Anthony . . . I can't do this anymore. I love you, God knows how much I love you, and I thought it was enough, but it's not. You have a problem, you hittin' on me whenever you get mad. You don't respect me. I think you'd do much better if you don't have a lady, or if you found another one, but I can't be with you no more," I said, breaking into tears.

"Oh, that's cute, Jasmyn. . . . You serious, huh?" he replied, laughing.

Before I could reply I felt his hand connect with my cheek. I saw stars. I reeled and fell to my knees. I quickly got to my feet so that I'd be ready to avoid any other blows he might want to deliver.

"Everybody thinks that you're so sweet and innocent. They think I'm lucky for having you. But if they only knew . . . that I'm not the lucky one, you are." His voice was quiet now. He seemed to be speaking more to himself than to me.

"You know what? I'm through. If you come near me again I'm going to the police. I am not playin'! I'll tell them you have a gun and that you threatened me with it!" I screamed.

"You think they'll go put me in jail based on something *you* say! Baby, I'm going number one in the draft. Do you know what that means? How many crazy females you think are gonna be coming up with fake mess and going to the police? Please. *I own you,* you hear me? *I own you* . . . I will *kill* you if you try to leave me." He was laughing and screaming now. I took that opportunity to slowly inch my way to the door.

"No, you won't. 'Cause I can ruin your career. I have your little freaknik at the lake on tape, sweetness. . . . Oh you didn't know there was a tape, did you?" I said quietly.

"What! You lyin!" he said, eyeing me.

"Whatever . . . it's in a safe place and no one has seen it except your little friend Sherina."

"I don't believe you, Jasmyn, you ain't that smart!"

"Oh, really? Two strippers, one of them in a red bikini, the other one in a silver one. Both of them pierced in places they shouldn't be, but you seemed to enjoy that." I smirked.

He was silent, and for one minute I thought he was about to get ignorant. He didn't, he just turned really cold.

"A'ight, so what is it gonna take?"

"All I want is for you to leave me alone. Pretend like you never met me." I was crying again. How could I say something like that about him? He was the only man I'd ever loved like that.

"A'ight. You don't exist. You know I'll just have to replace you. I thought you'd be good for my image. But I guess I chose the wrong one," he said sitting in a chair.

So it was that simple. I'd been for his image. He didn't

love me the way I loved him, and at that moment I wasn't sure he could love anyone.

"That's all I want. Oh, yeah . . . um, this whole conversation is being recorded. So if you start trippin', your little career is over, because I will tell all to your coach; then I'll put you on the evening news," I said, pulling out my activated cell phone. "Everything you said is on tape."

"Get out!" Anthony roared at me. I did, without further comment. I made my way to my car and put my cell to my ear.

"Girl, you a'ight! Chayenne screeched. I turned the volume down on my phone.

"It's cool, let's go to the bank and put the tape in the box," I said, turning off his street. I prayed that I'd made the right decision.

That night my mother called me. I'd gone home and taken a shower and crawled underneath the covers. It was around eleven when I answered the phone on my night table. It was my own private line. A gift from my daddy when we'd moved into the house.

"Hello, may I speak to Jasmyn?" Renai's voice was cultured.

"This is her," I said groggily.

"Hmm, you don't sound like a ray of sunshine today. Trouble in paradise?" Her voice was dripping with sarcasm. I chose to ignore it.

"What can I do for you?" I said coldly.

"Well, I found out some interesting information about your little friend Sherina. The one who helped you retrieve this tape."

"She's not my friend."

"Good. She's a little smart one. She set the whole thing up at the cabin. She paid those girls. They didn't even know they were being videotaped. She paid them five grand apiece. Well, really you paid them ten grand apiece. She merely recouped her spendings from your pocket. Watch your back." My mother sounded almost impressed by Sherina's efforts.

I was silent a moment. "I've taken care of that situation. I'm free of her and him and anything else sick and twisted that goes along with the game. You know what, Renai? I know you're still going to marry Matthew and that's cool with me, because I know that you don't care about anything but yourself. Just don't expect me to be a part of your life, unless you count the occasional phone call to let you know I'm breathing," I hissed.

It seemed that in my whole life, no one except my father and brothers really cared about me enough not to use me for something or hurt me.

"Excuse me?" my mother sputtered.

"You heard me. You marry the child molester if that's what you want, I'm just not going to be a part of your life," I said again.

"Well, I see someone finally read *Courage for Dummies*. Jasmyn, I didn't call to talk about my fiancé, so I won't, and if you need money or advice, call me."

"Okay, well, it's obvious you haven't read *Reality for Dummies,* because you still think problems go away if you run from them . . . or leave them on a doorstep. Bye, Renai." I felt good. I took a deep breath

"Jasmyn . . . " she said before I hung up.

"What?"

"You were a fool for leaving him. He's going to be worth millions," she said.

"Yeah, well, maybe I will be worth millions one day too," I said carefully.

"How?"

"When you die . . . hopefully you'll leave me in your will," I said coldly and hung up the phone.

Eighteen

The day of Anthony's big game that ESPN was actually televising, I went with Chayenne to meet the woman who would change my life and give my poor hot-combed, battered hair some tight microbraids . . . my therapist. I washed my hair and wrapped it Erykah Badu style (something Anthony hated) and rode with Chayenne to meet Ms. Elenora Paris.

Ms. Elenora Paris was a character if I'd ever seen one. She was about my height with beautiful caramel-colored skin. Her eyes twinkled when she spoke, and her hair hung past her shoulders in the prettiest locks I'd ever seen. They were neat and small. She wore a black dress that hugged all of her curves in the right places, and she was barefoot. Her home was tastefully decorated. It gave off a sense of warmth. Pictures of her family graced the walls, much like the walls at my own house. I felt comfortable there. Safe.

"Hey, Ms. Chayenne. Your mother and I just had lunch the other day. She said you're doing very well in school." Her voice was smooth and rich.

"I'm doing fine. Ms. Nora, this is my friend Jasmyn." Chayenne introduced me.

"Hi," I said politely.

She looked me in the eyes and gave me the brightest smile I'd ever seen. It lit up her whole face.

"Well, aren't you beautiful?" she said carefully.

That shocked me. Up until that point in my life the only people who had called me beautiful were my father and brothers. To hear it from a total stranger was a trip. I couldn't help smiling.

"Thank you," I murmured in response. What else could I have said?

"Ms. Nora, Jasmyn needs some healing. When can we make an appointment?" Chayenne asked, getting to the point.

"I had someone cancel just now, so if you have your hair I can get to work. You want what kind of braids?"

"Micros," I answered quickly.

"Let me see your hair, child," Ms. Nora said, walking over to me. She quickly divested me of my head wrap. She ran her hands through my hair. Pinched around the broken edges.

"You have some beautiful hair, that thick strong hair. We're going to grow it out okay. You washed it for me and you didn't put grease in it. Good." Her voice was businesslike.

"My hair is in the car." I had bought it earlier, not knowing when I'd be able to get an appointment. I retrieved it and Chayenne and I sat down in her basement converted to a studio. I got into the barber's chair and relaxed as she placed a cool black cape around my shoulders.

"What happened to your hair?" she asked as she clicked on the television. She opened up the bag of hair I'd handed her and began sectioning it into pieces.

I wanted to lie so badly. I hadn't expected her to ask me about it. But I decided to be honest.

"I was pressing it too much for my ex-boyfriend. He liked it real straight," I murmured.

She sectioned off a piece of my hair with a rat-tooth comb, and I felt her nimble fingers begin braiding my hair.

"He didn't treat me right. He mistreated me. I should have left him a long time ago," I said, controlling the tears in my voice.

Ms. Nora was quiet for what seemed like an eternity. The

only sound was our breathing, the steady hum of the news, and the smooth sound of her fingers braiding my hair.

"I'm not with him now though. I don't know if I can forgive him." I sighed.

"The first person you need to be forgiving is yourself, Jasmyn. It's not your fault, you understand? Look at what you did. He was controlling you, and look what happened to your pretty hair. What kind of sense does that make? You know why you did that? You did that because you thought if you did everything he asked, he would love you. Forgive yourself first." Her voice was low and smooth, but like steel nonetheless. I listened.

"It seems that men like to take advantage of me. . . . My grandmother's nephew by marriage . . . he . . . he used to mess with me. I told, and you know what happened? Nothing! We just moved. My mother got rid of me after that. Now my mother is going to marry the same man that messed with me. What kind of sense does that make? My life is just messed up." I was sobbing now. I'd never told anyone about Matthew, or my mother for that matter. That was one of those secrets I'd planned to take to the grave. It seemed that I didn't have any control over the words that had flowed out of my mouth. Chayenne was silent. I had never even told her.

"Honey, you aren't the only one that's been through something like that. For some reason there are women out there who just aren't fit to be mamas. See, love, when you first have a baby you get this attachment. Some women don't feel it until weeks after the baby is born. Some women feel it right when they see their baby. Some women never have it all. Your mama knows that she wasn't meant to be a mother. I bet you money that she didn't know about the situation with Matthew. Your grandmother probably asked her to leave to keep the peace, and didn't mention what happened to you."

"I'd never thought of that. I told her what happened to me. She just told me I was lying. She acted like she didn't know what I was talking about." I was dumbfounded. It had never occurred to me that my mother hadn't known.

"However, that doesn't mean that there is no justice.

Baby, what goes around comes around. I feel sorry for your boyfriend. He really doesn't know what love is. All the love he's received in his life has been conditional. His mama is mad at his father. So she just uses him. All the females that have ever been in his life are using him for the money and fame. Then along comes you, he didn't know how to treat you. He's selfish. Only person who loves him unconditionally is him. He can't conceive that you could."

"You know, that makes sense, Ms. Nora. But what about me? I love him and I still get the short end of the stick," I said through my tears.

"It's okay, baby, you'll find someone who loves you unconditionally. You just have to start to love you a little more, that's all. Do something for you. You live outside yourself, Jasmyn. You watch everything that's happened to you, but you don't want to let yourself feel. You run from your feelings. That can only work for a while. I know it's easy to pretend like the bad stuff is happening to someone else, but the thing about living outside yourself is you never get to experience the good stuff either. You have to start living it, baby, not just surviving it. Start with how you deal with this situation with your young man."

I listened intently. Then she was silent. I concentrated on the constant pull of her fingers on my scalp. By the time she was finished I felt better.

After nine hours she handed me the mirror so that I could admire my hair. For the first time in my life I felt just as beautiful as my mother. The braids looked good on me. I had gotten the curliest hair she could find. It looked almost natural. The braids were microscopic as they curled around my face, and my eyes seemed to stand out more. I looked like a woman. I decided it was time for me to start loving myself. I had already taken my first step, which was leaving Anthony. I paid Ms. Nora and I got into my car. We drove to Chayenne's house. She clicked on ESPN and we watched the game. She already knew I wanted to see it. And there he was as big as day. I saw the look of complete joy and control on his face. I saw why they called him Prodigy. I listened to his after-game interview when he stated he was single and focusing on school and basketball. Just that quickly I'd been erased. It felt good, I felt that I had a second chance. I had good grades. I was looking at schools, and my family was healthy and happy. Jasmyn was doing a'ight.

My mother called me that night. "I just wanted to say some things. I know our last conversation wasn't the most amicable. But I just wanted to say I didn't know that he'd done those . . . um, things to you. Ma Belle just told me it was time for me to go on my own," she stammered.

"Okay," was all I could manage.

"Jasmyn, you take care of yourself, okay? I know you're going to school, and you can just send the bill to me. Don't ever worry about money. If you need me, just let me know," she hurried.

"Okay, thank you," I said stiffly.

"Oh, and, Jasmyn, I remember when you used to cuddle with me at night. I wasn't really sleep and I, uh, wished I'd had the courage to hug you back, because I knew you were such a smart little girl. I was really proud that you were my kid, 'cause you were always so . . . um, smart. I have to go," she said, and I heard her trying to hold back the tears.

My face was already wet. "Bye."

So she'd remembered but didn't have the courage.

Nineteen

When I had gone back to Ms. Nora to get my braids re-done, my hair had grown nicely. I told her about what my mother said, and she'd smiled.

"You think you're cute with those braids, don't you?" Jordan teased me as we sat down at Chilli's.

I rolled my eyes.

"It's cool, you growin' up, little sis. I'm proud. See? Aren't you glad we decided to keep you when we found you on the porch that day?" He laughed.

I couldn't help laughing. I'll never forget the look on his face when I told him I was his sister. I realize that I have all the love I need right now. I have seven *J*'s including my daddy looking out for me. What else does a sista need?

Anthony plays now for that West Coast team he always wanted to play for. He's not married and is a consummate playboy. Marcus signed with New York. He married Sherina after his first season. Anthony hasn't contacted me since the incident. I sometimes wonder if he thinks about me. I know he probably doesn't. Anthony is one of those people that just knows how to look out for himself. Selfish. My experiences have taught me one thing. There is an art to being selfish. I try not to be selfish, but sometimes you have to be. If you aren't, then no one is going to give you what you need, they will only take what *they* need. I guess I'm a little wiser now. I concentrate on school and don't even think about the money I have saved in the bank.

I haven't met anyone either. I'm just taking some time to get to know me. See, now I'm actually living the movie, and let me tell you . . . I like how this story is turning out.

COMING IN OCTOBER 2003 FROM
ARABESQUE ROMANCES

__PASSION'S DESTINY
by Crystal Wilson-Harris   1-58314-286-X $6.99US/$9.99CAN
Jakarta Raven was never one to back down from trouble. Her determination to clear her sister of unjust charges puts her up against New Orleans district attorney Zane Reeves . . . and a sensual attraction neither can resist. Now, with Zane's future at stake, Jakarta must find a way to clear his reputation, even if it means heartbreaking loss.

__IF LOVING YOU IS WRONG
by Loure Bussey   1-58314-346-7 $6.99US/$9.99CAN
After years as a struggling screenwriter and the pain of a bitter divorce, Simi Mitchell has finally hit pay dirt—a major Hollywood studio has bought her screenplay for a feature film. As if that weren't enough, the man who's directing it—Jackson Larimore—is unbelievably sexy. But maybe Simi's attraction is more trouble than it's worth.

__THE BEST THING YET
by Robin H. Allen   1-58314-368-8 $5.99US/$7.99CAN
Fashion model Tangi Ellington has it all—youth, beauty, fame, and enough money to last a lifetime. Yet something—or more specifically, someone special—is missing. Until she meets District Attorney Steele McDeal. The hard-nosed prosecutor is one of the good guys—but that's the problem . . . because his latest case is against Tangi's brother.

__ENDLESS ENCHANTMENT
by Angie Daniels   1-58314-445-5 $5.99US/$7.99CAN
Keelen Brooks has been in love with his best friend Charity Rose since kindergarten. He never felt he could measure up to the standards of Charity's high-school clique, the Cutie Pies, or to a man like her ex-husband, Donovan. Now Keelen is ready to show Charity what she's missed when they reunite for their ten-year class reunion cruise.

Call toll free **1-888-345-BOOK** to order by phone or use this coupon to order by mail. ALL BOOKS AVAILABLE OCTOBER 01, 2003.
Name_____
Address_____
City_____State_____Zip_____
Please send me the books that I have checked above.
I am enclosing $_____
Plus postage and handling* $_____
Sales tax (in NY, TN, and DC) $_____
Total amount enclosed $_____
*Add $2.50 for the first book and $.50 for each additional book. Send check or money order (no cash or CODs) to: **Arabesque Romances, Dept. C.O., 850 Third Avenue 16th Floor, New York, NY 10022**
Prices and numbers subject to change without notice. Valid only in the U.S. All orders subject to availability. **NO ADVANCE ORDERS.**
Visit our website at **www.arabesquebooks.com.**